THAT KISS

"Just a minute," Nick said. He grasped Billie by the wrist and drew her to him. "I want that kiss you owe me."

"Let me go," Billie said, trying to loosen his grasp.

"Not just yet." He took her wrists in one big hand and grasped her chin with the other. "I want that kiss."

Billie opened her mouth to reply. Before she could utter a sound, his lips swooped down on hers. She made one muffled sound of protest, then she became lost in a flood of sensation.

He released her hands. She reached up to wind her fingers in the thick curls at the nape of his neck. She was kissing him back.

Nick groaned, lost in the sweet wonder of her response. He wanted her. She was trouble—big trouble—but he wanted her more than any woman he'd ever known. He exulted in the heat of her, the womanly perfume of her skin and hair. He pulled her closer and he could feel her body rubbing sinuously against his.

"Just like a cat," he murmured. "A sleek little cat."

CAPTURE THE GLOW
OF ZEBRA'S HEARTFIRES

AUTUMN ECSTASY (3133, $4.25)
by Pamela K. Forrest

Philadelphia beauty Linsey McAdams had eluded her kidnappers but was now at the mercy of the ruggedly handsome frontiersman who owned the remote cabin where she had taken refuge. The two were snowbound until spring, and handsome Luc LeClerc soon fancied the green-eyed temptress would keep him warm through the long winter months. He said he would take her home at winter's end, but she knew that with one embrace, she might never want to leave!

BELOVED SAVAGE (3134, $4.25)
by Sandra Bishop

Susannah Jacobs would do anything to survive—even submit to the bronze-skinned warrior who held her captive. But the beautiful maiden vowed not to let the handsome Tonnewa capture her heart as well. Soon, though, she found herself longing for the scorching kisses and tender caresses of her raven-haired BELOVED SAVAGE.

CANADIAN KISS (3135, $4.25)
by Christine Carson

Golden-haired Sara Oliver was sent from London to Vancouver to marry a stranger three times her age—only to have her husband-to-be murdered on their wedding day. Sara vowed to track the murderer down, but he ambushed her and left her for dead. When she awoke, wounded and frightened, she was staring into the eyes of the handsome loner Tom Russel. As the rugged stranger nursed her to health, the flames of passion erupted, and their CANADIAN KISS threatened never to end!

Available wherever paperbacks are sold, or order direct from the Publisher. Send cover price plus 50¢ per copy for mailing and handling to Zebra Books, Dept. 3482, 475 Park Avenue South, New York, N.Y. 10016. Residents of New York, New Jersey and Pennsylvania must include sales tax. DO NOT SEND CASH.

WENDY GARRETT
ARIZONA LOVESTORM

ZEBRA BOOKS
KENSINGTON PUBLISHING CORP.

*To Mom and Dad,
for always being there*

ZEBRA BOOKS

are published by

Kensington Publishing Corp.
475 Park Avenue South
New York, NY 10016

First printing: August, 1991

Printed in the United States of America

Chapter 1

Arizona Territory, 1881

"I won't go!" the stout woman cried.

"Oh, yes, you will. If I have to, I'll tie you like a hog and have you tossed in with the baggage," Billie said, flinging her braid back over her shoulder with an irritated toss of her head.

The older woman pressed her lips into a thin line, drawing the corners of her mouth down even farther. "You're a stupid fool. You'll never run that ranch without my help. A child like you—"

"I'm twenty-one, Althea. Hardly a child."

Her small hands firm on the reins, Billie guided the team across the cracked surface of Rojo Creek's dry bed, then turned them onto the track that led into town. The wagon jolted along the rutted strip of packed earth that served as Xavier's main street. Billie could see the weathered, dust-scoured buildings now, and behind them, the faraway purple outline of the Rincon Mountains. Relief washed through her. Only a few more minutes, she thought. During the three months Althea had lived with her, life had been pure hell. The woman had criticized, embarrassed or insulted everyone around her. Billie considered herself a fairly tolerant person, but not only did Althea possess the disposition of a rattlesnake, she hadn't done a lick of work. Enough was enough.

As they entered the town, Althea began dabbing at her cheeks with her handkerchief. Billie chucked the reins savagely, startling the team into a jolting trot. Bystanders looked up curiously as the wagon rolled swiftly past, lurching wildly over the deep ruts.

"Billie's really got her fur up today," one man commented.

"Ahh, she's had her dander up ever since that aunt of hers went to live at the Star M," his companion said. "I hear the old woman's a real bad 'un." The man shaded his eyes with his hand. "Hey! They're pullin' up at the stage depot. What do you want to bet Billie's puttin' the old gal out?"

"I want to see this!" the first man said, hurrying across the street to join the crowd that was gathering in front of the depot.

Billie ignored the gazes of the townspeople. Climbing nimbly over the seat, she hauled her aunt's trunk to the back of the wagon and heaved it over. It landed with a thump on the hard-packed dirt. A satchel, then another, followed it down.

Billie turned, arms akimbo, and said, "Get down, Althea."

"How could you do this to me?" the older woman wailed. Masking her mouth with the handkerchief, she spoke her next words so only Billie could hear. "You little bitch!" she snarled, her mouth twisted with hate. "You'll regret this!"

"The only regret I'll have is ever being foolish enough to have let you into my home," Billie whispered back with equal vehemence. "Now get down!" She took a step forward, and the old woman scrambled down

6

from the wagon with surprising agility.

With a satisfied nod, Billie jumped to the ground and sat down on the larger of the satchels to wait for the stage to arrive. Her hand absently crept upward to toy with the braid of glossy dark hair that hung over her shoulder. She was a small woman, but there were graceful curves beneath her faded, too-large jacket and the split skirt that was covered with dust from hem to knee. Beneath her battered Stetson, her face was delicately heart-shaped, her uptilted green eyes heavily fringed with thick, dark lashes.

Although Billie's attention remained fixed on the toes of her dusty boots, Althea played to the fascinated audience. Plumping her bulk down onto the trunk, she buried her face in her handkerchief. Sobs began drifting up from the dingy linen folds.

"There's the stage," someone cried, pointing to a cloud of dust at the outskirts of town.

Althea's sobs became louder.

Billie didn't look up, but her toe began to move up and down restlessly. Damn that Althea! she thought, her brows contracting in a scowl. The old bat is doing her best to make me out the villain. And, judging from the expression on some of the townspeople's faces, she was succeeding.

The stage pulled up with a great clatter of hooves and squealing brakes. Grateful for the distraction, Billie rose from her seat and went to speak with the driver. A few moments later she turned back to her aunt.

"I've paid your fare to Prescott." Billie held out a small purse. "Here's forty dollars to cover your fare from there to San Bernardino."

Althea continued to cry noisily. Unable to control her outrage a moment longer, Billie snatched the hand-kerchief from her and flung it away. Startled, the old woman looked up, revealing suspiciously dry eyes, and

7

the crowd's sympathy dried up like dew on a hot summer's day.

Althea heaved herself up from the trunk and walked toward the stage. Placing one foot on the step, she turned to look at Billie. The older woman's eyes had turned hard and cold, like blue pebbles buried amid the wrinkled folds of her face. The watching crowd sighed.

"I seen that look on a rattler jest before it struck," a man muttered. "Watch out, Billie, 'fore you get bit."

Billie just put her hands on her hips and glared back, unblinking and unyielding.

It was the old woman who looked away first. Defeated, she turned and clambered into the stage. After stowing the trunk and satchels in the compartment in the back, the driver climbed onto his high seat. With a flourish of his whip, he waved farewell. The vehicle rumbled into motion, leaving town in another cloud of choking dust.

As the crowd began to disperse, Billie bent to brush at the dust that coated the hem of her split skirt. Hearing a chuckle from behind her, she whirled to see a stranger leaning against a nearby hitching post. She straightened abruptly, scowling, then forgot her annoyance as she got a better look at him.

He was a tall man, long-legged, leanly muscled and whipcord-strong. Everything about him seemed warm and golden, like sunshine: tawny, sun-streaked hair, light brown eyes with flecks of gold swimming in their depths, skin tanned nearly the color of his hair by exposure to sun and wind. His bulging thigh muscles, the mark of a horseman, strained the legs of his jeans as he shifted position.

Her breath came shallowly, almost as if an invisible band had been wound around her chest, constricting it. She stood motionless as his gaze traveled from her head to her dusty boots, lingering boldly on the curves

8

between. Hot blood rushed into her face.

"Hey, Billie!" The voice came from right behind her, startling her out of her bemusement.

She whirled to see Emmett Lessing, the town's only doctor. He was a burly, red-haired man with big, gentle hands and a mustache that hung well below his chin.

"I hear you got rid of Althea," he said with a grin.

She grimaced. "Cully Frye and Lester Manon quit because of her, and some of the others were making noises about doing the same. Right before roundup, too. I had to get rid of her while I still had a crew left."

"Well, good riddance to her." He put his hands behind his back and rocked back and forth on his heels. "I've got a favor to ask."

"You know I'd do most anything for you, Emmett. What do you need?"

"Will you take the Laird girl in for a while?"

"She's still here?" Billie asked in surprise. "I thought she went to live with her brother in Kansas City."

"She's been sending telegrams to the fellow nearly every day, with no reply. Rachel says he travels quite a bit. Now, me and Jane'd be glad to have her stay with us, but she wants to get away from town. Says she doesn't like the way people stare at her."

"I bet she doesn't. They've got nothing better to do than mind someone else's business," Billie said, wrinkling her nose at the thought. "Is she all right? I mean, she's not—"

"For someone who was brutally ravished and forced to watch her family die, I'd say she's doing right well. There'll be a few scars, inside and out, but she'll survive. All she needs is time and a little caring from the people around her." Emmett chewed at the end of his mustache. "Well, what do you say? Will you take her?"

"Sure, I'll take her," Billie said, a bit surprised at the note of pleading in his voice. Surely he knew her well enough to realize that she'd never turn her back on another human being in need. But she had to admit to being a little nervous about it. She'd never met the Laird girl, and had no idea what to expect from such a soft, Eastern-bred lady. Would Rachel spend her time crying or staring off into space like Billie had seen other Apache victims do? The Star M wasn't a fancy place. Would the girl scorn her bare-bones accommodation as Althea had?

The doctor patted her on the shoulder. "You've got a kinder heart than all these so-called civilized folks put together."

"Don't tell anyone," she said, raising her hands in mock horror. "You'll ruin my reputation."

"Me? Reveal that you really are all soft inside? Never!" Grinning, he pulled his watch out and flipped it open. "I'll go tell Rachel to pack."

"Emmett," she whispered, putting her hand on his arm when he would have turned away. "Do you know who that man is? The one behind me."

The doctor looked past her, his brow creased in bewilderment. "What man?"

Billie glanced over her shoulder. The stranger was gone. Well, she thought, she'd probably never see him again, anyway. "Never mind," she said with a shrug.

The stranger stopped his horse on the rocky crest of a hill. Noting a plume of dust in the distance, he took a pair of field glasses out of his saddlebag and raised them to his eyes. In the center of the dust cloud he could see a wagon, driven by the Meyrick girl. Another girl occupied the seat beside her.

Drawing in his breath in a hiss of satisfaction, he lowered the field glasses. Everything was going as planned. All he had to do now was get himself hired on

10

at the Star M Ranch, and he'd be exactly where he needed to be. The only unexpected detail was the Meyrick girl's looks. She possessed such wild, untamed beauty that he'd felt an actual physical jolt at the sight of her. Despite her small stature, she was a delicious package of womanly curves. When she had bent over to brush her skirt, he had been strongly tempted to run his hands along the sleek swell of her hips. The creases on either side of his mouth deepened. Now, wouldn't that have caused a stir in that sleepy little town!

Whoa, boy, he thought. You're here to do a job. You can't afford to get involved with any woman, and that Meyrick girl is likely to get you so wound up you'll get careless. And a careless man in your profession is a dead one.

Even so, he couldn't help but wonder if that fiery temper of hers meant she'd bring equal heat to a man's bed. Shaking his head to rid himself of the disturbing thought, he urged his mount toward the wagon.

Chapter 2

Billie glanced at the girl who sat so quietly on the wagon's jouncing seat. Rachel Laird was an extremely pretty girl. Her hair was pale gold, her eyes as soft and brown as those of a fawn. She was tall and slender, with the sort of figure that made even the ill-fitting borrowed dress she wore look fashionable. Bruises marred her otherwise perfect skin, but they were fading now. A neat bandage covered her temple. It was a shame, Billie thought, that the girl's family had come all the way from Chicago to visit Rowan Laird, only to share in his violent death. Her father, mother and younger brother had all been killed. Eighteen-year-old Rachel had been raped and beaten and left for dead in Rowan's burning house. The girl had crawled out somehow, to be found by Bernard Greenhow and his wife Hermione, who had come to investigate the smoke.

"I'm real sorry about your family, Miss Laird," Billie ventured.

Rachel looked down at her clasped hands. Billie watched the horizon for a moment, then burst out, "Look, I don't want to pry and I don't want to upset you, but I can't tiptoe around this thing, not if you're going to live in my house."

"It's all right, Miss Meyrick . . . Billie," Rachel amended, correctly interpreting Billie's grimace. "What do you want to know?"

Billie sighed. "Nothing. I know what happened. I just don't want to go around pretending I don't, and neither will my men."

Rachel pressed her lips into a thin line. "You mean they won't talk about me behind my back like people did in Xavier? Will they pity the poor ruined girl, soiled by Apache hands? I heard the whispers, Billie, saw the pointing fingers, although I pretended not to. And they all wanted to know how many there were and exactly what they did to me."

"We all feel sorry for what happened," Billie said. "If that's pity, you'll have to learn to accept it. As for the rest of it, my men will stare at you because you're so pretty."

Rachel gasped. "You almost talk as though I'm a normal girl!"

"What else are you?" Billie demanded, slapping the ends of the reins against her boots in exasperation. "What happened to you could happen to me, to any of us who live out here. Those townspeople haven't been here very long. They don't remember the Apache Wars. But we do, and no one is going to say anything about you except how lucky you are to have survived."

There were tears in Rachel's eyes. "Oh, Billie! You don't know how wonderful it is to hear that!"

"Shhh! Look, up there." Billie pointed to a nearby ridge, where a mounted man was silhouetted against the cloudless turquoise sky. She reached beneath the seat for her rifle as he rode toward them.

"You're not going to shoot him!" Rachel cried.

"Not unless I have to," Billie said grimly.

She stopped the wagon and waited, holding the rifle

14

across her knees with apparent casualness. As he came nearer, she shifted the gun so it pointed, not precisely toward him, but close enough to be a warning. To her surprise, she realized that he was the stranger who had stared at her in town.

He stopped his mount beside the wagon and tipped his hat to her, then to Rachel. Although he ignored the rifle, Billie noticed that he was careful to keep his hands in plain view.

"Afternoon, ladies." His voice was deep and rich and slow, causing a strange little shiver to slide up Billie's spine.

"Afternoon," she replied, hoping that her awareness of him did not show on her face. "What can we do for you, stranger?"

He smiled, showing even white teeth. "We seem to be going the same way. I thought I'd ride along with you for a while."

"Mister, unless you're heading for the Star M Ranch, you're on your way to nowhere," Billie said.

"Then I'm heading for the Star M Ranch." His smile broadened.

Billie scowled. "Well, you can—"

"Besides," he said, glancing at her rifle again, "two pretty girls like you shouldn't be out here by yourselves. I'll just come along."

The arrogance of the man! Billie thought. She slapped the reins against the horses' rumps, urging them forward. Since she couldn't outrun him, and he hadn't given her any cause to shoot him, she'd just have to ignore him.

He urged his mount closer. "My name is Nick Larabee."

Billie pressed her lips together. To her surprise, Rachel answered him.

"I'm Rachel Laird," the girl said in a low, tentative

voice. "And this is—"

"Miss Billie Meyrick, of the Star M Ranch," he finished for her. Grinning at the surprised look on Billie's face, he added, "Your name was mentioned in Xavier. Often."

"Gossips, every one of them," Billie muttered, forgetting her resolve to ignore him. "Where are you from, Mr. Larabee?"

"Missouri mostly, Kansas some, Colorado a little," he said.

"You move around, I take it?" Billie asked. How old was he? she wondered. He didn't look to be over thirty, but he had an air of competence that belonged to a much older man.

"Some." He wasn't looking at her, but at the hills to the east.

A drifter, Billie thought. She felt a small stirring of alarm, which faded again as she noted that he was clean-shaven, his clothes well kept. His boots were new, made of the finest leather. In contrast, the butt of his pistol was well worn, and he was packing a Henry repeating rifle that looked as though it had seen plenty of use.

Her curiosity focused, sharpened. Her gaze moved to his horse, a tall buckskin gelding with a luxuriant mane and tail. Billie watched the animal move, noting its smooth, powerful gait and the spirited arch of its strong neck. A fine mount, she thought, several cuts above what most cowboys could afford. Several cuts, in fact, above what *she* could afford.

"That's a fine-looking animal," she said. "Is he any good with cattle?"

"Some." He glanced at her, noting the swell of her chest under the jacket. Damn, but she was one hell of an attractive woman. He was going to have a devil of a time keeping his hands off her. With a muttered curse,

16

he returned his attention to the hills.

Billie chewed her lip nervously. Ordinarily she didn't pry into other people's business, but this man roused her curiosity. On the surface, he seemed no different from any other drifter, uncaring of anything except where the next breeze was taking him. But she sensed depths in him beyond that outward nonchalance. There was a stubborn set to his broad shoulders, a look of determination in the line of his jaw that spoke of a man with something important on his mind.

"What were you doing in Xavier, Mr. Larabee?" she asked.

"Passing through," he said.

"Where are you headed?"

"Somewhere else," he said shortly, leaning his arm on his saddle horn and regarding her from under lowered brows. "You ask a lot of questions, Miss Meyrick."

Angry at the rebuff, Billie clamped her lips together and concentrated on her driving. There was no road here, just a faint track through the hills. It was rocky, rutted, and very steep in places. Wagons were not made for comfort, and as the jolting increased, she could see that Rachel was beginning to tire.

"Are you all right?" Billie asked in concern.

"I'm fine, really." Rachel braced her arms against the back of the seat. "Please, just keep going."

There were beads of perspiration on Rachel's forehead, Billie noted, and marks where the girl had sunk her teeth into her lower lip. She was obviously not as well as the doctor had thought, but she hadn't complained or given any indication of her discomfort. Billie felt a surge of admiration for her quiet courage.

The wagon lurched onto the last—and worst—section of track. As Rachel's face became whiter with each passing mile, Billie became more concerned.

Finally she pulled the team to a halt.

"Rachel, the next few miles are going to be pretty rough," she said. "Why don't you lie down in back? I'd stop and let you rest, but we'll barely make the ranch before dark as it is. This isn't a good place to spend the night."

"I'm all right," Rachel insisted. But her lips were pale, almost bloodless, and it was obvious she was in pain.

Billie opened her mouth to protest, but was forestalled by Nick Larabee. He stopped his mount beside the wagon and leaned over to pluck Rachel from her seat. Startled, Billie grabbed for her rifle. Holding Rachel in one arm, he reached out with the other and pulled the gun out of Billie's hands with the other.

Billie stared at him wide-eyed, her throat tight with fear. He had moved so fast that she'd lost control of the situation. Before she'd quite realized what was happening, she and Rachel were completely in his power.

"Relax, Miss Meyrick." He settled Rachel behind him. "She'll be more comfortable here."

Billie's fear turned to fury as she realized he'd only intended to help. He'd been right about Rachel being better off on horseback, but, damn it, he should have asked! "Give me back my gun," she snapped.

"Are you going to behave yourself?"

She took a deep, calming breath. "I don't shoot people just for being stupid."

His jaw tightened. Why, the little devil! He'd acted instinctively, doing what he felt was necessary for Rachel's sake, and this nasty-minded chit had nearly shot him for it! And now *she* was mad.

"Didn't your mother teach you not to call people names?" he asked softly. There was a hint of steel beneath the smooth timbre of his deep voice.

Billie drew herself up stiffly. "Didn't your mother

18

teach you not to go around grabbing people?"

Nick opened his mouth to reply, but closed it again when he felt Rachel touch him lightly on the shoulder. After a moment of struggling with his temper, he handed the rifle back to Billie and said, "Why don't we call a truce, Miss Meyrick? It's a pretty silly thing to get in an argument over."

"Well . . ." Truly, Billy didn't know why she had flared up as she had. He had only wanted to help. And anyone would have reacted to having a gun pointed at him—she was lucky he hadn't hurt her. With a sheepish smile, she held out her hand. "All right, Mr. Larabee. Truce. And I'm sorry I drew on you."

He took her hand. Instead of shaking it as he would a man's, he raised it to his lips. A jolt of warmth went through her at the feel of his mouth on the backs of her fingers. Snatching her hand away from him, she urged the team into motion. He smiled and spurred his horse after the wagon. Rachel, after a moment's startlement, wound her arms around his waist.

Billie couldn't keep herself from watching him. Although he rode in silence, seemingly lost in thought, she noticed that he picked the smoothest route possible over the broken terrain, reducing his passenger's discomfort as much as possible. At first Rachel sat stiffly, holding herself away from him. But soon her head drifted forward until it was resting against his back. Billie felt a stab of envy and a consuming curiosity. What would it feel like, she wondered, to be nestled so comfortably against that broad back, to feel that lean waist under her hands?

She shook her head irritably. She must have been out in the sun too long! With a sigh of exasperation, she focused her attention on the track ahead of her. But her gaze kept straying back to him, noting the easy way he rode, the strong-looking hands with the dusting of golden hair on their backs, the tawny hair that curled over the back of his collar.

The team set their chests into the harness and hauled the wagon up the side of the next hill. The wheels crunched noisily through the dry brush. It was going to be a hard summer for the cattle, she mused; there had been little rain this winter, and the crop of thick grama grass that usually sprang up among the browse was thin and scattered. As the rainless spring moved into the searing heat of summer, the little there was would dry up and blow away.

"It's going to be a dry summer," Nick Larabee said, as if reading her thoughts.

"Yes," Billie agreed somberly, urging the team up the last steep shoulder of the hill.

"Will the cattle make it?"

"Well, mine are range-bred. Most will survive if the drought doesn't last through the summer. But some of the other ranchers have been overstocking their ranges these past few years. Pa warned them, but they wouldn't listen. All they want is more cattle and more profit, and never believe that this land isn't always able to support that many head."

Nick rubbed his cheek thoughtfully. "Some are going to lose their ranches, then."

"I expect so." The wagon reached the crest of the hill. Billie pulled the team to a halt and pointed downward. "There's the Star M."

The ranch occupied the center of a broad valley that rose toward the foothills of the Tanque Verde Ridge. The pale adobe walls of the house almost seemed to glow against the darkening landscape. Two large corrals occupied a site not a stone's throw from the house. Flanking them were two small adobe buildings, smoke rising from their chimneys into the quiet air.

"Nice place," Nick said. He swung Rachel back into

the wagon seat, then urged his horse forward.

Billie slapped the reins against the team's rumps and followed him. A rider, his rifle held ready, came pounding toward them from the ranch.

"What's got you so nervous, Budge?" Billie demanded when the cowboy neared the wagon.

"Eliseo spotted a coupla Apach not ten miles from here. Where the hell have you been? When we got back an' found you gone, we nearly went crazy worryin' about you," he said, wheeling his mount to walk beside the wagon. He was a tall, rangy Texan in his mid-thirties. His eyes were a pale blue-gray, a startling contrast to a face that had been burned brown from a lifetime spent under a broiling Southwestern sun.

"I put Althea on the stage to San Bernardino," she said.

"'Bout time." He looked at Nick inquiringly.

"Nick Larabee, Budge Jewett, my wagon boss," Billie said. "Mr. Larabee rode out from town with us."

The Texan nodded. Although he and Nick didn't say a word, understanding seemed to pass between them. Budge leaned over to shake hands. "Obliged, Mr. Larabee," he said.

Billie indicated the girl beside her. "And this lady is Rachel Laird. She's going to stay with us for a while."

"Ma'am," the Texan said, tipping his hat. "I sure am sorry to hear what happened. Old Rowan was a good feller, helped us out plenty of times. Don't you worry none, sooner or later we'll track down ever' one of them murderin' devils and kill 'em fer you."

"Why . . . why . . ." Rachel glanced at Billie, then clasped her hands primly in her lap and said, "Thank you, Mr. Jewett. That is very kind of you. I'm sure Uncle Rowan would appreciate it."

"Damn right, he would," Budge growled.

When Billie saw the mingled horror and amused dis-

21

belief that warred in Rachel's delicate features, she was forced to bite her lip to keep from laughing out loud. Surely no one had ever offered to kill someone for this gentle, city-bred girl.

As it had done so often this afternoon, Billie's gaze sought Nick Larabee. He was staring into the orange half disk of the setting sun, his eyes half closed against its fiery glare. A muscle jumped spasmodically in his jaw, and there was a terrible cold anger in his face, a killing rage that made her stiffen in alarm.

He turned toward her so suddenly that she didn't have a chance to pretend she hadn't been watching him. The anger drained from his face as he met her curious regard. Then he smiled. A strange feeling rose in the pit of her stomach, a molten warmth that threatened to steal the strength from her limbs.

She stared back at him, wide-eyed and wary, and realized that his rage had not been meant for her—nor was it the most dangerous thing about him.

Chapter 3

It was dark by the time they reached the house. The door was open, sending a flood of welcoming yellow light across the dry ground. Budge swung down from the saddle and reached up to lift Rachel from the wagon.

She gasped, flinching away from his hands. The Texan dropped his arms to his sides and waited patiently while she struggled to regain her composure. After a moment she held her arms out to him, although she averted her face timidly. He helped her down, then unhitched the team and led them toward the corral.

Billie swung her booted feet over the side of the wagon. Just as she hopped down from the seat, Nick Larabee appeared in front of her, catching her before her feet hit the ground. Holding her easily with one arm, he took the reins from her hand and tossed them onto the seat.

Billie pushed ineffectually at his hard chest. "You can put me down now," she said stiffly.

"Yes, ma'am." He let her slide along the length of his body until her feet reached the ground.

Billie stepped away from him quickly and smoothed her skirt with trembling hands. Her whole body tingled from that brief contact. She ought to be angry at his boldness, but all she felt was confusion and a coiling heat deep within her. "You might give Budge a hand with the horses, Mr. Larabee."

His mouth curved with sardonic humor as he tipped his hat to her. "Anything you say, Miss Meyrick." He walked away, his dark clothes quickly blending into the shadows.

Billie turned to Rachel. "There's a barrel of water in the courtyard. We can scrape off some of this dust before going inside. We'd better hurry, though. It smells like supper's almost ready." She led the girl around the corner of the house and through the courtyard gate. "You're lucky you came to the Star M. Isabel is one of the best cooks in Arizona. Some of those other places . . ." She shook her head in disgust.

"Does she have a specialty?" Rachel asked.

"On a cattle ranch?" Billie laughed. "Beef, Rachel. Beef and more beef."

"Oh, dear," Rachel murmured, then added bravely, "It sounds wonderful."

Billie laughed again. "Liar." She dipped water out of the barrel and poured it into a battered tin basin that sat in a niche in the adobe wall. Towels had been hung on iron hooks nearby.

"Do you always bathe out here?" Rachel asked, peering nervously around the courtyard, which was dimly lit by two narrow gunports that pierced the thick outer wall of the house.

"I said wash, not bathe," Billie said, shrugging out of her jacket. "Don't worry. There's a tub in the house."

"That's a relief." Rachel dabbed at her face and hands with the harsh soap.

Billie took her turn at the basin, then unbraided her hair and ran her fingers through it quickly. Using her damp towel, she brushed the dust from her clothes as best she could. She looked up to see that Rachel was watching her, a quizzical look on her face.

Billie draped the towel over the makeshift wash-stand. She had never been bothered much by the decrepit old washbasin or the towels that had been mended so many times they were more patches than fabric. But now, seeing it through another person's eyes . . . How shabby it all must seem! "I know you're not used to this kind of life," she said. "But—"

"That wasn't what I was thinking at all," Rachel said, reaching out and taking Billie's hands in hers. "I was just wondering why you agreed to take a perfect stranger into your home."

"We all help each other out here. Anyone would have done the same."

"Anyone would not," Rachel said softly.

Billie shrugged, embarrassed. "Let's eat. I'm starving."

"I am, too." Rachel gave Billie's hands a squeeze before letting them go.

"You're all right, Rachel Laird," Billie said approvingly. She led the other girl into the house. The court-yard door, like the main entrance at the opposite side of the house, opened directly into the big central room that served as kitchen, dining room, and gathering place for the ranch's inhabitants. What would Rachel think, she wondered, when she realized that it was nearly all there was to the house, other than two small bedrooms and a tiny room for storage?

Eight men slouched wearily at the long table that occupied the center of the room. A rapid transformation came over them when they saw Rachel, however; their tired shoulders straightened, their hats were removed, revealing hair still damp from washing, and wrinkled shirts were swiftly tucked into their pants.

Rachel, seeing the host of admiring gazes that were

focused on her, blushed furiously.

"Easy, boys," Billie said, giving Rachel's arm a squeeze of encouragement. "This is Rachel Laird, and she's not used to being stared at by a bunch of cowboys. Now pull up some chairs for us."

There was a clatter as the men scrambled for the chairs that had been pushed against the far wall. The winner of the race carried a chair to the table in grinning triumph and set it down. Rachel took the offered seat, keeping her head bowed shyly.

In a low voice, she said, "Thank you, Mr. . . ."

"Art Bell, ma'am," he said, his face reddening.

"Thank you, Mr. Bell." Rachel put her hands in her lap and stared down at them.

Billie shooed Art back to his seat and bent close to Rachel's ear. "Would you rather go to your room?" she whispered.

"No, I'll be fine." Rachel took a deep breath. Although her lower lip trembled slightly, she raised her head and faced the watching men.

The cowboys began introducing themselves eagerly. They talked so fast that Rachel didn't have to say a word, only nod and smile at the appropriate times. Slowly, she began to relax.

Billie, satisfied, went to help Isabel with the cooking. As she passed the front door, Budge walked in, followed by Nick Larabee. It was the first time Billie had seen Nick without a hat. To her surprise, she realized he wasn't more than a few years older than she. His golden-brown hair was thick and wavy, curls springing up everywhere despite his attempt to slick them down with water. His forehead was broad, his nose straight and slim, and there was a sensual, slightly mocking tilt to his chiseled mouth that made her breath catch in her throat. He was an excessively handsome man, she thought, one who probably broke hearts wherever he went.

"Is Miss Rachel doing all right?" Budge asked.

"She's got them eating out of her hand," Billie said with a smile.

The Texan nodded and went to join the group at the table. Nick didn't move, but stood there looking down at Billie with a warm, caressing gaze that almost made her feel as if he were actually touching her.

"You left some dirt on your nose," he said.

"Here?" Billie scrubbed at her face with her sleeve.

"You missed it. No, let me." He took her by the chin and held her still while he rubbed the side of her nose with his thumb. His hands were hot against her skin.

Billie recoiled, her hand going up to cover the spot he had rubbed. It felt as though he had branded her with his touch, placed his claim right there on her skin for everyone to see. You idiot! she told herself sternly. The man only rubbed some dirt off your face! If he knew the effect he had on you, he'd probably bolt like a gun-shy horse. "Get yourself a plate and sit down, Mr. Larabee."

"You might as well call me Nick," he said. "I just hired on."

"You did?" she asked, then nodded. "Well, if Budge hired you, I'll assume that you know something about cattle."

"I spent a few years working on a Colorado ranch."

She folded her arms over her chest. "Recently?"

"Persistent, aren't you?" he asked, smiling down at her.

Billie scowled. "I just wanted to know if you're any kind of a hand," she snapped. Then she shrugged. If he didn't know cattle as he said he did, it would be obvious the moment he hit the range. As long as he did a good job here, his past was none of her business—as he had so bluntly indicated. "Welcome to the Star M, Nick,"

27

she said. She started to hold out her hand, then drew it back, afraid he'd kiss it again. Turning away abruptly, she headed toward the stove.

Nick watched her walk away, admiring the graceful swing of her hips. Now that she had shed her jacket, he saw that her breasts were full and high, her hips sweetly curved and her waist tiny enough for a man to span with his hands. Her hair was unbraided, falling down her back in a mass of shining dark waves. She was a lot of woman, he mused. Too bad he couldn't afford to do anything about her. Reluctantly, he turned away.

Since the other men had taken seats as near Rachel as possible, Nick had no trouble finding a place near the head of the table, where Billie was to sit. It was Rachel, not Budge, who introduced him to the other hands; the girl, responding to the courtly, respectful attention the men were lavishing on her, had opened up like a late-blooming flower.

Nick nodded, quickly tagging names to faces as Rachel pointed out each one: Art and Joe Bell, identical from their white-blond hair to the tips of their narrow boots; Bob "Stubs" Foley, short and stocky and going bald, with three fingers missing from his right hand; Eliseo Martinez, Isabel's husband, a small man with nervous hands; Creek Beuther, a large, young man with dark, curly hair and a mustache; Reuben Wheeler and Squint Conway, both tall and lanky and brown from the sun. Reuben had an open, boyish face, but Squint, true to his nickname, had a narrow-eyed, foxy look about him. At the far end of the table sat Freeman Jennings, his coffee-colored face alight with merriment as he watched the other men vie for Rachel's attention.

"Here comes the grub," Squint said, rubbing his hands together eagerly.

Isabel, a dark, pretty woman whose pregnancy was

28

just beginning to show, plunked a big, steaming bowl down on the table.

"It's them beans agin," Art groaned. "When are you gonna give up, Isabel?"

"When you eat some, Señor Art," she retorted, pointing a spoon at him before plunging it into the bowl. "Frijoles, they are good for you."

Budge reached across the table to take a steak from the platter, then spooned a large helping of beans onto his plate. "Beans is good for your bowels, Art. Us Texas fellers eat 'em all the time."

"Budge!" Billie put her hands on her hips and scowled at the lean Texan. "Isabel and I are old hands, used to your raunchy talk, but Miss Rachel is a lady. You don't want to make her swoon, do you?"

"I'm jest gettin' her used to things," Budge drawled, his accent growing thicker with every word. "Workin' her in slow like."

The men guffawed.

Nick glanced at Rachel. Her face was pink, but there was a smile twitching the corners of her mouth. Her delicate, white hands lay relaxed against the wide pine boards of the table.

"Miss Rachel, can I git you somethin' to drink?" Art asked.

"Why, thank you, Mr. Bell," she said. "Perhaps some cool water—"

Eight men instantly surged up from their chairs. Budge reached the moisture-beaded clay jar first. He glared at the others until they sat back down, then poured a dipperful of water into the Star M's only glass, a delicate crystal goblet that had somehow managed to survive years of clumsy male handling.

"Thank you," Rachel murmured, gravely taking the offered glass from the Texan. She cut a tiny piece of meat from her steak and lifted it to her mouth.

29

Nick grinned at the look of dismay that spread over her face as she chewed the leathery beef. She ate her beans, her tortillas and the limp canned peaches, then worried the steak here and there across her plate before bravely attempting another bite.

He chuckled. Reaching for a tortilla, he rolled it into a neat cylinder and took a bite as he took in his surroundings. The house was a fortress, built to protect its inhabitants through the wild, dangerous years of the Apache Wars. The adobe walls were nearly two feet thick, pierced at regular intervals with narrow gunports. Heavy shutters sealed the few small windows from the night. The ceiling, which looked to be a good fourteen feet high, was made of saguaro ribs laid atop massive wooden beams. There was a trapdoor in the center of the ceiling, and a wooden ladder hung against a nearby wall.

A spare dwelling, he thought. There were no decorations, no feminine touches of any kind, even curtains. His brow furrowed. If he didn't know better, he wouldn't think a woman lived here at all. What was the problem here? he wondered. He knew Billie was feminine from the top of her shining hair to her small, booted feet—and all the luscious curves in between, he was forced to add.

Billie, watching him surreptitiously from her post at the stove, interpreted his surprise as disdain. Picking up a plate piled high with biscuits, she walked to the table and put them down beside him. "You don't think much of my house, do you?" she demanded.

He twisted to look at her, hooking his arm over the back of his chair. "It's a fine house," he said. "I just wondered if you really live here."

"Of course I live here!" She stared at him as though he'd taken leave of his senses.

Briefly, he wondered why he was so curious about

her. He wasn't going to get involved with her, was he? Then why should he care about unraveling her mystery? But even as the thought passed through his mind, his mouth was asking, "Where are your parents?"

Billie hesitated, then sat down in the chair beside him "My pa's dead. Killed in a fall from a horse last September." The words, as they always did, brought a pang of loss. Anton Meyrick hadn't been the easiest person to live with, but she had loved him, and, perhaps even more importantly, had shared his dream of running a successful cattle ranch. Not because he was her father, but because it was her dream, too.

"And your mother?"

Heat rose in her face. "She ran off nearly ten years ago. Divorced Pa so fast he didn't know what hit him." Even now, all these years later, that hurt hadn't faded. Helena—she couldn't bring herself to call that woman "mother"—had left without a word to her own child. No explanation, no good-bye, nothing. Shrugging, she reached for a plate and utensils.

Was that shine in her eyes a trick of the light? Nick wondered. Or was it tears? He felt an upsurge of sympathy that made his hands twitch with the desire to comfort her. Resolutely, he pushed it away. "Have you had a lot of trouble with the Indians?" he asked.

"Sure!" Billie, eager for any distraction from the subject of Helena, put her fork down and turned toward him. "We bought this land in sixty-nine, three years before the end of the Apache Wars. For a while, they attacked the ranch regularly."

"Do they steal much stock?"

She laughed. "Not now. But the first year we were here, they stole *all* our cattle."

"All?" he demanded in astonishment.

"All. We managed to hold onto our horses, though.

Those we kept in the corrals and guarded at night. We had to fight for them nearly every night, too."

"We?" he repeated. "You were what—six or seven years old?"

"I was nine. Old enough to hold a rifle."

He took a bite of steak and chewed silently, digesting this information. He felt another jolt of emotion, but this time it was anger against her father. What was wrong with the man to put a nine-year-old girl in such danger?

"Why didn't you sell the place after he died?" he asked at last.

She put her head to one side and regarded him curiously. "Do you really want to know?"

He was startled by her question. On the surface, his part of the conversation seemed ordinary, but there was an undercurrent of emotion running beneath his seemingly casual words as he wavered between his interest in her and the need to hold himself apart. He hadn't expected her to be so perceptive, and it sharpened his interest as well as aroused his caution. He'd have to watch himself around her.

Realizing that she was staring at him, confused by his silence, he said, "Yes. I really want to know."

"Because I love it." She broke a biscuit in half and spooned molasses over it. "I don't think I'd be happy doing anything else."

"What about pretty gowns and parties? What about marriage?" What, he wondered, had made him mention that?

She shrugged. But he suspected she was not as uncaring as she'd have him think; her hands had crept down to smooth the front of her skirt.

"Who was that woman you brought into town today?" He smiled at the memory: the fat, old woman, quivering with outrage, being bullied onto the stage by the tiny, dark-haired girl.

"That was Althea Greeley. She called herself my aunt, but was she actually married to my mother's second cousin." Billie stabbed her steak as though wishing it had been some tender portion of Althea's anatomy. "A couple of months after Pa died, old Althea showed up, ready to run the ranch for poor little Billie. Well, I didn't need any help—hers in particular. But that sour old . . . biddy managed to run off two of my best hands before I could get rid of her."

He laughed, a deep, rich sound that sent another of those queer little shivers up her spine.

"She got a little more than she bargained for, didn't she?" he asked.

"It was a toss-up whether to pay her passage back to San Bernardino or stake her out for the Apaches." She smiled. "I wanted to stake her out, but Budge wouldn't let me."

He leaned his elbows on the table and stared at her mouth hungrily. Even now, smiling with malicious satisfaction as she was, her full, red lips fairly begged to be kissed.

Billie was immobilized by the raw passion on his face. Then she realized what a fool she must seem, sitting with her fork suspended halfway between her plate and her mouth. She laid it down hurriedly and scowled at him.

"Why am I telling you all this, anyway?" she demanded. "You're the one who says *I* ask too many questions."

"You do." He grinned, watching the way her chest swelled with outrage. Her full breasts strained the front of her blouse in a very intriguing manner. She took another deep breath, and his eyebrows went up. Very intriguing, indeed.

Before she could speak, he wrapped his long fingers

around her wrist and squeezed gently. Astonished, she stared at him, her mouth slightly open. Nick nearly groaned at the sight. It was tempting, so very tempting, to surrender to the desire she roused in him. And dangerous, he reminded himself. He released her abruptly.

Billie clasped her trembling hands in her lap. She glanced around warily, but no one else seemed to have noticed the tense little exchange.

Isabel began clearing the empty dishes from the table. Billie jumped up to help her, pausing to toss a deck of cards into Budge's hands. He shuffled them expertly and dealt five cards to everyone.

"What are you doing?" Rachel asked.

"Poker," Budge said. "We play every night. For matches, not money."

Rachel looked down at the cards in front of her. "I don't know how to play."

"We'll teach you," Reuben said.

"I'd rather not—"

"Everybody plays," Budge growled, reaching for the tin of matches. "Loser does the dishes."

Rachel looked up at Billie, who had come back to the table for another load of dishes. "Oh, Billie," she gasped, her face pink with repressed laughter, "not really!"

Billie nodded emphatically. "You don't think I'm going to do this pile of dishes every night, do you?"

Rachel ducked her head and picked up her cards. Billie glanced at Budge. The Texan winked, then turned his attention to his cards. Nick, glimpsing the exchange, realized that Rachel had been dealt a good hand, and would continue to be dealt winning hands for the remainder of the game.

Nick blinked. He hadn't seen that crooked deal, and he had played against plenty of gamblers, honest and dishonest and all the shades in between. Picking up his cards, he realized that the Star M's newest hired hand was fated to wash dishes tonight. He made a resolve to never, never play poker with Budge for money. Sighing, Nick resigned himself to his fate.

Budge divided the matches into equal piles and distributed them. "Nick, you stay here tomorrow and guard the women. It'll give you a chance to stow your gear and look over the spare horses. That buckskin your top mount?"

Nick nodded.

"Wal, you'll need four or five others. I warn you, they're the tail end of the lot, some only half broke. Billie kin tell you their bad habits."

Joe Bell spoke up. "Let him have a try at ol' Beelzebub, Billie."

She smiled, giving Nick a sly glance from beneath her lashes. "He'll have his chance."

"I can hardly wait," Nick murmured. His gaze went to her breasts, savoring the rich swell of them. Maybe, he told himself, he could be a *little* less cautious.

Chapter 4

Billie stepped out of the house and stretched, enjoying the cool morning air. The sun was just peeking over the eastern hills, a great yellow crescent that painted the sky a pale turquoise and gilded the shallow pools of water that were all that was left of Black Dog Creek. A rooster crowed mightily from the top of the corral gate, flapping his wings to greet the new morning. He ruled the chickens that ran loose around the little adobe house in which Eliseo and Isabel Martinez lived with their three children.

Billie walked toward the garden, which lay at the north end of the compound near the spring that supplied the ranch's drinking water. As she passed the bunkhouse, she heard water splashing. She peered around the corner, then stopped, staring.

Nick bent over a washbasin, bare from the waist up. His shoulders were very wide, tapering to a narrow waist and slim hips. Billie watched the muscles ripple in his back and arms as he scrubbed his face. Then, realizing that he might look up any moment, she took a step backward, intending to dart around the corner of the building.

"Don't go," he said, reaching for a towel.

Billie froze, staring at him while he dried his face and neck. He hung the towel over the side of the basin and came toward her, stopping not a foot in front of her. Billie couldn't take her gaze away from his strong, bronze-skinned chest, his flat belly with its hard ridging of muscles. His chest was lightly furred, and a line of hair ran down the center of his abdomen to disappear beneath the waistband of his jeans.

He reached out and straightened the collar of Billie's shirt. It was a man's yoked shirt, faded and much-mended, its voluminous folds gathered into pleats at her narrow waist. He noticed, however, that her breasts more than adequately filled her shirtfront.

"What's the matter, Billie?" he asked, touching his fingertips to his bare skin. "Does this bother you?"

She looked up into his face, startled by the boldness of his words. Amusement filled his tawny, gold-flecked eyes, as well as another, warmer emotion that made her legs tremble. But pride made her draw herself up stiffly and say, "Don't flatter yourself. I've seen plenty of men without their shirts."

"You have?" He took her hand and pressed it to the skin over his heart. "Then this shouldn't bother you, either."

"It doesn't." Billie knew she should pull her hand away, but something seemed to be wrong with her muscles. Her limbs felt weak, too leaden to fight him. Unconsciously, her fingers spread out across his skin.

He smiled. Slowly, he moved her hand from one side of his chest to the other, then ran it lightly down his flat belly to his navel. Billie stood still, frozen into immobility by the feel of the hard ridges of muscle beneath his sleek flesh, the prickling of hair under her palm. Then, seemingly of its own volition, her hand glided back up to his chest. She could feel his heart

38

beating rapidly under her hand, a counterpoint to the thunder of her own pulse.

Nick watched her during it all, noting the bemusement and look of wonder on her face. "Is this the first time you've ever touched a man like that?" he asked softly, pulling her closer.

Outrage surged into her. She snatched her hand away and leaped backward out of his reach. "You've got a lot of gall, Nick Larabee. If you think I'm stupid enough to get involved with a drifter who's going to move on as soon as the wind changes, you'd better run that notion right out of your head."

"You're trembling," he said. So was he. If he had any sense at all, he'd walk away from her now. But he just couldn't. He reached for her, needing to touch her again.

"Keep your hands off me," Billie warned, retreating hastily. "If you—"

Before she could get away, his hands clamped onto her shoulders. He drew her closer. Billie, furious, erupted in a wild flurry of flailing fists and kicking feet.

Her boot connected with his shin. With a curse, he let her go and took a step backward. "You little wildcat!"

"Don't ever try that again," she said through clenched teeth. "You come near me again and I'll—"

"Good morning," Rachel called, coming around the corner of the bunkhouse. "I thought I heard voices . . . Oh!" Seeing Nick's bare, broad chest, she put one hand over her mouth and blushed furiously. "Oh, dear!"

"Morning, Rachel," Billie said, wrestling her churning emotions into some semblance of order.

Rachel turned her back on Nick. "Mr. Larabee, I would appreciate it if you would put your shirt on."

"Yes, ma'am." He pulled his shirt over his head and tucked it into his jeans, winking at Billie, who was furious that she hadn't had the sense to look away, as Rachel had.

"You can turn around, Miss Laird," he said. "What are you doing out so early?"

Rachel turned to face him, the pink fading from her cheeks. "Why, I came to see you ride Beelzebub, Mr. Larabee."

"I'm not going anywhere near a horse named Beelzebub," Nick said.

"But everyone tries to ride him," Rachel protested. She blushed again and added, "Mr. Jewett said it's very entertaining."

Nick laughed. "I'm sure it is—for the fellow who's watching."

Billie stared at Nick thoughtfully. Like the other cowboys, he treated Rachel with tender courtliness, his whole demeanor softening when he spoke to her. For a moment, Billie wished she possessed whatever quality Rachel had that made Nick react that way. Billie shook her head, instantly ashamed of the brief moment of jealousy. Besides, what difference should it make to her if Nick liked Rachel, or even if he fell in love with her?

"Let's get to work," Nick said, breaking into her reverie. He retrieved his hat from the washstand and put it on.

Billie led the way to the corral, running ahead to greet her favorite mount, a compact black mare with a white blaze on her face. "Hello, Sunfish, old girl," she murmured, stroking the horse's velvet nose.

Nick's eyebrows went up. "Why Sunfish? If she was a palomino, I'd understand the name."

"Oh, it has nothing to do with her looks." Billie laughed. "I named her for her method of removing people she doesn't want riding her."

"I see." Nick reflected on the type of bucking called "sunfishing," where the horse flops wildly from side to side, bringing first one shoulder nearly to the ground, then the other, and decided not to try the mare. He indicated the other horses. "What about those?"

Billie looked them over expertly. "The roan is all right, once he's over his morning high jinks. Now that gray over there, he's got a bad habit of falling over backward, and so does that sorrel mare. The black gelding and the two bays have only been saddled once or twice, but I think they'll do fine if you treat them right. And then there's Beelzebub." She pointed at the big, strong-looking palomino stallion in the other corral. "He's also known by various uncomplimentary descriptions—in three languages, mind you. He's famous through the whole territory. I can't sell him or ride him, but he's just too pretty to shoot."

Beelzebub shook his pale golden mane and fixed Nick with a mournful brown gaze. Nick stared back, fascinated. "He looks docile enough," he said, walking over to the stallion's corral.

Billie smiled. "Oh, he's docile, all right. He'll follow you around like a faithful dog. He'll eat out of your hand and whinny a hello at you every morning. He'll even stand quietly and let you put a bit and saddle on him. But climb on his back, and he goes crazy." She sighed; every cowboy who came here wanted to tame the beautiful golden horse.

"If I can ride him, can I use him?" Nick asked. He turned to look at her, his eyes flaring with excitement and masculine love of a challenge.

Something in her responded to his emotion, something that compelled her to offer a challenge of her own. "If you can ride that horse, I'll *give* him to you."

Nick settled his hat firmly on his head and climbed into the corral. He took a bridle with him, holding it casually at his side as he walked toward the horse. Beelzebub let him approach, and even ducked his head so

41

that Nick could rub between his ears.

"Give me a saddle," Nick called softly, slipping the bit into the animal's mouth.

Billie was beginning to regret her impulsive words. He seemed to know something about horses, but if he didn't, he could get hurt. Even men who had been on horseback most of their lives had failed to master Beelzebub. "Nick, that stallion is as gentle as a lamb going his way and a hell-spawned demon going yours," she protested. "He can't be ridden."

"I'll never know if I don't try," he said. "The saddle, Billie."

She climbed into the corral. Lifting a saddle down from its perch on the top rail, she hauled it over to Nick. He heaved it gently onto the horse's sleek golden back and tightened the cinch, talking softly to the animal all the while.

"Open the gate," he said. "Give him some room."

"I wouldn't do that, if I were you," she protested. "He's going to—"

"Open the gate, damn it!"

"Yes, sir, Mr. Larabee, sir!" Serves you right, Billie thought. Arrogant peacock! She swung the gate open just as he climbed into the saddle.

The moment the seat of Nick's jeans hit the leather, Beelzebub snorted and gave three tremendous, stiff-legged leaps forward. Once clear of the corral, the horse ducked his head and headed south at top speed. Nick, his hat gone, his mouth open in astonishment, pulled up on the reins with all his strength. But it had no effect on Beelzebub. The big horse intended to go south, and no one was going to stop him.

Billie swung the gate closed and leaned against it to watch the pair disappear over the ridge. Nick's hat lay at her feet. She picked it up and brushed the dirt from it with her forearm. A clean, masculine scent rose from it, a scent that made her heartbeat quicken.

"Should we go after them?" Rachel asked in alarm.

"No one can catch Beelzebub once he's started. Don't worry, Rachel. They'll be back. Separately, of course, and Beelzebub quite a bit sooner than Nick." Billie laughed, but she stared a bit nervously at the spot where Nick and the horse had disappeared. For a moment she was tempted to saddle Sunfish and go after them, but then she remembered the way Nick had smiled when she had touched him, a knowing, self-congratulatory, infuriating grin that made her back stiffen even now. Dropping his hat back into the dust, she turned away.

The pair did not return that morning, nor that afternoon. When the other cowboys returned for supper, they immediately noticed that Beelzebub was not in the corral.

"How long they been gone?" Budge asked.

Rachel pressed her hands together. "All day. Do you think he's all right?"

"Sure," the Texan drawled. "It's jest takin' him awhile to walk back. What did you open the gate fer, Billie?"

"He told me to."

Budge pushed his hat back on his head and regarded her with amused blue-gray eyes. "You tell him about that critter's tendency to head south?"

"Sort of. He was real anxious to ride, though."

"The feller's probably halfway to Mexico by now," Stubbs Foley said, grinning.

"Mexico!" Rachel cried in horror. "He could be lost. Even hurt!" She turned to Budge in appeal. "Someone should go after him. Please, Mr. Jewett."

"All right, Miss Rachel." The Texan began snapping his chaps back on. "And call me Budge. I ain't been called Mr. Jewett since I mustered out of the army."

"Yes, Budge," Rachel said meekly.

"Will you look at that!" Squint exclaimed. "Swear to God, I never thought I'd see the day!"

Billie whirled. Her gaze followed Squint's pointing finger, and her mouth dropped open in astonishment. Nick and Beelzebub had just come into view on the slope of a nearby ridge. Nick was sitting in the saddle as casually as though he'd been riding the horse for years.

"Wal, I'll be goddamned," Budge said.

The cowboys watched in respectful silence as the pair approached. The slanting rays of afternoon sunlight caught the horse and rider, reflecting the gold of the palomino's hide and picking out the bronze highlights in Nick's tawny hair. Beautiful man and beautiful horse, Billie thought, and both as wild as the wind.

Nick pulled Beelzebub to a stop in front of the awed group. He dismounted stiffly. As he reached to unfasten the cinch, Squint stepped forward.

"I'll do that," Squint offered. "You look like you're hurtin'."

"He tried to scrape me off against a cholla cactus," Nick said.

"I never thought I'd see that horse broke," Reuben muttered.

"If you think he's broke, just climb on his back and see what happens," Nick said. Suddenly he turned to Billie. "Did you mean what you said?"

She nodded. "He's all yours. Now come inside and let me pull those spines out of your leg."

As Rachel darted ahead to open the door, he put his arm over Billie's shoulder and hopped beside her toward the house. He could have made it on his own. But he liked the feel of her tucked up against his side, the firm curves of her breast and hip rubbing against him as he walked.

Once inside, Billie eased Nick into a chair. He held

his leg straight out, wincing. She went to the cupboard and took out a long skinning knife, a bottle of whiskey and a pair of pliers.

"Rachel, get me some water and a clean cloth," she said.

"What are you going to do with that knife?" Nick demanded, half rising from the chair.

"I've got to cut your pants," Billie said, pushing him back down and thrusting the whiskey bottle into his hand. "Take a drink."

Billie knelt at his feet and pulled his boot off. She upended it, sending a shower of pebbles onto the floor. Then she turned her attention to his pants. Making a cut in the bottom of his jeans, she slit the fabric up to his thigh and carefully worked the fabric away from his leg. A little forest of cactus spines sprouted from his flesh from the top of his boot to just above his knee.

Rachel moaned. Billie looked up and, seeing how pale the girl's face had become, said, "Why don't you wait outside, Rachel?"

"No," Rachel said, pressing her lips together. "I'll stay."

Billie nodded. Bracing Nick's knee between her arm and the side of her chest, she plucked one of the spines out with a deft flick of the pliers.

"You've done this before," Nick said when he got his breath back.

"Hundreds of times." She plucked another spine. "What I don't understand is how you got rocks in your boots while you were mounted."

"Mounted!" He snorted. "That damned horse . . . Ouch! That damned horse all but crawled along the ground like a snake trying to get me off his back. Ouch! Goddamn it to hell!"

Billie ignored his curses and kept plucking. It was hard to keep her mind on what she was doing, for his thigh was hard with muscle, his skin smooth beneath a dusting of silky hair. His leg jerked every time she pulled a spine out, rubbing disturbingly against her breast. She shook her head in attempt to rid herself of the strange sensation that touch engendered in her.

With an effort, she pushed her discomfiture aside and bent to her task. When the spines were all out, she swabbed the punctures with soap and water. She would have preferred to clean them with whiskey, but Nick refused to let go of the bottle. By the time she was finished, he had downed half the liquor.

"There," she said at last, sitting back on her heels. "It's done. Are you hurt anywhere else?"

He pulled his shirt over his head and let it fall to the floor. Rachel, who was standing behind him, gasped and nearly dropped the basin of water she was holding.

Billie scrambled to her feet. "Let me look at that," she said, walking quickly around the chair.

A great purpling bruise covered his ribs in the back, and another was darkening on his shoulder blade. Billie pressed gently on his ribs.

"Does that hurt?" she asked.

"Ouch! Nothing's broken, if that's what you mean," he said, scowling at her over his shoulder.

Billie dropped her hands from his back. "Well, you're going to be mighty sore for a few days."

"I'll go dump this water," Rachel said in a strangled voice. She fled the room.

Billie stared after her. Why was the girl so upset? she wondered. "I'd better go see what—"

"Just a minute," Nick said. He turned and grasped Billie by the wrist and drew her around to the front of the chair. With a jerk, he pulled her down onto his lap.

"Let me go," she ordered.

The whiskey was working in him now, warming his insides, making him forget why he shouldn't be doing

46

this. But was it the liquor that was putting the fire in his blood, he wondered, or was it the delicious litle bundle of femininity who was perched on his knees?

She wriggled, but his grip was like iron, binding her in her place.

"I want that kiss," he said.

"What kiss?" She stared at him in astonishment.

"The one you owe me for opening that gate."

"I just did what you told me," she protested.

He leaned toward her. "Don't play innocent with me. You knew that horse would take off."

"You deserved it." She clenched her fists.

"Why? Because I touched you? Oh, no, you don't," hc growled, pinning her hands against the arms of the chair before she could strike him. He smiled down at her. "You really are a little savage, aren't you?"

"Let me go," Billie said with as much dignity as she could muster under the circumstances.

"Not just yet." He took her wrists in one big hand and grasped her chin with the other. "I want that kiss."

Billie opened her mouth to reply. Before she could utter a word, his mouth swooped down on hers. She made one muffled sound of protest, then she became lost in a flood of sensation. His tongue probed her mouth, seeking, tasting, running delicately along the edges of her teeth before moving back into the honeyed depths of her mouth.

He released her hands. Her fists unclenched, and she reached up to wind her fingers in the thick curls at the nape of his neck. Her tongue darted forward, playing shyly with his.

Nick groaned, lost in the sweet wonder of her response. He'd meant the kiss as much as a punishment as to taste her lips, but his anger was swept away in a tremendous surge of desire. He wanted her. She was trouble—big trouble—but he wanted her more than

47

any woman he'd ever known. He tore his mouth away from hers and began to explore the smooth skin of her throat with his lips. Her pulse beat wildly against his mouth, and he exulted in the heat of her, the womanly perfume of her skin and hair.

His hands moved up and down her back restlessly, and Billie arched to meet him.

"Just like a cat," he muttered. "A sleek little cat."

He pulled her against him, nuzzling at the neck of her blouse. His hands moved from her back to her waist, then rose to span her ribs. His thumbs brushed her nipples, finding them erect and swollen.

But the unfamiliar touch startled Billie, and she woke to reality with a rush. She leaped from her perch with a suddenness that took him completely by surprise. "You stay away from me!" she hissed. "I don't want you to touch me again, ever. Do you hear me?"

He leaned back and regarded her from under lowered eyelids. God, but he wanted her! "I hear you," he said. "I just don't believe you mean it."

Billie ran to the courtyard, slamming the heavy door behind her. She stood outside, her fists clenched, her breasts rising and falling with outrage. What was wrong with her? Had she succumbed to some sort of madness, to have let him touch her so intimately? Why, she'd never even kissed a man before. Her face burned. He'd known exactly what to do to inflame her senses, and was probably laughing at her right now.

Suddenly she heard the sound of sobbing and whirled to see Rachel crouched against the wall of the house, her face buried in her hands.

Billie knelt beside her. "What's the matter, Rachel?" she asked.

Rachel buried her face against Billie's shoulder and cried harder. Perhaps this was the first time the girl had wept since her family had been killed, Billie thought.

She'd never had much experience with tears; her father scorned such things as weakness, and she had quickly learned to keep her feelings inside. Her hand hovered uncertainly above Rachel's blond hair for a moment, then dropped down to stroke it lightly.

"Go ahead, let it all out," she murmured.

When the storm was at an end at last, Rachel lifted her head and rubbed the tears from her face with her sleeve. "I'm sorry," she murmured. "It was just the spines and the blood . . ." She took a deep, shuddering breath. "This is a terrible place, Billie, when even the plants can hurt people."

"But it's beautiful, too," Billie murmured. "Just look at that sunset, will you?"

Rachel leaned against the side of the house and gazed at the western horizon. The sky was a blazing glory of red and orange and bronze, against which stood the jagged silhouette of the hills. A hawk wheeled in a graceful circle before plummeting swiftly to his roost.

Suddenly Rachel took Billie's hands in hers. "Since the attack, I've been living in a dream. I walked and talked, but there was nothing but emptiness inside me. It was easier to feel nothing than to face the hurt. It's only since I came here that I began to feel again. Billie, I owe it to you. If you hadn't been the way you are . . ." she shivered. "Can we be friends?"

Billie resisted the impulse to turn away in embarrassment. Although she wasn't used to this sort of openness, Rachel's emotion was honest, her affection freely offered. It behooved her to accept it as freely. "Of course," she agreed, wondering what Rachel would think if she knew she was the first real woman friend Billie had ever had.

Chapter 5

Dawn was still an hour away when Billie hitched the team to the wagon and set off toward Xavier. This was her second trip in less than a week, but she'd been so furious at Althea that she'd completely forgotten to pick up supplies while in town. Billie shook her head in annoyance. Even in her absence, the woman managed to inconvenience people.

By the time Billie had crossed the second ridge, a soft apricot glow was lightening the eastern sky. She stopped the wagon and watched as the sun thrust its upper curve above the horizon. Yellow light seemed to spill over the edge of the world, rushing across the crumpled folds of hills toward her. Billie let out her breath in a long sigh.

"I see that you still love the land, Cactus Flower," came a soft voice from behind her.

Startled, Billie whirled to see a young Apache woman mounted on a thin brown horse. The girl didn't smile, but pleasure lit her dark face.

Billie responded in Chiricahua, the Indian girl's native language. "Hello, Laughing Woman. It has been a long time since our paths have crossed," she said, inspecting the visitor's face narrowly. The girl was as thin as her horse, the skin stretched tightly over her high cheekbones.

"Many, many moons," the girl agreed. "I have a son now."

"I rejoice for you. Are you well?"

"We are well." The young Indian woman urged her mount closer to the wagon.

Billie swiveled in the seat to face her. "You have been gone from the reservation many months. Do you need food?"

"Two cows."

"Take them. You know which of my men to stay away from."

Laughing Woman nodded. "We are grateful." She turned her mount toward the northeast, where a brave sat his mount at the top of the nearest hill.

"Your husband?" Billie asked.

"Yes. His name is Man-who-waits." Laughing Woman pointed over Billie's shoulder. "Yours?"

"What?" Billie turned to see a horse and rider standing upon the crest of the hill behind her. The horse was a palomino, its hide gleaming like purest gold in the sun. "No," she said. "He is not my husband."

"You should marry him. Only a very strong warrior could ride the Golden Demon. You need a strong man."

Billie was torn between outrage and laughter. Before she could reply, however, Laughing Woman turned away again.

"Come to me again if you have need," Billie called.

The Apache woman glanced at Billie over her shoulder. "Go in peace, Cactus Flower," she said in English.

"And you." But Billie knew there would be no peace for Laughing Woman's people.

Billie watched the Indian girl ride up the slope to join the warrior. Laughing Woman raised her arm over her head in farewell, then both Indians disappeared over the crest of the hill.

A horse's shod hoof rang against a stone behind Billie. Without turning her head, she said, "At least you had the sense not to come down here shooting."

"I'll take that as a compliment," Nick said. He nodded toward the spot where he had last seen the Indians, "Who are they?"

"That was Laughing Woman and her husband." Billie reached up to toss her braid back over her shoulder. "Six years ago I found a young Apache girl lying in an arroyo. She'd been shot in the back. I put her in the wagon and took her back to the house. She was six months getting well, and there were times when we thought she'd never walk again."

"I thought you were at war with the Apaches."

Billie shrugged. "Pa didn't hold with fighting women and children. But there are a lot of people who don't feel the same, so we hid Laughing Woman whenever anyone came to visit. She stayed with us until she was well enough to travel, then Pa gave her a horse and some food and sent her back to her people."

Nick leaned his forearm on the pommel of his saddle and stared thoughtfully into the distance. "What's she doing off the reservation?"

"She's Nana's granddaughter."

"Nana?" Nick demanded, surprise bringing him upright in his saddle. "The man who has been running the army, the Texas Rangers and the Mexican troops in circles?"

"Can you believe that old man?" Billie asked, her voice filled with grudging admiration. "He must be seventy or eighty years old, and I hear he walks with a cane."

53

"Do you know where they're hiding?" he asked.

"No," she said, picking up the reins. She wasn't exactly lying. She might have a very good idea, but she didn't *know*. Even if she did, she wasn't about to tell him, not when he'd kept his past—and his plans for the future—such a secret. Why she'd had the bad luck to have him catch her talking to Laughing Woman . . . No one, not even her father, knew how close she and Laughing Woman had become during the girl's long convalescence. Had that friendship become known, people would have tried to use it against the Apache— twist it, dirty it, turn it as ugly as their own hate.

"Do you see her often?" Nick asked, his voice as casual as it had been before.

"No." Billie urged the team forward. "All I can say is that it's a shame the whites and the Apache can't find a way to live together."

His eyebrows went up. "That's a mighty tolerant attitude, considering some of the things the Apache have done."

"I'm not defending their actions," Billie said, thinking of Rachel and her family. "But our people have done their share of brutal things, too. Hate turns men into beasts. It doesn't matter if they're red or white."

Nick rode beside the wagon, watching Beelzebub's ears for any sign of impending violence. He and the stallion had reached a fragile truce the day before, but it had been born of mutual respect and exhaustion, not from any capitulation on the horse's part. He was beginning to regret taking Beelzebub this morning; the palomino had started this ride as docile as a lamb, but had become increasingly hard to handle. It was like sitting on a barrel of gunpowder waiting for it to explode at any moment, Nick mused. God help him if someone fired a gun nearby.

"What are you doing here, anyway?" Billie demanded.

"Rachel was worried about you coming out here alone. She nagged Budge into sending someone after you."

Billie scowled. "Well, you can turn around and go back. I'm probably as safe out here as anyone can be."

"From Apaches, maybe. There are other kinds of predators."

"What kind are you?" she asked.

"Just a man."

She noticed that he didn't object to being called a predator. Most men would have. "Go away," she said.

"No." He reined Beelzebub in, forcing the prancing animal to match the wagon's lumbering pace, then lapsed into thoughtful silence. Billie's friendship with the Indians put a different light on just where she fit in the puzzle he had come here to unravel. He found her to be a mystery in herself, one he was compelled to solve. She was tempestuous, annoying, downright abrasive at times, yet her kindness to Rachel proved that there were depths beyond that tough façade. And now he knew her as friend to the Apache. In time, what other aspects of Billie Meyrick would he discover? Instead of making him draw back, that notion was powerfully appealing.

Billie chafed under the continued silence. Nick seemed to have forgotten her completely. She pulled her hat farther down on her brow and focused her attention on the track ahead, determined not to be the first to speak. But after a few seemingly interminable hours of listening to nothing but the rattle of the wagon's wheels, she couldn't help but start the conversation going again.

"Why did you come to Xavier?" she asked. "There's nothing here for a man like you."

He looked at her, his gaze as warm and as caressing

as his hands had been the day before. "I wouldn't say that."

"Will you stop it?" she cried.

Startled, Beelzebub tossed his head and pranced sideways. Nick soothed the palomino with his hands and voice, then glared at Billie.

"Don't do that again," he growled. "You spook this horse, you're going to be damn sorry."

Billie cocked her head to one side, wondering if the act would be worth the consequences. Oh, it was tempting! She couldn't help but speculate as to just how he might punish her. Would he kiss her again? It was the memory of that other kiss and her reaction to it, rather than his threat, that made her decide not to try anything. She fixed her attention on the track ahead and kept it there for the remainder of the trip.

It was nearly one o'clock when they entered Xavier. While Nick was looping Beelzebub's reins carefully around the hitching post, Billie jumped down from the wagon and took the list out of her jacket pocket.

Nick reached over her shoulder and plucked the paper out of her hand. "What do we need?" he asked. "Let's see . . . salt, sugar, flour, canned peaches—"

"Give me that!" Billie snatched the list back, irritated that he had taken over so casually. You'd think he was running things, she thought. "Why don't you go get yourself a drink? After I'm finished here, I have a few other things to do."

"Yes, ma'am, boss lady." He grinned, correctly reading her sour expression. "Touchy, aren't you?"

"Meet me back here in an hour," she snapped.

"I'll find you when I'm ready." He turned on his heel and walked away.

She watched him saunter down the street toward the saloon, his broad shoulders swinging easily with every step.

"New hand?" the storekeeper asked from behind her.

"Yes." Her face hot, Billie handed the man her list. "I'll need everything on here," she said.

He nodded. "You go on and tend to the rest of your errands. I'll have your order ready for you when you get back."

"I'd appreciate that."

"Say, isn't that Beelzebub?" the storekeeper asked.

"Yes."

"That new fella broke him? Well, I'll be damned!"

Billie smiled, thinking of how fragile Nick's control of the palomino really was. Then a shaft of pride for Nick's skill caught her unexpectedly, making her throat tighten.

Still smiling, she turned away and headed down the street to the telegraph office to see if there was a telegram for Rachel. To her regret, there was. Rachel's brother must have finally received word of his family's misfortune, and that meant she'd soon be leaving. Billie sighed; she'd enjoyed having the other girl at the ranch more than she would have thought possible. With the nearest neighbor more than twenty miles away, she'd become accustomed to the company of men. Oh, there was Isabel, of course, but the Mexican woman spoke little English and was usually too busy tending to the needs of her steadily growing family to provide much companionship. Until Rachel had come to the Star M, Billie hadn't realized just how lonely she had been. Lost in thought, she wandered slowly out of the telegraph office.

"Hello, pretty lady."

Billie whirled. The man who had spoken was leaning against a nearby hitching post, a cigarette dangling from the corner of his mouth. He was dressed in a white shirt and a pair of black jeans beneath leather chaps. Two gun belts were crossed over his hips, the holsters tied down on each thigh. He was slender and graceful, handsome in a sharp-featured way, but his smile was just a bit too eager for Billie's taste.

"I said hello, pretty lady," he drawled, lifting his hat to give her a glimpse of dark, straight hair. His voice was cultured, if a trifle high. His gaze lingered on her breasts for an insultingly long time.

Billie turned on her heel and walked away.

He abandoned his languid pose with startling quickness and blocked her path. "Not so fast, honey. I like you. Why don't we spend some time together?"

"I'm not interested." She took a step sideways, intending to dart around him, but he moved with her.

"My name is Carson Eames, pretty lady. What's yours?"

"None of your business."

He took her by the arm and turned her around. "Come on, honey. You can't refuse one drink with a lonely cowboy."

She jerked her arm out of his grasp. "You're no cowboy," she snapped. "You don't even know enough to take your chaps off when you come into town."

"You're a feisty one, but I like a woman with fire." He slid his arm around her waist and pulled her against him, ignoring her efforts to free herself. "I've got a room at the hotel. Let's go on up and—"

"You're not taking her anywhere," Nick said from behind the struggling pair. He pulled Billie away from the other man and shoved her out of the way.

"This is none of your business," Eames growled. "Walk away, stranger."

Nick smiled, but it was a humorless, feral smile that made Billie's heart pound with dread. "But she *is* my business," he said.

Eames took a slow step backward, then another. His fingers twitched slightly. Two men who had stopped to watch the argument turned and hurried into the nearest doorway. Billie pressed herself against the rough, weathered boards of the building behind her, trying frantically to think of a way to stop this madness.

Nick watched the other man's eyes, not his hands. His own hands were relaxed at his sides, his smile unfaltering. "Any time you're ready," he said.

"Eames!" a man shouted from across the street. He hurried across the stretch of rutted dirt and stepped between the gunman and Nick, his seamed, leathery face tight with concern and a little fear. "We don't want no trouble here!"

"He called me," Eames raged. "Get out of the way, Lew."

"You asked for it," the older man said. "Go on, get back to the ranch."

"I don't take orders from you."

"Yes, you do, young feller. You work for the Dolorosa Ranch. I'm foreman there, and you kin do as I say or git out."

"Stearns will set you straight soon enough, old man," Eames sneered.

"Mebbe so. But until I hear otherwise, I still run the Dolorosa, and I run you. Now, git!"

Eames hesitated for a moment, then strode to his horse and flung himself into the saddle. Before riding away, he fixed Nick with an icy stare and growled, "I'll be seeing you again, stranger."

Nick nodded. "Yes, you will."

Lew heaved a sigh of relief. "That was a close one. Sorry, Billie."

"What are you doing with a man like that?" she asked.

"The boss hired him back east, sent him to me." Lew shook his head in disgust. "I'd sooner bed down with a rattlesnake, but there ain't nothin' I can do."

"How long has he been around?" Nick asked.

"Mebbe a month." Lew hooked his thumbs into the waistband of his jeans and looked up at the taller man. "You jest bought yourself a mess of trouble, cowboy. That's one mean feller. You better walk careful."

Nick shrugged. "I always do. Who is this Stearns fellow?"

"New owner of the Dolorosa." Lew screwed his face up with disgust. "Some furriner. I ain't never laid eyes on him, but he's been givin' orders by telegram. Lots of orders. You wouldn't believe the things goin' on up at the house. And now he's comin' in today, complete with family and fixin's." He pulled out his watch and opened it. "Wal, I got to go, folks. Stage is due in a couple of minutes."

"Thanks, Lew," Billie called after him.

Nick rocked back and forth on his heels, whistling tonelessly.

Billie put her hands on her hips. "Are you crazy, taking on a man like Eames? What's wrong with you?"

"Would you rather have gone to the hotel with him?" Nick asked, raising his eyebrows.

"Of course not! But . . ." Billie's face grew hot. What was wrong with her? She'd been about to tell him how frightened she had been for him!

He smiled down at her tenderly, but his voice was teasing. "Were you scared? Dare I hope some small part of your concern was for me?"

Billie drew herself up, trying to maintain some semblance of dignity. There were times when the man seemed to actually read her mind. It was very disturbing, and yet, somehow, exciting. Pushing the thought aside savagely, she put her nose in the air and said, "I've got some more things to do. If you don't mind—"

"I don't." He took her by the arm. "Where are we going now?"

"*I'm* going to the dressmaker's," she said trying ineffectually to pull her arm out of his grasp.

"I'll take you."

She tried to dig her heels in, but he pulled her along easily. Finally she gave up and began walking beside him. He glanced at her, laughter twitching at the corners of his mouth, and let her go. To her chagrin, he followed her into the shop. His tawny masculinity was as out of place amid the satins and laces as a mountain lion in a henhouse.

"Why don't you wait outside?" she whispered.

"I'm fine right here," he said, leaning his broad back against the wall.

Billie turned her back on him to see Angela Felker, the dressmaker, and two other ladies watching the exchange interestedly. Judging from the amount of admiration in their faces as they inspected Nick, they didn't mind him intruding into this frilly, feminine domain.

"What can I do for you, Billie?" Angela asked, coming forward quickly.

Billie, anxious to get out of the shop and away from the women's curious gazes, quickly chose two skirts, three blouses, some underclothing and a pair of riding boots. Then her attention was caught by a yellow cotton dress, trimmed with narrow lace at the sleeves and demure neckline. It looked to be just Rachel's size. Near it was another dress, a pale turquoise that was just the color of the morning sky. Her hand lingered on the smooth fabric for a moment. She wanted the turquoise dress. She'd never had anything like it; she always bought clothes that were suitable for work around the ranch. But this . . . What, she mused idly, would she look like in it? Would Nick see her differently? Would he treat her with the same gentle respect as he did Rachel?

61

She stroked the sleeve, and the work-roughened skin of her palms caught at the delicate fabric. Idiot! she berated herself, putting the dress aside. You've got no business wanting anything like this! But she picked up the yellow dress and handed it to Angela. "I'll take this one, too."

"But none of these clothes are your size," Angela protested. "Are they for that poor girl you took in?"

Billie frowned. Angela knew very well the clothes were for Rachel. The dressmaker and her friends were terrible gossips. Give them the slightest encouragement, and they would begin asking a lot of questions about things that were none of their business. Billie considered several replies, none very polite, then reluctantly discarded them.

Angela, however, didn't wait for an answer. "Just think how awful it would be to have to live with such a memory. Those dirty Apaches . . ." She glanced at Nick. In a lower voice, she continued, "I heard there were six of them, and they—"

"You've got a filthy mouth and an even filthier mind," Billie snapped. "How much do I owe you?"

"Well, ah . . . that is . . ." Astonished by Billie's fury, Angela fumbled for words. "Thirty-two dollars."

Billie shot a glance at Nick. His face was impassive, but his lips were pressed in a thin line and his eyes were dark with anger. So, he'd heard. She tossed the money on the counter, scorning Angela's outstretched hand, then gathered up the parcels and dumped them into her escort's outstretched arms.

After loading the supplies into the wagon, they set off for the ranch. Nick rode beside her, seemingly lost in thought. Suddenly he leaned over and gave her a chaste peck on the cheek.

"What was that for?" she demanded, touching her fingertips to the spot he had kissed.

He smiled. "Someday, I might just tell you."

"I don't understand you at all," she said.

"No?" He raised her hand to his cheek, then pressed his lips to her palm. "I thought I'd been plain enough."

Billie jerked her hand away, closing it into a fist. Her skin tingled where his lips had touched it. "Stop it."

"Yes, ma'am."

He tipped his hat mockingly and moved away, but Billie knew he wasn't finished with her.

Those were kept in the corrals and guarded at night. We had to hunt for them nearly every night, too.

Chapter 6

"Rachel!" Billic called as she pulled the wagon to a halt outside the house. "There's a telegram for you!" She jumped to the ground before Nick had a chance to lift her down.

Rachel hurried out of the house, wiping her hands on her apron. Nick nodded casually to her and led Beelzebub toward the corral.

"I wonder . . . Oh, it's from my brother!" Rachel murmured, taking the telegram from Billie's outstretched hand.

An odd look crossed her face as she read, but it was gone so quickly that Billie couldn't quite decide what emotion had prompted that fleeting expression.

With a shrug, Rachel handed the telegram back to Billie. "Read it," she said.

"Cannot come now. Urgent business in Virginia," Billie read, her eyebrows going up incredulously. "Will send funds. Stay until I send for you. Love, Alan." She looked up at Rachel. "You told him about your family's death and everything?" she asked. "He couldn't have misunderstood?"

Rachel shook her head.

"Well, he's mighty calm about the whole thing,"

Billie said, looking down at her boots lest Rachel see the outrage and disbelief on her face. Why, the man hadn't said a word about his family's deaths! And his lack of sympathy for his sister's feelings . . . Suddenly she burst out, "What's wrong with him, Rachel? Can't he see that you need him?"

"He's a very busy man," Rachel said quietly.

Billie crossed her arms. "Busy" was not the term she would use to describe Mr. Alan Laird, but she refrained from saying any more lest she hurt Rachel's feelings.

"He'll be sending me some money soon," Rachel said. "I can take a room at the hotel—"

"Oh, no, you're not. You're going to stay right here."

"There's no way of knowing how long it will be," Rachel protested. "I can't impose on you like that."

"I'd do the same for anyone." Billie put her hands on her hips and glared at Rachel with feigned annoyance. "Besides, I like having you here."

"Oh, I see." Rachel smiled. "In that case, I'll be glad to stay." Suddenly she leaned forward and swept the smaller girl up in a tight hug. Before an astonished Billie could react, Rachel let her go and ran into the house.

"You didn't even stay to see what I bought you," Billie grumbled. But her smile belied the severity of her voice.

Leaving the supplies for the moment, she filled her arms with the lighter parcels of clothing and carried them into the house. Rachel wasn't in her room, however, so Billie dumped the packages on the bed and went out for another load. Noticing that the door to the courtyard was ajar, she went to close it. The soft murmur of voices came to her. Pushing the door open a few inches, she peered out into the courtyard to see Rachel and Nick deep in conversation. To her surprise, she realized that they were arguing.

Billie knew she should close the door and walk away, but she just couldn't do it. Although she couldn't hear what they were saying, Rachel was obviously upset about something, and Nick seemed to be trying to talk his way out of whatever trouble he was in. Rachel said something in a low voice, her hand chopping the air in anger. Nick shook his head in response. Speaking in a hushed whisper, he took the girl's hand in both of his.

Billie's heart felt as though it was turning over in her chest. It wasn't jealousy that she felt, but a realization and a grinding regret that she could never hope to compete with Rachel. She felt no animosity toward the other girl; Rachel was as gentle and kind as she was beautiful, and deserved every bit of happiness that went her way. But Billie's gaze kept going back to Nick's bronzed face, his broad shoulders and deep, powerful chest. The regret intensified.

Suddenly Rachel pulled her hand away. Turning her back on Nick, she marched toward the house. Abandoning her post by the door, Billie tiptoed across the room and slipped quickly out the other door.

The sun was just dipping beneath the western horizon, painting the sky with streaks of fiery color. But the sight gave Billie no joy; the whole world seemed gray just now, bleached of all color by the pain in her heart.

Budge raised his hand for quiet, an urgent, listening look on his lean face. The men immediately fell silent. Only their eyes moved, watching their boss for any sign.

"Art," the Texan said at last, "you and Joe git out there quietlike. See what's got them horses so jangly."

The twins rose in uncanny unison and slipped out the

back door. Billie rose from her seat and picked her rifle up from its place beside the door.

"Let's get the children, Eliseo," she said.

Nick pushed his chair back. "You stay here," he said, buckling his gun belt around his hips. "I'll go with him."

Outrage made Billie's cheeks burn. The man was giving her orders in her own house. What gall! She opened her mouth to retort, but before she could say anything, Art slipped back into the house.

"Relax, fellas," he said. "Just an army patrol looking fer a place to spend the night. They've been cut up some, had met up with the Apach."

Billie put her rifle down and opened the door. "Isabel, you'd better cook the rest of those steaks," she called over her shoulder. "We've got company."

There were eleven mounted soldiers in the group, leading six horses with empty saddles. The men were demoralized and bone-weary, drooping in their saddles like they had been riding forever. They were led by a grizzled old corporal whose face bore a network of whitened scars. He blinked wearily at Billie, obviously too tired to think what to do.

Nick took hold of the lead horse's bridle. "There's a hot meal waiting for you and your men, Corporal," he said. "We'll take care of your horses."

The mention of food brought the old man's head up with a jerk. "Dismount, men," he barked. "Let's eat."

A few minutes later, the soldiers were seated at the table, wolfing down a meal of steak, biscuits and Isabel's beans. The corporal stabbed another steak from the platter and cut off a huge hunk of meat. Working it into his mouth, he chewed blissfully, a stream of bloody juice running unheeded from the corners of his mouth.

"Thank'ee kindly, ma'am," he mumbled through the

68

mass of beef. "I near forgot what food tasted like."

Billie nodded. "What happened out there, Corporal . . . ?"

"Tillston, ma'am. Ira Tillston. We run into some Injuns over by Anteojo Peak. We been takin' regular patrols out that way ever since we heard old Nana's braves were holed up out there. Ain't seen hide nor hair of 'em until yestidday. Then all hell busted loose."

He paused to take a bite of molasses-soaked biscuit before continuing his story. "Damned—'scuse me, ladies—gol-darned 'Pach caught us in a blind canyon, fired down on us from three directions. We had no choice but to ride like hell and hope a bullet didn't find us."

Nick wrapped his hands around his coffee cup and leaned against the wall. "Are you sure they were Apache?"

"Hell, mister, we was too busy dodgin' bullets to say hello to the bas . . . fellers. But there ain't no one else out huntin' soldiers that I know of."

"I suppose not." Nick drained his cup and set it aside. He looked at Billie, frowning, but she was stubbornly keeping her back to him.

"Ain't nothin' worse'n the 'Pach," Tillston growled. "I purely hate to think what happened to those fellers what got left behind and wasn't dead." He reached for another biscuit. "I was plumb fond of Sergeant Joliet. He had horse sense. Now we'll probably git some greenhorn lookin' for glory who'll git us all kilt."

"Don't tell *me* about greenhorns," Budge said. "Let me tell you about the feller who . . ." Budge launched into a long, only remotely factual story about a tenderfoot, from his vast store of greenhorn lore. The tale became wilder and more improbable as he went on, aided from time to time by Squint and Reuben.

Billie paid little attention to the story, terrified that

Nick was going to tell Tillston about Laughing Woman. Although Nick was standing behind her, she knew he was staring at her. She could feel his gaze like a physical touch, reproaching her. Well, what am I supposed to do? she asked herself defensively. Laughing Woman is my friend! Should I hand her over to that man over there with his hate-scored face?

Finally, unable to resist any longer, she looked at Nick over her shoulder. With a slight jerk of his head, he indicated the courtyard door. She nodded. Casually, he pushed himself away from the wall and went out the front door. She waited several minutes, then rose from her chair and walked out into the courtyard.

"Over here." Nick's voice came from the shadows outside the courtyard gate.

He pushed the gate open and beckoned her outside. As she stepped through the opening, he took her by the arm and pulled her toward him.

He was much too close, and that now-familiar quiver of sensation went through her. Why was he the only man who'd ever made her feel this way? she wondered, pulling her arm out of his grasp. Why couldn't she have been attracted to some nice, steady rancher's son who would be willing to settle down in one place with her, instead of this will-o'-the-wisp who might disappear with the next sunrise?

His hat cast a band of shadow across the upper part of his face, giving him a secretive, faintly sinister look. Then he shifted, bringing his eyes into view, and he became once again merely a handsome cowboy. Billie blinked, deciding that the disturbing impression had just been a trick of the moonlight.

"What do you want?" she asked.

"We need to talk."

"I don't think we have anything to talk about," she said.

His eyebrows went up. "Then why did you come out here?"

She crossed her arms over her chest and gazed stonily out over the moonlit hills, wishing she hadn't followed him out here. She hadn't thought about what she was doing; he had beckoned, and she had come. It was as simple and as infuriating as that. She would have died before admitting it to him, so, with no convenient excuse for her action, she remained silent.

Nick let his breath out in a sigh. "Why didn't you tell them about your Indian friends?"

"Tell them what?" she asked warily.

"That you know where they're hiding."

Billie went very still, like a rabbit listening for sign of a predator's approach. "But I don't know where they're hiding."

Nick didn't know why he was so certain that she was lying, or why it bothered him so much. He didn't give a damn what she told Tillston; he wanted the truth for himself. It didn't matter that there was no logic in that notion, or that he was unfair to want the truth from her when he wasn't willing to give her the same in return. He wanted to know her, really know her. It was stupid and dangerous, but he couldn't help himself.

Although he knew he was provoking an argument, he couldn't keep from saying, "I think you do."

Her eyes narrowed. "Are you calling me a liar?"

"I'm calling you irresponsible," he growled. "If you can help the army capture the Apache and stop the killing—"

"You don't know a damned thing of what's going on here!" she hissed. "The Apache braves are always on the move, sometimes ranging seventy-five miles a day. Do you think they take the women with them?" She took a deep breath. "When you talk about a hiding spot, you're talking women and children. You heard

71

Tillston. He's an Indian hater. *If* I knew where Laughing Woman and the others were hiding, and I told him about it, what do you think he'd do?"

Nick shook his head. "I can't believe—"

"I've seen it happen!" she cried. "If I turned Laughing Woman in, it would be the same as killing her!"

He took her by the chin and tilted her face up. What would it be like, he wondered, to be given this woman's loyalty? She had paid a price for giving it to Laughing Woman. He could tell by the way her gaze wavered, as though she was expecting him to reject her for it. "It must be hard keeping a friendship going amid all the hate and killing. Don't you get confused?"

She slapped his hand away. What did he know about loyalty, confused or otherwise? His sort moved on whenever things got the least bit complicated. "At least I try to do the right thing. At least I care!"

"And I don't?" Almost of their own volition, his hands moved to settle on her shoulders.

"I know what kind of man you are, you . . . you damned drifter!" She put her hands on his chest and locked her elbows, holding herself away from him.

Nick clenched his jaw. By God, she was infuriating! If he didn't have a job to do here—if she wasn't so damned beautiful—he'd walk away and never come back. He pulled her closer, uncertain at the moment if he wanted to shake her or make love to her. Then her body came against his, and the uncertainty ended in a searing upsurge of desire.

"Do you have any idea what you do to me?" he groaned.

Billie could feel the steady beat of his heart beneath her breasts, his muscular thighs, the swelling hardness of his manhood as it rose up against her. A molten heat came into her limbs, weakening her, and she relaxed against him.

He ran his tongue lightly along the curve of her ear. his breath tickling her, then nibbled his way along her cheek to her mouth. Billie moaned softly and wound her hands in his thick, tawny hair. He kissed her, his lips slanting across hers, his tongue stabbing into the sweet depths of her mouth. Billie met him with equal intensity, straining against him, her tongue playing with his in a passionate dance.

Nick slid his hands upward along her ribs toward her breasts. When she didn't protest, he boldly cupped the rich weight of them in his palms. God, she was beautiful! he thought, his breath coming in ragged pants. With his thumbs, he teased her nipples into hard peaks.

Billie moaned against his mouth. His touch was almost unbearably exciting, but her body ached for still more. When his hands moved slowly down her body to grasp her buttocks, she gasped, astonished by the surge of liquid heat that rose in her. He pressed her into the cradle of his thighs, making her acutely aware of the rock-hardness of him. She trembled, nestling even closer.

"You're like fire under my hands," he murmured, tearing his lips from hers and burying them in the silky hair above her ears. "I've got to touch you, Billie."

She felt the cool evening air on her legs as he began pulling her skirt up, and that cold touch brought her back to reality with a jolt. How could he! How could he kiss her, try to make love to her, when only this afternoon he'd been holding Rachel's hand? Not only was he a drifter, he was an unprincipled lecher seeking the easiest route to his own gratification. And that was me, she told herself bitterly. Fool! She wrenched out of his embrace and stood glaring at him, her breasts rising and falling with her rapid breathing.

"What's the problem, honey?" he asked, reaching for her again.

She took a step backward. "The only problem I have is deciding whether or not you'll still have a job in the morning."

He stiffened. "What?"

"I don't like to be pawed," she said coldly, smoothing the wrinkles out of her blouse with shaking hands. "Especially by the hired help."

The passion in his eyes turned to anger. "If that's the way you want it, boss lady." He turned on his heel and started toward the bunkhouse.

"One more thing," she called.

He swung around to face her. His face was expressionless, but his hands were clenched into fists. "Yes, Miss Meyrick?"

"I don't want to see Rachel hurt."

"What's that got to do with me?" he growled.

"You know what I'm talking about," she said.

He came closer, towering over her intimidatingly. "What I do—other than my job—is none of your damn business."

Billie didn't retreat an inch. Putting her hands on her hips, she looked him up and down and retorted, "Anything that happens on my ranch is my business."

He grabbed her by the shoulders and picked her clear up off the ground. Then, seeing the fear that rose in her eyes, he set her back on her feet. He held her immobile, his fingers clenching and unclenching on her shoulders. What the hell was wrong with him? he wondered. She was a bad-tempered, sharp-tongued little baggage, who had lied to him, taunted him and insulted him, all in one evening. He couldn't trust her. She was distracting, perhaps even dangerous, and he shouldn't allow her to interfere with what he'd come here to do.

74

By rights, he should forget her. Although the Star M was ideal for his needs, he could run his operation from another ranch if necessary.

He stared down into her rebellious face, noting the sensuality of her full lips—even pouting as they were now—the silken creaminess of her skin, the soft, sweet curve of her cheek that was so at odds with the stubborn set of her firm little chin, and knew that he couldn't forget her.

"Billie—" he began.

"I'm sending you out to ride the southwest range as far as Twin Skulls Canyon. That ought to keep you away from here for five or six days. Time enough for you to think about keeping your hands to yourself," she snapped.

With a curse, he let her go and stalked away into the darkness.

Billie closed her eyes. Her heart felt as if it was about to pound its way right out of her chest. Even now she was tempted to run after him, to wind her fingers into his hair again and bring his lips down to meet hers. But she thrust the impulse aside brutally, telling herself that she was an utter fool to have come to care for a man like him.

"Damn you, Nick Larabee!" she whispered. "Damn you!"

Chapter 7

Billie and Rachel sat in the wagon and watched the herd slowly move closer. A thick cloud of dust, kicked up by thousands of hooves, nearly obscured the mass of dark, horned bodies. Shadowy shapes of horses and men rode beside the herd darting forward from time to time to turn an animal that tried to break away.

"Look at that one with the enormous horns!" Rachel cried. "What kind of cow is that?"

Billie glanced fondly at the girl beside her. Rachel had endured the heat, dust and rough terrain without complaint, and had even learned to drive the wagon over the smoother stretches. "Rachel," she said with mock sternness, "that's a steer, not a cow. A steer is a bull that's been—"

"Yes, I know," Rachel said hastily, pink rising into her cheeks. "Budge explained the process to me in lurid and quite unnecessary detail."

Billie laughed. "To answer your question, that's a Texas longhorn. They're mostly hide and horn, but they can live anywhere, eat anything, and are nearly as tough as the Apache."

Isabel pulled her wagon to a halt beside Billie's. "Señorita Billie, look!" she said, pointing to the ridge to the west of the herd, where six riders had just come into view.

Billie peered into the distance. "It's Lew Purcell and some of his men. I don't recognize the fellow in the fancy clothes, but I expect he's the new owner of the Dolorosa. You go on ahead, Isabel. Tell Budge that Mr. Purcell is here, will you?"

As the other wagon lurched away, Billie stood up and waved her hat overhead to attract the riders' attention. "Morning, Lew," she said when the men were close enough to hear.

"Mornin', ladies." Lew Purcell tipped his hat politely, then indicated the stranger beside him. "This here is Mr. Rosswell Stearns, owner of the Dolorosa."

Billie regarded the newcomer curiously. He looked to be about fifty, a big man, wide-shouldered and broad-chested, with a waistline that was just beginning to go to fat. Although his rather thin lips were stretched in a smile, his protuberant blue eyes held no friendliness. "Welcome to Arizona, Mr. Stearns," she said, holding out her hand. "This is Miss Laird, and I'm Billie Meyrick, owner of the Star M."

Stearns touched his fingers to hers briefly. "It is a pleasure to meet you both."

An Englishman, Billie thought, and rich as Croesus, or he wouldn't have been able to afford a spread like the Dolorosa.

Stearns pulled a handkerchief out of his pocket and wiped his forehead. "Mr. Purcell informs me that it is his duty to inspect your herd as it passes from my range to yours, since it is impossible for your men to avoid picking up a few of my cattle along the way."

Billie nodded. "It's one of those little courtesies we offer one another."

"A most necessary one, I would say." The Englishman pursed his lips. "I understand that you run the Star M yourself?"

"Yes."

"Isn't it rather unusual for a woman to shoulder such a responsibility?"

Billie shrugged. "Not as unusual as you'd think. Men die, leaving women to run things. It's that or give up, Mr. Stearns, and some of us just aren't able to do that."

"A most admirable attitude, I'm sure." Stearns flicked a speck of dirt from his lapel. "Mr. Purcell, lead the way. I am anxious to see my men in action."

"Just a minute." Billie regarded the Englishman's expensive clothing and polished, pristine riding boots. "Mr. Stearns, do you know anything about working cattle?"

"Of course not! That's what I hire men like Mr. Purcell to do for me."

"That's what I thought. I don't want to sound rude, but I'm going to have to ask you to stay here with us until Lew is finished."

Stearns's chin thrust forward pugnaciously. "Why?"

"Because you're what we call a tenderfoot," Billie said, "And I don't want you spooking my cattle."

"I assure you that I am an expert rider, Miss Meyrick."

"You don't ride cattle, Mr. Stearns." Couldn't the man leave it to someone who knew what he was doing? Billie thought sourly. God preserve us from greenhorns!

Lew moved his horse closer. "Boss, let me handle this," he urged. "Some of these brands kin be hard to spot. Me and the boys know what to look fer."

Budge galloped toward the wagon, perspiration making muddy rivulets through the coating of dust on his face. "Them cattle are being real fussy today. Lew, you ready? Let's get this done while they's still in one place." Without waiting for an answer, he wheeled his mount and headed back to the herd.

Lew glanced at his boss.

The Englishman nodded. "Carry on, Mr. Purcell," he said, releasing his men to follow Budge.

Billie and her companions watched the cowboys work the herd, expertly chivvying the Dolorosa cattle through the milling tangle of animals. Suddenly the whole herd threw up their heads, bawling in alarm.

"Hold them, hold them!" Billie cried, grabbing the reins.

The cowboys managed to soothe the herd, however, and the disaster was averted. Lew and his men began moving through the cattle again.

A rider, leading a spare horse, came galloping toward the wagon. As he came nearer, Billie recognized Nick beneath the layer of dust that covered his face.

"Budge wants you to hold the cut, Billie," he panted, tossing the spare horse's reins to her. Before she could react, he scooped her off the wagon's hard seat.

"Put me down!" she cried, slapping ineffectually at his hard chest. "Hey!"

With an easy heave of his powerful shoulders, he deposited her in the empty saddle. His teeth flashed whitely in the mask of dust covering his face, then he tipped his hat and headed back to the herd at a gallop. Billie glared after him for a moment, then spurred her horse in pursuit.

"I say!" Stearns exclaimed. "Shocking! A woman riding astride—"

"Not another word, Mr. Stearns," Rachel snapped, drawing herself up, prepared for battle. "Billie is here to work, not to worry about the conventions."

"I meant no insult, Miss Laird. I was . . . surprised, that is all."

"You will find many things surprising here," Rachel said. "But you will also find these Westerners to be fine people who will gladly share their superior knowledge with those of us with sense enough to listen."

He laughed, a harsh barking sound that was strangely at odds with his cultured appearance and manner. "I consider myself duly chastised, Miss Laird. Next time I shan't express my, er, surprise aloud."

"That would be wise, Mr. Stearns."

"I shall be . . . Good Heavens, but that girl can ride!"

Rachel turned to look at Billie, who had been assigned the job of keeping the Dolorosa cattle from rejoining the larger herd. She was lying along her horse's neck, urging her mount in a flank-to-flank race with a wayward cow. As soon as her horse was a hand span ahead, Billie slapped the cow in the face with a length of rope. Horse and cow reversed directions with a speed that made the watchers gasp with the certainty that the girl would fly from the saddle to be trampled beneath the pounding hooves. As the first cow rejoined the group of Dolorosa cattle, another decided to try for the big herd, and Billie was forced to repeat the maneuver.

Rachel turned to say something to her companion, but stopped when another rider came over the ridge. She shaded her eyes with her hand. "Mr. Stearns, is that one of your men?" she asked.

The Englishman glanced over his shoulder. "Yes." He waited until the newcomer had halted his mount beside the wagon, then said, "You're late, Mr. Eames."

"Sorry." The man tipped his hat to Rachel. "Ma'am."

Stearns did not offer to introduce him, so Rachel merely nodded and turned her attention back to the herd. Eames watched Billie work for a moment. Then, turning to his boss, he thrust his thumb in her direction and raised his eyebrows inquiringly. Stearns nodded curtly.

Unaware of the exchange, Rachel asked, "Do you see why Billie wouldn't let you near her cattle, Mr. Stearns? That is no place for an amateur."

"No, indeed," the Englishman said. Seeing Eames's barely disguised amusement, he fixed the gunman with a frigid stare.

Finally Lew was satisfied that all Dolorosa cattle had been culled from the herd. His men moved off, driving the cattle before them.

Billie took her hat off and used it to beat the worst of the dust out of her clothing. The Star M herd began to move past. The air was filled with the bawling of the cattle and the high-pitched yips of the cowboys.

Nick stopped his mount beside hers, offering her a drink of water from his canteen. Despite the acrimonious note of their last meeting, he had actually missed her.

"Thanks." Billie tipped her head back to drink, allowing some of the cool liquid to run down her neck to her chest.

"Where did you learn to ride like that?"

She shrugged. "We couldn't afford to hire many hands at first, so I had to learn to do a man's job." She glanced at him from under her lashes. "You don't ride so bad yourself."

The creases on either side of his mouth deepened. "I didn't realize you were watching."

Billie sighed; that deep, lazy voice of his still did strange things to her insides. She'd hoped that six days of separation would have cured her of whatever strange affliction came over her when he was near, but it seemed to have strengthened instead. Even her skin seemed to become sensitive in his presence, making her overly aware of every inch of fabric that covered her body.

Nick stared at the front of her shirt, where the wet fabric clung to the upper slopes of her breasts. Her nipples were erect, he noted, straining against her shirt as though begging for his touch. It took every ounce of his control not to reach out and caress those lush mounds. His caution fled beneath the goad of desire. God, he wanted her!

"You're beautiful," he said, a raw note of passion roughening his voice.

Billie gasped, unbearably stirred by the husky sound of his voice, the expression on his face. No one had ever called her beautiful! It was sheer cowardice, but she couldn't stay here with him lest she be forced to acknowledge the feelings he roused in her. She backed her horse away from him, then turned and headed back toward the wagon.

Surprised and annoyed to find Eames waiting beside the wagon, she reined in her mount and scowled at him. The gunman smiled, that same knowing, wet-lipped leer she remembered from their meeting in town.

"Hello, pretty lady," he said.

"I had no idea you two were acquainted," Stearns said.

"We're not," Billie snapped, aware that Eames was staring avidly at her breasts. Nick's gaze, though equally as bold, equally as demanding, had fostered an urgent warmth in her and a reckless longing to explore that surging response further. The lust on Eames's grinning face merely made her feel soiled.

Stearns raised his eyebrows. "I must say, Miss Meyrick, that I would like to see you ride to hounds one day."

"Hounds!" Billie gaped at him, all but forgetting

83

Eames in her astonishment. "You're not going to go fox hunting here!"

"I intend to enjoy civilized pleasures, even here." Stearns raised his hat politely before turning his mount toward the Dolorosa. "Good day, ladies. Come along, Mr. Eames."

Eames looked over his shoulder at Billie as he rode away, and his smile was a promise. Despite the hot sun, she shivered.

"Well, la-di-da to you, Mr. Stearns," Rachel muttered, wrinkling her nose in distaste.

Billie shook off the chill the gunman's leering gaze had caused. She even managed to laugh. "Civilized! Chasing some poor frightened fox to death, and he doesn't even intend to eat it! Give me an Apache any day."

"I think he's an odious man," the other girl said with uncharacteristic heat. "What a shame we have such a . . . a prig for our nearest neighbor."

Billie shrugged. "The house at Dolorosa is a good ten miles from ours, and Stearns doesn't appear to be the friendly sort. I wouldn't worry about seeing him all that often." But she suspected that Eames would be showing up again.

She tied her mount's reins to the back of the wagon and clambered nimbly from the saddle to the seat. Although he was unpleasant, she mused, Stearns was merely an annoyance to be avoided whenever possible. Eames, however, would have to be dealt with some day. Even Eames wasn't the worst of her worries. Nick was. What was she going to do about him?

With a muttered curse, she slapped the reins against the horses' rumps. The wagon lurched into motion, following the swath of trampled brush the herd had left behind.

Chapter 8

The cowboys stopped the herd on a broad plateau that was studded here and there with thick stands of mesquite trees. To the east, the mountains raised the dark blue bulk of their massive shoulders into the cloudless sky, seeming to frown upon the puny mortals who had the temerity to trespass upon their domain. To the south were the forbidding red humps of Bald Men Buttes, their bare, clean-lined outlines stark against the soft blue of the sky.

"Billie, pull them wagons up over there," Budge shouted over the din, pointing to a spot near the herd. "I need 'em to block one end of the brandin' area."

Billie obediently pulled her wagon to a halt behind Isabel's and jumped down to help the older woman unload the supplies needed for tonight's supper. The Martinez children, overexcited by the roundup, climbed over the vehicle like monkeys. There were three of them: Juana, the eldest at nine; Miguel, who at six was already an expert roper and the bane of the Star M's chicken population; and Maria, who was just learning to toddle on her fat little legs.

"Señorita Rachel, weel you watch them for a moment, *por favor?*" Isabel begged, pushing a lock of hair away from her sweaty face.

"Of course." Rachel climbed down from the wagon, calling to the children. With a handful of licorice drops, she lured them away from their exhausted mother. They sat down beside the American girl, chattering happily in Spanish, and watched the men work.

There was no corral, so the cowboys sat their horses in a ring around the branding area. Freeman Jennings and Squint tended the fire from which the ends of the branding irons extended, while Budge and Eliseo, the two best ropers, raced through the milling animals in pursuit of the calves. The cowboys' ropes whirled with uncanny accuracy, catching the bawling animals by their hind feet and stretching them full length upon the ground. Before the astonished calves could struggle back to their feet, they were dragged up to the fire and branded.

Dust rose in a choking cloud. With the lowing of the cattle and the frightened bawling of the calves punctuated by the cheers, curses and laughter of the men, it seemed to Rachel to be the dirtiest, noisiest spot on earth. Billie walked calmly through the midst of it all, keeping the tally while dodging plunging animals, dodging over and under and around a confusing tangle of ropes, and lending a hand wherever needed.

Isabel touched Rachel's shoulder. "I take her now," the Mexican woman said, taking little Maria from the girl's arms. *"Muchas gracias."*

Rachel nodded, then turned her attention back to the branding. Budge and Eliseo went after a larger animal this time, one man roping its hind legs, the other catching its forelegs.

"What are they doing?" she asked.

"They catch maverick," Isabel replied, then explained, "A bull of one year, Señorita Rachel. They missed heem last year. He grow pretty beeg now, takes two ropes."

There was a burst of laughter from the men as the bawling animal was branded.

Isabel put Maria down, but kept tight hold of the child's hand. "Now you see fun," Isabel said.

"Let 'er rip!" Freeman called, stepping back from the struggling animal.

Budge and Eliseo loosed the ropes and spurred their horses away. The bull scrambled to his feet, snorting with rage. Spying his nearest tormentor, Squint, the furious animal lowered his head and charged. The cowboy ran, his chaps flapping wildly around his churning legs. The other men hooted with laughter.

"Look at him go!" hollered Art. "Run, Squint! *Ruuun!* He's right behind you!"

Squint dove to one side, landing on his belly in the dust amid a chorus of jeers and high-pitched yips from the watching men. The bull kept moving, focusing his beady gaze on Freeman this time. The cowboy flapped his arms at the charging animal, then turned and ran. He darted behind Budge, whose horse reared before galloping out of the bull's narrow field of vision. The beast hesitated, peering nearsightedly about for another target.

"Papa! Papa!" shrieked Maria, pulling out of her mother's grasp. She ran beneath the wagon and out into the branding area, her arms outstretched towards her father.

The bull, catching the sudden flash of movement, wheeled and charged.

Isabel screamed and rushed toward Maria, but the wagon was between her and the child, and going around it slowed her down. Rachel jumped down from her seat and followed, shrieking for Budge to do something.

Billie took in the situation with one horrified glance. She dropped her ledger and ran toward the child, scooping the small form up in her arms and heading for

87

the protection of the wagon. Out of the corner of her eye, she could see the bull bearing down on her like a locomotive and knew she wasn't going to make it.

"Isabel!" she shrieked, tossing the child toward the woman with all her strength. She could hear the pounding hoofbeats behind her.

Something caught the back of her shirt, jerking her upward with terrific force. The bull's horns, she thought, waiting for the sharp tips to begin tearing into her body. She felt no fear, only a strange sort of detached awareness as she was lifted into the air. The world reeled around her in a slow-moving dance, as though time itself had been suspended. She caught blurred snatches of things—Rachel's face, her mouth open in a round "O" of horror; Budge, beating the ends of his reins on his horse's neck in a flat-out run toward her; the loop of Eliseo's cast rope floating gracefully overhead.

Instead of hitting the ground, however, she continued to rise upward. Then she felt someone's arms close tightly around her. She looked up, astonished, to see Nick's face, and abruptly realized that she had not been struck by the bull at all, but had been whisked neatly out of danger and deposited across her rescuer's saddle. There was a confused shouting behind her as the other men converged on the bull.

Holding her tightly against his chest, Nick spurred his horse out of the melee into the relatively quiet space behind the wagon.

"What are you doing?" she demanded, trying to push away from him. "Maria! What happened to—"

"She's fine, Billie," he said, restraining her easily. "You threw her right into Isabel's arms. The child didn't even get scratched."

He held her while Joe rode by in pursuit of an errant calf. When the cowboy had returned to the branding area, Nick slid down from his mount, pulling Billie with him. With the wagon on one side and the horse on the other, there was a tiny island of privacy around them. He released her.

"Why are you . . ." Billie looked down at herself and gasped. Every button had been ripped from her blouse, leaving her bosom covered only by a cotton camisole that was almost transparent from much washing. The upper curves of her breasts were bare, her rosy nipples plainly visible through the fabric.

She grabbed for the edges of her blouse, but he held her hands, drinking in the sight of her. His face tightened with desire. Billie stopped struggling and stared up at him with wide green eyes. He put his hand on her throat, testing her frantic pulse, then let his hand trail down across her breasts. His touch was gentle, but infinitely possessive. Billie moaned as her nipples rose up into taut, urgent peaks, betraying her.

Reluctantly, he let go of her and pulled her blouse closed. "You should wear more under your shirt if you're going to tangle with charging bulls," he said. His voice was calm, but there was a raging bonfire of frustrated passion in his eyes. He took a deep breath, then another, in an attempt to control his emotions.

Billie clutched the edges of the blouse together with white-knuckled hands and stared up at him. He was standing so close that their chests were nearly touching. Although there was plenty of room to retreat, she was held immobile by the feelings his touch had aroused in her.

He put his hands on her shoulders. They were hot, hotter than the blazing afternoon sun that beat down on her back.

"Billie, are you all right?" Rachel called, coming around the side of the wagon.

Her voice gave Billie the strength to take a step backward. "I'm fine," she said. Her own voice sounded strangely subdued, so she cleared her throat and spoke more firmly. "Rachel, will you get me a shirt from my pack?" She hoped her cheeks weren't as red as they felt.

As Rachel climbed into the wagon, Billie tried to gather her scattered wits. She wished Nick wasn't standing so close, or that his chest wasn't rising and falling so deeply. There was such a look of raw need on his face, she thought, that it must be obvious to Rachel what had been going on a moment ago.

"Here you are." Rachel pulled out a blue blouse and handed it to Billie, then tucked a pair of blankets under her arms and jumped down from the wagon. She shook out one of the blankets and handed it to Nick. "Hold this up, Mr. Larabee," she ordered. "Let's give her some privacy." She held up her own blanket, stretching it out in the space between Nick's horse and the side of the wagon.

Billie glared at Nick, who had copied Rachel's actions with one exception: he was facing into the makeshift dressing room, not out. "Turn the other way, Mr. Larabee," she said.

He smiled sardonically at her, then turned around. She took the ruined blouse off and tossed it up into the wagon. Slipping the clean shirt over her head, she quickly did up the laces and tied them into a tight knot at the neckline.

"You'll probably have to cut that knot to get it off," Nick said when he saw her handiwork.

Rachel laughed. She folded the blankets and tossed them back into the wagon. "I'd better help Isabel with the cooking. We're going to have a bunch of hungry men here in a moment."

"It's that late?" Billie glanced up at the sun, surprised to see that it was well along its downward arc. "I've got to finish the tally before it gets too dark to see." She took a few steps toward the tangle of men and animals beyond the wagon, then turned to face Nick. "I want to thank you for what you did back there," she said.

He tipped his hat. "All in a day's work, boss lady." He swung back into the saddle and rode off, leaving her staring after him.

The exhausted cowboys rolled themselves in their blankets and were immediately asleep. Nick, however much he would have liked to emulate them, tossed and turned restlessly in his hard bed. Thoughts of Billie tormented him—the memory of the full, white curves of her breasts, the way her nipples had risen up in response to his touch and her lips had parted in unconscious invitation. Although he was probably cutting his own throat by getting involved with her, he couldn't help himself. He wanted her, wanted her more than any woman he'd ever known.

A soft footstep nearby alerted him. He froze, holding his breath so he could hear better. He heard the faint sound again, but farther away this time. Whoever had made it was moving away from camp. Marking the direction from which the noise had come, he waited a few moments, then eased out from under his blanket and slipped out of the camp. There was a trail, easily visible in the bright moonlight, leading to a pile of boulders a few hundred yards away. The footprints had been left by a small, booted foot. He grinned; there was only one person here who could have made that trail. Moving as silently as any wraith, he followed the line of prints.

Billie was sitting on the ground on the far side of the rocks, gazing out over the moonlit hills. Nick moved to stand behind her. She was brushing her hair, and the unbound tresses looked like finest silk in the pale light.

Suddenly she whirled, warned of his presence by some sixth sense, and Nick found himself looking down the barrel of a small but deadly looking derringer.

"Oh, it's you," she said, lowering the gun. "Don't you know not to sneak up on a person like that? It isn't healthy."

Nick's heart began beating again. "What are you doing with that?" he demanded.

"It comes in handy sometimes." She shrugged, slipping the little gun back into her jacket pocket as she rose to her feet. "I'm a dead shot, you know. Pa taught me. Rifle or pistol or even this." She patted her pocket.

"What are you doing out here, anyway?"

Billie shrugged. "Can't a person enjoy a little privacy and a look at the night sky?"

"I suppose." He picked up the brush she had dropped and handed it to her.

Then he froze, staring at her. His heartbeat quickened. Her long hair fell over her shoulders in a cascade of dark, glossy waves. The moonlight softened the roguish expression in her eyes and made her skin seem to glow with its own soft, pearly light. She lowered her eyelids, shy under his rapt perusal, and her lashes cast long, spidery shadows across her cheeks. It seemed as though she'd been created for him. Born of his dreams and his desire, he thought, innocent, lovely and infinitely sensual. For this one magical night, he decided, let her be nothing more than what she seemed. A woman. His.

"Billie," he breathed, "you're beautiful."

Again his words stirred her, making her heartbeat pound in her ears. Resolutely, she controlled her reaction. "You've been out in the sun too long," she scoffed.

He sat down, leaning his back against the rock, then reached up and pulled her down beside him. "Don't

92

you believe me? You've just gotten so used to hiding your beauty that you can no longer see yourself as you really are."

"Oh, come now!" She tossed her head, flinging her hair back away from her face. Why wasn't she running? she wondered. This was crazy! But her legs had gone weak, and she didn't think she could have run from him if she'd wanted to.

He took her hand and turned it palm upward. With his finger, he began tracing small, tickling circles against her skin. That small touch was so simple, yet so very intimate, that Billie closed her eyes, trying to control the swirling heat that rushed through her body.

"But you *are* beautiful," he murmured. "You live a hard life among hard men. You've had to seem as hard as they to be accepted. But you know, and I know, that there's more to you." He raised her hand to his lips and began kissing her fingers one by one. "There's softness and kindness and"—he touched the tip of his tongue to her wrist, smiling when a tremor went through her— "responsiveness."

Billie gasped as his tongue moved farther up her forearm. Pulling away, she clasped her hands in her lap. "There's something I have to ask you," she said.

"What?" Hearing the note of breathlessness in her voice, he smiled and took her hand again.

"Why didn't you . . . ah"—she caught her breath as his tongue laved over the sensitive tip of her fore-finger—"tell Tillston about Laughing Woman?"

"I don't hold with fighting women and children any more than your father did. And I couldn't betray you, honey." He hadn't thought much about it before, but to his surprise, he realized that he'd told her the truth. What was it about this woman, he wondered a bit dazedly, that made him want to protect her—even when her motives were suspect? He shook his head to clear it. Right now he didn't want to think. All he wanted to do was to drown himself in her. Tonight was his. Tomorrow would have to take care of itself.

He moved to kneel in front of her, taking her by the chin and forcing her to look at him. "I have to kiss you, Billie." Gently, he placed his lips on hers.

Almost of their own volition, her arms crept up around his neck. She parted her lips, giving him free access to the honeyed secrets of her mouth. Instead of taking what was offered, he nibbled teasing little bites along her lower lip and kissed the tiny dimple at the corner of her mouth. A wave of heat surged through her. Winding her hands in his thick hair, she pulled him closer, seeking more of him. His mouth opened over hers, slanting passionately across her parted lips, his tongue delving into the warm depths of her mouth. A soft moan rose upon the quiet night air, and Billie was astonished to discover that it had come from her.

Nick kissed his way across her cheek to her ear, where he ran his tongue in steadily decreasing circles. His hands went to her waist, pulling her still closer. Billie felt her shirt being drawn out of her waistband, briefly felt the cool night air on her skin before the heat of his hands replaced it. Slowly, he worked his way up her ribs to her breasts. His fingers stroked her hardening nipples through the thin fabric of her camisole. Billie arched her back in mindless ecstasy.

With an impatient movement, he untied the laces of the shirt and pulled it over her head. The camisole quickly followed, leaving her breasts naked to his heated gaze. For a moment he sat back on his heels, just looking at her. Then he leaned forward, kissing her hungrily.

Frantic to reach his skin, Billie pulled his shirt up and pressed her breasts into the furred hardness of his chest. He held her to him, rubbing himself with

94

exquisite gentleness against her erect nipples until she cried out softly. Then he gathered her into his arms and tipped her backward onto the cool ground.

He stripped his shirt up over his head and tossed it away. Holding his weight off her with braced arms, he continued teasing her breasts with his body as he watched her face, loving the way her eyes half closed with her passion, the way her lips pouted, begging for him to teach her all the secrets of desire. It took every bit of control he possessed not to take her now, this instant, but he wanted to make this last.

Billie was beyond thought, beyond control. A coiling tension had taken hold of her lower body, forcing her hips to move upward against his, seeking something she didn't yet know but needed in every fiber of her being. She moaned again, running her hands over the hard, flexing muscles of his arms and chest in gentle retaliation.

"Oh, God!" he groaned, coming down on her at last. "Billie!"

He pulled her skirt up over her hips. Kissing her deeply, he ran his hands over the slim curves of her thighs and calves, then returned to her waist to pluck at the strings of her drawers. Loosening them, he slid his hand down her flat belly. For a moment she hesitated, then opened herself to his seeking hand. He explored lower, his fingers gliding deliciously over moist, warm flesh and silky hair.

Billie surged upward against his hand, wild with passion. When his fingers found her most secret spot she stilled, gasping with the shock that bold touch engendered. But as he explored her with gentleness and barely contained desire, a kind of madness came over her.

"Please, oh, please," she moaned.

"Yes, honey," he murmured hoarsely, reaching

between their straining bodies to unfasten his jeans. "It's going to happen. Neither of us can stop it now."

There was the sound of a rifle shot nearby, its sudden crack splitting the silence of the night. The herd was up and running an instant later. Billie pushed frantically against Nick's chest. Cursing, he scrambled to his hands and knees and reached for their scattered clothing.

"My herd!" Billie cried, grabbing her shirt out of his hands and pushing him aside.

She cursed, watching the terrified cattle flee east. The cowboys pounded after them, trying desperately to turn the herd before it reached the rough country of the foothills. The shouting, bawling mass of men and animals disappeared behind the shoulder of the nearest ridge. Billie pulled her clothes on hurriedly and ran toward the wagons, tucking her shirt in as she ran.

"Wait!" Nick shouted. "Billie!"

She ran faster, the need to get away from him almost as strong as her concern for her herd. The realization of what had happened between them rushed in on her. She had been willing to let him do anything to her, anything! It hadn't mattered that her men weren't two hundred yards away, and that any one of them could have come out to those rocks. It hadn't mattered that Rachel seemed to care for Nick, or that he was a drifter who'd take off the moment the notion hit him. At that moment, Billie hated herself. She was no better than the girls who worked in the saloon, selling their bodies—worse, in fact, for at least those women didn't claim to be other than what they were. Tears sprang into her eyes, blinding her.

Nick caught up with her, grabbing her by the arm and swinging her around to face him. "Stay here. You can't do anything now!" Startled to see tears running down her face, he demanded, "What's the matter with you?"

"What do you think is the matter with me?" she cried furiously. "How could you do that to me? I've never . . . Just stay away from me!"

"Billie—"

She tore out of his grasp and ran toward the horses. Rachel was sitting in the wagon, a blanket wrapped around her shoulders. Spying Billie and Nick, she stood up and waved.

"Billie!" she cried. "Over here! Budge said you're to stay with us. Nick, you're supposed to go after them and bring as many spare horses as you can handle, he said."

Nick hesitated. "You'll be alone—"

"Oh, go on, get out of here!" Rachel ordered, putting her hands on her hips. "Billie, come up here with me."

Billie obeyed, glad it was too dark for Rachel to see the flush that heated her cheeks.

Nick pulled his Henry repeating rifle out and tossed it to Billie. "Just in case," he said. "There are more bullets in my saddlebag if you need them."

Billie nodded, running her fingers absently over the smooth stock of the gun. She watched Nick ride off into the hills, leading several spare mounts. Two hot tears trickled down her cheeks, and they were not for her lost cattle.

Chapter 9

"Billie, look! There's someone at the house," Rachel said, shading her eyes against the noonday sun.

Billie stood up to see better. "I wonder who . . . What kind of vehicle is that?" she demanded, pointing to the high, two-wheeled cart that occupied a tiny wedge of shade at the north end of the house. "Budge, can you see who it is?"

The Texan slowed his mount to match the wagon's pace. "Nope. I ain't never seen anything like that. But what do you want to bet it belongs to the English feller?"

Billie pressed her lips together and urged the weary team to a faster pace. After chasing through the hills and canyons for her scattered cattle, she wasn't in any mood to deal with Rosswell Stearns. And to make her temper even more volatile, Budge had ordered Nick, of all the men, to help guard the woman on the trip back to the ranch.

She had remained close by Rachel's side during that four-day journey, successfully keeping Nick at a distance. But she knew she had only delayed the confrontation that was sure to come, for there was a stubborn set to Nick's jaw that promised trouble. No matter how badly she might want to forget what had happened between them out on the range, it was obvious that he had no intention of doing the same. He wanted her. The flaring desire that burned in his eyes every time he looked at her proved it.

The knowledge of what she had roused in him gave her a little thrill of dread and yes, she was forced to admit to herself, of anticipation. She'd never thought a man could make her feel so good. And she realized that she had only tasted the very beginning of passion's measure. What would it have been like had nothing interrupted them?

Pushing that dangerous thought aside, Billie pulled the wagon to a halt beside the strange vehicle and jumped down. Suddenly her chest grew tight. Oh, God, it couldn't be!

She hardly noticed the younger of the two women perched on the cart's high seat, for all her attention was focused on the other visitor's lovely countenance. Although the woman was nearing forty, her skin was unlined and creamy, her stunning beauty undimmed by time. She was exquisitely dressed, her hair artfully coiffed, and even her parasol was a dainty, lace-trimmed affair. Her hat was an absurdly small scrap of felt, decorated with feathers dyed to match the vivid blue of her dress. Billie could smell the French perfume even at this distance.

For a moment, she could only stare. This was the woman who had once been her mother. The woman who had turned her back on her husband and young daughter and ran away to the arms of a dandified nobleman. It had happened ten years ago, but seeing her like this brought Billie's pain back as though it had been yesterday. All the things she had wanted to say, all the tears she'd never shed rose in her throat in a hot, choking flood. Somehow she managed to wrestle them back down and face her visitors with some measure of calmness.

Taking a deep breath to compose herself, she took another step forward. "Hello, Helena," she said. To her relief, her voice was cool and emotionless, giving nothing away of the emotions raging wildly inside her.

"It's been a long time, Wilhemina," the lovely woman replied.

"Wilhemina?" Nick demanded incredulously. He dismounted and went to stand beside Billie. Rachel, sensing Billie's discomfiture, climbed down from the wagon and stood at her other side, flanking her protectively. Although she would never have admitted it, Billie was comforted by their presence.

Helena closed her parasol, then held out her hand imperiously. Nick strode forward and lifted her down from the cart, then reached up to aid her young companion.

"I hate being called Wilhemina," Billie snapped.

"Billie, then." The older woman made a tentative gesture, as though to reach out to Billie, then dropped her dainty, gloved hand back to her side. "And I would prefer that you call me Mother," she said.

Nick, who was in the process of lifting the girl down from the cart, nearly dropped her into the dust. He set her on her feet and whirled to look at Helena and Billie. Superficial differences aside, they resembled each other closely, he realized now. Although Billie's hair was dark and her mother's an unusual and striking reddish gold, both were small, sweetly curved women, possessing the same delightful tilt to the eyes and the same wide mouth that seemed to beg for a man's kiss. But Helena's beauty was full-blown and self-aware, while Billie exuded a kind of sensual innocence that was even more appealing.

Billie crossed her arms over her chest and remained

101

silent. Helena's smile faltered. It was Rachel who rushed into the awkward gap in the conversation. She introduced herself and Nick, then added, "It's a pleasure to meet you, Mrs. Meyrick."

Helena turned to her gratefully. "Thank you, Miss Laird. But my name is Stearns now."

"You're married to *him?*" Billie demanded. "What happened to that count you married after you shook free of us?"

"He died." Helena indicated the girl who had accompanied her. "This is Julia, my stepdaughter."

Billie looked at the young woman. She was a tall girl, with black hair and brows that contrasted sharply with her white skin and pale gray eyes. She was striking, and would have been beautiful if it weren't for the petulant, downward turn to her rather thin mouth.

Rachel squeezed Billie's elbow, hard, then asked, "Won't you ladies come in out of the heat?"

"Thank you, Miss Laird." Helena moved toward the house, followed by Julia and Rachel.

Billie hesitated for a moment. For years the desire to punish Helena had haunted her. She had prepared for this meeting. Over and over she had practiced her speech, her gestures, her contemptuous expression. Over and over she had envisioned her final, triumphant leave-taking, walking away as Helena had walked away from the Star M so many years ago. And now, when her chance had finally come, all she wanted to do was hide.

"Afraid?" Nick asked.

She turned to glare at him, outraged that he could read her so clearly. How dare he poke his nose into her problems! "Of what? A couple of women in fancy dresses?"

"You know what I mean."

"I know that this is none of your business."

102

"Everything you do is my business, honey," he said.

She turned her back on him and started walking toward the house. Nick strode beside her, whistling under his breath. As they entered the dim coolness of the house, he touched her lightly on the shoulder, shaking his head in silent warning. She scowled at him, then turned and tossed her hat on the table. The Stetson made a dusty trail as it slid across the rough, clean-scrubbed boards.

Julia sat down gingerly in the chair Nick held out for her, a moue of distaste on her mouth. But Helena moved slowly around the room, touching a colorful Indian blanket, running her fingers across the sturdy oak sideboard, then putting her hands behind her back and inspecting the utilitarian kitchen area where fire-blackened iron pots and skillets hung from hooks on the wall.

"It's just as I remembered," she murmured. "But I see that Anton finally put a wood floor in," she said, indicating the wide pine boards.

Billie clenched her fists. Helena hadn't changed a bit, she thought sourly. The woman still had no understanding of what made a house a home or the standards by which a successful ranch—or a good man—was judged.

"I heard about Anton's death," Helena murmured. "I'm so very sorry."

"Why? He meant nothing to you."

Helena removed her gloves and folded them neatly. "That isn't true."

"What do you want, Helena?" Billie burst out.

The older woman sighed. "Is it so unusual for a mother to want to see her daughter?"

"One like you, yes," Billie snapped.

"That's not—" Nick began, but stopped when Billie whirled to face him.

103

"Go help Budge with the wagons," she said.

He cocked his head to one side and looked at her. Her face was expressionless, but her eyes were huge, her face completely drained of color. Cold rage almost seemed to radiate from her in waves. He'd faced men across drawn guns who had looked like that. In another situation he would have challenged that anger and tried to turn it into something else, but this was not the time. With a muttered curse, he put his hat back on and went outside, slamming the heavy door behind him.

"I must say, Miss Meyrick, that you have marvelous taste in hirelings," Julia said in a quick, high voice that grated across Billie's nerves like rusty iron. "Oh, I should call them cowboys—that is the term used to describe them, is it not? Are all your men as handsome as Mr. Larabee?"

"My men are good at their job, Miss Stearns," Billie replied. "I don't hire them for anything else."

"Shall we offer our guests some refreshment, Billie?" Rachel asked rather loudly, rummaging in the depths of the sideboard. "I'm certain there's some sherry in here somewhere."

"Do you have tea?" Helena asked.

"Tea!" Billie stared at her. "We drink coffee out here. And I'm sure all we have is whiskey."

"Whiskey! Good Heavens!" Julie exclaimed.

"Ah, here's the sherry!" Rachel said, pulling a bottle from the depths of the cabinet. "Billie, would you please get something to serve this in?"

"Oh, goodness! Where are my manners today?" Billie cried, her voice going up in her attempt to imitate the English girl's lighter tones. She took down two battered tin cups and sloshed a few ounces of the sherry in each. "Here," she said, banging the cups down in front of her guests.

Julia set hers aside with a shudder, but Helena merely smiled and took a sip, her pinky held daintily in the air. Billie squeezed her eyes closed and prayed for control.

"Billie, dear, we are planning to host a gathering of the local ranchers and townspeople," Helena said, setting her cup on the table. "I would be pleased if you and Miss Laird would come."

"I don't think I'll have time," Billie said.

"Oh, it won't be until next month." Helena lifted one shoulder in a graceful shrug. "There should be plenty of time for you to prepare."

Julia brushed a nonexistent speck of dirt from her glove. "I understand it will take at least that long for the local, ahhh, gentry to obtain suitable attire. Why," her gaze brushed over Billie's plain, utilitarian skirt, "I've seen clothes here that surely must be fifty years out of date."

"There's a reason for that, Miss Stearns," Rachel said. "The current fashion"—she indicated the English girl's pencil-slim skirt with its burden of ruffles, flounces and delicate lace—"doesn't lend itself to work on a ranch."

"Perhaps." Julia sniffed. "But perhaps it is merely an unwillingness to make the extra effort required to be feminine amidst primitive conditions."

"That's enough, Julia," Helena said.

Julia's thin brows lowered. "I do not take orders from you, Stepmother." Her upper lip curled in distaste.

Helena turned her back on the English girl. "Now, Billie, I don't expect you and Miss Laird to rush out and order gowns. You and I seem to be the same size, and Miss Laird should be able to wear Julia's clothes. We'll be glad to lend you—"

"*If* we go," Billie snapped, "we'll wear our own

105

clothes, thank you. I'm not so poor that I need your charity."

"Very well. But the offer remains, if you happen to change your mind," Helena murmured. "Come, Julia. We have a long ride ahead of us. Let's collect Mr. Eames and—"

"You brought *him?*" Billie demanded. "Where is he?"

"Why, I believe he said he was going to take a look at the spring or something. I really paid little attention—"

"Get him off my property." Billie put her hands on her hips. "Now! And don't bring him back."

Helena drew herself up, offended. "Really, we couldn't come out unescorted, Billie. My husband has assigned Mr. Eames to protect us."

"Fine." Billie stalked to the door and opened it. "Then you can stay away, too."

Helena walked out, her head bowed. Julia nodded coldly and followed her stepmother. Billie slammed the door closed.

"I've never seen you act like that," Rachel scolded. "You were awful to her."

Billie went to the table and picked up the two cups the unwelcome visitors had used. "She deserved it."

"No matter what she's done, she's your mother."

"Not anymore." Billie flung the cups into the fireplace, spilling a glistening brown arc of sherry across the floor. "She divorced us, don't you understand? She ran away to Europe to marry some French nobleman. Now she's sunk her claws into a rich Englishman. It's always money with her—jewels and clothes and a fancy house. You know she couldn't have married Stearns for his charm."

Rachel clasped Billie's hands in hers. "She must have been very young when she left you. People make mistakes, Billie. Can't you find it in your heart to forgive her?"

"No!" Billie pulled her hands away, unable to bear the other girl's sympathy. "She wasn't there when we needed her. Now I don't need her."

"You can't turn your back on your own mother."

Billie pressed her lips together stubbornly.

"I think we should go to that party," Rachel persisted.

"Are you out of your mind?" Billie cried, startled. "You expect me to go there and watch her lord it over everyone? And that stepdaughter of hers . . ." Billie threw up her hands, unable to think of an epithet bad enough for Julia.

"Yes, I think you should," Rachel said.

"Well, I won't."

"Just think about it."

Billie scowled. "No. Absolutely not. And what about all those people? You said you couldn't stand them staring at you."

"I'm getting tough, Billie," Rachel said. "As long as you and the other people I care about like me," she blushed prettily, "I don't care what anyone else thinks."

Billie stared at her. For a moment, Rachel's face had fairly glowed with emotion. Was it pride, perhaps? Or was it love? Love for Nick?

"I suppose I can wear my yellow dress," Rachel murmured, lifting her arms to an imaginary partner, then swirling around the room in a smooth, graceful glide. "And if you want me to, I'll teach you to dance."

"I know how to dance!"

"Can you waltz?"

"Waltz!" Billie yelped. "I'm not about to—"

"You'll have to waltz, you know." Rachel put her arm around Billie's waist. "Here, let me show you. It's really very easy."

107

Billie stared at Rachel in astonishment. The girl was actually bullying her! And although Rachel was being as sweet and soft-spoken as always, she was obviously determined that they go to that party. With a sinking feeling in the pit of her stomach, Billie also realized that Rachel was the only person who could actually make her do it. "I don't want—"

"And if you won't borrow anything from Helena, we'll have to buy you a dress. Most of your things are years' old."

"I don't want to buy, borrow or even wear a dress. I don't want to go to the damn party at all!" Billie shouted.

"Of course you do." Rachel swung Billie around in another graceful turn.

"I do not!" Billie shrieked, recoiling from her friend. She rushed outside, slamming the door behind her. "Budge! Where are you?"

"Here," he called from the corral.

"Did you see that woman?" she demanded, running to the gate and leaning her elbows on the top board.

He nodded. "She 'membered me right off. Just as purty as ever, ain't she? I recollect the first time I saw her, just nineteen years old and as purty and graceful as a queen."

"A queen!" Billie scoffed. Then she added, "And it's easy to keep your looks when all you have to do is tend to your 'toilette.'"

"I s'pose." He leaned his elbows on the top rail of the gate. "I caught that Eames feller snoopin' around the bunkhouse. Said he was lookin' fer some rope to fix a busted strap." With a contemptuous snort, the Texan spat into the dust. "He ain't no cowhand."

"He's trouble, that's what he is. And so is Stearns, if that's the sort of men he's bringing in. I don't know what he's up to, but you tell our boys to watch themselves."

He nodded. "I surely would like to know who fired the shot that spooked the herd," he said.

"Well, whoever it was, they picked the worst place for it. We're going to be weeks finding our cattle and rounding them up again."

He pushed his hat back with his thumb. "Mebbe the best spot, from his look-see. As it is, we're gonna be one of the last ranches to get our cattle into Tucson."

Billie plucked thoughtfully at her lower lip. Her cattle usually were sold to the army at Camp Lowell, but with so many new ranches starting up in the area, competition for local markets was becoming fierce. If she was late bringing her herd in, she might have to send her cattle by rail to California or even Kansas City. It would be an expensive and time-consuming trip which would reduce her year's profits badly.

"We'll just have to do the best we can," she said at last. "I want you to go into town tomorrow and see if you can hire a few more hands. Maybe we can pull our herd in faster than our 'friend' expects, hmmm?"

He nodded. Billie started to turn away, but Budge tapped the back of her hand to stop her.

"There's bad blood between Nick and Eames," he said. "I thought they was gonna have it out right here."

"Well, keep them apart if you can." Billie walked away, scowling. She'd had enough for one day, and Nick's feud with Eames was one problem she was not prepared to deal with just now.

Billie tossed and fretted far into the night. Finally she climbed out of bed and opened the shutter to allow the cool night air into the room. She took a deep breath, then another. Seeing her mother had been much more disturbing than she would have believed. Why couldn't the woman have just stayed away?

Propping her elbows on the deep windowsill, Billie

109

stared out over the hills. The moon, looking like half a silver dollar in the velvet nest of the sky, shed a faint platinum radiance over the land. Suddenly she straightened, peering intently at the top of the ridge to the west, where a rider had been silhouetted against the horizon for an instant. She knew who he was, knew by the set of his shoulders and the angle of his hat. But why was Nick leaving the ranch so late? She knew he was supposed to go into town with Budge tomorrow, for she had heard the Texan tell him so.

"Just what are you up to, Nick Larabee?" she muttered.

With a hiss of frustration, she pulled her nightgown over her head, gooseflesh rising up on her body as the cool air touched her bare skin. She donned her undergarments and blouse, then slipped on a pair of men's jeans.

After rolling a change of clothes and some extra bullets in her bedroll, she secured the shutter and quietly slipped out of the house.

"Shhh," she murmured to the horses as she climbed into the corral. "Easy, Sunfish old girl, it's me."

The mare whickered a greeting. Billie glanced at the bunkhouse, then threw a blanket onto the horse's back. A saddle soon followed, and a moment later Sunfish and her mistress were heading west.

Chapter 10

Billie leaned over the mare's neck, peering at the ground in an attempt to pick out Nick's trail among the rocks. She had followed him for more than twenty miles now, and had entered a very broken section of hills, riddled with arroyos, canyons and treacherous, shifting rocks. Now she had lost his trail completely.

"Damn, damn, damn!" she hissed through clenched teeth.

Suddenly she spied the yellow glow of a campfire in the canyon below. She urged the mare closer to the edge and peered into the dark depths of the canyon. Silhouetted against the fire were the shapes of three—no, four—men. And beyond them, half hidden among the scrubby piñon trees, were fifty or sixty head of cattle. My cattle, she thought.

The mare's hoof slipped, sending a shower of pebbles down into the canyon. There was a shout from one of the men, then a fusillade of shots. Bullets pinged loudly on the rocks near Billie and went ricocheting off in every direction. The mare reared, sending Billie hurtling to the ground with numbing force, then galloped away, neighing in terror.

"You little fool!" Nick said from behind her.

Billie gasped. Before she could say anything, however, he hauled her roughly to her feet.

"Come on!" Holding his revolver in one hand, he grasped her wrist with the other and jerked her after him.

He kept to the shadows as much as possible, slowly working his way to the mouth of another canyon.

"Not in there!" Billie cried. "What if—"

"Shut up!" he growled, pulling her after him with a jerk that snapped her head backward. "It's the only cover around. Damn it, girl, how many of them do you think I can take with you slowing me down?"

Billie stumbled, going painfully down on one knee upon the rocks. There was a shout behind them. It brought her back to her feet with a rush.

"They've seen us!" she panted.

They reached the mouth of the canyon just as their pursuers began firing. Nick shoved Billie behind a boulder and began shooting back. There were shouts and a great crashing of brush as the rustlers dove for cover.

"Three shots left," Nick muttered grimly.

Billie glared at him. "Didn't you bring any spares?"

"I was only watching them, you little idiot, not preparing for a damned war."

"I'm sorry."

He drew in his breath sharply, surprised by her sudden capitulation. "Okay, honey," he said, leaning beyond the protection of the rocks to snap off a shot. "Shit. Missed again."

Billie took her revolver from her belt and tossed it to him. He hefted it silently, staring at her, then thrust it into the waistband of his jeans and joined her behind the boulder. Lifting her to her feet, he held her tightly against his chest for a moment before pushing her ahead of him into the depths of the canyon.

"Come on," he said. "Let's see if we can lose them in here."

Billie followed him silently. There was a stealthy crackle of brush as the rustlers came in behind them. Fortunately, the moonlight didn't reach down here; the darkness folded itself around the fugitives, a welcome refuge just now. Nick held Billie's arm with one hand and felt his way along the winding wall of the canyon with the other.

Suddenly he stopped. "Goddamn," he whispered. "It's a dead end."

Billie leaned against the rough rock wall, fighting for breath. "Can we climb out?" she asked.

"No. Too steep." He moved away from her for a moment. "Billie? Come here, honey."

She reached out blindly, to have her hand captured in his large, strong one.

"There's a crack here," he whispered, squeezing himself sideways into the crevice and pulling her after. "It might be big enough for us to . . . ah!" The crack widened abruptly, almost sending him sprawling onto the soft sand floor of the cave that lay beyond.

"Where—"

"Shh!" He put his hand over her mouth.

The rustlers were right outside. Their voices echoed in the confined space.

"Ahhh, they ain't here!" one of them complained. "You said they come in here, Jack."

Another man snorted. "You gonna believe him after all that whiskey he guzzled?"

"Ahh, go to hell," a third man, presumably Jack, said. "I told you what I saw."

"Well, we lost 'em," the first man said. "Let's get outta here. The boss is gonna be mighty upset."

"*I* ain't gonna tell him. What about you, Jack?"

"Not me. That feller gives me the creeps, anyhow."

The men left, cursing each other good-naturedly. Nick slowly removed his hand from Billie's mouth.

"We were lucky they were too drunk to shoot straight," he said. "What are you doing out here?"

"What are *you* doing out here?" she countered. She wasn't about to tell him she'd been trailing him.

"Following up on some tracks I ran across a few days ago."

"You didn't see fit to tell the rest of us about them?" she asked.

He shrugged. "I thought I'd check them out first."

Billie nodded slowly. It was a plausible enough reason, she supposed. But he'd been just a little too sneaky about it for her taste; as long as their work was done, her men could come and go as they pleased without any interference from her. And she was uncomfortable here with him in the silent darkness. Some strange, powerful force seemed to be drawing her toward him as though his flesh called to hers, beckoning her to touch him.

Nick sat down on the floor of the little cave that had saved their lives. There was light coming from somewhere; now that his eyes had adjusted, he could make out some of his surroundings. Their refuge was perhaps ten by twelve feet, cut into the rock by water long ago. Tipping his head back, he could see a small opening high above. A single star was framed in the aperture. He turned to look at Billie. She was still standing near the entrance, poised to flee like some shy desert animal. His gaze took in her disheveled hair, her heaving chest and, with fascinated leisure, her jeans. Although they were rather loose on her, they revealed far more of her shapely curves than he'd ever had the pleasure to view before.

"What's the matter, Billie?" he asked.

"Nothing." Her voice was breathless, as if she'd been running a race.

Nick smiled, realizing what was bothering her. They were completely alone for the first time. And they couldn't go anywhere until morning. They had hours with nothing to do but be with each other. Passion stirred in him, making his heart race and his blood flow like fire in his veins. There was no caution in him, only a reckless desire to possess her. He *would* have her tonight, and damn the consequences.

The sight of the naked hunger on his face drove all rational thought from Billie's mind. Her breath came shallowly, as though a hand of iron was squeezing her chest. She wanted to run from that primitive masculine desire, and yet she also wanted to give herself up to it.

He patted the sand beside him. "Sit down, Billie."

Moving slowly, as though caught in a dream, she took her hat off. She had just enough presence of mind to sit down as far away as the confines of the cave allowed. The tiny hideaway was warm and quiet and intimate, the pale sand beneath her as soft as any bed. Now, that's a hell of a dangerous comparison, she thought, her heart kicking into a gallop. Unsure what to say or do, she began toying with the end of her long braid.

Suddenly Nick moved to kneel before her, placing his hand on hers, stilling her nervous movements. With his other hand, he untied the ribbon that secured the end of the braid and shook her hair free of its restraints. The glossy tresses slid over his hands like the finest silk, cool from the night air. He lifted one of the long curls to his nose, inhaling the fragrance of it.

"Lovely," he murmured, leaning toward her.

Billie's pulse thundered in her ears. She was helpless to speak, to do anything but watch as his mouth came

115

closer. Then his lips were on hers, teasing her, then parting her lips with urgent gentleness as his tongue delved deeply into her mouth.

"Wait!" she panted, wedging her arms between them. "What about Rachel?"

He pulled back in surprise. Then he took her chin in his hand and looked deeply into her eyes. "Billie, I want you, not Rachel. I want you more than any woman I've ever known."

"Are you sure?" she whispered.

"I'm sure."

Billie stared up at him. His face was serious, his gold-flecked gaze fairly blazing with desire. For the first time in her life she felt truly beautiful. Feminine. Wanted. It was an irresistible lure.

She wound her hands into his hair, knocking his hat off, and pulled him closer. His hands seemed to be everywhere at once, caressing her ribs, her hips, her breasts. His hot mouth trailed a fiery path over her chin and down her throat, lingering for a moment at the wildly throbbing pulse point. He unbuttoned her blouse, pulling the garment slowly over her shoulders. The straps of her camisole went with it, winding into a constricting tangle at her elbows. She moved to free herself, but Nick stopped her, pinning her wrists together with one big hand.

He moved back a few inches to look at her. Her full breasts were nearly bared now, the tightly stretched camisole pushing the soft white flesh upward and showing the top curve of her rosy nipples. With a groan, he bent forward and ran his tongue along the crevice between her arm and the side of her breast, then traced a moist, tormenting trail along the top of the camisole. He used his chin to work the fabric down over her breasts, finally revealing the full mounds and

116

the erect peaks to his famished gaze.

Billie moaned as his mouth closed over one of her nipples, tugging gently, licking, sucking until she was nearly wild with desire. He let go of her arms then, stripping the blouse from her with an impatient tug. Her camisole followed. Her arms freed, she rose up on her knees and unlaced his shirt, then pulled it up over his head and discarded it. He cupped her face between his big hands and kissed her tenderly. Billie pressed close, loving the feel of his throbbing manhood against her thighs.

"Ahh, Billie!" he groaned, cupping his hands beneath her buttocks and pulling her even closer.

Suddenly he tipped her backward so that she was sitting, then tugged her boots off and tossed them aside. He unbuttoned her jeans and pushed them down, lifting her briefly to slide them over her hips and down her legs. His hands came back to caress her slender ankles, her shapely calves and the sensitive places behind her knees. As his fingers slid upward along her thighs, Billie arched her back and cried out softly. With a groan, he laid her down on the pile of discarded clothing. He untied her drawers and slid them down, kissing every inch of flesh as it was exposed.

Billie was lost in sensation, tossed in spiraling passion like a ship on a stormy sea. She ran her hands over the coiled muscles of his thighs and hard male buttocks.

It was almost too much for him. Striving for control, he pulled her to a sitting position and buried his face in her hair. "You're driving me crazy," he rasped. "I've never felt like this before—never!"

She could actually feel the thunder of his heartbeat. Awed and a little frightened by the force of the passion she had called up in him, she tried to push him away, to get some control over her raging emotions.

"Ah, no!" he whispered, laying her back down. "Not again. I have to have you, Billie. We were meant for this."

Billie tried to cover her nakedness, but he held her hands away. Intent on devastation now, he kissed her breasts, her ribs, ran his tongue down her belly to her navel. Billie sank once again beneath the tumultuous waves of desire, arching to meet his mouth. His hand slid across her hip and over the dark triangle of hair at the juncture of her thighs, then delved into the tender folds of flesh below to find her wet and welcoming. He stroked her with gentleness and finesse, bringing her to a state of quivering eagerness.

Billie writhed as the coiling sensation in her abdomen tightened. She wanted, she wanted . . . "Please!" she cried. "I need—"

"Yes, yes, yes!" he groaned, stripping his boots and pants off and freeing his erect, throbbing manhood.

Naked, he knelt between her parted thighs. Kissing her deeply, he grasped her hips and pulled her up to him. He held himself gently against her opening, testing her response. Billie felt no fear, no hesitation. She dug her nails into his back and rubbed herself against him.

"Oh, God, Billie!"

He thrust deep within her, feeling her maidenhood tear. She gasped once, then recovered from the brief pain and began to enjoy the feel of the hardness within her. Nick stroked her gently with his body, careful of her newly breached innocence. He kissed her eyes, her forehead, the corners of her mouth, then buried his face against the side of her neck.

Billie clasped him to her, listening to the rasp of his breathing, feeling the spiraling sensation grow in her lower body as he loved her. His breathing quickened, became labored as his strokes became deeper and faster. The coiled tension became unbearable, and Billie wound her legs around his hips, seeking something she didn't yet know, but realized he could give her. Then it happened, a wild, shuddering release that made her cry out in surprise and ecstasy.

At the feel of her silky legs around him, the tight, pulsating depths of her enclosing him, Nick lost any hope of maintaining control. He thrust into her with unrestrained passion, groaning as he, too, was claimed by that powerful, final release.

He supported his weight on his elbows and looked down at her. "Are you all right?" he asked.

Billie nodded, resisting the impulse to cover her face with her hands.

Nick smiled, correctly guessing her thoughts. "There's no reason for shyness, my wild little virgin, nothing to be ashamed of. Men and women have been making love since the beginning of time, although"—he kissed her gently—"I bet many of them have not had as much fun."

She blushed. "Well, what do we do now?" she asked. It wasn't that she was expecting him to propose marriage, exactly, but surely there must be some sort of commitment between two people who had shared something so wonderful.

"Next?" Nick asked, raising his brows. "You're a greedy baggage, but I'll try to be accommodating." He thrust with his hips to indicate what his intentions were.

"I didn't think it was possible . . . Oh! Oh, Nick!" Billie gasped as he gently pushed her breasts upward so he could suckle the hardening peaks one by one.

"Anything is possible," he murmured, releasing her nipple to kiss the underside of her jaw as the motion of his hips quickened. "And I find that I'm even greedier than you are. We have the rest of the night to learn about each other, Billie. Let's not waste a minute of it."

Billie closed her eyes and surrendered to the passion that was already rising within her. Her hands closed over his flexing buttocks, and her awareness of the rest of the world faded.

Chapter 11

Billie sighed and rolled over, reaching out instinctively for Nick. Her hand encountered only cool sand, however, and she woke up with a start to find herself alone in the little cave. A faint tang of smoke drifted on the cool morning air. She put her scattered clothing on hurriedly and slipped outside. Nick squatted beside the fire he'd built against the far side of the canyon. The carcass of a rabbit, cleaned and skinned, hung on a makeshift spit above the flames.

The smell of roasting meat brought Billie farther out of the cave. Nick looked up at her briefly, then returned his attention to the flames. She felt a jolt in her mid section. Not even a smile from him, she thought. Is this the way a man was supposed to act after a night spent making passionate love to a woman? Feeling hideously uncomfortable, Billie sat down on a rock on the other side of the fire from him.

"Such a nice, tidy fire," she said, watching the smoke trail upward along the canyon wall, then rise into the air in a nearly invisible shimmer. "Nearly as tidy as an Apache could make it. Where did you learn to do that?"

"Here and there," he said, glancing up at her again.

"I'm a man of varied experience."

Billie blushed, remembering the things they had done and said during the fevered hours of the night. Oh, yes, he knew many things, and had been eager to teach her all of them. But he seemed to be completely unaffected by what had happened between them. If anything, he looked as sated and comfortable as a cat after a big meal. No, she corrected herself with a pang of apprehension, not a cat, but a great, tawny mountain lion that, having made a successful stalk and caught its prey, had turned its attention to other things.

"Where are the rustlers?" she asked.

"Gone. At least for now."

"With my cattle."

"I'm afraid so." He pulled the steaming meat away from the fire and laid it on a nearby rock to cool. After cutting it into chunks, he speared one on the point of his knife and offered it to her. Billie shook her head, then pulled her own knife out of her boot and helped herself.

Nick was startled by the knife's sudden appearance. Until now, he'd been basking in a heady, masculine feeling of possession and contentment. The weapon reminded him that Billie was no soft piece of fluff who needed his protection, but a canny young woman who was most likely better equipped to survive out here than he was.

Her next words proved him right.

"If you cut one of those," she said, pointing to a nearby clump of cactus, "you'll find the flesh edible and full of water."

Nick had had enough dealings with those damned, murderous plants to last a lifetime. Flipping his knife, he offered it to her hilt first. "You're the expert."

"Coward."

"Damn right."

Ignoring the proffered knife, she squatted beside the cacti and cut several chunks with swift, expert movements. As he watched her flick the spines out with the point of her knife, Nick reflected that her friends the Apache had probably taught her. What else had they taught her? he wondered. How had she managed to keep that forbidden friendship a secret all this time? And why? The thought made him want to hold his emotions in check even as he noted how her position stretched her jeans tightly over the sleek swell of her behind. Damn it, he had the feeling he was going to regret getting this involved with her.

Taking his revolver out, he checked his remaining bullets. Two shots left, he thought sourly. Even though Billie's pistol was fully loaded, they'd be easy pickings.

"We're going to have to leave soon," he said gruffly. "Those outlaws may decide to come back once they sober up."

Billie sat down beside the fire again, her heart clenching in misery. Wasn't he even going to mention what had happened between them? Hadn't it meant anything at all to him? She looked at him, searching for some desire, some small awareness of her in his face, but there was nothing. This was terrible! And even worse was the realization that she wanted him again, wanted to feel the fierce gentleness of his caresses. To possess and be possessed in the light of day so she could watch his face while he made love to her. You idiot! she railed inwardly, the man hardly knows you're alive this morning. Scowling, she stabbed another chunk of meat onto her knife and worried at it with her small, white teeth.

"Is there water anywhere near?" Nick asked.

"Not that I know of," she said, keeping her gaze on her food. Oh, God, this is humiliating! What do I say to this man now that I've shared his bed? How do I act?

"Damn! I wish we had our horses!" He smacked his fist into his other palm.

"What about yours?" she asked. "Didn't you tie him when you came up here?"

"Of course I did. But there isn't a tether made that could have held Beelzebub once all that shooting started." He watched her breasts rise and fall with her breathing, noting that the nipples had risen up in hard little peaks beneath her shirt. His manhood stirred as he remembered how he had suckled those luscious mounds, and how she had cried out her pleasure, holding his head against her in a wordless plea for more. He'd like to peel that shirt off her right now and do it all over again. Absently he fed a stick to the fire, burning his fingers in his bemusement.

"Ouch! Goddamn it to hell!" He surged to his feet. "Are you finished?"

"Yes." For a moment she'd thought desire had come back into his eyes. And then he'd cursed, shriveling her newborn hope. She must be even more of a fool than she'd thought, to mistake annoyance for passion. She slipped her knife back into her boot and rose, keeping her head down so he wouldn't see her flush of mortification.

After smothering the fire with dirt, Nick strode toward the mouth of the canyon. Billie jammed her hat on her head and hurried after him, cursing him under her breath.

Suddenly he stopped and turned toward her, holding out his hand. "Come on!" he growled impatiently. One more minute here and he'd be making love to her again. How had he gotten so wound up with her in just one night?

Astonished by the savagery of his face, Billie nearly stumbled. He set her upright, then took her by the hand and pulled her after him. She followed docilely, thoroughly confused by his actions.

124

If she thought some revelation as to his feelings might burst upon her like lightning, the next few hours disabused her of that notion. Although Nick retained hold of her hand as they walked, he might have been leading his horse for all the effect that contact had on him. He was once again the preoccupied male, she thought, intent on business. His hold on her was impersonal, and his gaze constantly scanned the hills around them. She revised her opinion; surely Beelzebub would have commanded more of his attention than this.

Nick was bewildered by his feelings this morning. He'd thought that making love to her would have cooled this strange obsession he had with this willful, sharp-tongued but sensuous girl. He had taken women where he had found them—sweet, bad-tempered, honest and scheming, he'd made love to all kinds. A man who thrived on challenge, he had looked on lovemaking as a kind of conquest. After the women had given themselves, they had become more clinging, more demanding, while he had begun to disengage himself from the relationship. But things hadn't worked that way with Billie. If anything, the desire to possess her had grown stronger. Even now, when he should be paying attention to what was going on around him, his mind kept straying to the memory of her fiery response last night. Every time he looked at her, his gaze roved over the breasts he ached to touch, the wide mouth he longed to kiss. Damn it, he thought savagely, it was getting so bad he'd be lucky if he could put one foot before the other without falling.

They walked for another hour, then another. Billie's boots felt like vises, squeezing her tired feet into burning lumps of agony. When he finally stopped to rest, she sank down on the nearest rock and pulled her boots off.

Nick knelt and took her feet in his hands, kneading

her aching flesh with his strong fingers.

"Oh, that feels good," she murmured, closing her eyes.

The memory of another time when she had said that washed over him, bringing his manhood to instant attention. His hands strayed up under the legs of her pants to stroke her curved calves. Suddenly remembering where they were and what they were supposed to be doing, he jerked his hands away from her and rose quickly to his feet.

"We'd better get moving again," he growled.

Billie put her boots back on, sudden hot tears stinging her eyelids. He didn't want her anymore! Making love had bound her heart to him as thoroughly as it had joined their bodies. And the pleasure they had shared had been special; despite her innocence, she couldn't have been mistaken about that. But a small, nagging doubt blossomed and began to grow. Could it have been different for him? Perhaps it was, she thought. Perhaps her virginal ineptitude had bored him. Dully, she followed him as he began walking again.

The sun was at its zenith now, bringing a shimmer of heatwaves to life. Billie doffed her hat and wiped her sleeve across her brow. Nick stopped so suddenly that she walked right into his broad back.

He reached behind him and grasped her by the arm, pulling her around to his side. "Up there," he said, pointing.

Billie saw a faint track running north. It snaked across the lower slope of a nearby hill and disappeared in the dark depths of a canyon.

"It's a cattle track," she said. "Do you think there might be water up there?"

"I think we should find out," he said, drawing her after him.

They found a spring tucked in the far end of the

canyon. The rocky ground around it was crisscrossed with the tracks of many cattle, and there was a small grove of sturdy pines nearby. Billie walked across the trampled ground, stopping only long enough to remove her boots before wading right into the water. The spring was little more than a shallow pool, but the water was as clear as glass and very cold, bringing gooseflesh to her overheated skin. Billie filled her hat with the precious stuff and poured it over her head, letting it sluice the dust from her body. Three more times she did it, soaking herself to the skin. Just before she bent to fill her hat again, Nick's bare arms came around her waist.

With a gasp, she realized that the rest of him was as bare as his arms. She could feel the iron muscles of his thighs flex as he drew her against him, then the hard brand of his maleness pressed urgently against her back, bringing a surge of liquid heat to her lower body. Her head fell back against his chest. He did want her! She was aware of a brief moment of triumph before she forgot everything in a surging rush of desire.

His hands came up to caress the slim white column of her throat, then moved to her breasts. Billie could feel the heat of his fingers through the wet fabric of her blouse. To her surprise, she realized that he was trembling. She moaned, unbearably moved by that knowledge. Her nipples rose up to meet his palms.

Drawing his breath in with a hiss, he unbuttoned her blouse and spread it open. When the ribbons of her camisole resisted him, he broke them. Billie was too lost in passion to protest. She closed her eyes as his fingers sought and found her nipples and teased them into turgid peaks.

"God, you're beautiful!" he muttered into her ear. "I can't think of anything but touching you." Then his tongue replaced his breath, and Billie gasped.

"Let me turn around," she pleaded.

"Not yet."

He unfastened her jeans and drawers and slipped his hand beneath the fabric. As his fingers stroked along her flat belly and over the soft curls below, Billie's legs began to give way. He wrapped one arm around her waist to support her while his other hand delved yet farther into her moist secrets. Billie moaned as his fingers parted her woman's flesh, seeking the source of her heat. Still he forced her to stand there, her back to him, while he brought her to a fever pitch of passion.

Billie reached behind her, desperate to touch him, but he was pressed so tightly against her that she was unable to reach her true goal. So she ran her hands over his lean thighs, then clasped his muscular buttocks to pull him even closer.

"Billie!" he groaned, spinning her around to face him.

His hot tongue played a sensual game with her parted, eager lips, rubbing, teasing, sliding over the rosy flesh, then stabbing deep inside her mouth with bold possessiveness. Billie clung to him tightly, her hips gyrating in helpless response.

The movement against his swollen maleness was more than he could resist. Scooping her up into his arms, he strode out of the water and headed for the trees. Billie pressed her lips against the spot where his neck joined his shoulder. Her tongue darted out to taste his skin, then daringly slid along his neck toward his ear.

"I'll drop you if you keep that up," he said huskily.

"You did it to me," she murmured, looking up at him from beneath her lashes. Her eyes had darkened nearly to emerald from passion.

He reached the trees at last. Still clasping her in his arms, he sat down on the thick bed of needles that carpeted the ground.

"Now you can do whatever you want," he said.

Billie pressed her breasts against his chest, feeling the crisp hair tickling her sensitive nipples. She traced his ear with her tongue, then nibbled on the lobe, hardly aware that Nick had lifted her lower body and was divesting her of her jeans and drawers.

He set her in his lap again, making her suddenly, acutely aware of the thick, hard shaft that was pressed against her naked hip. She kissed her way slowly, teasingly along his jaw toward his mouth. Too impatient to wait a moment longer, he sank his hands into her hair and pulled her head back to kiss her with savage urgency.

"I want you too badly," he muttered against her mouth. "Tell me you want me, too. Please, Billie!"

"I want you!" she gasped. "More than anything, anything!"

He laid her on her back and slid between her thighs. His manhood entered her easily this time, driving deep. Billie moaned and wrapped her legs around his waist.

"Ah, yes, perfect! That's the way, honey," he muttered. Her tight flesh closed around him, drawing him even farther into the sweet, sweet depths of her. This tiny girl was more woman than he had ever known before, more than he had ever dreamed could exist. He fought for control. Then her nails raked his back with tender savagery and he was lost. "Oh, God!" he groaned, driving into her with passionate abandon.

Billie met his every thrust, seeking the fulfillment she knew waited for her. He carried her higher and higher, until she thought she would faint from the pleasure of it. Then the shuddering release caught her, and her voice rose in a wail. Nick smothered the cry with his mouth, drinking it in avidly, then lunged against her as his own fulfillment came.

He kissed her again and again, murmuring her name between kisses. Billie put her arms around his neck, shocked by the realization that she loved this man. Love. She rolled the word over in her mind, trying to understand what it meant to her, to Nick. She had expected love to be some pleasant, tidy emotion that could be understood and handled, not this combination of exasperation, desperation and the terrible, wonderful passion that drowned all thought in its tumultuous passage. Did Nick feel the same? she wondered. Would he stay with her, or would he ride away when the urge came to move on?

"What are you thinking about?" he asked, propping himself on his elbows and staring down into her face.

"About this." She blushed. "About what's happened between us."

"I know you liked it," he teased.

Her color deepened. "I was wondering if, well, if it's going to continue once we get back."

"I certainly hope so!" He grinned, then suddenly rested his weight on her possessively. "Try to keep me away, Billie. Just try!"

She stared into his gold-flecked eyes, seeking the emotion behind that bold claim. "What does that mean?"

"Mean?" he asked, astonished by her question. He'd never had a woman ask him such a thing before. But then, he reflected, Billie was different from any other woman he'd ever met. He rolled over onto his side, bringing her with him and tucking her into the curve of his arm. "Haven't I demonstrated how much I want you, over and over again? What more do you want from me?"

Billie sighed. He didn't understand. Perhaps he would never understand. Perhaps he only thought in terms of possessing a woman, of making love to her body, not being in love. Love would be a terrible inconvenience to a man who never settled anywhere. "We'd better get going," she said, trying to slip out of his embrace.

He pulled her back, restraining her with his arm around her waist. "Not yet. It's hot, and I'm damned tired."

"Someone is stealing my cattle and you want to sleep?" she demanded. "Get up, Nick."

"An hour isn't going to make any difference." His eyes drifted closed.

Billie lay against him, entrapped by the iron strength of his arm. His breathing deepened. After a few minutes, she managed to wriggle out of his embrace. As she dressed, she noticed that his holster was lying within easy reach of his hand. Even during their love-making, it had been there. Was it merely prudence after their encounter with the rustlers the night before, or was it something else entirely?

Chapter 12

Nick and Billie struggled down the slope of a hill. Her boot caught in a crevice, and she would have fallen if it weren't for Nick's strong arm around her waist.

"It won't be much longer, honey," he said, setting her upright. "We've only got an hour or so before we reach the spring in Dogleg Canyon. We can spend the night there."

Billie nodded. The thought of another night out here with him made her shiver with anticipation. Would he make love to her again? Would he cradle her in his arms as he'd done the night before, then wake her so he could love her all over again? A flush rose into her cheeks. Without thinking, she leaned toward him, her lips parted in silent invitation.

Nick groaned at the sight. His arm went around her again, crushing her against his chest. As he bent toward her, he saw the figure of a mounted man appear on the crest of a distant hill. He stiffened, pushing her behind him. "Someone's coming," he said, his hand moving toward his holster.

"Rustlers . . . No, it's Budge." She squinted at the faraway figure. Even from here she could see the outline of the Texan's cowboy hat. "I swear I've never seen a prettier sight," she said fervently. They'd been walking in the broiling afternoon sun for two hours without a rest, and her body felt like one big ache.

Nick grunted. "Looks like he's only brought one spare mount. Sunfish must not have made it home."

"The rustlers must have found her." Billie snatched her hat off and threw it down. "By God, I'd rather the Apaches have her than those bastards!"

Nick laughed, more amused than shocked at her profanity. Picking up her hat, he brushed it clean and put it back on her head. "Come on, honey."

Billie sat down on the nearest rock. "Someone's stealing my cattle and my best horse is gone, probably to end up pulling some farmer's plow down in Mexico somewhere. My face is sunburned and my feet hurt. I'm not walking another step."

He picked her up, then sat down on the rock with her in his lap. "You look beautiful to me," he said, leering at her. "Want me to prove it?"

"Stop it." Billie pushed at his chest. "Let me up. Do you want Budge to see us?"

"So it's to be boss lady and cowhand again, is it?" he asked softly.

Billie scowled. "Maybe you'd like me to put a notice up in town telling everyone what happened out here?"

"That might not be a bad idea." Anything that might keep other men away from her was a damned good idea, he thought, caught by a surge of fierce possessiveness. She might be a whole lot more trouble than he had any business taking on right now, but he wanted her.

"Let me up," she snapped. She pushed at his chest again.

"Not yet." He cradled her head in the crook of his arm and kissed her. His mouth plundered hers leisurely, bringing her to a state of trembling desire.

134

When he lifted his head, she lay against his arm help-lessly, her eyes closed, her lips parted. He smiled and set her down on the rock beside him.

Billie clasped her hands over her knees and stared at her boots, wondering if she would always be so vulner-able to him. It wouldn't be so bad if he didn't know the effect he had on her. What was really infuriating about the whole mess was that *he* seemed so calculating and controlled, bringing her to a fever pitch with that single, flaming kiss just now, then turning away, seem-ingly unaffected, to idly toss pebbles at a nearby cactus.

"Why is this so complicated?" she demanded, flinging her arms out in frustration.

He turned to her, grinning. "But it isn't complicated at all, honey. You want me, I want you. Very simple, as far as I can tell."

"You call that simple?" she cried.

He nearly said "yes" again, but then turned away from her and began throwing rocks at the cactus again. Damn, he'd better convince himself before trying to convince her. He'd thought bedding her would solve his problem, not add to it. But then, he'd thought he could rid himself of his need for her by making love to her. No more mystery, no more nights spent trying to escape dreaming about her. But it hadn't worked that way. He wanted her more than ever, and that desire was like a net drawing around him, distracting him from what he needed to do.

Billie glanced at him and, realizing that she'd lost him again, lapsed into sullen silence until Budge rode up. The Texan leaned his forearm on the pommel of his saddle and looked down at the tired, dusty pair.

"Lose your horse, Nick?" he asked. "Or did your horse lose you?"

"He lost me," Nick said cheerfully. "I take it Beelze-bub showed up at the house?"

135

"Don't he always?" Budge turned to Billie, glaring at her from under lowered brows. "What the hell are you doin' out here, gal?"

"I was trailing some rustlers," she said. "I found them camped in a canyon just south of Pima Mountain. They had at least fifty head of cattle tucked away." Quickly, she told him what had happened the night before. Most of it, that is.

Budge tossed his canteen down to her. "Wal, that explains who fired the shot what spooked the herd. And we ain't the only ones they hit, neither; Lew Purcell stopped by this mornin', said the Dolorosa is missin' more'n a hundred head of Herefords, prime breedin' stock, and Stearns is madder'n a hornet. I better send a man around to the other ranchers to warn 'em." He took his foot out of the stirrup and held out his hand to Billie.

"She'll ride with me," Nick said. When Budge's eyebrows soared, he quickly added. "Your horse is tired enough without having to pack another rider."

The Texan nodded. Putting his foot back into the stirrup, he watched with interest as Billie's face turned scarlet. Nick took the canteen from her and tossed it back to Budge, then mounted the spare horse. Grinning, he reached down with one hand to pull Billie up behind him.

Budge wheeled his mount and headed back toward the ranch. Ignoring her attempts to resist, Nick drew Billie's arms around his waist. The horse lurched into a jolting trot, and she had no choice but to hang on.

"You're enjoying this," she whispered fiercely, wishing she could shout at the top of her lungs. Damned infuriating man! Wouldn't he allow her any dignity at all?

Nick smiled at her over his shoulder. The feel of her breasts bouncing against his back was indeed enjoyable. So enjoyable, in fact, that his manhood was growing hard in response. He wished he could stop the horse, pull her down and make love to her all over again. And again. His body burned at the thought. He faced forward and tried to keep his attention on the landscape ahead, but his mind was filled with plans of getting her alone once they were back at the ranch, and what he was going to do to her when he did.

At first Billie sat stiffly, but the horse soon abandoned the spine-jolting trot and settled into a smooth walk that rapidly lulled her. As the hot afternoon wore on, her eyelids grew heavy, too heavy to keep open. She leaned wearily against Nick's back and slipped into a doze. One hand slipped downward from his waist and came to rest against the bulge of his manhood. She woke with a start. Feeling the hardness of him under her palm, she snatched her hand away and glanced at Budge. To her relief, the Texan wasn't looking.

Nick chuckled. "See what you do to me?" he murmured.

"Lecher!" she hissed. "Can't you think of anything else?"

Grinning, he leaned back into the cushion of her breasts, forcing her to grasp his belt to keep from sliding off the horse's rump. "Budge, what do you think those rustlers will do with the cattle?" he asked.

The Texan shrugged. "Most likely they'll take 'em down to Mexico where they ain't so fussy about brands."

"They must be pretty well organized, to be able to take that many in one night."

"Yep." Badge's pale eyes were full of cold anger. "And we can't do a damn thing to stop 'em. There ain't enough men in the whole territory to patrol this here range."

137

"What about the army?" Nick asked.

"Them?" Budge snorted contemptuously. "If it ain't wearin' war paint, they ain't interested. Anyhow, I doubt they'd have any better luck with these fellers than they've had with the Apach."

Billie pinched the muscular flesh of Nick's waist as hard as she could. He sat forward abruptly. With a nod of satisfaction, she turned to Budge. "How many head have they taken from us?" she asked.

"I ain't had time to finish the count, but my guess'd be three hundred and fifty, mebbe as much as four hundred. So far."

"Four hundred!" Billie groaned. "That does it. The minute we get back we're heading for town. I'm going to hire anyone who can sit a horse, or even anyone who thinks he can."

Budge shook his head. "Billie—"

"What?" she shouted.

"A bunch of greenhorns ain't goin' to do a damn bit of good agin those rustlers."

"He's right," Nick said. "It'll be a waste of time and money."

Forgetting herself for a moment, she pummeled Nick's broad back with her fist. "Well, what am I supposed to do? Sit back and let them steal all my cattle?"

"No," Nick said, glaring over his shoulder at her. "But a few experienced men are going to do more good than a whole army of amateurs. You let us handle it."

"It's my ranch," she snapped. "I'll do as I see fit."

Nick shrugged, feigning indifference, although he would have liked to shake her until her teeth rattled. "What would your father have done?"

"Pa would have taken his rifle and his best horse and hit the range. When he came back, there wouldn't have been any more rustlers." A speculative light came into her green eyes.

"Don't try it," Budge said, scowling at her. "I'll tan your hide, boss or no boss."

"Pa—"

"Your pa would have whipped you good fer even thinkin' about it."

"Pa isn't here," she muttered, fuming with impatience. She wanted to scream, to lash out at someone, anyone. She'd worked hard nearly all her life to build the Star M, and she wasn't about to let a bunch of thieves take it away from her.

Nick rubbed his hand over his cheek as he stared at her, his fingers rasping over two days' growth of beard. Although Budge hadn't heard that low comment, he had. Ordinarily he'd have thought she had more sense than to consider going out against a gang of armed men, but there was a speculative look in her green eyes that he didn't like at all.

"Take it easy, honey," he murmured. "We'll stop them."

She closed her eyes, her limbs becoming weak at the sound of his lazy, caressing voice. She leaned forward and pressed her forehead against his back. Briefly, he let his hand stray backward, his fingers trailing lightly along her thigh. It was good to have him here, she mused. Good to have someone to share her troubles with, to lean against when times got hard.

She straightened abruptly, however, shy about showing her feelings in front of Budge. But when the Texan spurred his horse into the lead again, she laid her cheek back onto the warm sturdiness of Nick's back.

Perched on the horse's rump as she was, it was a long, uncomfortable ride. She sighed with relief when the house came into view at last, its white adobe walls gleaming like porcelain in the fading afternoon light. First a bath, she thought, then about a dozen hours' sleep in the comforts of a clean bed.

Nick stopped his tired horse in front of the house and

dismounted. Reaching up, he pulled Billie down from her perch behind his saddle.

"I'll take care of the horses," Budge said. "Y'all git somthin' to eat."

Nick tossed the reins to him. Billie turned toward the house, stopping in surprise as the door was flung open with such force that it slammed back against the wall. Rachel came running out, her skirts flying wildly behind her. She rushed past an astonished Billie and flung herself into Nick's arms.

"I thought something terrible had happened to you!" she sobbed, burying her face against his chest. "Beelzebub came back . . . Oh, Nick! I thought you were dead!"

"Shhh," he soothed, stroking the distraught girl's hair. "Easy, Rachel. Come on now, everything's all right."

But she couldn't stop crying. Great, gasping sobs were torn from her, and her fingers clutched the fabric of his shirt with desperate intensity. Nick put his arm around her waist and led her toward the house.

He didn't look at Billie as he passed. A moment later the door closed behind him.

"Hello, Billie," Nick said, stepping into the house early the next morning. He sniffed at the delicious aroma of baking biscuits. "Mmm. That smells wonderful!"

Since Rachel was still asleep, exhausted by a night spent crying, Billie dried her hands on her apron and pushed him out the door. She stood on the porch, arms akimbo, and asked, "You wouldn't care to explain yourself, I suppose?"

"Explain what?"

"What happened yesterday with Rachel."

Nick adjusted his hat, causing its shadow to fall over his eyes. "I don't think I have anything to explain."

"I do."

"You're not jealous, are you?" he asked, the creases at the corners of his mouth deepening. "You don't have to be."

She was confused and more than a little disturbed by his attitude. He seemed to be taking this so lightly! Didn't he think she would be upset by what had happened? Just yesterday he had made love to her. He had taken her virginity, her heart, and then taken Rachel into his arms in front of her. Surely any reasonable person would think that demanded some explanation.

"What kind of game are you playing?" she asked.

He let out his breath in an explosive sigh. His next words were spoken slowly and distinctly as though she were hard of hearing. "I don't play games, Billie. As you ought to know, I make it quite clear when I want a woman."

"I want to know if you made it as clear to Rachel as you did to me." Billie hooked her thumbs in her belt to keep her hands from trembling. She was determined to get the truth from him, and half afraid to hear it. What if he told her that he *did* care for Rachel? The girl still hadn't recovered fully from the attack. She was fragile, emotionally and physically. What would it do to her to find out that the man she cared for had been making love to her best friend? What kind of man would do something like that to either of them?

"I haven't touched her," he said through clenched teeth.

No, Billie thought, Rachel is a lady. She deserves respect. But he hadn't had the same reservations with *her*. "I think she'd need a very good reason—and a lot of encouragement—to be so free with her affection."

"I haven't encouraged her!"

"Don't lie to me!" Billie snapped.

He moved forward with uncanny quickness and grabbed her by the shoulders. His biceps flexed, and he pulled her right up off the ground. Furious, she found herself dangling like a toy in his big hands.

"Put me down!" she ordered, undaunted by her undignified position.

"I ought to—"

"Oh, dear, am I interrupting something?" Julia Stearns's high, breathy voice contained a great deal of amusement.

"Yes," Billie said rudely.

Nick set her down. "Mind your manners, Billie." He turned to Julia, damping his anger down to greet the visitor. "What can we do for you, Miss Stearns?"

"Oh, please, call me Julia," she said. "And I shall call you Nick."

"That suits me just fine, Julia." Nick gave her his most sensual smile. Call me a liar, will you, Billie? he thought, stepping forward to hold out his arm to the English girl. "Come in out of the sun."

"Thank you." Julia tucked her gloved hand in the crook of his arm and let him lead her into the house. She smiled maliciously at Billie as she passed.

Billie nearly booted the girl's artfully swaying behind as it went by, but restrained herself and followed them inside. Nick escorted Julia to a chair, then went to get her a drink of water.

Billie propped her hip on the corner of the table and crossed her arms over her chest. "Did you come alone, Miss Stearns?" she asked. By God, she thought, if the girl had brought Eames back to the ranch . . . !

"Actually, yes, although Father will be furious when he finds out. But one cannot allow oneself to be confined to a rude and ugly house merely because of some savages, you know."

142

Billie stared at her in astonishment, more because of her description of the Dolorosa's house as rude and ugly than because of her utter stupidity in ignoring the danger posed by the Indians. "The Dolorosa is the most luxurious house outside Tucson," she said. "Most people would feel lucky to live there."

"Indeed? I suppose that depends on one's point of view." Julia looked around at the stark interior of the house, then at Billie's dress, several years out of fashion, and curled her lip superciliously.

Nick returned, carrying a cup of water. "Here you are, Julia," he said, setting it in front of her.

Billie looked at him, then at the door. "Don't you have some work to do?"

He ignored the less than subtle hint, however, and sat down at the table. "To what do we owe the honor of this visit, Julia?"

"I just thought to be neighborly, as you say." Julia looked at him from under half-closed lashes, pulling her gloves off slowly, as provocatively as though she were undressing for him. "We will be hosting a ball at the Dolorosa in a few weeks, Nick. I'd like to extend my personal invitation."

He leaned back in his chair. "I thought it was for owners and the local gentry, not for cowhands."

"I can invite anyone I wish," she said. "Will you come?"

"How about it, boss lady?" He looked at Billie, mischief in his tawny eyes. "You won't mind, will you?"

"Of course not." Billie took a deep breath. She would not lose her temper in front of the haughty English girl, she vowed.

"Excellent." Julia rose to her feet and reached for her gloves. "Are you planning to come, Miss Meyrick?"

"Yes, I am." Billie was astonished by her answer. The words had sprung from her mouth, unbidden and unwelcome, just because it was so obvious that Julia would rather she stay away.

Julia looked disappointed for a moment, but the cold hauteur soon returned to her face. "Helena will be pleased. I shall tell her for you."

"Thanks." Billie felt as though she was strangling, and the mocking smile on Nick's face didn't help.

"I'll see you to your buggy," Nick said, taking Julia by the arm.

Billie followed them outside, fuming. What perverse demon had possessed her in that moment, causing her to commit herself? She'd rather cut off her arm than attend the party.

Budge came around the corner of the house. "Your horse picked up a stone, Miss Stearns," he said. "I put him in our corral and hitched one of our mounts to your cart. Ol' Samson don't look like much, but he'll git you from here to there without too much trouble. I'll have one of our hands bring your horse out to the Dolorosa in a coupla days."

"That would be very kind of you." Julia's smile made it clear which of the Star M's men she would like to perform that particular errand.

"I'll ride back with you," the Texan said. "A lady got no business wandering out here alone."

"I was not wandering," Julia snapped. "I shall do very well by myself, thank you."

Budge shrugged. "I got to talk to Lew Purcell anyhow."

"Miss Meyrick," Julia hissed through clenched teeth, "this fellow doesn't appear to understand English. Please explain to him that I do not want his company."

"He probably doesn't want yours, either," Billie said. "But it's our responsibility to see that you get home safely."

Julia presented her back to Billie and the Texan and held out her hand to Nick. Smiling, he lifted her into the buggy.

"*Au revoir*, Nicholas," she murmured.

Nick bowed. "Adieu, mademoiselle," he replied in perfectly accented French. He looked past Julia to Billie and Budge, who were staring at him as though he'd taken leave of his senses. When Billie's mouth silently shaped the word "mademoiselle," then puckered into a grimace of disgust, it was all he could do to keep from laughing.

"My, my," Julia breathed, unaware of what was going on behind her, "you are indeed an interesting man. I may just learn to like Arizona." She smiled up at him. "With the proper inducement, of course."

Nick was very much aware of Billie's gaze boring into his back. He smiled, as self-satisfied as a cat after a full meal. Julia picked her parasol up and held it across her knees.

"I wouldn't use that if I were you," Billie said. "Samson isn't used to—"

"Really, Miss Meyrick, I wouldn't think of exposing my skin to this horrible sun." Julia slapped the reins against the horse's rump. As the cart pulled away, she opened the parasol with a sharp snap.

Samson looked over his shoulder. Spying the strange, fluttering object that seemed to be following him, he snorted and picked up his pace. Still the frightening thing followed. He moved into a trot in an attempt to leave it behind, ignoring the human female's shrill cries and her frenzied pull on the reins.

Billie watched the cart clatter off in the opposite direction from the Dolorosa. Cupping her hands around her mouth, she shouted, "Get rid of the parasol!" She burst into laughter, leaning against Budge for support.

145

Julia opened her hand, letting the parasol drop to the ground. Samson slowed, and she was able to turn him toward the Dolorosa. "You're going to pay for that, Miss Meyrick," she hissed, glancing over her shoulder at Billie. "I promise, you will pay."

Nick, noticing that malevolent stare, said, "You've made yourself an enemy, boss lady."

"If that . . . woman wanted to be my *friend,* I'd be worried." Turning her back on him, she headed back toward the house. "We're going into town tomorrow, Budge," she called over her shoulder. "Be ready at dawn."

"Stubborn as a mule and madder'n a bobcat with its tail in a campfire," the Texan muttered. "We got problems fer sure." He started toward the corral, then turned and regarded the younger man thoughtfully. "You think Eames is trouble? Wal, you ain't seen nothin' yet."

Nick laughed.

Chapter 13

"I wonder what they're doing here." Billie nodded toward the six men who loitered outside the telegraph office.

It was the second such group she'd seen, composed of men whose low-hung guns and hard faces proclaimed their violent profession. They turned to watch the wagon as Billie and Rachel drove past.

One of them called, "Wal, lookee whut we have here, fellers." He had a harsh, guttural voice, almost like an animal's growl. "Come on over here, gals. We's mighty lonely." A burst of rude laughter followed his words.

Nick interposed his mount between the watching men and the wagon. He stared down at the one who had spoken, his face impassive, his eyes as flat and cold as a winter sky. The stranger met that boreal gaze challengingly for a moment, then shrugged and turned away. Nick urged his mount after the retreating wagon, keeping his hand near his gun and his attention on the men he'd left behind.

Billie turned the corner, putting a building between the wagon and the strangers, then stopped and waited for Nick to catch up.

"I hope Budge doesn't run into trouble at the

saloon," Nick said, pulling his horse to a halt beside the wagon.

"Budge knows enough to steer clear of men like that." Billie looked at Nick's hand, which was still hovering near his pistol. "I hope you do."

His face was as unreadable as stone. "They haven't come here looking for work. Someone hired them."

"Yes. People are afraid," Billie said, indicating the nearly empty street.

"You and Rachel shouldn't have come," Nick growled. "Budge and I could have handled this."

"You and Budge don't run the Star M. I do," she snapped.

"Then you ought to have more sense."

She scowled at him. Who was he to give her orders when he wouldn't even tell her the truth about his relationship with Rachel? "I'm not going to . . . Rachel, what's the matter?"

There was no answer. Rachel was gripping the wagon seat with trembling hands. Terror filled her eyes, and her face was as pale as death.

With a gasp, Billie dropped the reins and grabbed her by the shoulders. "Rachel!"

Awareness slowly came back to Rachel's eyes. "Wha . . . what?" she mumbled, her hands relaxing their clutch on the seat. "I . . . it's just that coming back to town reminded me of . . . everything came back to me for a moment. Billie, I . . . I'm afraid."

"It's all right. No one's going to hurt you." Billie put her arms around the distraught girl and held her close. She looked over Rachel's shoulder at Nick. His face was a mask of rage, and he gripped the butt of his pistol with white-knuckled force. The tendons in his hands stood out like wires. "Nick!" she called, alarmed by the barely leashed savagery in him.

148

Rachel pushed away from her. "Please, Nick!" she said, reaching toward him in entreaty. "I'm all right, really."

The violence faded from his face, although a bonfire of anger still burned in his eyes. He urged his mount closer to the wagon and took Rachel's outstretched hand in his. "Tell me what frightened you, honey," he murmured.

"That man's voice. It was like an animal's, and his eyes . . . they were, too. Feral and hungry, like . . ." She pulled away from him and clasped her hands in her lap. "Never mind me. It was just a . . . a hysterical girl's fancy."

"Anyone with any sense would be afraid of a man like that," Billie said, hoping her face didn't show the stabbing pain that gripped her heart. "Honey," Nick had called Rachel. Oh, God!

"I think we'd better get our business done and get back to the ranch," Nick said. "I'll take you girls over to Doctor Lessing's house while Budge and I take care of business."

"I'm coming with you," Billie said.

Nick leaned out of the saddle and reached across Rachel to grab Billie by the upper arm. She tried to pull away, but his grip was like iron.

"Nick, what are you doing?" Rachel cried, pulling at his sleeve.

"Stay out of this, Rachel," he snapped, causing the girl to shrink back in the seat obediently. He gave Billie a shake. "You're going to do what you're told, for once in your stubborn life." By God, he vowed, if she gave him any more trouble, he was going to turn her over his knee right here and give her the walloping she deserved.

"You're hurting my arm!" Billie hissed. His knuckles were rubbing the side of her breast, and his touch—

even like this, in anger—brought her nipples into aching attention. She didn't dare struggle lest that bring even more contact between them and reveal her for the fool she was.

"I'm going to hurt a lot more than just your arm if you don't do what I tell you." He shook her again, harder this time, and a muscle in his jaw twitched.

Billie started to shake her head, but the look on his face frightened her. Besides, common sense forced her to admit that he was right. So she nodded instead. "All right, we'll go to Doctor Lessing's."

He held her gaze for a moment. His tight grip eased, and his hand moved just enough to show her that he was as aware of its contact with her breast as she was. A flame of desire leaped into his tawny eyes, threatening to draw her in, to consume her in that searing heat. Billie turned her face away.

"Come on," Nick said, urging his mount toward the northern edge of town where the doctor's house was located.

With a sigh of exasperation, Billie chucked the reins against the horses' backs and followed him. When they reached the newly whitewashed adobe house in which Emmett Lessing and his wife Jane lived, she scrambled down from the wagon and tied the team up.

"I'll see if anyone is home," she said, climbing the three shallow steps in front and knocking on the door. There was no answer. "They must be out back in the office. I'll go around."

Nick nodded, swinging down from his saddle to help Rachel down from the wagon. When Billie disappeared around the corner of the house, Rachel clutched Nick by the forearms.

"Please, Nick, don't start anything!" she whispered, her fingernails digging into the fabric of his sleeves.

"The man with the raspy voice—he's one of them, isn't he?"

She nodded.

"What about the others?"

"I . . . I can't be sure. They were wearing war paint, and their faces were nothing but nightmare masks. I only remember that two of them had blue eyes and one . . . that hoarse voice, like an animal growling. I'll never forget it. I'll never forget his laugh as he . . . as he . . ." She took a shuddering breath.

"Bastards." Nick's hands clenched and unclenched. "Was he the leader?"

"No. Another man gave the orders, while he and the other two just . . . Oh, please, don't do anything!"

Nick stared down the street, his face bleak. "Do you want him to get away with what he did?"

"The sheriff—"

"The sheriff is hiding like a frightened rabbit. And I've got no proof to show him even if he had the spine to face them."

Rachel shook her head wildly. "I won't risk losing you, I can't! You're all I have left, my only brother—"

"Don't say it," he growled. "Don't even think it."

"Who's going to hear? Billie? She'd never betray us."

"We can't trust anyone. Not even her," he said, thinking of Billie's ties to the Apache. But damn it, he still desired that maddening little wench! What was wrong with him that he wanted to make love to a woman he couldn't even trust with his name?

"We can trust her, I know it," Rachel said stubbornly.

"No!" He took her by the shoulders and shook her. This wasn't the first time they'd argued about this very thing. But his little sister was too trusting, too naive about the complicated desires that sometimes drove

151

people to do things that were seemingly out of character. "Listen, Rachel, do you want to get me killed?"

She shook her head.

"Then promise me you won't tell anyone. Not Billie, not anyone!" His fingers tightened. "Promise me!"

She tipped her head back to look at him. "I'll make you a bargain," she said. "I'll promise to keep our secret if you'll promise not to go after those men."

"Damn it—".

"I agreed to help you bring those men to justice. I even agreed to weasel my way into a rancher's home so we'd be right in the middle of things. But I will not countenance you getting into gun battles with outlaws. As much as I want to see those men pay for what they did to our family and me, I don't want it at the price of your life. If I have to forgo justice to protect you, so be it."

"Blackmail, Rachel?" he asked softly.

"Indeed it is."

He raked his hand through his hair. With another woman, he'd be tempted to call her bluff. But he knew that his little sister, despite her soft heart and quiet manner, was a very stubborn young woman and would do exactly as she'd threatened.

"All right," he growled. "You win. But if they ever try to get near you again—"

"If they do try"—her face was as white as the adobe wall behind her—"you have my permission to do whatever you feel is necessary."

Hearing voices inside the house, he stepped away from her. "Sounds like Billie found Mrs. Lessing. You'll be all right here." He swung back into the saddle and turned his mount back toward the center of town.

*　　*　　*

152

After placing glasses of cool water before her guests, Jane Lessing plumped down in a chair and fanned herself with her handkerchief. "Do you remember it ever being so hot in May, Billie?"

"Can't say that I do." Billie nibbled appreciatively at a lacy, molasses-rich cookie, one of Jane's wonderful concoctions.

Jane straightened and reached to touch Rachel's hand. "I'm pleased to see you looking so well, Rachel. Living at the Star M seems to be good for you."

"Billie has been wonderful to me," Rachel said.

Billie ducked her head, embarrassed, and reached for another cookie. "How long have those men been in town, Jane?"

"Two days now. It's been terrible. It isn't safe for a decent woman to walk the streets, and the sheriff hasn't done a thing about it."

"There isn't much he can do except get himself killed," Billie said.

"I suppose not. But he hasn't even sent for help. I've never thought Jared Wallace much for principles, and I suspect someone has paid him to mind his own business." Jane scowled, an unusually fierce expression for her broad, placid face. "Emmett left for Fort Lowell this morning to ask the army for help, but it will be days before he can get back."

The door swung open suddenly, and three men walked into the room. One was the man with the rasping voice who had spoken to them earlier. "Howdy, ladies," he said. "Now, ain't this our lucky day? Three of us an' three of you. How 'bout that?"

Jane gave a squeal of alarm. Rachel jumped to her feet, her hand going up to cover her mouth. Billie rose too, placing herself between the other two women and the intruders.

153

"What are you doing in here?" she demanded. "Get out!"

The man with the odd voice laughed. "We got us a feisty one here, boys."

Billie looked longingly at the rifle that was leaning against the wall beside the door. One of Raspy Voice's companions caught her glance. "Hey, I think the little gal'd like to use that there rifle on us. This filly needs to be broke to the saddle a mite, what do you say?"

"Who gits to be first?" the third man said, showing his yellowed teeth in a grin. He shut the door and leaned his back against it.

"You leave her alone!" Rachel cried fiercely. "If you dare lay a hand on her you'll be sorry!"

Billie stared over her shoulder at her companion, astonished by the other girl's flare of temper. Rachel was no longer afraid; her usually gentle face was white with fury and towering outrage. It was as though a rabbit had turned upon a wolf, teeth bared, ready to do battle.

"Will you listen to that?" Raspy Voice said in mock admiration. "I know who you are, gal. You're the one who likes 'Paches. Whut's the matter? Ain't we good enough fer you, or do you only spread them legs for Injuns?"

Billie dove for the rifle. With a startled shout, Raspy Voice went after her, catching her by the shirt and pulling her back against him.

"Now ain't this nice?" he demanded, anchoring her with one arm around her waist while his other hand came up to fondle her breasts roughly. The other men laughed.

Billie struggled wildly, ducking her head in an attempt to bite his hand. He cuffed her, making her head swim. She heard Rachel's voice rise in a shriek—not of terror, but of rage, like the clear, fierce call of a hawk, and turned just in time to see the other girl hurl a vase, flowers and all, at her captors. Raspy Voice cursed as it slammed into the side of his head. Billie jabbed backward with her elbow, catching him in his ribs. He dropped her, cursing.

She scrambled toward the rifle just as the door opened with terrific force into one of the men, knocking him into his companions. All three went down in a heap, clawing for their guns.

Nick catapulted into the room, pistol in hand, and hurdled the struggling group of the floor. "Get out!" he shouted to the staring women.

One of the men managed to draw his gun, but his struggling companions jarred his arm and his bullet ploughed a ragged groove in the floor between Nick's feet. Nick dropped to one knee and put two bullets in the man's chest, knocking him backward out of the tangle of arms and legs. He lay spread-eagled near the open door, his life running out in a scarlet flood.

"Hold it!" Nick shouted, but another man whipped his gun up. Nick fired again, and this one, too, gasped out his life on Jane's parlor floor.

Raspy Voice tossed his gun down and rose slowly to his feet. "Don't shoot!"

"Why not?" Nick asked. His voice was mild, even pleasant, but a cold, killing rage was on his face.

Billie stood beside the door, the rifle forgotten in her hands. The fight was over so quickly she hadn't even had a chance to cock it. She looked into Nick's tawny eyes, reading death there, and a shiver went up her spine. "Nick—"

"Pick up the gun," Nick said, his gaze never leaving the other man's face.

"What?" The hired gunman's mouth dropped open in surprise.

"You heard me. Pick it up."

"Nick, don't!" Billie took a step forward, her hand outstretched.

"Shut up, Billie," Budge said from the doorway behind her.

She turned to glare at the Texan in outrage, but her protest died in her throat when she saw that his face was as set and as cold as Nick's.

Budge gave her a shove. "Git in the back with the other women," he growled.

"No." She crossed her arms over her chest. "I'm staying."

"This gonna be two agin one?" Raspy Voice snarled contemptuously. "T'ain't hardly fair."

"It'll be fair," Budge said, turning his back on the man. "I'll watch the street, Nick."

"Thanks." Nick pointed to the pistol.

Slowly, Raspy Voice bent and picked the gun up by the barrel.

"Put it in your holster," Nick ordered.

The man obeyed, and Nick holstered his own weapon.

"You sure are stupid," Raspy Voice said, grinning. His hand flashed toward his pistol.

Nick's gun roared, seeming to appear in his hand as if by magic. A crimson stain appeared in the center of Raspy Voice's chest. He stared down at himself, astonishment on his face, then slumped to the floor. His gun hadn't even cleared the holster.

Billie stared at Nick, her heart clenching at the look of savage satisfaction on his face. She had seen that expression on other men's faces. They had been outlaws—killers, the human wolves of the desert. Never in all her wildest imaginings would she have thought to see such a look on the face of the man she loved. She whirled to place her cheek against the cool wall behind her. Silent sobs shook her. Nick stepped over Raspy Voice's body and took her in his arms. She flinched away from him, but he pulled her close, stroking the hair back from her forehead.

"It's all right, Billie," he murmured, misunderstanding the reason for her tears. "It's over."

"You killed him. You were glad to kill him!"

"Yes, I was glad! Do you think I'd let him live after what he did?" His fingers tightened on her waist until she gasped. Even now, the memory of what the man had done to Rachel and had nearly done to Billie caused a red mist of rage to rise before his eyes.

Rachel and Jane came running from the back of the house. Nick tucked Billie against his side and held out his other arm toward Rachel. She rushed to him, pressing her face against the front of his shirt to blot out the sight of the sprawled bodies, then reached out to put her hand on Billie's shoulder.

"Are you all right, Billie?" she asked, her voice muffled.

"Yes," Billie said, although she felt anything but all right. What in heaven did Nick think he was doing? Did he expect to share the two of them like he did his horses? Did he think she and Rachel would ever agree to such an arrangement? Then, looking down at the three men he had killed, she decided that perhaps he did.

"Sheriff's comin'," Budge said. He gently pulled Rachel away from Nick. "Miz Lessing, you take Miss Rachel back to the bedroom and git her to lie down. She don't need to see this."

Jane put her arm over Rachel's shoulders and led her toward the back of the house. There was the sound of boots pounding the walk outside, then Sheriff Wallace came around the corner and skidded to a halt in the doorway. Rosswell Stearns and Carson Eames peered over his shoulders.

"What happened here?" Sheriff Wallace demanded. "Budge, you do this?"

"Nope." The Texan thrust his thumb in Nick's direction. "He kilt 'em. Didn't like the way they was talkin' to the ladies."

Wallace looked at Billie, noting the tear at the collar of her shirt and the bruise that was just beginning to show purple against the pale skin of her jaw. "I'm going to have to—"

Rosswell Stearns pushed past him and walked into the house. "Three against one," he said, surveying the lifeless bodies and bloodstained floor with calm detachment. "A clear case of self-defense, wouldn't you say, Sheriff?"

"Yes, sir." Wallace hitched his gun belt higher and turned away. "Well, I've got some things to do. I'll swing by the undertaker's and tell him he's got some customers." His footsteps faded into the distance.

The Englishman clasped his hands behind his back. "You handle yourself well, Mr. . . . ?"

"Larabee. Nick Larabee."

"I could use a man like you, Mr. Larabee," Stearns said, his cold gaze flicking briefly to Carson Eames, who was lounging indolently in the doorway. "Would you be interested in a position of some responsibility?"

"I thought Lew Purcell ran things for you," Nick said.

"Mr. Purcell takes care of my cattle. But I need someone to head my household guard, and I think you can handle the job."

Eames stiffened in surprise.

"A hundred dollars a month, and you won't be breathing the dust of the cattle trail," Stearns continued, a cold smile stretching his thin lips.

Nick cocked his head to one side thoughtfully. He wanted to get closer to Stearns—and to Eames. Someone was turning the territory upside down. The Englishman was as suspicious as hell, with his cold, conniving nature, and Eames, well, Eames was a killer, plain and simple. Nick just couldn't figure what either of them would want here. Besides, the longer he stayed at the Star M, the more likely Rachel was to give their secret away. Once it became known that they were brother and sister, he could forget ever finding out who had killed his family.

Abruptly, he became aware that everyone was looking at him. He glanced at Billie, then away. He wanted to take Stearns's job. She had no hold on him, he told himself firmly. He couldn't even trust her. But when he spoke, it was to say, "It's a very tempting offer, Mr. Stearns, but I'll have to think about it. I'll let you know in a day or two."

"That will be fine." The Englishman turned away. "Come along, Mr. Eames. Good day, gentlemen, Miss Meyrick." He strode down the street, Eames trailing behind him.

Billie glared at Nick in outrage. "How can you even think about working for that man?"

"I didn't say I would," he growled, furious at himself for his lack of self-control. Damn it to hell, she had him so tied up in knots he couldn't even control his own tongue!

"You didn't say you wouldn't."

"True." He picked up his hat and put it on. Without another word, he left.

"I'm not finished with you!" she cried.

Budge grabbed her arm to stop her from following Nick. "Leave it be, Billie."

"Leave it be?" she repeated. "How do you expect me to leave it be?"

There was sympathy in his pale eyes. "If a man wants to go, there ain't nothin' you kin do to hold him. Especially a man like that."

She felt as though the breath had been knocked out of her. Then she straightened her shoulders. Budge was right. If Nick wanted to go, let him! She had more pride than to go running after him. "Were you able to hire any men?" she asked.

"Three. Cully Frye and Lester Manon—"

"I thought they headed for New Mexico!"

Budge spread his hands. "Wal, they's back now, and glad enough to come back to the Star M now that that ol' woman is gone."

"Well, that's a stroke of luck. They're both good hands," she said with satisfaction. "Who's the third man?"

"Henry Davalos."

"But he's been working for the Dolorosa for nearly five years. I never thought . . ." Billie grimaced. "I see. Stearns doesn't like half-breeds."

"Seems he hates Mexicans and Indians, and Henry jest happens to be both."

Billie shook her head in disgust. "Well, I'll be glad to have him. Are those three the only ones available?"

"Yep. Stearns hired everybody else. I was lucky to catch Cully and Lester jest after they hit town, or they'd be workin' fer him, too."

"The more I hear about Stearns, the less I like him," Billie said.

Budge grunted. "Better git used to him. He's your stepfather now."

"Don't ever say that again!"

"And that Julia gal is your stepsister." There was a

look of pure mischief in the Texan's face as he added, "She's a mighty purty woman, if you ask me. I expect she'll be right pleased if Nick goes to work for the Dolorosa. Him workin' so close to the house and all."

Billie stalked from the room, slamming the door behind her.

Chapter 14

"Rachel, you don't want to go to the dressmaker's now!" Billie cried.

"Yes, I do," Rachel said, rising from her chair to wipe a few crumbs from the big oak table in Jane Lessing's kitchen. "If we're going to have gowns made in time for the Stearns's party, we've got to order them today. And don't worry about being safe. Budge said that every one of the ruffians left town in a hurry after Nick killed those three."

Billie doubted Budge had called the gunmen anything so polite as ruffians, and doubted even more that they had left because of a little killing. "Well, after what's happened, I think we should get you back to the ranch."

"You don't understand me very well at all, do you?" Rachel sat down again and reached out to take Billie's hands in hers. "I was frightened at first. But when that man insulted me, then laid his dirty hands on you, I got mad clear through. If I'd had a gun, I would have killed him myself."

Billie stared at the other girl in confusion and dawning admiration. "You sure have changed."

"Oh, Billie, I haven't changed. Something happened

to me, something that nearly broke me. But I survived, and now I'm getting better. The shy, timid girl who came to the Star M isn't me, but someone created by the men who attacked me. She's fading now, and only comes back with the nightmares. I am . . . Well, Papa . . ." she faltered for a moment, then lifted her chin and went on. "Papa always teased me, saying that I was much too bossy and opinionated for my own good, and a terrible nag as well."

Billie couldn't think of a reply to that astonishing statement. Rachel, bossy? Well, she mused, reflecting on some of the changes that had occurred at the Star M under Rachel's gentle insistence, maybe a little. But the bossing was done so subtly, with such sweet persuasion, that nobody seemed to mind it a bit.

"Billie, are you in love with Nick?"

The abruptness of the question took Billie's breath away for a moment, then heat rushed into her face, bringing with it a vehement protest. "Of course not!"

The words seemed to hang in the room, the overly passionate denial in them branding them a lie. Billie hunched her shoulders. "What about you, Rachel? Are you in love with him?"

"No," Rachel said. "I am not."

"Then why do you run to him?" Billie demanded.

Rachel looked down at her hands, dry and reddened from the harsh lye soap she had used to scour the blood from Jane's parlor floor. "He makes me feel safe. He always has."

There was an off note in her voice that made Billie straighten in her chair, startled. "Rachel—"

"Let's not beat it to death, Billie." Rachel said, pushing her chair back with an irritated gesture. Drat that brother of hers! Suspicious of everybody and everything, he had tied her to a promise that was getting harder and harder to keep. "I haven't a shred of a claim on Nick Larabee. If you care for him, nothing would make me happier than to see the two of you together."

Generous, loyal girl, Billie thought, but a poor liar. It was obvious that Rachel felt so obligated that she'd willingly step aside to let her friend have a chance with Nick. Could she allow the girl to make such a sacrifice? Did she have the strength not to? Remembering the look of savage satisfaction on Nick's face when he had killed those men, she cursed herself for a fool. Of all the men to have given her heart to!

Rachel took her by the hand and tugged her out of her chair, interrupting her somber reflections. "Come on. Let's get to the dressmaker's while there's still time."

"All right. But I warn you, I'm not about to let you talk me into anything fancy."

"Nothing fancy," Rachel agreed solemnly, twining her arm with Billie's and pulling her outside.

As they approached the dressmaker's shop, Billie saw Carson Eames leaning against the hitching post outside. He abandoned his languid pose as they drew nearer, and a disgusting leer appeared on his face. Billie thought of the way Nick's mouth curved upward when he smiled. Whether his humor was teasing or mocking, there was a world of difference between his grin and the lechery on Eames's narrow face.

"Ladies," the gunman said, touching his hand to his hat.

"Good afternoon, Mr. Eames," Rachel said.

Billie remained silent, and Eames's smile faded. "Not very sociable, are you, Billie?" he asked.

"Not very." She scowled at him. "And I don't remember us being on a first-name basis."

"You ought to be nicer to me, honey," Eames said. The grin came back, but it was more angry than lustful

165

now. "We're going to be very good friends some day, and you just might regret some of the things you're doing now."

"I'll take the chance," Billie said, turning toward the shop.

Eames grabbed her by the wrist. "Now just a minute—"

The door to the shop opened. Helena stepped over the threshold and scrutinized the three young people. "Take your hand from my daughter's arm, Mr. Eames," she said. "And then you may find my husband. I won't be needing you for a while."

He stalked away, the sun glinting off the polished silver and that encircled his hat.

"Thank you, Mrs. Stearns," Rachel said.

Helena smiled. "You're very welcome. Miss Laird, is it not?"

"Please, call me Rachel." Rachel's answering smile was warm, and even a bit sympathetic.

Billie grimaced. In a moment they'd fall into each other's arms and vow undying friendship. Couldn't Rachel see that the woman wasn't worth it? Damn it, how had she let herself get talked into this, anyway?"

"It's unfortunate that you have attracted that man's interest, Billie," Helena said, stepping back to allow the girls to enter the shop.

"Very," Billie muttered shortly.

Julia was inside, draped across a chair with indolent grace. She looked up briefly, then turned her attention to some imperfection on one of her fingernails.

"Julia," Helena said, a hint of steel in her soft, refined voice, "you seem to have forgotten your manners."

The English girl straightened slowly. "I did not forget them, Helena. I am merely learning to be as boorish as the other residents of this benighted place."

166

With a sniff, she stalked toward the door. She paused before Billie, inspecting the smaller girl with sneering contempt. Then, with a toss of her beautifully coiffed head, she left the shop.

"I'm sorry," Helena murmured. "Arizona doesn't seem to agree with Julia. It seems to have made a rather, ah, acerbic personality even worse."

Billie put her hands on her hips. "A good kick in the—"

"Billie!" Rachel cried.

". . . behind would do her a world of good," Billie finished.

Angela came hurrying out of the back room. "Here are the buttons, Mrs. Stearns. I'm sorry it took so long to find . . . Oh, Billie! I didn't know you were here." She stared at Rachel curiously.

"We've come to order dresses for the party," Billie said gruffly. "Go on, finish up with Mrs. Stearns. We'll come back some other time."

"Oh, no we won't," Rachel said. She smiled, then added, "Mrs. Stearns has such lovely taste. Perhaps she will be kind enough to give us some advice."

Billie stared openmouthed at her friend, astonished by her betrayal. But there was nothing she could say, no protest she could make that wouldn't seem rude and which Angela wouldn't relay to everyone in town. The only thing worse than having to endure Helena's advice would be to provide fodder for the town gossips' flapping mouths.

"I'd be happy to help," Helena said. "Miss Felker, would you bring out some fabric? Perhaps that pale green satin we saw earlier would do for Billie, and for Rachel"—she tapped her chin thoughtfully—"that marvelous piece of pink silk. And let me see that ivory velvet ribbon and that lace over there. No, not that, the wider one—"

"Whoa!" Billie cried. "No frills!"

Helena turned to her. "But these aren't frills. These are necessities."

"She's right," Angela said. "I won't have time for anything fancy, not with eight other dresses to make. But I'll do right by you, don't worry."

Billie crossed her arms over her chest and watched silently as the other women chose her gown for her. Helena *did* have taste, she thought grudgingly. When the design was complete, Billie couldn't see a thing she didn't like about it.

So she said, "I'll probably fall flat on my face trying to walk in that skirt."

Rachel laughed. "Oh, do shut up, Billie. It's going to be a wonderful dress." She help up a bolt of creamy ribbon. "What do you think of this, Helena?"

"No, I think the pink will do better." Helena put her head to one side. "White lace, and white satin roses."

Rachel nodded enthusiastically. "Oh, Billie, I nearly forgot! What about undergarments? Petticoats?"

"Petticoats!" Billie wailed.

An hour later she walked out of the shop, shaking her head in bewilderment. Somehow she'd been talked into buying a great many things she'd never needed before and would never need again, most likely. "Let's get out of town while I still have a few dollars left to my name," she complained. "Perfumed soap! Two new blouses I don't even need. Silk underwear, by God! I could have bought a Hereford bull for what I spent in there." Suddenly she turned to Rachel, scowling. "You *are* bossy!"

"Yes, Billie," Rachel said. "I know."

Billie shuffled her cards irritably while she waited for

Budge to finish dealing. She was beginning to regret allowing Rachel to talk her into wearing one of her new blouses tonight. It was simply made—by Helena's standards, that is—with only a few lines of ruching to adorn the crisp white cotton. But it fit perfectly, hugging her waist and the full curve of her bosom, and Nick had been staring at her all evening. There was a flare of desire in his gold-flecked eyes, and a promise. He leaned his elbows on the table as he talked to Budge, but his attention remained on Billie.

His sleeves were rolled up nearly to his elbows, exposing the sinewy muscles that moved smoothly beneath his skin, the dusting of golden hairs on the back of his arms. Billie watched his hands, the strong squareness of them, the long, sensitive fingers that were so gentle, yet so arousing upon her body.

Heat rushed into her face at the thought, flushing it a delicate pink, and it was not from embarrassment. She wanted him, wanted him with an intensity that was almost painful, and it made her furious. She shuffled her cards again.

"You oughta look at your hand, Billie," Budge said. "It's your bet."

"Oh." Hurriedly she fanned her cards open. Three queens, her best hand yet. "What's the call?"

"Rachel jest raised. It's goin' to cost you twenty to stay in."

Billie counted out twenty matches and pushed them toward the pile in the center of the table, then added twenty more. "I'll meet that, and raise you twenty."

"Hell, she's bluffin'," Squint scoffed.

"Wal, it'll cost you forty to find out," Budge said. "Let's jest see if you got the ba . . ."—he stopped, glanced at Rachel's stern face, then amended—"guts to stick it out."

169

While Squint counted his small hoard of matches, Billie decided to broach the subject that had been nagging at her all evening.

"I've been thinking about Redesware's cattle," she said.

"Uncle Rowan's?" Rachel asked, startled. "What about them?"

"They're yours now, yours and your brother's." Wherever *he* might be, Billie thought sourly. Out east somewhere, leaving his sister to fend for herself.

"Yes, I suppose they are. I hadn't thought about it," Rachel said.

Billie laid her cards facedown on the table. "Budge, did Rowan's foreman try to get a count of the herd before he left?"

"I kin find out," the Texan said.

"Is there a problem with the herd?" Nick asked.

"Maybe." Billie frowned at him. What business was it of his, anyway? "I talked to Frank DeWitt over at the bank today, and he said nothing can be done about Rowan's estate until Rachel's brother gets here. The house is gone, and all that's left is the land and the cattle, and no one expected either to go anywhere. But if the rustlers are working that range as well as they're working mine, they could run off with half the ranch's capital."

"We ain't got enough men to work our range and Redesware's, too," Art said. "We still ain't got all our own cattle rounded up yet."

"We've got most of them, though." Billie drummed her fingertips on the table. "We've got the three new men. Art, you and Joe and I will start riding Redesware range tomorrow. We can round up Rachel's cattle next week and run them into Tucson with ours."

"It's near thirty miles away," Budge protested. "You ride here, and I'll take Redesware. I expect Bernhard

Greenhow or Hank Beadle will let me use a couple of their boys if I get in a bind."

"I can help," Rachel offered. "Between Billie and me, we can replace one cowboy."

"No!" Nick and Budge spoke together.

"They're my cattle," Rachel said. "You have no right to tell me what to do, either of you. I said I'd help, and that's what I'm going to do."

Budge shook his head. "She been livin' with Billie too damn long," he growled, adding a handful of matches to the central pile. "Call."

"Full house!" Rachel cried to a chorus of groans. "Nick, you lose."

Isabel walked by, drying her hands on her apron. "You wash, Señor Nick," she said. "Again. You sure have eevil luck with the cards."

"I know." Nick shook his head in disgust. One of these days he was going to figure out Budge's crooked deal, and then he'd see who did the dishes!

Billie rose from the table and went outside. She needed a chance to think. What was she going to do about Nick? she wondered. Things couldn't go on like this. Half the time she was looking for a way to get free of him, the other half she spent remembering what it was like to make love to him, and yearning to do it again.

She wandered past the bunkhouse toward the spring, enjoying the velvet coolness of the night wind. There was a thin sliver of moon overhead, just enough for her to see where she was going. A jackrabbit burst into motion under her feet, his white tail a rapidly disappearing blur as he bounded away.

She sat down on a rock and crossed her arms over her chest. Forget Nick for a minute! she told herself firmly. There was something more important to think about just now. She'd gotten herself into a tight spot tonight with her decision to take Redesware's cattle to market along with her own. Despite the confidence she'd shown the others, she was afraid she had taken on more than she could handle. Redesware's range was even rougher than hers, and it might take weeks to find the scattered cattle. If she didn't at least try, however, it would be like handing Rachel's legacy to the rustlers without a fight. And knowing how uncaring the girl's brother was, it was obvious that someone had to help her.

Nick, hidden in the shadows nearby, watched her. He'd come out here to tell her he was taking the job at the Dolorosa, but her expression was so full of uncertainty that he suddenly doubted the wisdom of his decision. She needed him. Could he walk away, even to take the opportunity to wend his way into Stearns's confidence?

The wind shifted, bringing to him the scent of perfume. His chest swelled as he savored it. It seemed like years since he'd touched her. Such wild beauty, such fiery response . . . his manhood rose up at the memory of their lovemaking. Silently, he moved closer.

He stood staring down at her dark, shining hair, then wrapped his arms around her and pulled her up against him. She gasped, startled, then began to struggle.

"Stop it," she protested. "Let me go!" Already her heart was pounding, her blood racing through her veins in a surge of heat.

"You don't mean that." He shifted her so that she was facing him, her breasts pressing into his chest. Ignoring her struggles, he ran his tongue lightly around the delicate curve of her ear.

Billie stopped fighting. His tongue dipped slyly into her ear, then teased the sensitive earlobe. Smiling, he enjoyed the faint shiver that went through her. He set

172

her back onto her feet. With incredible possessiveness, his hands smoothed slowly over her breasts and ribs, coming to rest at last at her waist. He buried his face in her luxuriant dark hair. "You smell good."

"It's the soap." She could feel the hardness of him against her belly, urgent, demanding things she was afraid to give.

He chuckled, nuzzling her hair aside to kiss the tender spot where her neck and shoulder joined. "It's the woman."

His lips trailed up her throat to her chin. He kissed his way to her mouth, gently parting her lips with his tongue, then slipping inside to taste the sweet depths of her mouth. Billie leaned into him helplessly, her fingers twining in his thick, tawny hair. Then she stiffened, remembering the men he had killed just a few short hours before. Tightening her hold on his hair, she used it to pull his head back.

"I said stop it!" she snapped.

His jaw tightened. "What the hell is the matter with you?"

"A lot of things. Stearns for one."

"What does Stearns have to do with us?" he asked, his hands coming to rest on her shoulders.

"Are you going to work for him?"

"Is that what's bothering you?"

"That, and a lot of other things." She tried to step backward, but his hands tightened, anchoring her in front of him.

His anger rose, fueled by frustrated desire and his own guilty conscience. It would be so easy to fix things between them. A few words. Words he couldn't bring himself to say. "Stearns is offering a lot of money."

"A hundred dollars a month," Billie agreed, looking deeply into his gold-flecked eyes. He couldn't be just another hired gun available to the highest bidder. He

173

couldn't! Please, she prayed silently, give me a reason to believe in you. No, she amended, give me a reason to believe in your feelings for me. Put me above money, above anything. "I can't pay that much, and you know it," she said.

"True."

"Does that mean you're going?"

"I'm just pointing out the reasons why I might." He crossed his arms over his chest. "What if I do?"

Billie turned her back on him, not trusting herself to answer. He took her by the shoulders again and forced her to face him.

"Will you stop seeing me?" His voice was soft. Too soft.

Billie was glad the darkness hid her expression. She was terrified of being with him, of losing herself in him, and equally terrified of being without him. As she had learned to do long ago, she used anger to cover her fear. "I don't want anything to do with Stearns or anyone who works for him," she snapped.

"You don't own me, Billie. No woman does."

"Then go!" she cried. "Go make your hundred dollars a month. Go work for that, that—"

"All right, I will!" he shouted, jamming his hat on his head and turning on his heel.

She followed him, her hands clenched into fists. "Go on, then! Maybe you'll enjoy working for Julia more than you did me!"

"Maybe I will! She's a damn sight more agreeable, I can tell you that."

"Get off my ranch!" she shrieked.

He stalked toward the corral, his long strides quickly leaving her behind. A few minutes later, mounted on Beelzebub and leading the buckskin, he rode off into the darkness, headed toward the Dolorosa.

Good riddance! Billie raged silently. What did she

care, anyway? He was a gunman, a proven killer! She was better off without him. If she was lucky, she'd never lay eyes on him again.

She sat down abruptly. Wrapping her arms around herself, she began to rock back and forth, too miserable even to cry.

Chapter 15

"I don't think I've ever been so tired," Rachel moaned, wriggling in a futile attempt to find a comfortable spot in the sidesaddle. "Are we home yet?"

"Just over this ridge." Billie smiled at her companion. She was very proud of Rachel. The girl had ridden the range with the cowboys, enduring heat, dust and bone-deep weariness without a single complaint. She wasn't skilled enough to make a hand yet, but she had a lovely, crystal-clear singing voice that seemed almost to put the cattle in a trance at night. As her father used to say, Billie mused, anyone who could sing was always welcome on a cattle ranch.

"I hate cattle," Rachel said, breaking into Billie's reverie. "I never want to see another cow as long as I live! The rustlers can have them all."

"Now, you don't mean that a'tall, Miss Rachel," Squint said. "You know you'll be out there tomorrow, jest like the rest of us."

Rachel shifted position yet again. She wished fervently that she could rub the part of her anatomy that hurt the worst. Glancing at Squint to make sure he wasn't looking, her free hand crept down to her

177

posterior. "I don't think I'm cut out for this life," she muttered.

Squint looked over at her, surprised. "'Acourse you are, Miss Rachel. You're 'xactly the kind of woman this here country needs." He swept his arm in a wide arc, indicating the jagged line of the peaks, the broken, tilted land with its dusting of piñon pines and the tall, thin shapes of the saguaros, gilded by the rays of the setting sun. "See this? There's nothin' as purty an' wild nowhere else. If'n you go back east, you'll never be restful with the city agin. Cain't you see that?"

Rachel's mouth dropped open. She'd never thought of staying here. She had planned to finish what had begun that terrible day at Uncle Rowan's, then go back with her brother to the ordered, comfortable life she had left behind. But a seed had been planted in her without her knowledge or consent, and this cowboy's words had brought it into bloom. "You're a poet, Squint," she murmured.

He ducked his head, pleased. "Pshaw. I cain't even read, Miss Rachel."

Billie stood up in her stirrups. "Look! There's someone at the house. Squint, can you see who it is?"

He pulled his hat off and shaded his eyes against the orange blaze of the setting sun. "It's Budge. And if I guess aright, that's Larabee with him. Whoa! They're carryin' somebody between 'em!" He clapped his hat back on and spurred his mount.

"What's *he* doing here?" Billie muttered, urging her tired horse into a gallop. She glanced over her shoulder to make sure Rachel was following. The girl had her mount in a flat-out run, slapping its withers with the ends of her reins. Squint had been right about her, Billie thought briefly, then returned her attention to the rocky ground.

They skidded down the flank of the ridge in Squint's

wake, then pounded across the valley toward the house. Even before her mount came to a complete stop, Billie jumped down from the saddle and ran into the house.

Budge and Nick had deposited their burden on the table. Squint lit the lantern and raised it high, peering down at the injured man.

"Who is it?" Billie demanded, pushing at Nick's broad back. He moved aside, and she gasped. "Emmett!"

"He took three bullets," Nick said. "One in his leg, two in his shoulder."

"Budge, heat some water and get me some clean cloths. Quick, now," Billie snapped. The lanky Texan moved away.

Billie drew in her breath sharply at the sight of the gaping wounds. The doctor had lost a great deal of blood. Perhaps too much. She plucked her knife out of her boot and began cutting his clothes away. "Where did you find him?"

"Near Machorro Canyon," Nick said.

Billie glanced up, surprised. "But that's nearly ten miles north of Xavier. What was he doing there?"

"He was running from the Apaches." Nick took the sodden rags that had once been the doctor's shirt and put them aside. "He said they attacked him a few miles outside of town and chased him nearly twenty miles."

"He said? He was conscious?" Billie probed the wounds gently, and Emmett groaned. "Was he coming back from Fort Lowell, or going?"

"Going."

Billie chewed at her bottom lip nervously. "He's been out there for three days, then. No wonder he's burning with fever. Rachel?"

"Yes, Billie." Rachel spoke from behind her.

"Get the laudanum from the trunk in my room."

179

Billie brushed a stray hair away from her forehead with the back of her hand, not realizing that doing so left a streak of blood across her forehead. "Squint, go tell Jane what's happened."

"Yes, ma'am!"

"Billie . . ." The doctor's voice was faint, almost too low to hear.

"Emmett?" Billie bent close. "Can you hear me?"

He gave a tiny nod.

"The bullets passed clean through. But the wound in your leg has begun to fester."

"Cau . . . cauterize. I . . . trust you." The doctor's hand fumbled along the table. Billie reached out to clasp it in hers. He took a deep breath. "Clean . . . it . . . good. Hot, so . . . hot." His eyes drifted closed.

Billie squeezed his hand gently and laid it down. She didn't want to do this. Nick or Budge would take over for her if she asked, she knew. But Emmett trusted *her* to do it right, and she was not about to let someone else take responsibility for her. "We'll take care of you, Emmett," she said, not knowing if he could hear her or not. "Build up the fire, Nick."

Rachel stood frozen in horror, the laudanum forgotten in her hand. "You're not going to do it yourself!" she cried. "Not here, not like this!"

"We'd have to go clear to Tucson to find another doctor, Miss Rachel," Budge said. "Even if we talked him into comin' all the way out here, which I sorely doubt, Emmett would be dead afore he got here."

Rachel sighed. "How much laudanum should I give him?"

"As much as you dare," Billie said, washing her hands thoroughly with lye soap, then drying them on a clean rag. Nick's arms came around her, making her gasp with surprise, but he only slipped her apron around her waist and tied it. "Thanks," she murmured, returning her attention to her patient.

Even with the laudanum, however, the doctor moved uncontrollably when she started cleaning the wounds on his shoulder. His eyes flew open, although it was obvious that he wasn't seeing anything but his own pain. When the time came to tend the festering wound in his thigh, Billie washed her hands again and began cleaning as much of the diseased flesh away as she could. Emmett thrashed in agony, and Nick and Budge were forced to hold him down until she finished. Billie stood for a moment, taking several deep breaths to calm herself.

"Do you want me to do it?" Nick asked softly.

"No. I'll be all right." Billie straightened her spine and held her hand out for the knife. Rachel wrapped a cloth around the handle and drew the red-hot blade from the fire. After giving it to Billie, she ran from the room, her hands covering her mouth.

Billie carefully drew the knife across the gaping wound, ignoring the agonized screams that rose with the smoke. The stench of burning flesh filled the room.

"There, it's done." She bandaged the doctor's leg, then indicated that the men should take him to one of the bedrooms.

She collected the bloodstained linens and dropped them into a barrel and poured water over them. With any luck, they'd come clean again. Suddenly her hands began to shake, slopping water down the outside of the barrel and onto the floor.

She rushed outside and dropped to her hands and knees. Tears blinded her, running down her face in a stream to spatter the dust between her hands.

Strong hands pulled her up, and a moment later she was cradled against Nick's hard chest. "Easy, honey," he murmured. "Easy. You're a brave girl, and I'm proud of you."

Billie drew a deep, shuddering breath and buried her face against his shoulder. It felt so good to be held, so good for someone to understand. Her father would have walked away from her tears, scorning them as weakness. When Nick set her back on her feet, she gave a little murmur of protest.

Instead of letting her go, however, he took her face between his hands and lightly kissed her brows, her eyelids, her straight, fine nose, the delicate curve of her cheek. She stood frozen, immobilized by the tenderness of his touch. Closing her eyes, she let herself enjoy his butterfly-gentle caresses, the upsurging of the molten warmth of desire.

Suddenly that light touch was not enough. Wrapping her arms around his neck, she pulled his head down and rubbed her open mouth against his. His hands clamped on her waist tightly. With an easy flex of his sinewy arms, he brought her up to his level and held her there while he kissed her hungrily, almost savagely. She clung to him, her tongue meeting his in an eager dance of passion.

Then Rachel's voice came from inside the house, shattering the sultry mood. Billie pushed away from him.

"Put me down," she ordered.

Nick set her back on her feet, shaking his head to clear it. Damn, but she'd had him going! For one precious moment, she had clung to him, needing him. And his need to comfort her had been irresistible, and so had the passion that always seemed to grip him whenever she was near. Realizing suddenly that his hands were still on her shoulders, he stepped backward, creating the distance physically that he seemed unable to maintain emotionally.

Billie smoothed her blouse with shaking hands. This was weakness! she thought. How could she have let him come near again? But there was no anger in her, just disgust at her own lack of control. "What are you doing here?" she asked. "I thought you were going to work for Stearns."

"I did. But I told him I couldn't start until next week, so I thought I'd give Budge some help with the Redesware herd." He spread his hands.

"Oh." Billie untied her blood-spattered apron and folded it over her arm. "I didn't have a chance to pay you the other night," she said, turning away. "Come into the house. I have your money ready. I was going to send someone to the Dolorosa with it, but we've been a little busy."

He followed her, a smile curving his well-cut mouth as he watched the graceful sway of her hips. "How has Rachel been doing out on the range?"

"Rachel is all right," Billie said. "She's becoming a real ranch woman. Why, in the past few days she's heard language that would have made her faint a month ago. But she just blushes and keeps working."

He pulled her to a halt just outside the door. "You care for her a great deal, don't you?"

"I admire her more than anyone I've ever known." Billie stared into the gold-flecked depths of his eyes, unaware that her hands were twisting together in front of her. "You see, Pa wasn't ki . . . he wasn't a man who had much sympathy with soft things like emotions and . . ." she paused, uncertain for a moment exactly what she was trying to say.

"Women's tears?" Nick prompted, taking hold of her hands to stop their agitated motion.

She nodded. "Rachel is soft and feminine. She cares for people's feelings, she cries. But she's brave. There's steel in her, a quiet kind of courage that doesn't depend on fists or loud words or a gun." Billie spoke the next words slowly, so that Nick would be very sure of her feelings. "Rachel is the sister I never had. I'm going to make sure no one hurts her, is that clear?"

To her astonishment, he raised her hand to his lips. She snatched it away and put it behind her back. But she could feel the imprint of his mouth on her skin like a flame, and her heart raced as though she'd run a mile.

He smiled down at her. "You know, you're nicer than you'd like people to think."

"Don't be an idiot," she said, grimacing in irritation. "In a minute you'll start talking French or something." Why did he have to be this way—hot-eyed killer one day, kind and understanding the next? If he would stick to one or the other, she could decide whether to hate him or to love him and leave this horrible indecision behind.

She opened the door and walked in, to see Rachel and Budge seated cozily at the table over steaming cups of coffee. They looked up when she and Nick came in.

"Is Emmett sleeping?" Billie asked.

"Yes, but his fever is rising," Rachel said. "He'll have to be tended closely the next few days."

"Don't worry about that," Billie said. "Jane will be here tomorrow, ready to tend her beloved's every need. He'll work her like a plow horse."

Rachel clasped her hands before her on the table. "Billie, is he going to die?"

"If I did a good enough job on the cauterizing, and if he doesn't get pneumonia from lying out in the open for three days, he'll make it." For Rachel's sake, Billie forced herself to laugh. "Don't worry about him. He's tough as old leather. And old Ira Maher owes him twenty dollars—Emmett will never let himself die before collecting it."

Rachel gave a peal of laughter. "Billie, you're insane!"

"Well, that's the truth, if I ever heard it," Billie

muttered under her breath. She went to the cabinet and took out a small rawhide bag. With a deft flick of her hand, she tossed it to Nick.

He hefted it, then opened it and looked inside. "You don't owe me this much," he said.

"There's another week's pay there. You're helping Budge, aren't you?"

"Yes." He counted out the forty dollars that represented his pay for the time he had worked at the Star M, put it in his pocket, then tossed the pouch back to her.

She frowned. "I don't take charity. Take the money."

"It's not charity," he said. "I'm doing it as a favor for Rachel." He smiled over at the girl and received a brilliant smile in return.

Billie felt as though she'd been punched in the stomach. He certainly made his loyalties clear, she thought in sudden misery.

Chapter 16

"Billie, are you sure we're not needed out on the range any longer?" Rachel asked hopefully. It was eight days after Billie's makeshift surgery. Doctor Lessing was up and around, criticizing the way she and Billie ran the house, giving his wife orders, interfering with Isabel's cooking—in general, making a complete nuisance of himself.

"I'm sure. Budge should have our herds combined by now and on their way to Tucson." Billie felt a little stab of loss; with the Redesware cattle rounded up, Nick had quietly taken his leave and headed for his new job at the Dolorosa. She hadn't heard from him since. His absence nagged at her. She tossed and turned in her bed at night, plagued by her need of him, a physical craving that was almost painful in its intensity. Telling herself that she was better off without him didn't help at all.

"There must be something I can do out on the range. Cook for the men, maybe mend a shirt or two," Rachel said.

Billie shook her head to rid herself of her disturbing thoughts of Nick. Then she saw the desperate expression on Rachel's face and smiled. "Rachel, you're not getting impatient with Emmett, are you?"

"Yes!" Rachel spoke with uncharacteristic violence. "This morning, when he was complaining about his eggs, it was all I could do not to hit him over the head with the frying pan. And I saw Jane clutching her knife as though itching to stab him with it."

"Maybe we can get Isabel to dose him with one of her sleeping potions. A double dose, to make him sleep for the rest of the week."

"Have I been that bad?" the doctor asked from behind them.

Rachel blushed furiously, but Billie turned to look at him, her eyebrows raised.

"You've been miserable, Emmett," she said. "I'd almost rather have Althea back in the house."

"Candor is always best between friends," he growled. "But you push it, Billie."

"Then you shouldn't have asked," she said, the corners of her mouth twitching with repressed laughter.

He leaned both hands on the cane Budge had whittled out of mesquite. "I want to thank you for saving my life. You did a good job. It could have been neater, but it's still a good job for an amateur."

This time Billie did laugh aloud. "That's a real compliment, coming from you."

Jane came out of the bedroom, a bulging carpetbag in her hand. "I'm taking him back to town before someone shoots him again," she said. "May we borrow your wagon?"

Billie nodded. "Sure."

"Thanks, Billie. For everything." Jane transferred the heavy bag to her other hand. "Come on, Emmett, while we can still call these people our friends."

The doctor grinned sheepishly at Billie and tipped his hat to Rachel before following his wife outside. "Are you sure you girls and Isabel will be safe alone here with the Apaches rampaging across the country? Maybe I should stay until—"

"That's all right," Billie said quickly. At this moment, she'd rather face a hundred screaming Apaches than another day with the doctor under her roof.

She and Rachel watched the wagon roll toward town. The moment it disappeared over the crest of the ridge, they grasped each other's hands and did a little dance of delight.

"Free at last!" Rachel cried. "Now we can do anything we want!"

"Now we can wash clothes," Billie said.

"Oh, no!"

"Oh, yes." Billie linked arms with the other girl and pulled her around the house to the courtyard. "This is something every frontier woman must know."

Rachel tried another tack. "But Isabel always does the wash. You pay her!"

"I'm paying her today, too, but we're going to do the work. She's got two sick children on her hands."

Rachel groaned, but helped willingly as Billie dragged the three big washtubs to the center of the courtyard and filled them with water. Billie built a fire beneath the two largest tubs and began shaving slivers from a cake of hard lye soap into the water of one as it heated.

When the water was nearly boiling, she dumped a double armload of clothing into the washtub. Taking a stick, its wood bone-white from much immersion in water, she poked the clothes beneath the surface. She watched them cook, mesmerized by the roiling bubbles. Would she ever be free of Nick? she wondered. Would the sound of hoofbeats approaching the house always make her heart pound with the hope that the visitor might be him?

"How long do you plan to cook those clothes, Billie?" Rachel asked.

Billie gave a guilty start and doused the fire. "Fetch

me that washboard, will you?" she asked, stirring the clothes before pouring three buckets of cool spring water into the tub. By God, she thought, staring mournfully into the depths of the washtub, this must be the worst torture ever devised by man!

She pulled a shirt out of the still-steaming water and slapped it onto the washboard. The vigorous act of scrubbing gave her a chance to vent some of her frustrations, and she went to it with a will. After it was as clean as she could manage, she handed it to Rachel, who stirred it into the hot, clean water of the next tub, then plunged it into the cool water of the third and left it to soak. Billie reached into the tub for another piece of clothing. Damn that Nick Larabee! she muttered under her breath as she scrubbed. Damn him—with his sun-warmed looks and that deep, beguiling voice that turned her knees to water! Sauntering into her life and stealing his way into her heart, then walking out as though he didn't notice or care what she had given him. She would meet him again at the Stearns's party. Would he smile at her with that caressing grin, then turn away to take another girl into his arms? That thought gave rise to another, and she looked over her shoulder at Rachel.

"Now wouldn't a fancy dress do well in a wash like this? And you wondered why I don't bother to buy impractical clothes," she said, savagely squeezing the last of the soapy water out of a pair of jeans and tossing them into the rinse water with a splash.

"There must be a gentler way of washing clothes, fancy or otherwise," Rachel said, eyeing the tangled ball of abused clothing. "Whose neck were you thinking about wringing?"

"Mine, for being stupid enough to agree to go to that damned party."

"Now, Billie, don't be a sourpuss," Rachel chided, a

smile twitching the corners of her mouth. She wiped a lock of sweaty hair away from her forehead with the back of her hand. "How are we going to hang these clothes to dry?"

For answer, Billie stretched a lariat across the courtyard. Since there were no clothespins, the girls merely hung the clean clothes over the rope, hoping the wind wouldn't knock them off into the dust.

"Hello!" a woman's voice called from the front of the house. "Is anyone home?"

"It's Helena," Billie said sourly, glancing down at herself. The front of her blouse was soaked, her hands were red and blistered from heat and the harsh lye soap and her hair lay in wet strands along her cheeks. Why did the woman always manage to find her in such a state? Why did she keep coming around at all?

"We're in the courtyard, Helena," Rachel called. "Come on back."

A moment later the courtyard gate opened, and Billie called, "Mind the wash!" before turning back to the tub to scrub the last of the jeans.

Helena came into the courtyard, another of those ridiculous parasols held overhead. She was wearing a day dress of ivory silk, its many flounces accented with expensive French lace. Every hair was in place, and she looked as cool and perfect as though she had just stepped from her house. Her perfume pierced even the smell of lye soap.

Nick was with her. He ducked under the clean laundry and stopped a few feet from Billie. Hooking his thumbs in his belt, he looked her up and down and drawled, "Having fun?"

At the sound of his deep, lazy voice, Billie's heart felt as though it was going to beat its way right out of her chest. She cursed under her breath and wrung the water out of the pants carelessly, sending a cascade of dirty

191

soapsuds onto her boots. All she needed now, she thought in disgust, was to trip over her own feet and fall on her face in the dirt.

"Helena, how nice to see you again," Rachel said, coming forward, her hand outstretched.

Helena smiled and took Rachel's hand in both of hers. "Thank you, my dear."

"What are you doing here?" Billie asked rudely.

Helena's smile faltered. "I was in town today to pick up something at the dressmaker's. When Miss Felker mentioned that your gowns were finished, I took the liberty of bringing them out to you."

"Oh. Well, that was very kind of you." Billie's cheeks burned scarlet, for Helena's graciousness only pointed out her own rude behavior.

"It was no trouble, really. Mr. Larabee told me that you've been extremely busy with the Redesware herd as well as your own."

Billie's brows contracted. Busy, was she? Well, Nick ought to know, since he'd walked out on her and left her shorthanded.

Nick reached out suddenly and grabbed her hand. She stood, immobilized by surprise, as he stroked his fingertips lightly over her blistered palms. He turned her hand over and inspected it, drawing in his breath when he saw that her fingers were bleeding around the nails.

"Don't you have sense enough to quit when you're hurting?" he asked, his voice harsh.

"Let me see." Helena stepped forward and gasped when she saw the condition of Billie's hands. "Take her inside and tend to her, Mr. Larabee," she ordered. "Miss Laird and I shall finish up here."

"You, do laundry?" Billie scoffed.

Helena lifted her chin defiantly, a gesture that made her look even more like her daughter. "Contrary to

MORE PASSION AND ADVENTURE AWAIT... YOUR TRIP TO A BIG ADVENTUROUS WORLD BEGINS WHEN YOU ACCEPT YOUR FIRST 4 NOVELS ABSOLUTELY *FREE* (AN $18.00 VALUE)

Accept your Free gift and start to experience more of the passion and adventure you like in a historical romance novel. Each Zebra novel is filled with proud men, spirited women and tempestuous love that you'll remember long after you turn the last page.

Zebra Historical Romances are the finest novels of their kind. They are written by authors who really know how to weave tales of romance and adventure in the historical settings you love. You'll feel like you've actually gone back in time with the thrilling stories that each Zebra novel offers.

GET YOUR FREE GIFT WITH THE START OF YOUR HOME SUBSCRIPTION

Our readers tell us that these books sell out very fast in book stores and often they miss the newest titles. So Zebra has made arrangements for you to receive the four newest novels published each month.

You'll be guaranteed that you'll never miss a title, and home delivery is so convenient. And to show you just how easy it is to get Zebra Historical Romances, we'll send you your first 4 books absolutely FREE! Our gift to you just for trying our home subscription service.

BIG SAVINGS AND FREE HOME DELIVERY

Each month, you'll receive the four newest titles as soon as they are published. You'll probably receive them even before the bookstores do. What's more, you may preview these exciting novels free for 10 days. If you like them as much as we think you will, just pay the low preferred subscriber's price of just $3.75 each. *You'll save $3.00 each month off the publisher's price.* AND, your savings are even greater because there are never any shipping, handling or other hidden charges—FREE Home Delivery. Of course you can return any shipment within 10 days for full credit, no questions asked. There is no minimum number of books you must buy.

4 FREE BOOKS

TO GET YOUR 4 FREE BOOKS WORTH $18.00 — MAIL IN THE FREE BOOK CERTIFICATE T O D A Y

Fill in the Free Book Certificate below, and we'll send your FREE BOOKS to you as soon as we receive it.

If the certificate is missing below, write to: Zebra Home Subscription Service, Inc., P.O. Box 5214, 120 Brighton Road, Clifton, New Jersey 07015-5214.

FREE BOOK CERTIFICATE

4 FREE BOOKS

ZEBRA HOME SUBSCRIPTION SERVICE, INC.

YES! Please start my subscription to Zebra Historical Romances and send me my first 4 books absolutely FREE. I understand that each month I may preview four new Zebra Historical Romances free for 10 days. If I'm not satisfied with them, I may return the four books within 10 days and owe nothing. Otherwise, I will pay the low preferred subscriber's price of just $3.75 each; a total of $15.00, *a savings off the publisher's price of $3.00.* I may return any shipment and I may cancel this subscription at any time. There is no obligation to buy any shipment and there are no shipping, handling or other hidden charges. Regardless of what I decide, the four free books are mine to keep.

NAME _____

ADDRESS _____ APT _____

CITY _____ STATE _____ ZIP _____

TELEPHONE ( ) _____

SIGNATURE _____
(if under 18, parent or guardian must sign)

Terms, offer and prices subject to change without notice. Subscription subject to acceptance by Zebra Books. Zebra Books reserves the right to reject any order or cancel any subscription.   019102

what you may think, I am not totally useless." She turned away.

Nick clamped his hand on Billie's wrist and pulled her after him like a recalcitrant child, slamming the door behind him with his heel.

"Do this, Mr. Larabee. Do that, Mr. Larabee. Jump, Mr. Larabee," Billie sneered, twisting her wrist in a futile attempt to free herself. "She sure has you trained. Maybe I should take lessons."

"If you're trying to make me angry, you're succeeding," he said, pulling her across the room and thrusting her into a chair. "Sit down."

"I don't need to be tended, especially by you," she said.

"Shut up." He brought the water jug over to the table and washed her hands with cool, fresh water. "Do you have any liniment?"

"In the cabinet over there." She was actually trembling. Despite his scowl, his touch had been infinitely gentle, reminding her of other times . . . She shrugged the memory away. That was over and best forgotten.

Nick found a battered tin and opened it, wrinkling his nose at the highly aromatic smell that wafted out. "What's in it?"

"Oil of sassafras, sweet oil and beeswax. Isabel swears it will cure anything, from sore muscles to frostbite."

He sat down beside her and began rubbing the ointment into her hands. His scowl deepened. Damn, he hated to see her hurt! Why she had to work like this, push herself beyond all reasonable limits . . . Stupid, stubborn, beautiful girl. Suddenly he raised her hand to his lips and kissed her fingertips one by one.

"Don't!" She snatched her hands out of his grasp.

His eyes narrowed. By God, he thought, she was the

most maddening woman with whom he'd ever had the misfortune to become involved. His nights had been full of dreams of her, her arms outstretched toward him, her legs clasping him eagerly as he came into her, her mouth calling his name in ecstasy. It had been he who suggested they deliver those gowns to the Star M, for he hadn't been able to stay away from her another day.

"Are you still playing that game?" he growled.

"It may be a game to you, but not to me," she retorted. "So this is your oh-so-important job? Escorting Madame Stearns on her shopping trips?"

"And don't forget Julia," he said, needing to hurt her. "Some of my duties include her."

Billie's chest heaved with outrage, but she remained silent, determined not to be drawn into his baiting.

"Where's Emmett?" Nick asked, suddenly realizing how quiet the house was.

"Jane took him back to town, and none too soon."

"You're here alone? Just you women?" His voice rose to a roar. "What the hell is wrong with you?"

She clenched her hands into fists. "I suppose I should have put Emmett on a horse and sent him to ask Budge to come back here and play nursemaid."

"You could have asked me to help!"

"You!"

"Me." He thrust his chair backward with a scrape and stood up. "I'll have a man out here this afternoon."

"I don't need your help," she said.

He put his hands on his hips. "You're going to get it anyway. And if you give my man any trouble, he'll be under orders to truss you like a chicken for market until you can behave."

"Let me tell you this, Nick Larabee—" The door opened, and she broke off, scowling. Helena and Rachel stepped into the house.

194

"Are you having a nice chat?" Helena asked.

Billie opened her mouth to answer, but Nick forestalled her by saying, "Your dress is ruined, Mrs. Stearns."

Helena looked down at the wet spots that marred the front of her beautiful gown, then back at the train, which was thickly encrusted with dust. She shrugged. "Mr. Stearns will buy me another. I do believe I smell more like lye than perfume now, however."

"Is that all you think about?" Billie demanded. "Money, dresses and perfume?"

"Do you care?"

"No."

Helena's lips thinned. "Then don't say anything at all if you can't show common courtesy to a guest in your house."

"Guest!" Billie shouted. "You call yourself a guest?"

Nick took hold of her shirt collar and pulled her out of her chair. Although she tried to push him away, he clamped his hands on her upper arms.

"Go out to the buggy, Mrs. Stearns. Rachel, go with her. I want to have a little talk with Billie." Although he spoke calmly, his jaw was clenched with anger. The two women obeyed quickly.

Billie didn't even glance at them. All her attention was fixed on Nick's angry face. "You can go straight to hell," she hissed. "You don't scare me."

Furious, he shook her so hard that the combs fell out of her hair, letting it escape from the knot at the back of her neck to spill out over his hands in a silken flood. When he stopped, she tossed her hair back over her shoulders and glared at him as defiantly as ever.

"Take your hands off me," she said.

He let go of her, not because she had told him to, but because he was so angry that he didn't trust himself. He had never beaten a woman in his life, but she had pushed him farther than anyone ever had before. And still he wanted her. Perhaps more than ever, because he admired her spirit as much as he was enraged by it.

"I'll see you at the party." His voice was hard—a threat, not a promise.

Billie shrugged and turned away. The self-conscious swing of her hips was an insult. Scowling, he swung his palm against her rounded behind in a slap that brought her up on her toes with a shriek.

He slammed the door behind him on his way out of the house, feeling a great deal better. Inside, he could hear Billie curse him, his ancestors and several generations of his descendants, then shout something about getting her rifle and shooting him like the dog he was. He noticed, however, that she didn't quite dare to come out of the house after him.

"What did you do to her?" Rachel demanded, her hands on her hips.

Nick just smiled. His palm throbbed from the force of that blow, but he suspected Billie's posterior hurt even worse. His grin grew wider. He climbed into the buggy beside Helena and drove off, leaving Rachel to deal with the furious mistress of the Star M.

Chapter 17

As Nick headed the buggy away from Billie's house, he became aware that Helena was crying. "Mrs. Stearns, why do you put yourself in a position to be hurt?" he asked.

She fumbled blindly in her reticule. With a sigh, Nick pulled his handkerchief out and handed it to her.

She sobbed into the white linen, great gasping sobs that made Nick itch to comfort her. Before he could reach out to her, however, she regained a measure of control.

"I know Billie can be rather, ah, difficult—" she began.

"Is that what you call it?" Nick snorted in derision. "She needs a good walloping, if you ask me."

"I'm afraid I shall have to leave that to someone else," she said. "You see, I deserve every bit of Billie's scorn, Mr. Larabee." She hiccuped, tried to smile, then drew in her breath in a ragged gasp that ended in a sob.

"Because you ran out on her?" he asked with deliberate bluntness, trying to stem the imminent tide of weeping. He wanted to hear this story, for it was Billie's, too.

"You don't know what Arizona was like back then.

If you think it's bad now . . ." She held the handkerchief to her eyes as though to press the tears back in. "We didn't have the money to hire many hands, so Anton began training Billie to do a man's work. Nine years old, and she was riding a horse like an Indian, shooting a rifle that was nearly as big as she was and—at least when she thought I couldn't hear—cursing like an infantryman. And when the Apaches attacked the ranch, she would go up on the roof with the men. At first it was only to reload their rifles for them, but then she began fighting on her own. Anton was terribly proud of her. She was the best shot in the territory, he said."

She swiveled to face Nick, moisture welling in her eyes again. "One night she came down from the roof shouting, 'I got four myself, Mama!' My beautiful little girl had just killed four men, Mr. Larabee! At that moment, her eyes were as cold and hard as her father's. I knew I had to get her out of there. But when Anton heard what I was going to do, he threw me out of the house. He said I was too soft, a coward. And neither Billie nor he needed me any longer. She was visiting some neighbors at the time, and I never even had a chance to say good-bye."

Nick cursed under his breath.

"He was right. If I had had any courage I'd have fought for my child. Instead, I let him drive me to town and put me on the next stage headed east. He said if I ever tried to take Billie from him, he'd kill me. Still the coward, I was afraid to take that chance, even for my daughter."

Nick's hands tightened on the reins until his knuckles were white. "That's not the story he told Billie."

"I expect not. But she worships her father. If I tell her what really happened, she may hate me even more for changing her memory of him." Helena dabbed at her

198

eyes again, then crumpled the handkerchief into a ball. "Anton was not always like that, but more than a year in a Yankee prisoner-of-war camp changed him, hammered every bit of softness out of him. He despised weakness, in himself and in others."

A muscle twitched in Nick's jaw as he remembered how Billie kept her feelings twisted up inside. What a battle must be going on inside her! he thought in sudden understanding. The sensitive young girl had struggled to suppress her very nature to please a man who could never understand what she was. Now that he was dead, she didn't quite know who to be. The notion made his heart ache with pain for her. No wonder she had fought him every time he'd tried to unleash that softer side of her. It made the times he'd managed to reach her all the more precious.

Helena, realizing that his silence was that of thought and not of condemnation, continued. "When Mr. Stearns told me he had bought the Dolorosa, I thought destiny was bringing me and my daughter back together. I suppose it has in a way. I just never expected it to hurt so much."

"Give it time, Mrs. Stearns."

She bowed her head. "I only hope there's some small part of my daughter beneath what Anton has made."

Nick drew in his breath sharply. She'd hit the target dead center. Billie was such a collection of diverse reactions that sometimes he thought she was as likely to shoot him as kiss him. And, God help him, he found her so intriguing, so compelling, that he couldn't seem to stop coming back for more. She had him stretched ten different ways, drawing him into her web like some beautiful but deadly spider.

Nick managed to stay away from the Star M exactly

five days. Then, cursing himself for a fool, he saddled Beelzebub and went to see how Billie and Rachel were getting along.

As he neared the house, he saw the wagon parked outside. The team was still hitched to it, their reins dragging in the dust beside the vehicle. The front door was ajar, a stark black outline against the pale adobe of the wall. There was no one to be seen; even the Martinez children, usually playing outside at this time of the day, were absent.

His pulse hammered in his ears. Completely forgetting caution, he spurred Beelzebub into a gallop. The stallion skidded to a stop outside the house, half rearing in outrage at his rider's abrupt pull on the reins. Nick hit the ground before the animal finished moving, hurtling across the dry ground to burst through that open doorway with his pistol at the ready.

Someone had emptied every cupboard, every chest, throwing the contents aside like so much garbage. Plates were smashed, chairs broken, bags of flour and sugar broken open and strewn across the floor. The metal strongbox had been broken open and emptied. He heard voices in Rachel's bedroom, hers and Billie's, and his shoulders sagged with relief. His boots making tracks in the floury mess, he strode across the room and flung open the door to the bedroom.

Billie and Rachel supported a man between them, trying to get him onto the bed. He was trying to help them, but his legs buckled whenever he tried to hold his own weight. Startled by Nick's precipitous entrance, the three nearly went down in a heap.

Nick slipped his gun back into his holster and took the man from them, noting a dark splotch of blood in the fellow's bright red hair. "Pat, are you all right?" he asked.

"Yeah. Jest a little dizzy, is all." With Nick's help, he

managed to sit on the edge of the bed. "How long was I out?"

"I don't know," Billie said. "We just got here a minute ago, and . . . Oh, my God! Isabel and the children!" Whirling, she ran through the front room and darted outside.

Her heart going even faster than her breath, she headed for the Martinezes' little house. Please, God, she prayed. Let them be all right! Dreading what she might see, she pushed the door open and went inside.

Isabel was lying on her side beside the bed, three small shapes beside her. All four had been tied and gagged, but to Billie's utter relief, they were alive and unhurt. As she bent to release them, she heard Nick come in behind her.

"What . . . Oh, thank God!" he said, going to his knees beside Juana. After he cut her bonds, the child swarmed up into his arms, sobbing.

Cradling the small form against his chest, he moved to Miguel and cut him free, too. But the boy, young as he was, had already learned a man's pride. Holding himself stiffly, he took the knife from Nick's hand and went to help Billie with Isabel's bindings. It was just as well, Nick thought; Maria, once free, joined her sister in the comfort of his arms. He sat on the hard dirt floor, rocking them.

Somehow Billie managed to protect both Isabel and herself from Miguel's overeager attacks on the rope. When the woman was free, she began babbling in a wild conglomeration of English and Spanish.

"Easy, Isabel," Billie said, patting the older woman's hand comfortingly. "Slow down, now. Tell me what happened."

But Isabel broke down into sobs, and it was Miguel who told the story.

"Three hombres, Señorita Billee," the boy said.

201

"They come out of nowhere, tie us up."

"Did you see what they looked like?" Nick asked.

Miguel shook his head regretfully. "They have bandannas here." He covered the lower half of his face. "I fight them, bite, scratch, kick, but they are too many."

Billie put her hands on his shoulders. "You are very brave, Miguel. *Mucho hombre.* Your father will be proud."

The boy puffed out his chest. "Juana! Maria! Mama needs you," he ordered.

His tone was as authoritative as any calvary officer's, and Billie was forced to turn away to hide her smile. Soon Isabel grew calmer.

"Isabel?" Billie knelt beside her and patted her shoulder to comfort her.

The older woman sniffled. *"Si?"*

"Eliseo will be back tomorrow. I'm going to have him take you and the children down to his brother's farm in Agua Prieta. When things are safe, you can come back. *Comprende?"*

"Si. Muchas Gracias." Isabel held her children close.

Nick pulled Billie to her feet. "They'll be all right now," he said. "Let's get back to the house and see how Pat is doing."

They found him, his head neatly bandaged, sitting at the table with Rachel. Billie sighed with relief to find him looking so well. Although she'd been furious at first that Nick had followed through on his threat to post a man at the Star M, she'd come to like Pat for his wit and easy charm. In addition, he was a terrible poker player, and neither she nor Rachel had done dishes since he'd come.

She stood, arms akimbo, and surveyed the wreckage of her home. "They didn't leave much, did they?" she asked.

202

"What did they git?" Conway asked.

Billie tossed her braid back over her shoulder. "Forty dollars, more or less. I haven't been keeping much in the house since Pa died."

She turned and walked back to her bedroom, hardly aware that Nick followed her. The breath went out of her in a gasp when she saw what the intruders had done there. They had ripped the stuffing out of her mattress, torn the pages out of the few precious books she owned, and had broken or poured out all her medicines. Even her new gown had been slashed with a knife, the lace torn from it and shredded, and, as a final insult, molasses had been poured over it. Her Bible lay in a forlorn heap of torn and crumpled paper. She picked one of the mangled pages up and tried to straighten it. Someone had stepped on it, leaving a molasses-sticky imprint of his boot across it. Her hand trembled.

"I'm sorry, honey," Nick said, putting his arm around her shoulders.

Billie shook him off, unable to bear his kindness just now. Why did he seem to show up just when she was weakest, when she needed someone to lean on? And she knew just how limited his concern really was; he always managed to find a way to slip out from under whenever she made any sort of emotional demand on him.

"What are you doing here?" she asked as nastily as she could.

Nick scowled, ready to reply in kind, but then noticed how woebegone her face was. Realizing that she was using anger to keep from breaking down, he reached for her again.

She stepped away hastily. "I asked you a question."

"I came to make sure you and Rachel were all right," he said. "What were they looking for?"

"I don't know." She hoped the lie didn't show on her

203

face. Oh, she knew, all right; this wasn't the first time someone had come looking for the gold coins her pa'd had the foresight to bury out on the range. Damned useless stuff, she thought sourly. Finding it had been a curse. She couldn't spend it, for that kind of news traveled faster than any other. And then a passle of fortune hunters would come down on her; no one ever believed a person found a *little* gold. And speaking of fortune hunters, Nick was awful curious about what might be hidden in her house.

Nick regarded her narrowly, watching the play of emotions on her face. Something wasn't quite right, but that could be the effect of what had happened here. He'd give her the benefit of the doubt just now, but tomorrow he was damn well going to ask her again.

"Pat was supposed to guard you," he said. "Why did you and Rachel go off without him?"

"Should I have left Isabel and the children alone, then?" she demanded. "And as you can see, we were safer out on the range than here."

He raked his hand through his hair, wishing he could open that pretty head of hers to see what was inside, what she thought and felt and believed in, what the truth about her really was.

"I'll go see if they've left me enough makings for a pot of coffee." She turned away from that too-penetrating gaze of his.

He followed her out to the other room. "You girls can't stay here," he said. "Come back to the Dolorosa with me, and I'll send someone out to clean this mess up for you."

"No, thanks. I can handle it," Billie said, her brows lowering. He had a lot of gall coming in here and taking over like this! "But take Rachel back with you; this isn't the place for her right now."

"I'm not leaving you here with this!" Rachel cried,

outraged that Billie would even suggest she leave.

"I can handle it!" Billie insisted.

Nick began rolling up his sleeves. "Don't be an ass."

She turned to glare at him, but before she could think of a suitable retort, Rachel tugged at her skirt and said, "Help me go through these tins, Billie. They're dented, but still useable."

Billie sighed. She was too tired to fight both of them. Feeling like she'd lost complete control of her life, Billie bent and helped Rachel rummage through the pile of tins. It looked like beans and peaches for supper, she mused. She shrugged; she'd eaten worse before, and probably would again.

Rachel straightened. Wiping her hands on her apron, she said, "The Stearns's party is tomorrow. I wonder—"

"We can't go, of course," Billie said quickly.

"Of course we can." Rachel picked up the broom and began sweeping the mess on the floor. "Helena offered to lend us some gowns, remember?"

"I'm not going to borrow anything from either of those two . . . fancy ladies. You go if you want, but I'm staying here."

Rachel frowned. "If you don't go, I won't, either. But, really, Billie—"

"I'm taking both of you back to the Dolorosa with me in the morning," Nick growled. "Pat, I want you to stick close to the house here. If those men come back, I want you to make things damned hot for them."

"Let 'em come," the cowboy said. "I'm ready for 'em."

Billie put her hands on her hips and glared at Nick. "Who gave you permission to give orders around here?" she demanded.

"I don't need permission. You're coming back with me, and that's final." He folded his arms over his chest

205

and looked at her from under his tawny eyelashes. "Rachel has been looking forward to that party for weeks now. I'm not about to let you ruin her fun just because you don't have the guts to face your own mother."

It was the truth, and it hurt. Billie's innate sense of honesty would not let her deny that she'd been looking for an excuse not to attend that party. And one glance at the hopeful expression on Rachel's face proved that he was also right about her wanting to go.

"Oh, all right!" she shouted. "Damn it!" Grabbing the other broom, she marched toward her bedroom.

Nick watched her go, enjoying the sway of her hips as she walked. His hands twitched with a sudden desire to touch her again. What would she do if he kissed her? Would she melt against him as she'd done out there on the range, or would she fight him? For a moment, he considered following her and finding out. Then prudence took over, and he remained in the front room with the others.

Chapter 18

Billie woke just after dawn. She yawned and scrubbed at her eyes, wishing she'd had about ten more hours of sleep. They had spent most of the night cleaning what was salvageable and dragging the rest outside to be burned later. Nearly everything she owned had been consigned to the bonfire. They had managed to restuff the mattresses and sew up the tears, but the result was lumpy and hard, nearly as unwelcoming to the body as the ground outside. This morning she was stiff and sore, and her sour mood mirrored her discomfort.

She lay for a moment, listening, but the house was completely silent. Outside the narrow slit of the gunport, she could hear the low drone of an insect. Groaning, she climbed out of bed and splashed water on her face in an effort to shake her fatigue, then pulled on a blouse, jeans and her most comfortable boots—traveling clothes. With everyone asleep, this was the perfect chance to see if she could pick up the intruders' trail. After picking up her pistol and Stetson, she tiptoed through the quiet house and slipped outside.

"Going somewhere?" Nick drawled from somewhere behind her.

With a startled gasp, Billie whirled. She was just in time to see him detach himself from a patch of shade that clung to the western wall of the house and saunter toward her. His dark clothing had blended into the shadows so perfectly that she doubted that she would have seen him even if she had looked directly at him.

"I warned you once about sneaking up on me like that," she said, frowning to cover her discomfiture.

"You won't shoot me." He stopped in front of her and inspected her attire. She was wearing the same loose jeans he remembered from the night he had first made love to her, the same much-washed blouse and battered Stetson. The memory of the towering passion they had shared during those heated hours made his body tighten, but he could tell by the set of her jaw that she wouldn't be receptive to reminiscing about times past.

Billie shrugged and turned away. He grabbed her by the arm and spun her back to face him.

"I asked you where you were going," he said softly.

She wrenched free. "Can't a person go for a morning ride without being set upon?"

"You weren't planning to follow that set of tracks heading northeast, by any chance?"

"You've already been out." She put her hands on her hips and glared at him.

Taking her arm again, he led her a short distance past the bunkhouse and pointed to a set of hoofprints in the dust. Billie bent to look closer. There had been three of them, as Miguel had said, and they'd headed northeast in a hurry. One of their mounts had a notch in its left front shoe, making a distinctive track. She glanced up at Nick, her eyebrows raised.

He nodded. "They split up just north of Ovillo Canyon, but I wasn't able to track them farther. It's nothing but rock up there."

208

"Maybe you just aren't a good enough tracker."

He laughed. "Maybe you just want to disappear until after the Stearns's party is over." Suddenly all humor dropped from him. "What were those men looking for, Billie?"

She regarded him from under her eyelashes. "What do thieves usually look for?"

"Do you always answer a question with a question?"

"I do when the answer is obvious," she retorted. "Or ought to be." She looked at him levelly, daring him to call her a liar. He'd be the last person she'd tell about the gold. He'd probably strip her of that faster than he had her virginity. She'd been stupid once, but not again.

He put his finger under her chin and tilted her face up. "Is that the truth, Billie?" he asked.

"Of course."

Although she met his gaze steadily, he knew she was lying. Looking right into his eyes and lying! A burning ache spread from his heart to the pit of his stomach.

"You kept the strongbox in the cabinet above the stove. They would have found it right away," he said, gauging her reaction carefully. "But they ransacked the house, even going so far as to slash the mattresses. They were looking for more than just your cash."

Her expression didn't flicker. "Well, maybe they were after my map showing the location of the Lost Dutchman Mine. Or maybe Montezuma's Gold. It's buried right under the kitchen table, you know."

"Damn it, Billie!" He took her by the shoulders and gave her a shake. "This isn't a game! If you fool around with something like this, you're going to get hurt."

"I'm not playing a game, and despite what you think, I'm not a fool. At least not anymore," she said coldly. Her eyes darkened nearly to emerald with malice and a slow-burning anger. Reaching up, she pushed his hands from her shoulders. She gave him one last, withering glare, then turned and stalked back to the house.

Nick watched her go. Frustration tightened his chest and made his hands clench into fists. What the hell was she hiding? What secret could be so important that she'd put herself and her household at risk to keep?

"Goddamn it!" he muttered, jamming his hat farther down over his brow. "Why the hell should I care?"

He turned on his heel and strode toward the corral, wishing he could saddle up and head straight out of Arizona and never come back. After the party, he was damn well going to stay clear of her until he purged himself of this idiotic fascination, he vowed. She was nothing but trouble.

Billie stared at the huge Dolorosa ranch house, her brows lowered in concentration. "Something is different about the house, but I can't quite place it."

Nick slowed Beelzebub to match pace with the wagon. "Stearns changed damn near everything. I think he would have torn the whole thing down if he could. He hates adobe."

"What did he say when he found out that the stable was attached to the north end of the house?" Billie asked, rolling her eyes.

Nick shrugged. "The stable has been moved."

"Lord, but he must have money to burn!" Billie said incredulously. She would have been thrilled to have a stable at all, and to have one so handy to the house would be downright heavenly. Who in their right mind, she wondered, would mind the smell of horses? Suddenly she straightened, squinting at the house through the distortion of the heat waves. "I see it now; the gunports have been cut larger to make windows!"

210

Nick nodded. "The windows that look into the patio are even bigger. They're glass, too, and not a shutter in the place, just curtains."

"Why, anyone could just walk in any time it pleased them!" Billie gave an involuntary shudder, despite the heat. "I don't think I can sleep in that house. I'll be waiting for an Apache to slip in and cut my throat."

"He says he hires enough men to protect the house and grounds, even from the Apaches."

"He doesn't know spit about Apaches," Billie said.

Nick chuckled. What a little savage she was! He looked at her from under half-closed lids, enjoying the way her breasts bounced with the motion of the wagon. By God, she was a delicious package of womanhood! Already his vow to walk away from her was beginning to waver under the whip of desire. If only he could get his emotions under control, learn to enjoy her for the moment, then leave her when something more important needed to be done. He'd managed it before with other women. But he knew deep in his heart that it would not be possible with Billie. It was all or nothing with her. Right now, he decided, it would have to be nothing. He'd never regretted a decision more. He thought of all the women he'd known, and couldn't think of one who was half as entertaining as Billie. Mendacious, yes, infuriating, certainly, but at least she wasn't boring.

It would be interesting to be able to listen in to the conversation at dinner tonight, he thought. Billie against Rosswell Stearns; tiny, opinionated spitfire against cold British sarcasm, with Julia's waspish comments thrown in for seasoning. Yes, it would be most interesting. Grinning, he turned the wagon into the drive leading to the house.

A neatly whitewashed fence had been erected around the house and grounds. It was nearly the height of a

211

man, and there were two guards stationed at the gate. Although Billie looked askance at the whitewash, knowing how brief its life would be in the brutal Arizona sun, she approved of the fence. Perhaps Stearns wasn't quite as stupid as she had supposed.

Nick slowed the team as they passed through the gate. The guards nodded to him, touching their fingertips to the brims of their hats in deference to the ladies.

Rosswell Stearns came out of the house as they drove up. "I'm glad you decided to come, Miss Meyrick, Miss Laird," he said, reaching up to help them down from the wagon. "Welcome to the Dolorosa."

"Thank you," Billie said. The man's frigid formality put her back up. Was he this way with everyone, or did he just dislike her in particular?

Stearns turned to Nick. "Mr. Larabee, I've been told that the gentlemen will expect to wear their weapons into my home tomorrow night. Is this true?"

Nick nodded.

"See that they do not. Politely." He swiveled suddenly to face Billie again, startling her. "I trust this will not make me a pariah, Miss Meyrick?" he asked.

She cocked her head to one side. Was he making a joke? she wondered. If so, his was the stiffest poker face she'd ever seen. "If you serve enough liquor, they'll forgive you anything," she said at last.

"Excellent." He swept his arm toward the entrance. "Ladies, come inside. You just have time to freshen up before supper."

Billie followed the Englishman inside and nearly gasped at the sight that greeted her. A crystal chandelier hung in the hall, casting shards of rainbows over the room. On the opposite wall was an elaborate coat-of-arms, and beneath it, a pair of graceful chairs, richly upholstered in gold brocade. The expense of bringing such things out here was staggering, and this was only the entryway!

212

The housekeeper, a thin woman with gray hair pulled back into a tight bun, rushed in to greet them, followed by two young maids. All three were strangers to Billie. It seemed that Stearns liked to import his help along with his furniture, she thought.

"Ruth and Constance will show you to your chambers," Stearns said, dismissing them with a wave of his hand.

Billie and Rachel followed the two silent maids to the rooms that had been prepared for them. Billie sat on her bed, testing its softness, and sighed. The furniture in this room had surely cost more than her yearly income. She looked at the tall window with its shrouding of green velvet draperies, and wondered what it must be like to have Stearns's unshakable confidence in the safety he could provide his household. For Billie, who could hardly remember a time when she didn't have to sleep with a pistol beside her bed, when the howls of the Apache and the sound of gunfire was as likely to wake her as the sun, it was a novel thought.

No wonder Helena had left the primitive little house Anton had built! She recoiled from her own thought; what was she doing making excuses for the woman who had run out on them? Remembering the times when she had cried herself to sleep after a night spent on the roof fighting the Apache—killing in order not to be killed, but sick with a gut-clenching terror her father would have scorned—those were the times when a mother's soft, comforting arms had been needed most. But Helena had gone to pursue her dreams of luxury unencumbered, leaving her daughter to face the horror alone. Billie would never, never forgive her.

Rachel tapped lightly on the door, then opened it and poked her head inside. "Are you ready?"

"Almost. Come in and wait for me." Billie jumped up from the bed and splashed water onto her face, then quickly changed into a fresh blouse and skirt.

"What do you think about all this?" Rachel indicated the rich furnishings.

"I think even the maids are dressed better than I am," Billie said, grimacing. "And the size of that window makes my skin crawl."

"We'll be perfectly safe. Nick told me that Mr. Stearns keeps thirty men just to protect the house." Rachel took her by the arm and pulled her toward the door. "Come on. I can't wait to see what's for supper."

The dining room was what had once been the sitting room. The wall had been removed from between it and the room beyond, making one enormous, cavernous chamber. A mahogany table, large enough to seat at least twenty people, occupied the center of the room. Above it hung a massive chandelier that was twice the size of the one in the hall. Two sideboards occupied the walls flanking the table, their tops covered with heavy silver serving dishes. At the far end of the room was a piano, artfully surrounded by twin Chippendale sofas and a number of chairs.

Billie hesitated in the doorway, intimidated by the luxury that was displayed so flagrantly here, but Rachel pulled her into the room.

"Look, Billie, a piano!" she cried, rushing toward the instrument. "I haven't played in ages!"

She sat down on the seat and began to play. Billie closed her eyes and enjoyed the lilting music.

"That was lovely, Miss Laird," Rosswell Stearns said when the song was over.

Billie opened her eyes in surprise. He moved quietly for so big a man; even with the music, she would have heard most people approach.

"I, too, am fond of Mozart. Perhaps you would play another?"

"Certainly," Rachel said. "Do you have a favorite—"

"Who is playing my piano?" Julia's high voice came

214

from the doorway, too loud in the quiet room.

Rachel rose and stepped away from the instrument.

Stearns turned to look at his daughter. "Miss Laird, and very well, too."

Julia, ignoring Rachel completely, came farther into the room and inspected Billie without favor. "What are you doing here?" she demanded.

"We're here for the party, of course," Billie said.

Julia's eyes widened. "But I thought . . . Nick said your gowns were ruined."

"You thought we would stay away just because our dresses were ruined?" Billie asked, thinking that Nick had said too damned much about something that wasn't any of his business.

"Well, you certainly can't expect to attend in"— Julia's lips curled in contempt—"those things."

Billie smiled broadly. "We're not. We're going to wear some of yours."

Helena came into the room then, and the English girl bit back her retort. Billie noticed that her mother's eyes were reddened as though she'd been crying. Was the luxurious life she'd made for herself not quite as idyllic as it seemed? Perhaps money hadn't bought her as much happiness as she'd thought.

A surge of sympathy went through Billie. "Hello, Helena," she said.

Helena, responding to the lack of rancor in her daughter's voice, reached out to take her hand. "Hello, dear."

Billie stepped backward quickly, instantly regretting that one moment of understanding. "Dear," was she? Well, Helena had better save it for old Rosswell over there.

Sighing, Helena turned to her husband. "Perhaps our guests would like a glass of wine before dinner, Rosswell."

215

"An excellent idea." Stearns swept his hand toward the table. "Come, ladies."

They sat at the table, Stearns at the head, Helena at the far end, Billie and Rachel on one side and Julia on the other. The housekeeper came into the room, a wine bottle cradled in her arm. After her employer nodded his approval, she uncorked it and poured a glass for everyone.

Stearns picked up his glass and held it to the light, enjoying the rich, ruby color of the wine. "A fine vintage," he murmured. "To your health, ladies."

"Helena, what is this I hear about you giving my clothing away?" Julia demanded, ignoring her father's frown.

"I did not give your clothes away, Julia," Helena said. "I merely offered Miss Laird the use of one of your gowns for the party tomorrow night."

"Without asking me?"

"Yes. Without asking you." Helena nodded to the housekeeper. "You may serve the meal, Mrs. Davenport."

When the woman was gone, Helena turned to her stepdaughter once again. "I didn't think it would be a hardship for you, Julia, since you have a multitude of gowns."

"It isn't the gown." Julia's pale gaze slid over Rachel, then returned to Helena. "It's the person to whom you offered it. Why, I heard the Apaches actually—"

"That's enough!" Billie was shaking with rage. She set her glass to one side lest she hurl it at Julia's nasty, simpering face. "Out here, it's considered bad manners to insult a guest at your table. Maybe your standards are different in England, but I can assure you that if you say one more word I'll teach you a lesson you'll never forget."

Stearns thrust his chair back and rose to his feet. His

216

face expressionless, he went to stand beside his daughter's chair. "Manners are no different in England, Miss Meyrick. Julia, you will apologize to Miss Laird."

"I certainly will not!"

His hand flashed out, catching her in the mouth. Julia's head jerked backward with the force of the blow.

"Apologize to Miss Laird," he said again.

Julia held her napkin to her lips for a moment. Then she dropped her hands into her lap and bowed her head. "I apologize for my hasty words, Miss Laird," she said. "My behavior was inexcusable. Please forgive me."

Stearns nodded and returned to his place. Julia jumped to her feet, knocking her chair over backward in her haste, and rushed from the room.

Billie glanced at Julia's discarded napkin. A crimson stain marred the snowy fabric. She gave a convulsive swallow, bothered, not by the fact that Julia had received a sorely deserved punishment, but by the unemotional way in which it had been delivered. Stearns hadn't even frowned. Maybe that was the way the upper classes handled their problems, but Billie would have preferred a good, screaming fight and a beating with a strap to that chill ferocity.

Helena rose to her feet. Silently, she removed the reddened napkin and set Julia's chair upright. "I'd better see if she needs anything."

"She will not appreciate your help, my dear," Stearns said. He finished his wine and set the glass to one side. Laying his thick, well-kept hands on the table, he leaned toward Rachel. "Please forgive my daughter's outburst, Miss Laird. I am extremely embarrassed that you were forced to endure such abuse in my house."

Rachel's face was as white as the tablecloth. "It isn't

217

the first time I've heard it, Mr. Stearns."

"Well, it shall be the last, at least from any member of my household." He looked up. "Ah, here comes our soup. Perhaps after dinner you will deign to play a little Mozart for us, Miss Laird?"

"Of course."

Billie looked down as the housekeeper deftly slid the bowl of soup before her. There was a confusing number of forks and spoons on either side of the plate, more silverware in this one place setting than the Star M owned. She watched Rachel out of the corner of her eye to see which spoon she picked up, then imitated her.

"The soup is very good tonight, isn't it, Rosswell?" Helena asked.

"Yes. I must remember to compliment Cook." Intent on his meal, he spoke without looking up.

Billie glanced from him to his wife. Helena hadn't touched her soup at all; her hands were clasped in her lap. A diamond and ruby necklace encircled her slim throat, its fire-and-ice glitter echoed by the earrings she wore. She looked very beautiful and astonishingly youthful, the faint lines around her eyes erased by the flickering candlelight.

She was staring at her husband, and there was fear in her eyes.

Chapter 19

"Get that thing away from me!" Billie shouted. She was clad only in a camisole, drawers and the sheerest of silk stockings. Her dark hair fell around her shoulders in a shining aureole.

Helena's French maid, a corset clasped in her arms, protested, "But, mademoiselle, you must wear it."

Billie shook her head.

"You *must* wear the corset," the Frenchwoman said, louder this time. "Every woman wears one."

"I don't." Billie crossed her arms over her chest.

"But the gown, she needs a corset. See, mademoiselle, the waist—"

Helena came into the room, closing the door behind her. She was wearing an elaborate silk gown that exactly matched her red-gold hair. Every seam, every flounce—even the train—was edged with delicate Point de Tulle lace and tiny velvet bows. "What is the problem, Sophie?"

The maid responded with a flood of rapid French.

Helena nodded, putting her hand consolingly on the maid's arm. "It's all right, Sophie. Bring the topaz necklace from my room. It will go well with my daughter's gown."

"I'm not going to wear a corset," Billie said.

Helena walked around her slowly. Truly, she mused, Billie had a marvelous figure, with her full, upstanding breasts and supple waist, the slender curves of her hips and shapely legs. "I don't think you need it," she said at last. "I think you'll fit into my gown beautifully just as you are. But you will undoubtedly scandalize everyone you dance with."

Billie shrugged. "I don't plan on doing much dancing."

"Mr. Larabee will be there."

"*He'd* hate the corset even more than I would." Billie clapped her hands over her mouth, appalled at what she had said.

Helena laughed. She laughed until the tears ran down her face and her knees began to buckle. "Oh!" she gasped, groping behind her for the chair. "Oh, Billie!"

Billie grinned shamefacedly. "I don't know why I said that."

"I do." Helena wiped her eyes with her handkerchief. "If ever I saw a tomcat on the prowl, Nick Larabee fits the picture."

Billie shrugged, feigning indifference, but Helena's words made her heart contract with dread. Was Nick really like that, just a predatory male looking for a willing bed partner? Would any woman do—Rachel, Julia, Helena, herself?

"Are you interested in him?" Helena already knew the answer, for she had seen the truth in Billie's eyes when she had looked at Nick, had seen the raw hunger on Nick's face, the yearning that went far beyond the mere physical attraction of a man for a pretty girl. But still she asked; if Billie could learn to confide in her, perhaps they could find a way to repair the relationship that had been severed by time and anger.

Billie's brows contracted in a scowl. "What the hell

business is it of yours?" she snapped.

"None. I'm sorry I pried." Helena folded the handkerchief into a neat square, her face showing nothing of the hurt she felt. "May I give you a bit of advice, not as a mother, but as a woman of the world?"

Billie nodded grudgingly.

"Don't be so honest."

"What?" Billie gaped at her in astonishment.

"You carry your heart in your eyes, dear. It's obvious that Nick's touch affects you deeply. If I can see it, so can he."

Oh, he could, could he? Billie thought savagely. The only thing worse than feeling like she did was having him know it. Oh, but he must be damned pleased with himself! "What do you suggest?" she asked.

Helena stood up and smoothed the front of her skirt. "I've always found that men are far more intrigued by what they think they cannot have than what they can."

"You mean say no? Tell him I don't want to see him?"

"Absolutely not. Tell him maybe. Then dance with other men, talk with them, flirt with them. Make him think you're not quite as interested as he's assumed."

"What am I supposed to do? Trail around after every man in sight, laughing and fluttering my eyelashes? They'll run like calves at branding time!"

"You won't have to do the chasing." Helena closed the distance between them and took Billie's chin in her hand. "Oh, Billie, don't you realize how beautiful you are? If you would relax for one moment, you'd have more men than you'd be able to count."

Billie pulled away from her. "Don't be an idiot." The anger in her voice was not caused by the other woman's words, but from the memory of what *had* happened to her the one time she had let her guard down. She had ended up in Nick's arms, loving him, letting him love her.

Helena sighed and dropped her hand to her side. "Tonight you are not the owner of the Star M, the girl who can outride and outshoot most of the men here. Tonight you are merely a beautiful woman. Beauty is power. Enjoy it. Use it to your advantage. Make them dance to your tune."

With a rustle of silk, she moved away, leaving Billie alone in the quiet room. Billie crossed her arms over her chest and looked down at her stockinged toes. After a moment, she went to the mirror and stared at herself. Beautiful? She bent closer, but saw only her accustomed features in their accustomed places.

Then a sly, calculating look came into her face. So, Nick thought he had her in the palm of his hand, did he? Maybe he was used to women who lost themselves under the spell of his tawny good looks and roaming hands. Well, maybe it was time he learned a lesson.

Billie smiled at her reflection. A corset was just what she needed to erect a barrier between her and Nick, although she suspected she would need a suit of armor to keep her body from reacting to his touch. But, as Helena suggested, she didn't actually have to change her responses, just make Nick think she had.

Billie and Rachel stood just outside the doors leading to the patio, listening to the swirling music that wafted faintly through the thick wood.

"Are you as nervous as I am?" Rachel murmured.

"More. I feel like a damned fool in this getup." Billie swept her hand downward at her gown. It was so tight around her knees that she was forced to take tiny, mincing steps, and the train slithered behind her like some malevolent creature just waiting for a chance to trip her up. And the maid, calmly ignoring Billie's loudly professed hatred for finery, had eased her into this froth of silk, delicate ivory lace and tiny pleats. Billie grimaced. She was terrified of taking too long a stride and tearing the fragile gown from stem to stern, or worse, having her bosom pop right out of the low-cut bodice.

Rachel put her hand over her mouth. "Oh, you really ought to see the horrible look on your face! Come now, Billie. You might at least pretend that you're having fun."

Billie shrugged, then grasped frantically for the top of her bodice.

Rachel laughed. "Don't worry, you won't fall out." Then she added, "But I wouldn't shrug quite so emphatically if I were you. A dainty lift of the shoulder will do." She demonstrated.

Billie tried the gesture, staring down at her chest as she did. "I still jiggle." She looked up at Rachel, scowling. "*You* don't jiggle."

"More's the pity," Rachel murmured.

"Well, you certainly look beautiful," Billie said. "That dress looks like it was made for you."

Rachel dipped into a graceful curtsy. She was wearing one of Julia's best gowns (over that young lady's strenuous objections), a confection of ruffled peach satin and creamy lace. A pearl necklace, lent to her by Helena, adorned her long, slim neck.

The doors swung open suddenly. Nick stood framed in the opening, his broad shoulders looking even broader in his well-cut evening coat. He was even more handsome in formal dress, Billie thought, for the narrow trousers and high collar of his shirt only accentuated the feral grace of his leanly muscled body. The candlelight picked out the bronze highlights in his hair and turned his light brown eyes to amber. Heat rushed

223

through Billie's body at the sight of him, making her feel as if she was going to melt right out of the constricting corset.

"I was just coming to get you," he said.

He grinned down at Rachel, then turned to Billie. The smile faded from his face as his gaze swept over her. By God, he thought, she was so beautiful he hated for other men to see her! Her midnight-dark hair was pulled back from her face in a simple chignon that accentuated her delicate bone structure and made her green eyes look enormous. And the gown! It was made of the lightest, most delicate silk he had ever seen, in a burnished shade of bronze that made her skin look like creamy satin. Her topaz necklace, with its large, pear-shaped central stone, drew attention to the deep cleft between her rounded breasts. The sight of all that luscious flesh infuriated him. How dare she expose herself like this!

"Shall we go?" Rachel took his left arm, indicating that Billie should take the other.

Remembering her resolve, Billie tucked her small gloved hand into the crook of his arm, making sure her breast brushed against him as she did. His muscles tightened under her hand, and she smiled.

They stepped out onto the wooden floor of the portal, the covered walkway that surrounded three sides of the patio. Lanterns had been hung at regular intervals along the overhand, filling the patio with golden light. A wooden platform had been built over the dust of the courtyard, and the musicians sat upon a raised stage at the far end. The dance floor was crowded with couples swirling to a graceful waltz, and even the walkway was thronged with people.

A woman called a greeting to Nick, but his attention was fixed on Billie's breasts. "You're going to come right out of that gown," he growled.

"Nick!" Rachel hissed, blushing scarlet.

Billie ignored him. She took a deep breath and bestowed what she hoped was a dazzling smile upon the nearest thing wearing pants, which happened to be old Hank Beadle of the Triple Fork Ranch. Hank stopped to stare at her, his mouth open in astonished admiration. He nudged the man beside him, who glanced over his shoulder at her briefly, then turned to take another, longer look.

"Nick! Oh, Nick!" Julia waved at him from the edge of the dance floor, her high-pitched voice carrying clearly over the music.

Nick turned and walked toward the refreshment table, pulling Billie and Rachel after him.

"Your boss is calling," Billie said sweetly.

"She isn't my boss!" Nick scowled at her. "I've worked for one woman, and that was enough to last me a lifetime."

"My, how charming you are tonight," Rachel murmured. My, she thought, her brother was certainly squirming under the whip of jealousy. He had always been so controlled with women, had always managed to keep his heart unencumbered. Rachel smiled; it was wonderful to see that it was Billie who had finally brought him down.

"Nick!" Julia tapped him on the shoulder with her fan. "Didn't you hear me calling you?"

All three turned to face her. Julia curled her lip at Rachel, unwilling to admit that the other girl looked prettier in the peach gown than she did herself. Then her gaze went to Billie, and her face tightened.

"I see that you share your mother's fondness for exhibiting far more of yourself than anyone would wish to see," she said, her voice seething with malevolent anger.

"Is that so?" Billie lifted her shoulder in a languorous

225

shrug, drawing not only Nick's gaze, but also the fascinated attention of several other men. The gesture—and its results—proved how inaccurate Julia's statement was.

The English girl lifted her chin haughtily and put her long, gloved fingers on Nick's arm. "You promised to dance with me, Nick."

"So I did." He nodded briefly to Rachel and gave Billie a hard, warning stare before letting Julia lead him toward the dance floor.

"What's got his dander up?" Billie asked.

Rachel laughed. "As if you didn't know." She cocked her head to one side and regarded Billie from beneath half-closed lashes. "Not that he doesn't deserve it."

A young man rushed up to them. "Good evening, ladies," he said, sweeping a graceful bow.

Billie nodded regally. "Miss Laird, Jack Kempker."

"Ah, Miss Laird, you're the . . . I mean, I always wanted to tell you . . ." he floundered to a stop. A flush rose into his face as he struggled for words. He had been appalled at the callous way some of the townswomen had behaved toward the unfortunate girl, and wanted somehow to tell her how sorry he was without reminding her of the terrible experience.

Rachel, seeing the sincere distress on his face, took pity on him. "It's a pleasure to meet you, Mr. Kempker," she said, extending her hand.

He gave a great sigh of relief. "Would you like to dance, Miss Laird?"

"Yes, I would." Rachel smiled, seeing that an impatient swain hovered just behind Billie. She took Jack Kempker's arm and let him lead her away.

"Miss Meyrick?"

Billie turned to see Stephen DeWitt, the handsome son of the bank president. He was poised, charming, and considered the most eligible bachelor in Xavier.

226

Usually, he ignored her. She tried the brilliant smile on him and was pleased to see his chest expand several inches in response.

He raised her hand to his lips. "You look very beautiful tonight, Miss Meyrick," he murmured. "Will you dance with me?"

"Sure." Billie let him take possession of her arm. Just before they stepped out onto the dance floor, however, she held back, whispering, "This is a waltz. I can't—"

"I'll show you. It's easy." He swept her into his arms and into the swirling crowd.

Billie easily mastered the steps. In moments she was dancing effortlessly, enjoying the lovely, swaying movement of the waltz. What would it be like to dance with Nick? she wondered, whose leonine grace occupied his every movement.

She spotted Nick at last. Julia was draped across his chest like a waistcoat, smiling seductively up into his face. And the girl had twitted me about showing a few inches of my breasts! Billie thought sourly.

"You need a man," Stephen said.

She looked up in astonishment; she had almost forgotten he was there. "I beg your pardon?"

"You need a man to handle the ranch for you," he repeated, tightening his hold on her possessively. "A tiny woman like you is much too fragile for that kind of rough work."

Why, you arrogant rooster! she thought. I can work you into the ground any day of the week! She almost said it aloud, but then she remembered Helena's words and smiled coyly up at him instead. God forbid that Nick wasn't watching; she didn't think she'd be capable of doing this twice. To her relief, the song ended.

"I'd like something to drink," she said, batting her eyelashes at him. "And I see that Miss Laird is waiting for me."

"Will you honor me with another dance?"

"Later, perhaps."

He escorted her to the edge of the portal, then turned and disappeared into the crowd. Billie, seeing several young men approaching, hastened to rejoin Rachel before she ended up on the dance floor again.

Rachel sat down on one of the wooden chairs that had been placed against the wall of the house and pulled Billie down on the one beside it.

"Well, did you like Jack?" Billie demanded. "What did he say?"

"He apologized for the things some of the towns-people said to me after . . . after the attack. He asked me not to judge them all by the stupidity of a few."

"And?" Billie prompted.

Rachel blushed prettily. "He told me I was beautiful."

"I knew it! You've made a conquest already."

"Oh!" Rachel looked down at her clasped hands. "He's very nice and seems to be a steady, sincere young man, but he wouldn't be the one I'd choose, not at all."

Billie's stomach twisted. No, she mused, nice, steady, sincere Jack Kempker would never replace Nick Larabee in any woman's heart.

Another young man came to beg Rachel for a dance. She hesitated, glancing at Billie.

"Go on," Billie said, giving her a push. "I'd just as soon not dance for a while."

A moment later, however, she noticed young David Beadle coming toward her. She could tell by the look on his face that he was going to ask her to dance. With a sigh, she wriggled her toes, trying to make a bit of extra room in the pointed toes of her high-heeled slippers. Suddenly David stopped, a look of dismay on his face, then turned and bolted back into the crowd.

Billie's hand automatically went to her bodice. Then

someone chuckled behind her, so close that she could feel his warm breath in her ear. She recoiled, swiveling in the chair to see who it was.

"You!" she snapped.

Carson Eames laughed. He was dressed, not in formal attire, but in narrow black trousers and a black shirt with silver studs. He hadn't even taken his gun belts off.

Billie scowled. "What are you doing here?"

"I came to see you in a dress." His gaze leisurely took in her delicate, heart-shaped face, her rounded breasts and tiny waist. "It was worth the trip."

Billie slid across the chair away from him and rose to her feet. "I'd better—"

"Not so fast, beautiful lady." Moving so quickly that she didn't have time to react, he straightened and took her arm in a grip that made her wince. "Let's dance." He tossed his hat onto the seat of the chair she had just vacated and pulled her onto the dance floor.

Billie stood stiffly within the circle of his arm, wishing the musicians were playing anything but a waltz. But Eames only smiled and drew her closer, his pomaded hair shining greasily in the soft light.

"You ought to give me a chance, honey," he said. "None of my women have ever complained."

Billie tipped her head back to look at him. "Looking to add me to your herd? That's not exactly flattering."

"But you're special." His hand caressed her back lightly. "If you decided to be nice to me, I might be persuaded to hang up my hat in one place."

"I see. And if I refuse?"

"Then I'll see to it that you change your mind." His eyes burned with consuming desire. "I always get what I want, honey. Somehow, some day, I'll have you. Make it easy on me, and I'll make it easy on you. I might even be gentle." Grinning, he let his hand drift down to the beginning swell of her buttocks.

"Get your filthy hands off me," she hissed, pushing ineffectually at his chest. "You damned rattlesnake! You, you . . . *hijo de la chingada!*"

Although Eames didn't understand Spanish, it was quite clear that Billie hadn't used an endearment. Crimson stained his pale cheekbones. "You little devil! You'll pay for every word, do you hear?"

The gunman flinched as Nick's big hand fell heavily on his shoulder.

"Billie," Nick said, his voice rough with anger. "Go get something to eat." He watched her until she was safely in Rachel's company.

He kept his hand on Eames's shoulder, urging the other man toward the portal. "I thought I told you to watch the gate," he said.

"I put Harvis there, don't worry." Eames shrugged, but the grip on his shoulder remained. "I just came to see the Meyrick girl." He smiled at Nick, a brief showing of teeth that had nothing of humor in it. "A mighty fetching piece of baggage, that girl, once you peel a few layers of clothes off her."

Nick's fingers tightened.

Eames winced, then slid out from under that numbing grasp. He turned to face Nick. "You wouldn't be wanting her for yourself, would you, Larabee? If so, you'll have to go through me to get her."

Nick crossed his arms over his chest. He was unarmed. Without a gun, there was nothing he could say to this man.

Another smile creased Eames's narrow face. "I'll wait while you get your gun," he offered. "Meet me at the—"

"Is there a problem, gentlemen?" Rosswell Stearns's voice came from behind Nick.

230

Nick glanced over his shoulder at the Englishman. "Nothing I can't handle."

"I shall handle this, Mr. Larabee." Stearns fixed the younger men with a cold stare. "There will be no fighting, now or later. Is that clear?"

They nodded reluctantly.

Stearns plucked a bit of lint from his otherwise immaculate sleeve. "Very good. Now, Mr. Eames, I believe you are supposed to be elsewhere?"

Eames turned on his heel and headed for the door.

"He's a hothead," Nick growled. "You're going to have trouble with him."

"That is why you are in charge, Mr. Larabee. I expect you to see that I *don't* have trouble—with him or anyone."

"Nick!" Julia's high voice cut clearly through the murmur of the crowd. "Where have you been hiding?"

Nick glanced around, judging the best route of escape, but it was already too late. Julia descended on him in a flurry of lace and velvet ribbon, taking a firm hold of his arm. "It's time for another dance," she trilled.

A muscle in Nick's jaw tightened. "Your father is paying me to make sure everything runs smoothly here, not to dance."

"I expect you can do that as well from the dance floor as anywhere," Stearns said. He leaned closer, adding in a low voice, "Do see if you can keep my daughter from making a fool of herself, Mr. Larabee."

It was far too late for that, in Nick's opinion. But, unable to think of a polite way to refuse, he let Julia lead him among the dancers. She pressed herself so tightly against him that he could feel the twin peaks of her small breasts against his chest. If only the girl would stand on her own feet!

231

Seeing Billie whirl by in the arms of yet another man, he sank into brooding silence. That was her third partner in as many dances, and there didn't seem to be a dearth of fellows waiting to take their turn. Nick ground his teeth in frustration. Damn young bucks, all of them itching to get their hands on her. Damn her, too, looking up at them with that sultry smile on her face, the rounded curves of her breasts barely covered by that gown. If he had to see her swing by in the arms of another man one more time, he'd . . . Goddamn it to hell, there she went again. Her partner was all but drooling into her bodice, and his hand had crept downward to the small of her back. Nick glared at that straying hand. Another inch or two farther, and he was going to be forced to do something about it.

"Why the hell are they playing nothing but waltzes?" he demanded.

"Don't you like waltzes? I think they're divine." Julia breathed, leaning even more fully against him.

Nick cursed under his breath and shifted her back onto her feet. Taking her by the hand, he led her over to the refreshment table. "Wait here." A moment later, he disappeared into the crowd.

He returned a short time later. Grabbing Julia by the hand, he towed her back to the dance floor.

"My, are you always so impetuous?" She laughed breathlessly. "It bodes well for the future . . . Good Heavens! What is that?" she asked, hearing the musical screech of a fiddle.

One of the ranchers climbed up onto the stage, and the crowd howled with delight.

"Ladies and gents, find yer partners!" the man shouted at the top of his lungs.

There was a shuffling among the revelers as they paired up. The musicians struck up a rollicking tune. Nick saw Billie pick up her train and sling it over her

232

arm, revealing shapely calves and dainty, high-heeled shoes.

"Ladies, do-see-do!" the caller howled. "Birdie hop out and the crow hop in, three hands around and go it agin!"

Julia stared at the dancers in bewilderment. "Nick, what on earth is that?"

"It's called 'Sandy Land,' and it's a hell of a lot of fun." He swung her onto the dance floor, ignoring her protests.

The caller was really getting into the song, clapping his hands as he screamed the words. "Four hands around and around, change them partners and swing them 'round!"

Billie twirled toward her next partner and found herself suddenly in Nick's arms. He grinned down at her, swinging her out, then bringing her against his chest with a solid thump.

"Idiot!" she gasped.

"Lover." He whirled her to one side, putting his hand on her waist to steady her for a promenade. She put her nose in the air and ignored him as she danced beside him. Nick grinned. She was adorable, and for two cents he'd kiss her right here. By God, he thought, that would really get folks jumping!

Before he could succumb to the temptation, however, the caller cried for everyone to switch partners again.

"Watch yourself, honey, or you're going to buy more trouble than you can handle." Nick held onto her a moment longer, then reluctantly let her go on to her next partner.

Billie glared at him over her shoulder. The gall of the man! If he ever, ever came near her again, she vowed, she'd make him regret it.

Chapter 20

Billie sat down at the dressing table and took the pins out of her hair. It was long past midnight. Her back was sore from the unaccustomed restriction of the corset, and her feet were twin lumps of agony from dancing in those high-heeled shoes. Although the party was far from finished—no one would leave until nearly dawn, travel at night being too dangerous—most of the women had retired to the bedrooms to catch a few hours of sleep. The men would drink and talk and drink some more. Come morning, they'd head out toward home, blinking and bleary-eyed, trusting their wives and horses to get them pointed in the right direction.

Billie smiled at her reflection in the mirror, wondering if Rosswell Stearns would ever agree to having another party. She laughed softly and began brushing the thick, luxuriant length of her hair.

There was a faint stirring of the curtains behind her. She froze, the brush poised above her hair, as Nick stepped out from behind the draperies. He had changed from evening dress to boots and jeans and a yoked shirt, all dark blue to blend in with the shadows. His hair had been slicked back with water, darkening it as well, although the lantern light picked up a few bronze strands amid the brown.

Laying the brush aside, she pushed the chair back and stood up. "Get out," she snapped.

Nick restrained a smile; she was standing in front of the lamp, not realizing that the light made the silhouette of her shapely body clearly visible through her nightgown. His hungry gaze roved over her, noting the full outline of her breasts, quivering a bit just now with indignation, lingering for a moment on her tiny waist and the smooth curve of her hip, coming to rest at last on the spot where her thighs joined. God, she was beautiful! he thought, his manhood springing to urgent attention at the sight of her.

"We have to talk," he said.

Billie shook her head. Judging from the look on his face, talk wasn't what he had in mind. He wasn't going to do this to her, not again! If only she could run, call for help, anything! But she could only stare at him as he came closer, mesmerized by the heat in his gold-flecked gaze.

"It's your fault," he said, stopping a scant foot in front of her.

"What?" she asked in bewilderment.

"You shouldn't have flirted with other men."

Her temper flared. "Why the hell not?"

"Because you're mine," he growled. "You're lucky I didn't turn you over my knee out there, the way you acted."

"Get out!" She pounded his chest with her fists. "Get out this minute!"

With a muttered curse, he grabbed her wrists. He knew he was a damned fool for coming in here. But after watching her play her little game all night, smiling, flirting, making his soul burn with jealousy, he

236

had to claim her again. God help him, for he couldn't help himself.

"Don't you know how beautiful you are?" he murmured. "I want to make love to you again, Billie."

She stopped struggling, astonished by the pleading in his voice. He brought her fists to his mouth and kissed her knuckles one by one. Slowly, her hands opened. His hot mouth moved across her palms, nibbled at the fleshy pad beneath her thumb.

A wave of desire went through her, and she gazed up at him from under half-closed lids. How could she resist the need in him, the need in herself? Truly, they belonged together, forged by the white-hot heat of their passion. He had to love her, she thought, he had to! Perhaps he just wasn't comfortable speaking the words, but the feelings had to be there.

"Nick," she whispered. "Nick." It was a capitulation, and a promise.

He drew her arms around his neck, bringing their bodies together with delicious slowness. The moment she came against him, however, she became aware of the rock-hard shaft of his manhood. He was raging with long-withheld desire, she realized, and that knowledge was infinitely exciting.

His hands stroked slowly down her back to her waist. "I can't think of anything but you," he said, his deep voice rough with passion. "I can't eat, I can't sleep from wanting you."

A surge of triumph went through her. But she resisted the forgiveness that welled up in her, the quickening of her pulse in anticipation of what that forgiveness would bring. "Is that why you were fondling Julia Stearns every time you hit the dance floor?" she asked, tipping her head back to look at him.

"Honey, of all the things you could worry about, you

sure picked the least important. And she was fondling me, not the other way around."

He kissed his way around the curve of her ear, his breath tickling deep inside. Billie shivered as the coiling desire rose in her, a flame deep within her body that only he could quench. Teasingly, he ran his fingers along the cleft between her buttocks.

She cried out softly, all thought drowned beneath a flood of sensation. His mouth claimed hers with searing heat, his tongue stabbing deeply into her mouth as he lifted her nightgown up over her head and tossed it away.

He stepped back a pace to look at her. Automatically, she tried to cover herself, but he grasped her wrists and held her hands away. "Don't," he muttered. "Don't hide yourself."

Unable to refuse him, she relaxed. He let go of her and stared at her hungrily, his hands twitching with the desire to touch her. But he forced himself to wait, to enjoy this perusal of her. But his self-imposed restraint crumbled when he saw her nipples darken and rise up under his regard, beckoning him irresistibly.

With a groan, he dropped to his knees before her, his hands claiming the rich weight of her breasts, his mouth trailing upward along the silken skin over her ribs. His tongue traced a line of moist heat across the underswell of her breasts, coming near the straining peaks but not actually touching them.

"Oh, God, I can't stand it! Please, Nick!" Billie bent forward and grabbed his hair, guiding his mouth toward her aching nipples.

Obediently, he tasted first one nipple, then the other. When his mouth finally settled firmly on one, suckling, she gave a sigh and clasped him to her. Too soon, however, he released her, and she gave an inarticulate moan of protest.

"You're so beautiful, so perfect for me," he muttered, kissing his way down her abdomen toward her navel. Then his hot mouth moved again, trailing a moist path across her flat belly to her hip, where he traced the contours of the bone with soft, gentle love-bites.

"I'm going to love every inch of you tonight," he murmured against her skin. "I want you to be as crazy for me as I am for you."

His hand delved through the soft curls of her mound, urging her thighs apart. He parted the folds of her secret flesh gently, then slid two fingers into her. Billie's knees gave way beneath that loving assault. He rose, sweeping her into his arms, and carried her to the bed. Laying her down, he began stripping his clothes off.

Billie rose to her knees to help him, her hands fumbling a little in her eagerness. He dropped his hands to his sides and bent his head to watch as she undressed him. Trembling, she pulled his shirt up over his head and discarded it, then unfastened his jeans and pushed them down over his narrow hips. He bent and pulled his boots off, tossing them carelessly over his shoulder. She sat back on her heels and looked at him, just as he had looked at her a few minutes before. And just as he had been unable to keep from touching her, so too was she forced to reach for him.

She came to him in a rush, her skin like silk against him. He sank one hand into the rich darkness of her hair and pulled her head back for his kiss, while his other arm went around her waist, sliding her deliciously upward along his body. Billie arched into him, listening to the passionate rasp of his breath, feeling the urgent hardness of him beneath her belly, the trembling of the strong arms that clasped her so tightly. She clung to him in helpless abandon, incredibly excited by the turbulent desire she had aroused in him.

He let her slide back to the bed. Before he could lay

her down, however, she put her hands on his chest and murmured, "No, it's my turn now."

"Your turn?" His eyes were heavy-lidded with passion, his chest rising and falling rapidly with his labored breathing.

Billie traced the line of his love-softened mouth with her finger. His tongue darted out to taste it, bringing a shiver to her spine. "Let me touch you," she said softly.

Nick took a deep breath, holding his raging desire at bay with iron self-control. He kissed her palm lingeringly, then put her hand back onto his chest. Lightly, she traced the swelling muscles there, then ran her thumbs across the flat male nipples, drawing in a sharp breath of wonder as they hardened into tiny points.

"So, it happens to you, too!" she murmured.

"Yes." His voice was a strained whisper.

Her hand trailed lower, moving downward over his lean waist and taut belly. His muscles quivered under her palm, and she hesitated.

"Losing your nerve?" he asked, smiling tenderly at her.

She bent her head to hide her flaming face. "A little."

He put his hand beneath her chin and forced her to look at him. "Then I'm going to lay you down and love you until you beg for mercy."

She grasped his wrists. "Not yet." Her hands slid up the coiled muscles of his arms, reveling in his strength, then moved slowly down his ribs to his belly and beyond. Encouraged by his soft groan of pleasure, she clasped the rigid shaft of his manhood.

As she caressed him, his hands moved restlessly over her breasts, lifting their ripe, passion-swollen weight, his fingers teasing the dark pink tips. Suddenly he pulled her hands away from him, lifting her easily and bearing her backward to the bed.

"You're driving me crazy," he rasped, holding himself over her with braced arms.

Billie smiled up at him. Winding her arms around his neck, she pulled him down to her.

"Ahhh, honey!" He claimed her lips, plundering her mouth with gentle savagery, then moved slowly down her body until he reached her breasts. "Now it's my turn," he muttered.

"You had your turn already," she teased.

"I'm taking another." He took her nipple into his mouth, suckling for a moment, then turned his attention to the other.

Billie writhed under him, roused beyond control by the feel of his strong body between her thighs. With a muttered exclamation, he moved lower. His tongue traced a fiery path downward from her navel, then brought a cry from her as it delved into the secret heat below.

"What are you doing?" she gasped, her hands clenching in his hair. Then, as his tongue darted out to taste the warm silk of her again, she let go of him and cried. "Oh! Oh, Nick!" Her hips bucked as a whirlpool of shuddering tremors caught her. But still she needed something, something only he could give. She pulled at his shoulders, urging him to come to her. "Please, Nick!" she murmured.

"Do you want me, Billie?" he asked hoarsely. "Do you want me to love you?"

"Yes, yes, yes!"

He slid up her, and into her. Billie gasped at the feel of him inside her, the potent promise of him. He thrust into her deeply, slowly, savoring her, wanting to bring her to the fever-edge of passion again before giving in to his own needs. Holding her tightly, he rolled over onto his back.

Billie's eyes opened in surprise, then closed again as he grasped her hips, holding her still as he stroked her with his body. She gasped, spreading her fingers out across the flexing muscles of his belly. Unable to hold back, she began moving against him, taking control of the pace of the lovemaking. He let her do what she wanted, his eyes slitted almost closed with passion. Finally, driven beyond his endurance, he clasped her against him, stilling her movements, then rolled over to place her beneath him. He stared down at her for a moment, his face taut with long-restrained desire.

Then he began to move with rhythmic power, driving into her, and she wrapped her legs around his waist to welcome him. A familiar ache built up in her lower body, and her hands moved restlessly on his back as she sought the release she knew was coming.

Driven over the edge of control, Nick buried his face in her hair and thrust into her wildly. As she arched beneath him, crying out, he was caught in his own devastating climax. He clasped her to him, shuddering, calling her name over and over.

He lay on her for a moment, unable to move, then recovered enough to roll to one side. Billie murmured a protest when he moved away, but he brought her with him, tucking her securely against his chest.

"Our first time in a bed," he said.

"Which do you prefer—the ground or the bed?" she asked sleepily.

He chuckled. "Both. Any way I can have you is the best."

"Mmmmm." She nestled against him and was immediately asleep.

Nick kissed her forehead and settled the pillow more comfortably beneath his head. But sleep eluded him. He lay, staring into the darkness, and listened to her quiet breathing. Even now, although he should be exhausted, desire was returning to him.

He looked down at her, marveling at her beauty, at

242

her strength and fiery courage. A thought came to nag him, the notion that perhaps she was enough to sweep aside everything else. Frowning, he pushed the notion away. What the hell had happened to him? He was caught in a deadly game among rustlers and Apaches and mysterious hired guns, and he couldn't afford any distractions. Especially, he mused, remembering how she had lied to him, since he didn't know what role she was playing in this contest of wits and power. Somehow he had to break free of whatever spell she'd cast over him.

Against his will, his hand moved to cover one of her lovely breasts. Her nipple hardened, and she sighed. His manhood stirred. Even asleep, she responded to him. Tomorrow would be time enough to deal with his ambivalent feelings, he decided, bending his head to flick her other nipple with his tongue. Tonight was his.

There was a knock on the door, startling Billie awake. She looked around wildly, but Nick was gone, only a dent in the pillow beside hers to show he'd ever been there.

"Billie!" Helena called, knocking again. "Budge just rode up. Hurry—I think there's something wrong."

"I'm coming!" Billie scrambled into her blouse and split skirt, then pulled her boots on with quick, efficient movements. She headed for the door, then turned back and grabbed her Stetson. If there was trouble, she'd better be ready to ride.

Helena was still waiting, the dark circles under her eyes showing how little sleep she'd gotten. As Billie rushed past, the older woman fell into step beside her, lifting her skirts to give her more freedom of movement.

Reaching the front door at last, Billie flung it open

and stepped outside into the searing sunlight. Budge sat slumped in his saddle, too tired even to dismount. A coating of dust and sweat crusted his face.

"What happened?" Billie demanded.

Nick came around the corner of the house, carrying an earthenware jug. "Let the man have a drink of water first," he said.

The Texan accepted the jug gratefully and tipped his head back to drink. "Thanks," he said, handing it back.

"Well?" Billie asked, her heart going so fast it felt as though it was going to beat its way right out of her chest.

Budge wiped his sleeve over his mouth. "The Apach attacked the herd night before last. Scattered 'em over half the territory."

"Was anyone hurt?" Billie rushed forward to take hold of his horse's bridle.

"Art and Joe are dead, kilt as they stood back to back agin the Injuns. Henry Davalos an' Stubbs was kilt, too, and Reuben and Freeman hurt."

"Oh, God!" Billie closed her eyes for a moment. "How bad are Freeman and Reuben hurt?"

"Bad. We brought 'em back to the house an' sent fer Doc Lessing."

Billie turned to look at Helena, and was surprised to see that Rosswell Stearns had come out and was standing beside his wife.

"Did you hear, Mr. Stearns?" Billie asked.

He nodded.

"I need to borrow two mounts—range horses," she corrected, remembering some of the fancy horseflesh she'd seen in his stable. They were pretty to look at, probably fast, and surely all but useless on the range.

"Of course." The Englishman raised his voice, calling to one of the men at the gate. "Mr. Janssen!

Saddle two of our working horses and bring them here, will you?"

"Thanks. Would you mind if Rachel stays with you for a while?"

"We'd love to have her," Helena said quickly.

"Why can't she go back with you, Billie?" Nick demanded.

"Once Reuben and Freeman are fixed up, we'll be heading out to find the cattle. Once we get them rounded up again, we'll take them straight on to Tucson. I won't be able to spare a man to stay at the ranch with Rachel."

He took her by the arm and pulled her aside. "You can't go out there, not with the Apache on the warpath!"

"I've got to find my cattle." Gently but firmly, she pulled her arm from his grasp. "And this isn't your business."

"Don't be a fool," he growled.

She tipped her head back to look at him. "You can make it your business, if you want to," she said softly.

He knew what she wanted, what she was offering. All he had to do was follow her, to claim her openly, and she would share with him her love and loyalty, even her ranch. But would she? a small, cynical voice whispered in his mind. Remember the lie! Even without that doubt, he knew he couldn't leave the Dolorosa until he'd gotten what he'd come here to find.

"I can't," he said, wishing he could have said anything but that. A muscle jumped in his jaw.

Billie stared at him, unbelieving for a moment. She'd offered everything she had, and he'd turned her down. The lovemaking that had meant so much to her had been just play to him, a tumble in bed with a willing female. The pain in her heart was so bad that it nearly

245

made her sick to her stomach. She turned away lest he see how badly he'd hurt her.

Stearns's hired man came with the horses, and she took the reins of the nearest and swung into the saddle. She waited while Budge changed mounts, then spurred her horse toward the gate, the Texan a length behind her.

Chapter 21

Billie held bandages ready while Doctor Lessing probed Reuben's shoulder for the bullet lodged deep inside.

"There!" the doctor exclaimed, holding up a lump of bloody metal. He tossed it into a nearby bucket in which several other bullets already lay, then began stitching the edges of the wound together. "Why he's still breathing, I'll never know. I've never seen a man take six bullets and live."

"Will he make it?"

Emmett grunted. "It's a roll of the dice. There isn't anywhere for him to go but dead or better." He tied off the thread and stood up. "You can bind him up now."

"Wait." Billie crumpled the bandages nervously. "What about Freeman?"

"He's gut-shot, Billie. There's nothing I can do except give him morphine to ease his dying." He gave Billie a gentle push toward the bed. "Go on, take care of Reuben. I'll sit with Freeman for a while." Shaking his head sadly, the doctor headed toward the bedroom where Freeman Jennings lay.

When Billie finished bandaging the injured man, she sat down at the foot of the bed with the tattered remains of the family Bible on her lap. Its pages had been torn out by the men who had ransacked her house, its cover mutilated, but she had gathered the scattered pieces and wrapped them in a strip of soft deerskin. Now she searched through the loose pages until she found the one where six generations of Meyrick names had been recorded. She wrote in the names of the cowboys who had already died and, after a moment's hesitation, added Freeman Jennings's to the list. Doing so while the man still breathed sent a chill down her spine, but Freeman had no kin and no home but the Star M, and this would be the only record of his brief existence on this earth. Before he died, he'd want to know it had been done.

Tears suddenly sprang to her eyes, making her vision blur. Nick, Nick, Nick! His name seemed to flow through her with every heartbeat. For the hundredth time, she berated herself for being a fool. He turned away from you when you needed him most, she told herself. You have to forget him. But how? The memory of his hands caressing her, his strong, bronzed body pressing her into the mattress, possessing her, loving her, was going to remain with her for a long, long time.

Hearing the creak of wheels outside, she wiped her eyes and hurried to the door to see the Dolorosa's two-wheeled cart just pulling up in front of the house. Nick was driving. Rachel sat on the high seat beside him, a carpetbag on her lap and a frown on her face.

Rosswell Stearns, mounted on one of his handsome, long-legged imported horses, was with them. He touched two fingers to his hat brim. "Good morning, Miss Meyrick."

Billie nodded briefly. "Mr. Stearns."

"I wondered if we might talk," he said.

"Sure." She glanced at Nick, then at Rachel's angry

face. "Would you mind waiting inside for a minute, Mr. Stearns?"

The Englishman dismounted, graceful despite his size, and walked into the house.

Nick propped his foot on the side of the wagon and looked down at Billie. "Hello, Billie," he said. "Are you doing all right?"

"I'll get by," she said, trying to keep her voice from trembling. It made her statement sound flat, even to her. And the tears were so near the surface now that she had to feign anger to keep from bawling out loud. "I told you not to bring her here," she snapped.

"Hah! She doesn't listen any better than you do," Nick growled, irritated that she didn't seem to want any comfort from him. He jumped down from the wagon, then reached up and swung Rachel to the ground.

Rachel put her hands on her hips. "How dare you leave me there!" she cried. "As if I'd allow you to face this alone!"

"You can't stay here right now. It's not safe," Billie said.

"If you can leave Isabel and the children here—"

"I didn't. I sent them to Eliseo's brother's place down in Agua Prieta." Billie flung her arms out in frustration. "Can't you see, Rachel? I've got six men to find nearly two thousand head of cattle that are scattered all over creation. I can't spare anyone to guard you while the rest of us are out on the range."

"Then I'll just have to go with you," Rachel said with placid determination.

Billie glared past her at Nick. "Take her back."

"Take her yourself," he retorted. "I've never seen two such damned stubborn women in all my life."

Rachel sniffed in disdain, then linked arms with Billie and pulled her into the house.

"I'll talk to you later, Billie," Nick called.

Billie grimaced; he made it sound more like a threat than a promise. Infuriating, arrogant man! Even so, the sight of him had made her pulse beat faster and that treacherous molten heat rise into her body. Would she never be free of it? Annoyed, she slammed the door closed behind her.

"May I get you something to drink, Mr. Stearns?" she asked. "Whiskey or water is all we have, I'm afraid."

"Whiskey, please."

His pale gaze flicked to Rachel, who smoothed the front of her skirt and asked, "Billie, do you know where Budge is?"

"He was in the bunkhouse the last time I saw him," Billie said.

"I'll go see if he's still there." Rachel turned to the Englishman. "Thank you for your hospitality, Mr. Stearns."

He nodded. When the door closed behind her, he put his hands flat on the table. "You're in a great deal of trouble, Miss Meyrick."

"Surely you didn't come here just to tell me that, Mr. Stearns."

"No." He smiled briefly, a polite stretching of his lips that had no humor in it. "I feel a certain amount of responsibility toward you. We *are* related, after all."

Billie set a cup of whiskey in front of him and sat down across the table, her arms crossed over her chest. "I'd call it a pretty distant connection, wouldn't you?"

"One can never have too large a family," he said.

Oh, no? she thought. Stearns was fairly oozing affability all of a sudden, and it fit about as well as a saddle on a rattlesnake.

She rubbed her temples with her fingertips. She

really wasn't up to this, not today. "Listen, Mr. Stearns. I'm tired and very busy. I'd appreciate it if you'd get to the point."

"Very well." Stearns took a sip of whiskey. "I want to buy the Star M, Miss Meyrick."

She shook her head. "I'm—"

"Why don't you listen to what I have to offer before you refuse?" He placed his big, square hands on the table in front of him and leaned forward. "If you sell to me, you can buy a house in town—in Tucson, if you would prefer. And I, as your stepfather, will see that you lack for nothing. A life of ease, pretty clothes and, in time, a husband. Your mother would like to see you settled in safety—"

"My ranch is not for sale," Billie snapped.

"My dear, you can't possibly expect to keep it running now! We're in the middle of a drought, you're shorthanded, and your cattle are too scattered to get to market on time."

Billie shrugged. "If you really want to be helpful, lending me about twenty men will do me more good than offering to buy my ranch."

"And leave my own property unprotected? No, Miss Meyrick, I couldn't possibly do that."

Fury rose in her. How dare he! What kind of a sneaky, crawling weasel would wait until she was down, refuse to help, then try to buy her property? She hid her hands in her lap so he wouldn't see how they trembled.

"Surely you must understand my position, Miss Meyrick," he said.

Her gaze locked with his. For a frozen moment they stared at each other, assessing one another's strength, searching for one another's weaknesses. Slowly, Billie nodded. This was war. He wanted something from her, and would stop at nothing to get it.

"I understand," she said.

He rose to his feet and reached for his hat. "My offer stands. But don't wait too long to change your mind." A hard note crept into his voice. "Yours wouldn't be the first property I've acquired because the owner couldn't meet his financial obligations."

Billie tilted her head back to stare at him. "Just because I don't fill my house with fancy gadgets doesn't mean I'm poor."

"I never said you were," he replied, raising his eyebrows. "But I'm worried about you. With the rustlers taking so much of your stock, I wonder how you'll hold on to your property."

With iron self-control, she wrestled her temper into submission. Anger would only give him an advantage; to beat him, she had to think like him—cold and sneaky. "You're a real thoughtful fellow, Mr. Stearns," she said, her voice emotionless. "But I'll manage somehow. No one is going to take this ranch from me. Not the rustlers, not anybody."

"Very well, Miss Meyrick."

Stearns gave her a slight bow before striding to the door. Billie stared at him, surprised. It had been an almost courtly gesture, not at all mocking as she would have expected. What was the meaning of it? she wondered as she followed him outside. Acknowledgment of her declaration of war? What a strange man! A shiver of fear went through her. He had money, men, resources she'd give her right arm to possess. How was she going to stop him? In that moment, she felt more alone than she'd ever felt in her life.

Nick, who had been leaning against the side of the cart, straightened. He couldn't tell if their conversation had gone well or not, for Billie's face was as impassive

252

as Stearns's. Had they argued, or had they come to some sort of agreement?

Stearns swung into the saddle. "Coming, Mr. Larabee?"

"In a minute."

"Don't be long." Stearns's gaze swung to Billie. "I am glad, Miss Meyrick, that we had the opportunity to have this conversation. It makes things much easier for both of us, does it not?" He smiled then, the first genuine smile Billie had ever seen on his face.

Billie smiled back, although she would rather have screamed her anger to the sky. "It was real enlightening, Mr. Stearns," she said. Pa would have shot his fancy ass, she thought savagely, damning herself for being a woman, damning herself for being too soft to do what ought to be done.

"Farewell." The Englishman spurred his horse into a canter, and soon disappeared over the ridge.

Nick's eyebrows went up. Well, they surely seemed to be pleased with one another, he mused. I wonder what kind of deal they've cooked up? The very thought made him furious. How dare she hook up with that cold bastard?

"Did you get what you wanted out of him?" he asked, taking a grip on her elbow.

She tried unsuccessfully to pull away. "Get your hand off me," she snapped. He'd made his choice. Now he could damn well stay out of her business.

Nick took a firmer hold on her arm and stalked toward the relative privacy of the spring, pulling her behind him like a recalcitrant child. He sat her down on a rock and stood in front of her, his legs spread belligerently.

Why did he keep involving himself in her life? he wondered. Why did her face, her body, the memory of their loving haunt his days and make his nights unbearable?

"What did Stearns talk to you about?" he demanded.

"What makes you think it's any of your business?"

"I told you once, Billie, that everything you do is my business," he said, leaning over her intimidatingly.

"Things have changed." *You* changed them, she thought bitterly. I offered you everything I had, and you turned away. She needed him more than anyone she'd ever known, and he had let her down.

Nick clenched his fists. He wanted to take her in his arms and promise to make everything right. He wanted to love her, to protect her, to stand with her against the rest of the world. But he couldn't, even if she would have let him. The souls of his murdered family cried out for justice, and by God, he was going to see that they got it.

"Is Pat Conway still here?" he asked.

She nodded.

"You can have him for as long as you need him," he said, keeping his voice cool with an effort. "Stearns won't miss him. I've been paying him out of my own pocket."

Billie looked up at him in surprise. Then her eyes narrowed. "Oh, really? Are you starting your own little army?" she asked.

Nick groaned inwardly at his slip. His concern for her safety was making him careless. "You sure are nosy," he said, his brows contracting in a scowl.

"So you've told me before." Ah, but then he'd been teasing. And then she'd thought he wanted her. She looked at him, noting the anger that flared in his eyes. She remembered other emotions she'd seen in him— passion and caring and teasing humor, and her heart twisted with pain for what she'd lost. No, she corrected herself firmly, what she'd never had. She lifted her chin defiantly. "I don't see where Pat is going to be of any help to me."

"He can guard Rachel. I don't want her out on the range right now. It's too dangerous." He didn't want Billie out there, either, but he knew it was useless to say so. He shook his head, stopping the protest he knew was coming. "If you won't let him stay at the house, he'll be guarding her from out here. Take your pick, Billie."

"All right, damn it!" she hissed. Cold rage filled her, closing her throat against words. Well, that surely ought to tell her exactly where she stood with him! There was a knot in her stomach, and in her heart. She turned on her heel and marched back toward the house.

Nick caught up with her, grabbing her arm and spinning her around to face him. "Don't walk away from me!"

"What is it?" she asked coldly, holding her arm far out to the side so his hand wouldn't make contact with any other part of her body.

He scowled down at her. By God, she was spoiling for a fight! Well, if that's what she wanted, that was what she'd get. "As soon as things don't go your way, you go stomping off, cussing me under your breath."

"Maybe I'm just tired of you telling me what to do," she hissed.

"Somebody has to try and talk some sense into you!"

"How's this for sense: you stay out of my business and I'll stay out of yours. That ought to solve both our problems." She jerked her arm out of his grasp.

He clamped his hand on her shoulder before she could slip away from him. "I'm not finished with you," he growled.

She glared at him over her shoulder, and the violence in her green eyes made him take his hand from her arm. "Yes, you are," she said.

This time he let her go. He watched her disappear into the house, then turned away, raking his hand through his hair in frustration.

With a muttered curse, he stalked back to the wagon, intending to return to the Dolorosa and try to forget the whole thing ever happened. It would be even better if he could forget Billie, too, but he knew that was impossible. She was in his blood, in his heart, and he'd never be able to get rid of her. Fool! he told himself savagely. You're a grown man. You can handle your emotions. Ride away. Ride away, and don't look back.

Billie left the door open a crack so she could watch him go. She saw Rachel come around the corner of the house and stop him as he climbed into the wagon. The two talked, their heads close together, then Rachel put her arms around him and held him close. And Nick responded, his arms going around Rachel in a tight hug, his head bent solicitiously over hers. Then he put her aside gently and climbed into the cart. With a flick of the reins, he started the team moving, leaving Rachel staring after him.

Billie closed the door softly and went back to Reuben. She sat down on the bed again and clutched the Bible to her chest, unaware that tears were coursing down her face.

". . . 'And we commit his body to the ground; earth to earth, ashes to ashes, dust to dust.'" Billie tossed a handful of dry Arizona soil onto Freeman Jennings's grave. "Good-bye, Freeman," she murmured, tears stinging her eyes.

Rachel bent to tie a silk rose, salvaged from her

slashed gown, to the simple wood cross at the head of the grave. Then she straightened and took Billie's arm. "He was so young," she murmured. It's such a shame."

Billie thought of the four graves out on the range, lonely resting places for the other Star M men who had died. "It's a waste, is what it is," she said, unshed tears making her throat ache. "Twenty years old, and a gentler, quieter man there never was."

Glancing over her shoulder, she saw Budge and the other cowboys lined up behind her, their hats in their hands. "He was their friend," she said. "Let's leave them alone for a while."

They returned to the house, arm in arm, drawing comfort from each other.

"When do we leave for Tucson?" Rachel asked, pouring herself a cup of coffee before sitting down at the table.

"The day after tomorrow. Reuben says he can stand a few hours' travel; we'll drop him off at the Triple Tree Ranch on our way. They'll take care of him for us."

Rachel spread her hands out on the tabletop. "The house will be unprotected while we're gone. What if those men come back looking for whatever they missed the first time?"

"The herd is more important than the house right now. Now that we've got the cattle rounded up, I want to get them into Tucson before something else happens. We'll just have to take a chance . . . who's that?" Hearing the sound of galloping hoofbeats, Billie ran to the door.

Rachel peered over Billie's shoulder. "It's Squint! I wonder what's wrong?"

The cowboy pulled his mount to a halt in front of the house and swung down from the saddle. "I found Lew Purcell out on the west range," he gasped. "Dead. Shot in the head."

Billie closed her eyes for a moment. Poor Lew! Then she opened them and asked, "You didn't bring him in?"

"Nope. There wasn't enough . . ." Squint glanced at Rachel and cleared his throat. "Coyotes been at him. I buried him right where I found him."

"You did the only thing you could," Billie said. "Go get something to eat, if you can. I'll tell Budge."

Rachel turned away, holding her apron to her mouth. Billie didn't feel too well herself, but she retrieved her hat and headed toward the knot of men gathered beside Freeman's grave. Quickly, she told them what had happened.

"Gettin' so there's more dead men than live in this here territory," Budge waid. His voice was calm, but fury lit his pale eyes. "What you plannin' to do, Billie?"

"I've got to go to the Dolorosa and tell them what's happened," she said.

The Texan shook his head. "Not alone." He poked his thumb toward Creek Beuther. "Saddle up, Creek. You're goin' with her. The rest of ya'll git out on the range. You see anybody—anybody, hear?—who ain't supposed to be there, you start askin' some hard questions."

"But take it easy," Billie warned. "No shooting unless you have to. We don't want the territory going up in flames around our ears."

Even as she said it, she realized that it already might be too late.

Chapter 22

Nick walked down the hallway toward Rosswell Stearns's study, not trying to hide especially, but not making any noise, either. He paused outside the door and took a quick glance up and down the hallway before slipping inside. Catching movement out of the corner of his eye, he dropped into a crouch and drew his gun.

"Oh!" Julia gasped, stepping away from the desk hurriedly.

Nick straightened and slid the pistol back into the holster. "What are you doing in here?" he asked.

"What are *you* doing here?" she countered.

"I just wanted to find out why you sneaked into your father's study." It was an out-and-out lie, but he couldn't very well admit that he was here to snoop, just as she was.

She drew herself up. "I did not sneak. I have a perfect right to be here."

"Yeah?" Nick's eyebrows went up. "I'll just ask him about it when he gets back, then."

"No, don't do that!"

"Then tell me what you were looking for," he said.

"If you must know, I was looking for money.

Enough money to get me back to England. I can't stand this horrible, barbaric place a moment longer, and Father refuses to let me leave!"

He threw back his head and laughed. "You're really something, Julia. Robbing your own father!"

"It's his own fault." She came around the desk and put her arms around his neck. "Help me, Nick. He's got thousands in here somewhere. We can go together!"

"I don't want to live in England."

She pressed herself against him, running her lips along the line of his jaw. "Then we'll go somewhere else. Anywhere you want!" Her hand strayed downward along his chest, deftly unbuttoning his shirt. She reached beneath the fabric to caress the muscles of his chest. "I can make you happy, Nick."

Despite the brazen wantonness of her actions, Nick could sense no desire in her. Truly, he thought, she was as cold as her father, understanding other people's emotions only as a means to further her own ends. Whatever else Billie might be, at least her passion was honest and warm and human.

As Julia's hand moved lower to unbuckle his belt, Nick grasped her by the shoulders and pushed her out to arm's length. "No, thanks."

"Still enamored of the Meyrick chit?" She smiled and leaned her weight against his hands. "I can make you forget her."

"I doubt it," he said, showing the edges of his teeth in a contemptuous smile. "You can't hold a candle to her."

"Indeed!" She pulled away. "And just what is it you like about her?" she sneered. "Is it her bovine charms, or perhaps her filthy language that attracts you? It certainly isn't her innocence, not with all those men she lives with. Which one—or rather, which ones—were before you?" She laughed shrilly. "Perhaps that is what excites you! I've heard that some men actually prefer—"

"Shut your damned foul mouth!" he growled, grasping her wrists in a painful hold.

The door swung open. Nick turned, still holding Julia's wrists, and saw Billie standing on the threshold. He let the English girl go abruptly.

Billie's stunned gaze took in Julia's flushed face, Nick's unbuckled belt and the shirt that gaped open, showing most of his muscular chest. How could he! She ought to slap his face, shoot him, anything! But her feet might as well have been nailed to the floor; she could only stare stupidly, held frozen by the pain in her heart.

Julia smoothed her hair. "Well, I had better be going. We'll finish this . . . discussion later, Nick."

She stopped in front of Billie, a mocking smile on her face. "You really shouldn't blame him for looking elsewhere, Miss Meyrick," she said, indicating Billie's faded blue blouse and homemade skirt. "You should take better care of yourself if you want to hold on to a man." With a malicious laugh, Julia brushed past and walked slowly down the corridor.

Billie hardly even heard her. Her attention was focused on Nick. He didn't even have the decency to put his clothing to rights, but stood with his hands on his hips, staring at her as if she, not he, were in the wrong.

To her surprise, there was no anger in her, only a sort of cold despair. It gave her a strange sense of clarity, allowing her to see at last what sort of man he really was, and how little the gift of her body and heart had meant to him. She clung to that thought, for it gave her the strength to meet his gaze with dignity. There would be no shouting this time, no opportunity for comfort or reconciliation.

"Spreading yourself kind of thin, aren't you, Nick?" she asked. First her, then Rachel—or was it the other way around—and now Julia. Drifter, moving from woman to woman just to change the scenery.

"It isn't what you think," he said. Somehow he had to make her understand. The look in her green eyes tore at his guts. Anger he could take from her, even hatred, but not this chill dignity that rose between them like a shield.

"Then why are you all but undressed?" Billie was proud to hear that her voice didn't tremble at all. "I don't think even Rachel would believe you now."

"Rachel has nothing to do with this," he growled. "She's only—"

"Another woman you were playing with, just like me." Billie was suddenly very tired. Tired of fighting him, tired of loving him. "You don't have to explain. I understand."

Nick wanted her to shout, cry, anything but this dry-eyed, dead-voiced calm. He had told himself he wanted to break with her. He'd ridden away from the Star M determined not to have anything more to do with her, no matter how badly it hurt. But not like this. Not with her thinking that their loving had been nothing but a game, or that she'd been nothing but a convenient partner. He had watched her blossom with every touch, every kiss, realizing her womanhood right before his eyes. And now it had all been taken from her. By him.

"Billie—" he began.

"I don't want to hear it, Nick. There's nothing for either of us to say any longer." There was a knot of pain in her chest. She had to get out of here before she suffered the final humiliation of tears. Whatever else he might think of her, she wasn't about to let him pity her. "I didn't come here to talk about this," she said. "I came

262

to tell Stearns that we found Lew Purcell's body out on our west range."

"Lew!"

She nodded. "He'd been shot in the head."

Nick let his breath out in a sigh. Lew had been a good, honest man and a top cowhand. More, he had been trailing the rustlers, determined to find out who'd been skimming some of the Dolorosa's best stock. Perhaps he'd gotten too close. Another debt to be paid, Nick vowed. How many more was he going to have to add to his list? He began buttoning his shirt. "I'll go get him. He'd want to be buried here."

"It's already been done."

He lunged forward and grabbed her by the shoulders. "Why? What didn't you want me to see?"

Billie stood stiffly between his hands. "A body that the coyotes—"

"Goddamn it to hell!" His fingers clenched and unclenched on her shoulders. "Billie, listen to me. I want you to—"

"No!" A wave of white-hot fury tore through her, sweeping the icy calm away in a whirlpool of hurt and outrage. "I've done a whole lot more listening to you than is good for me. You're a liar and a cheat. No more, Nick!"

"Now just a damned minute—"

"Stay away from me, and stay away from Rachel. We deserve better than you!" Her chest heaved. "If you set foot on my ranch again, I swear I'll shoot you!"

She tore out of his grasp and ran for the front door. Nick started after her, but was forced to stop and fasten his belt lest he lose his pants on the way. That few seconds' head start gave Billie the chance to mount and whip her horse into a gallop before he made it out of the house.

"Close that gate!" Nick roared.

The men hastened to obey. But Billie spurred her horse, scattering the guards as she pounded toward the barrier. The horse sailed over the five-foot gate without hesitation, and soon the fleeing pair disappeared over the nearest hill in a cloud of dust. Creek Beuther stood, openmouthed with surprise, and stared at the spot where his employer had vanished.

"In a damned sidesaddle!" one of the men shouted in admiration.

"What the hell . . . ?" Creek Beuther said, recovering enough to reach for his gun.

Nick grabbed his arm. "Relax, Creek. It's something personal between Billie and me."

"Yeah? Well, it sounds damn strange to me." The cowboy jammed his hat on his head and swung into his saddle.

Nick waved for the guards to open the gate. "It *is* damned strange," he muttered. Although every fiber in his body urged him to follow Billie, he forced himself to turn back to the house. He had a job to do.

The Star M seemed deserted when Billie rode up, not even a thread of smoke coming from the chimney. Stopping her mount some distance away, she drew her pistol and approached the house on foot.

She eased the door open a crack and peered inside, then straightened in shock. Budge and Rachel were sitting at the table—or rather, Budge was sitting at the table and Rachel was sitting on his lap, her arms around his neck.

As Billie watched, the girl pushed the Texan's hat off his head and pressed her lips to his. Budge's arms, until now held stiffly at his sides, went around Rachel as he began kissing her back. Then he stood up with the girl still clasped in his arms and turned toward the bedroom.

Billie closed the door silently and sat down in the dust outside. "Budge?" she whispered, numb with astonishment. "It was Budge?"

She brought her knees up and rested her chin on them. This was surely a day for revelations, she thought. She'd been so sure that Rachel was in love with Nick, and half convinced at times that he'd returned her love. In a way, that had been easier to accept than the fact that he was just a rutting tomcat looking for a few hours' fun.

With a muttered curse, she rose to her feet and went to unsaddle her horse. She'd never understand, never. What was wrong with her that she couldn't win Nick's love? What did Julia have that she didn't? Was it the feminine airs, the batting eyelashes and shrill giggles?

"What does he want?" she asked the horse. "Is it the fancy clothes and the fancy manners? Or her daddy's money?" The animal turned and snorted into her hair as though to comfort her. Tears rolled down her cheeks, infuriating her, and she dashed them away with the back of her hand.

Damn that stupid party! she raged inwardly, taking the reins and leading the horse into the corral. It brought him into her arms one last, disastrous time, deluding her, making her think she could possibly compete with women who'd spent their lives learning how to catch a husband. And damn Nick, too! He was as bad as Helena, judging people for what they wore or what they had, not whether they had a good heart.

"Damn him, damn him!" Her hands working with rapid, agitated movements, she rubbed the horse down with a piece of blanket.

That chore done, she climbed to the top rail of the corral and looked out over the valley, trying to submerge her sadness in the beauty of her land. But the scenery was blurred by the tears that kept welling into her eyes no matter how she tried to keep them back.

Creek rode into view. Determined not to show how hurt she was, she pressed the heels of her hands against her eyes. She was Anton Meyrick's daughter! No man was going to break her! She had her ranch, and that would have to be enough. By the time Creek reached the corral, she had herself under control.

"I might has well have tried to ketch a sandstorm," the cowboy complained.

"Sorry." Reaching up, she tossed her braid back over her shoulder. "Why don't you get yourself some rest before heading out to the range?"

"Yes, ma'am." He unsaddled his mount and turned it into the corral, then strode toward the bunkhouse.

Billie noticed a plume of smoke rising from the chimney. With a sigh, she climbed down from the fence and headed for the house. Budge came out just as she reached the front door, a look of consternation crossing his sun-browned face when he saw her.

"How long ya'll been back?" he growled.

"Long enough."

"Cain't a feller have any privacy a'tall?" he asked.

"Not when I have to spend the afternoon in the corral because I don't dare go in my own house."

"Scamp." He scowled at her with mock ferocity. "You ain't too old fer a hidin'."

Billie forced herself to smile, not wanting to lessen his happiness with her own low spirits. "I'm happy for you, Budge. She's a fine girl." Reaching up, she patted him on the cheek before going inside.

Rachel was puttering with the stove. Without turning around, she asked, "Did you forget something, darling?"

"Yeah," Billie drawled.

"Oh!" Rachel whirled. "You surprised me!"

"No more than you surprised me." Billie put her hands on her hips. "So it's Budge you love."

"Oh, yes. Ever since I first met him, when he . . ."— Rachel's face turned a pretty shade of pink—"when he offered to shoot those men who killed my family."

After a moment of atonishment, Billie doubled over with laughter. "Oh! Oh, Rachel! And I thought you were such a proper, civilized lady!" She wiped her streaming eyes. "You sure had me fooled. And Budge! I'd never have guessed he was pursuing you."

"He wasn't." Rachel smiled. "He was being respectful. *I* was the one who did the chasing."

"I thought you loved Nick," Billie said.

"Nick?" It was Rachel's turn to laugh. If only Billie knew! Oh, the trouble Nick was going to be in when she found out! "Oh, no. I care very much for him, but I could never be in love with him!"

Billie turned away. Too bad she couldn't say the same; loving Nick Larabee was mighty hard on a girl's heart

Chapter 23

It was getting dark. All that could be seen of the sun was a thin, fiery crescent barely peeking over the jagged silhouette of the mountains. A wagon lurched along the faint track leading to the Star M, its vastly elongated shadow rushing ahead of it as though impatient to reach its destination.

Hearing Budge's warning whistle, Billie stepped out of the house, her rifle held ready. "Can you see who it is?" she called to the Texan.

"Not with the sun behind 'em." Budge led his mare from the corral and saddled her quickly. "I'll go take a look," he said.

He rode out to meet the wagon. After a moment he wheeled his mount and galloped back to the house. A young boy was sitting behind him, clutching the Texan's belt.

"Why, it's Shep Harndon!" Billie cried. "Is that your ma coming?"

"Yes, ma'am," Shep said, sliding down from his perch. He came to stand in front of Billie. "Garve and Sulie, too."

Billie put her hand on the boy's shoulder. Thirteen years old, she thought, and already he was taller than she was. "Did something happen, Shep?" she asked.

"We was burned out night afore last. Apach." There was no youth left in his eyes, only bitterness. "Pa's dead. If'n Ma and we'uns wasn't visiting the Greenhows' we'd all have been kilt."

Billie glanced up at Budge. "Tell Rachel to put her things in my room. She can bunk with me while they're here."

Budge nodded and swung down from the saddle. Keeping her hand on Shep's shoulder, Billie waited until the wagon rolled to a stop in front of the house.

The woman laid the reins aside. "Shep tell you?" she asked, her voice harsh with fatigue.

"Yes. I'm sorry, Emma Lee." Billie took the reins and tied the team to the hitching post. "Are the children sleeping?" she asked.

Emma Lee nodded, pointing to the back of the wagon where two small bundles lay. Slowly, she climbed down from the wagon. She was a spare woman in her midthirties, her strong, plain face already deeply etched by a lifetime of hard work.

"Come inside, Emma Lee," Billie said. "Dinner's ready."

"Thanks. Shep, bring the young 'uns in."

Billie led the way, pointing out the room that was to be the newcomers'. She pushed Emma Lee into a chair, while Rachel went to help Shep put the children to bed.

It was a quiet meal; Emma Lee, never much of a talker, was even quieter than usual. She kept her gaze on her plate most of the time, eating mechanically.

Shep tried to push his food away, but his mother looked up briefly and said, "Eat, son. You got to keep your strength up. I'm dependin' on you."

When the meal was over, Rachel left the room, murmuring that she wanted to check on the children again.

270

Budge took Shep outside with him, leaving Billie alone with Emma Lee.

Billie poured two cups of thick, steaming coffee and brought them to the table. When she was seated again, she asked, "What do you want me to do for you, Emma Lee? Shall we bury Eustace for you?"

"Shep an' me already took care of Eustace," the older woman said. "I want you to buy my ranch. I cain't run it myself, not with three young 'uns."

Billie stared at her, astonished. "Buy your ranch? Emma Lee, didn't you hear about my herd?"

"I heard." Emma Lee clasped her square, work-hardened hands on the table before her. "Whatever you kin afford will do."

"Emma Lee—"

"Let me finish, Billie. You see, I only want you to buy it for a while. Then I'll be wanting it back."

"I don't understand."

"I don't 'spect you do," Emma Lee said. "That fancy Englishman was out to see us today—"

"Stearns!"

"Yep. He wanted to buy me out. I tell you, Billie, Eustace wasn't hardly cold!"

Billie clenched her fists. First her, then the Harndons. Just what was Stearns after, an empire? On reflection, she decided that maybe he was.

Emma Lee took a sip of coffee. "I got kin in Kaintuck who'll take care of me and the young 'uns. But Shep says he wants the place someday, and I got to figger a way to keep it for him. Now, I seen fellers like that Englishman before. They don't come at you from the front. No, they git you in the back, all legal and proper. They git in cahoots with the bankers, the lawyers 'n the sheriff, an' the next thing you know, papers get all messed up, payments get lost, God knows

271

what-all. I'll lose the place before I ever hear there's trouble."

"But, Emma Lee—"

"You buy my ranch," Emma Lee said stubbornly. "You ain't Anton Meyrick's daughter for nothin'. You'll hang onto my place, if anybody kin. An' Shep will come back when he's sixteen an' pay you every cent he owes you."

Billie chewed her lip thoughtfully. Emma Lee was putting her son's future in her hands, trusting her to preserve it for him. The Harndons had been her neighbors for more than ten years. They had shared hardships most people couldn't even understand. They were the same kind, a kinship of survival that went beyond friendship. "How much do you need?" she asked.

"Whatever you kin pay," the older woman said. "I'll get by."

Billie nodded. "All right. Tomorrow we'll go into town and draw up the papers."

"Thank you kindly." Gracelessly, but with great dignity, Emma Lee rose to her feet and went into the bedroom.

Billie poured another cup of coffee and propped her elbows on the table. She knew she had no business taking on the responsibility of another ranch, not when the success of her own was by no means assured. But she'd agreed to do it, and the thought of thwarting Rosswell Stearns was nearly as gratifying as helping a neighbor in need.

She sighed. Maybe Emma Lee had enough confidence in her to ride away, leaving everything in her hands, but Billie knew things weren't going to be quite as easy as the other woman thought. Emma Lee had said that any amount of money would be enough, but she had no way of knowing just how hard up for cash Billie was just now. After she paid her cowboys—an expense that couldn't be delayed for anything—it would be all she could to pay the Harndons' fares to Kentucky.

In sudden decision, Billie stood up and collected her hat, rifle and bedroll, then slipped out of the house. Pa's gold had been sitting in a hole in the ground for years. It was time it did someone some good. She'd managed all this time without it, after all; why not let Emma Lee have the use of it?

She saddled one of the horses, a sturdy gelding whose one bad habit had earned him the name Chomper. Just as she put her foot in the stirrup, the horse twisted his head to look at her. "Don't even think about it," she whispered, doubling her hand into a fist.

Chomper faced forward obediently, knowing Billie would be certain to carry out her threat. A moment later she was in the saddle and urging him north, into the hills.

An hour later, she turned him into the mouth of Desolado Canyon. After tethering him to the twisted branch of a mesquite tree, she walked slowly into the fissure, carefully counting her paces. Her boots kicked up little gouts of dust, pale clouds in the faint moonlight.

"Five, six, seven . . . where the hell is it?" she muttered, peering into the shadows at the base of the cliff wall. Suddenly she straightened, spying a cat-shaped rock above her, crouched precariously at the top of the cliff as though ready to spring at any moment. "Ah! There it is!"

She fell to her knees in the dust directly below the rock and began to dig. A foot below the surface she uncovered a small deerskin pouch. It was heavy, and clinked when she hefted it.

"I'm sorry I have to use this, Pa," she murmured. But even as she said the words, she realized that Anton would have agreed with what she was doing.

She slipped the pouch into the pocket of her jacket. Working quickly now, she pushed the loose dirt back into the hole and smoothed it over.

When she returned to the spot where she'd left Chomper, she saw a woman standing beside the horse. Her hair gleamed like polished ebony in the moonlight.

"Greetings, Laughing Woman," Billie said in Chiricahua.

The Apache woman stepped forward and put her hands on Billie's shoulders. "Greetings, Cactus Flower."

"How did you find me?"

"I followed you. I have been waiting to speak to you, but there have always been others nearby." Laughing Woman dropped her hands to her sides and regarded Billie quietly, as though assessing her mood. Then she said, "It is always thus between us, is it not? Always this small bit of friendship in the midst of the hatreds of men."

Billie nodded, then reached out to clasp her friend's arm briefly. "What was so important to tell me that you followed me all the way out here?"

"It was not the Apache who burned that woman's house, Cactus Flower."

"What?" Billie stared at her in astonishment. "Then who did?"

"I do not know," Laughing Woman said. "But there is danger for you. Come." She faded quickly into the shadows, heading for the mouth of the canyon.

Billie hurried after her. The Apache woman led her to a nearby arroyo. Billie leaned over the side and saw a man's body lying at the bottom, his sprawled limbs dark against the pale sand. An arrow stood out from the middle of his back.

The skin at the back of Billie's neck crawled. Pushing

274

her nervousness aside, she climbed down into the arroyo and turned the corpse over. She didn't recognize him, but she knew his type all too well. Gun for hire.

Laughing Woman pointed to the corpse. "He followed you, I followed him."

Billie wiped her hands on her jeans. She realized that Laughing Woman—or whoever was with her—had probably just saved her life.

"There was another man as well, but he went that way"—the Indian woman pointed west—"leaving this one to track you."

"Can you take me to the spot where they separated?" Billie asked.

"Yes."

Billie tossed her braid back over her shoulder, impatient to get started. "Where's your horse?"

Laughing Woman disappeared into a nearby canyon. She reappeared a few moments later, mounted on the bare back of a piebald mare.

Billie retrieved Chomper and swung into the saddle. "You don't have to tell . . . anyone where you're going?" she asked, restraining the impulse to look around; the only Apache who could be seen was one who wanted to be seen.

Laughing Woman smiled. "No, they will know."

"Come on, then," Billie said, urging Chomper forward. "They," Laughing Woman had said! Just how many Apaches were trailing them, anyway? Again the skin on the back of Billie's neck crawled, but she managed not to look behind her.

The spot where the men had separated was about two miles back toward the ranch. Billie dismounted to see the tracks more closely, and saw that one of their horses had a notch in its left front hoof.

Billie crouched to touch the distinctive track. "This

was one of the men who broke into my house."

"You are in even greater danger than I thought, then." The Indian woman drew in a sharp breath. "These men—they were looking for you?"

Billie reached into her pocket to touch the bag of gold coins. "No. Something else." She rose to her feet. "I'm going to follow him."

"Be careful, Cactus Flower."

"I'm always careful." As the Apache woman turned her mount and began to move away, Billie called after her softly. "Thanks. I'll return the favor some day."

Laughing Woman raised her hand in acknowledgment, but didn't turn around. A moment later she disappeared around the side of a nearby ridge.

Billie trailed the man deep into the hills. Seeing the faroff glow of a campfire at last, she tethered Chomper and approached on foot. When she was close enough to smell their meat cooking, she dropped to her stomach and wormed her way as close as she dared.

She counted three men. Beyond them were the shapes of several horses, but it was too dark to see how many there were. Carefully, she scanned the surrounding rocks, but she could see no sign of a guard.

She eased her rifle forward and aimed at one of those man-shaped silhouettes between her and the light of the fire. If only she had Nick's Henry repeating rifle, she could drop all three before they knew what was happening.

Her target moved, and she eased her pressure on the trigger. A moment later he sat down again. Billie drew a bead on the center of his body. Was it his back or his chest? she wondered. Sweat broke out on her forehead.

"It's no different from shooting the Apaches when they attacked the house," she muttered, settling her

276

elbows more firmly against the ground. But it *was* different; before, she had been protecting her home and family. This was cold-blooded killing.

"Pa would," she told herself in a fierce whisper. "It's the only sensible thing to do."

Her finger tightened on the trigger. Then, with a curse, she lowered the rifle. She couldn't do it, couldn't plant a bullet in a man's back without giving him a chance to defend himself. It was stupid, and she would probably regret it. If Pa were here, he'd turn away from her in disgust.

She squirmed backward until she was far enough away to stand up, then made her way quietly toward the far side of the camp where the men had tied their horses. The least she could do was run off their mounts.

As she slipped around the eastern end of the area, she heard a horse whicker softly at her from the darkness beneath a grove of piñon pines. She followed the noise, to find Beelzebub tethered to a low hanging branch. Her knees grew weak as she realized the extent of Nick's betrayal. He'd been rustling her cattle while he'd been making love to her! The bastard!

Beelzebub nuzzled her, his breath blowing hot through her shirt. "Not getting along with one of the other horses, hmmm?" she whispered absently. "Is that why you're out here?"

She was so furious that she was hardly aware that she was babbling nonsense into the horse's uncaring ear. By God, she thought, she'd make Nick pay for doing this to her!

Whirling, she peered toward the campfire, trying to distinguish Nick from the others. But the men had retired to their blankets and it was impossible to know one from another. Then she untied Beelzebub's reins and tossed them around the saddle horn so as not to trip up the big horse when he took off.

He moved a few steps and began placidly cropping the few straggling blades of grass that still survived. Billie slipped through the shadows to the spot where the rustlers' horses were tied. She slid her knife out of her boot. One of the men stirred, mumbling, and she froze. But he settled back down, and she quickly cut the tether rope before hurrying back behind cover.

When she was out of sight of the camp, she aimed her pistol over the horses' heads and squeezed off three shots in quick succession. Instant bedlam arose. Squealing, bucking horses burst through the middle of the camp, one jumping clear over the fire in his panic to get away. The men cursed and dodged the flailing hooves.

Under the cover of the noise, Billie ran back to the spot where she had left Beelzebub. To her surprise, the stallion was still there. But he was extremely nervous, and sidled away from her when she approached. She fired another shot into the air, and the stallion reared. With a bugle of fright, he whirled and plunged into the darkness.

"That'll fix you, Nick Larabee," she muttered as she ran toward her own mount.

"Oh, yeah?" he growled, appearing out of the shadows and catching her arm in a numbing grip.

Billie gasped. With her free hand, she raked for his eyes, only to have him knock her hand aside easily.

There was a crashing in the brush behind them. "Come on," he hissed, pulling her after him ungently. "Where did you leave your horse?"

"I hear 'em!" one of the men shouted. "This way, boys!"

"Over there," Billie gasped, pointing to the left. This was not the time to argue, not with the other men not twenty yards behind them. But she intended to settle up with him later. Oh, yes, indeed!

Nick let go of her hand when she began to run with him. As they neared the spot where Chomper waited, she pulled slightly ahead of Nick and swung into the saddle, intending to leave him behind if she could. Before she could urge the horse into motion, however, Nick had vaulted up behind her.

"Move," he growled.

Billie spurred Chomper into a gallop. Their pursuers howled in rage, firing their pistols as they ran. But the fleeing pair soon disappeared behind a hill and the shouts faded behind them.

After a few miles, Billie slowed the horse to a walk. She could feel Nick's hands on her waist. The firm possessiveness of his grip made her furious all over again.

"What were you doing there?" she asked. Go ahead, she thought, lie to me again! But I know you now, Nick Larabee, and it's not going to work.

"I was watching them," he said.

"You do an awful lot of watching. I don't suppose it ever occurred to you to actually *do* something about them?"

"Like shoot them in the back?" he asked softly.

Billie stiffened, but before she could get a word out, he added, "I saw the moonlight reflecting off the barrel of your rifle. Damn, but I was furious at whatever fool was out here messing things up. But I was on the other hillside and couldn't work my way around fast enough." His hands tightened. "If I'd known it was you—"

"Messing what up?" she demanded, prying at his fingers ineffectually with her free hand. "Your little deal with the rustlers, maybe?"

"I was planning to use my head, you little fool! I was going to trail them tomorrow to see if I could find their hideout."

"Sure you were." Billie's lip curled contemptuously. Oh, his words made sense! If another man had spoken them, she might even have believed them. "Get your hands off me," she hissed, raking the back of his hand with her nails.

With a swift movement, he captured her clawing hand and pinned it to her thigh. "Damn it, Billie, are you out of your mind, going after those men alone?"

She shrugged.

He took a deep, calming breath, then another. "Do you know what would have happened if they'd caught you? Do you have any idea what they would have done to you?"

"What the hell do you care?" she hissed.

Ah, he thought, Julia. He cursed under his breath, damning the English girl for her sly machinations. "There's nothing between Julia and me."

Billie jerked in surprise. In her outrage about his more serious betrayal, she'd forgotten that little scene with Julia. Her anger went up another notch. "Oh, really?" She gave him a scathing look over her shoulder. "You must really think I'm stupid." But why shouldn't he? she asked herself harshly. Even now, when he'd shown himself to be the worst sort of rogue imaginable, she couldn't stop herself from loving him.

"I'm telling you the truth," he said, striving for patience. If this were any other woman, he wouldn't bother to explain himself. But her closeness was already having an effect on him, making him overly aware of the clean, fresh scent of her hair and the delicious curves of her body. "I'd caught her snooping in her father's office, and she was trying to distract me."

"Well, its a damn good thing you were interrupted before you got any more distracted, or you'd have had her there on the floor," she snapped.

"Billie, I swear there's no other woman," he said,

280

leaning forward so that his warm breath tickled her ear. He let go of her hand, transferring his grip to her waist. "Not Julia, not anybody."

His hands slid upward to her ribs. A shiver went through her, and unconsciously she leaned back against him. Remembering herself abruptly, she stiffened.

"No, don't pull away," he murmured huskily, moving his hands so that the rich weight of her breasts bounced against them.

A wild mixture of emotions flooded through Billie: fury, outrage, hurt and, yes, desire. After everything he'd done to her, everything he'd cost her, that liquid heat still rose into her at his touch. She must be as stupid as he thought, to let him do this to her again! But she couldn't seem to stop him—or herself.

His hands were cupping her breasts now, lifting them, his thumbs going up to caress the hardening peaks. He kissed his way down her neck to her shoulder, nuzzling her shirt collar aside so he could touch her pulse point with his tongue.

Still veering from one reaction to the next, Billie was unable to move, unable to speak.

Nick's hand glided down her body and slipped between her legs, rubbing her mound through her pants. Desire was riding him now, his manhood so hard within his jeans that it was actually painful. His chest was rising and falling like a bellows, and he couldn't wait to be inside her, loving her, claiming her.

"Stop the horse," he rasped. "Get down, honey. I'm going to lay you down right here."

His words broke the spell of passion that had held Billie in thrall. A great tide of outrage surged through her. How dare he use her again! How dare he try to take everything from her—her body, her love, her self-respect?

"No!" she shrieked, jerking upward on the reins with all her strength.

Chomper whinnied in protest and reared, spilling Nick from his perch behind the saddle.

"Hey!" Nick shouted, sprawling on his back in the dust.

She jabbed the horse's flanks with her spurs. Chomper plunged into a gallop. Billie could hear Nick's shouts fading into the distance behind her.

"A nice, long walk will do you good," she muttered. Tears were running down her face now, and she scrubbed ineffectually at them with her sleeve. "Bastard!"

Chapter 24

Billie got back to the house just after daybreak to find Budge waiting for her.

"Where the hell have you been?" he shouted. "Rachel's been half crazy worryin' about you!"

Rachel rushed out of the house and grabbed Billie by the shoulders. "Thank God you're back! Where's Nick? Is he all right?"

"Why would anything be wrong with Nick?" Billie demanded.

Budge hooked his thumbs in his belt. "Beelzebub came trottin' in about two hours ago. Lookin' mighty pleased with hisself, too."

"What's that got to do with me?" Billie asked, crossing her arms over her chest.

"'Cause you got the damndest strangest look on your face, part guilty, part cryin' and part as pleased with your devilment as that damned palomino, and I ain't seen nobody but Nick Larabee put such a look there," the Texan drawled. "You think you kin fool ol' Budge?"

"Billie, what have you done?" Rachel's fingers tightened.

Billie shrugged. "Nothing much. I just thought a bit

283

of a walk would do him some good, so I left him about six miles back in the hills."

"You left him defenseless out there?" Rachel demanded.

"Defenseless?" Billie cried. "Him?"

Rachel opened her mouth to protest, but then she looked more closely at Billie, noting her reddened eyes and the faint trails left by tears. "What's the matter, Billie?"

"Nothing," Billie said, looking up to see Pat Conway walk around the corner of the house and come toward them. Nick's hired hand, she thought sourly, put here to tell his boss her cowboys' comings and goings so he could steal her cattle in safety. "Pat, get our horses and Emma Lee's wagon ready, will you?"

His brow furrowed thoughtfully, Budge watched the cowboy as he moved away. "Rachel, darlin', go pack your gear," he said, giving her a gentle push toward the house.

Rachel walked away reluctantly, casting worried looks over her shoulder as she went. When she was out of earshot, Budge confronted Billie, his hands on his hips.

"What happened out there?" he demanded.

Billie took a deep breath and told him the story, omitting the part about the heavy little pouch that was tucked into her pocket. He grunted in surprise when she told him that the Apaches hadn't attacked the Harndon place, but remained silent until she finished her tale.

He shook his head. "Nick, rustlin' your cattle? I find that a mite hard to believe. I jest don't think he's the type to be rustlin' cattle," he said, then added, "'specially yours."

"Do you think he'd leave my herd alone just because I was . . . I was"—she took a deep, shuddering breath,

284

just managing to turn a sob into a bitter laugh—"distracted? Hell, Budge, you're a bigger fool than I am if you think that."

Budge's hand slid down to grasp the handle of his pistol with white-knuckled force. "What're you plannin' to do about him?"

"What would Pa do?"

"Shoot 'im," Budge said. "But Anton could be a mite hasty sometimes."

"Did he ever regret it?"

"He never regretted nothin'." Budge met her gaze steadily, his face creased with concern. "But he never worried about nothin' but this ranch. You cain't say the same, kin you?"

Billie looked away from his too knowing regard. "I . . . I'm going to tell the sheriff. Let him handle it."

"I don't know." The Texan rubbed his jaw thoughtfully. "The way everyone's been losin' cattle, they're likely to lynch him first an' ask questions later. That what you want, Billie?"

Billie looked up at him with wide green eyes. Was it what she wanted? Could she live with herself afterward? She lifted her chin defiantly, remembering how Nick had used her and cast her aside. "Those men have got to be stopped. If he's with them, maybe even leading them—"

"You better be damned sure," Budge growled. Turning on his heel, he strode to the bunkhouse.

Billie pounded the wall of the house with her fist. Why was it so hard to do what needed to be done? Nick had planned this whole thing. He had chosen her deliberately, figuring a naive girl like her would be easy pickings. And he'd been right, she mused bitterly. He'd played her emotions expertly, confusing her, heating her blood until she couldn't wait to give herself to him.

The truly infuriating thing about it was the fact that

even now she wanted him. During their time together, he had made her feel beautiful, womanly . . . desirable. All those things she thought she'd never be, never have. And now they were gone, as fleeting and as insubstantial as heat waves over the sand.

Damn him.

With a sigh, she turned and went into the house. Emma Lee was seated at the table, mending one of the children's garments. She set her needle aside when Billie came in.

Without a word, Billie pulled the pouch out of her pocket and set it on the table. The other woman untied it, fumbling a little with the string, then upended it over her cupped hand. Coins spilled out, the buttery yellow of gold catching the light.

"Five hundred dollars," Billie said. "It's little enough for your land."

Emma Lee stared at the money. "You cain't afford it any better than I kin."

"I'll do all right once my cattle are sold." Billie closed the other woman's fingers gently over the coins. "Go on, take it."

Emma Lee ducked her head. "Thanks. Looks like you done bought yoreself another ranch."

"Yeah," Billie said. "And Emma Lee—don't tell anyone where you got this."

Emma Lee nodded. Billie held the pouch open so the other woman could pour the gold back into it. A faint breath of wind touched Billie's back, and she whirled. But the door was closed, the house completely still, so she just shrugged and turned back to her task.

Outside, Pat Conway stood for a moment with his back to the door, then headed for the corral. A short time later he was following Billie's trail back into the hills, leading Beelzebub behind him. It took him some time to ferret out the tracks on the hard, cracked

286

ground, and it was afternoon before he spotted a small, plodding figure in the distance. When he was close enough to see the figure closely, he saw that it was Nick, dust stained, thirsty, weary, and very, very angry.

Pat pulled his mount to a halt and looked down at the other man. "Hello, Nick," he said.

Nick took Beelzebub's reins and swung into his saddle. "How did you know I was here?"

"I'm damned good at eavesdropping." Pat unhooked his canteen and offered it to the other man.

"Thanks." Nick took a long drink, letting the water trickle down his neck to his chest, then handed the canteen back. "When I get my hands on that little—"

"She thinks you been rustlin' her cattle," Pat said, keeping his face turned away so Nick wouldn't see his smile. "She's plannin' to tell the sheriff all about it."

"Goddamn it to hell!"

"And," Pat coughed to disguise a chuckle, "it's too late to stop 'em now. They already left for town."

Nick grimaced. He'd have to hope Billie would have cooled off by the time she got to town, or his neck would soon be a lot longer than he'd like.

"'Member the folks who got burned out the other day?" Pat asked, turning his horse toward the Dolorosa.

"The Harndons? What about them?"

"Billie bought their ranch. Paid 'em five hundred dollars for it"—Pat took a deep breath, pausing for dramatic effect—"in gold."

"Gold!" Nick stared at the other man in astonishment. "What kind of gold?"

"Coins. Looked Mexican to me."

Nick scratched the stubble on his jaw. Gold, he thought. It had to be the key to this whole thing. "Well, at least we know why those men tore her house up."

Pat nodded. "Think there's more of it?"

"Probably." Nick's hands clenched into fists. Damn that Billie! he raged inwardly. What the hell was she doing? She'd paid five hundred dollars for the Harndon place, cattle and all. Just the land was worth several times that amount. Could she be capable of asking her Indian friends to burn the Harndons out so she could acquire their property? His heart said no, but his brain, that cynical, all-too experienced organ, said maybe she had.

He frowned down at Beelzebub's silken blond mane. How could she have fooled him so badly? Could he have mistaken her fiery response for calculation, kindness for scheming shrewdness? Had her generosity to Rachel only been a ploy to somehow acquire Redesware as well? If that were true, he'd never trust his instincts again. For such a young, seemingly inexperienced girl, she'd sure managed to turn him inside out. By God, he'd even felt sorry for her for putting aside all her softer feminine emotions to please her father. Fool that he was, he had fallen in love with that inner, hidden Billie. Yes, he had to admit to himself now. He loved her. And now he discovered that the woman who had captured his heart might not exist at all.

"Where we goin'?" Pat asked, breaking into Nick's reverie.

"What? Oh." Nick shook his head to clear it of those annoying thoughts; he had a job to do. "You know, Pat, I need to go to Xavier today. Funny, isn't it? Almost as if it were Fate taking me there."

"Well, you'd better hope Fate ain't plannin' to have you hung," Pat said. "What exactly happened out here, anyway?"

"Billie followed one of the rustlers to the camp. While she was sneaking around, she found the spot where I'd hidden Beelzebub." Nick ground his teeth together. "Damn her! I trailed one of them from the place where Lew Purcell had been bushwacked, and was planning to stick with them until I found out who was leading them."

Pat coughed to disguise a chuckle. "Ran their horses off, she said."

"Yeah," Nick growled. "Mine, too."

A smile twitched Pat's mouth. Nick glared at him, daring him to say anything.

"How long do you think it will take Billie to get that herd to Tucson?" Nick asked.

"Her boys have rounded up most of the cattle already. I'd say ten days—if they don't have any more problems."

Nick nodded. "Stearns is planning to go to Tucson next week. Eames left for Tucson yesterday."

"Interestin', ain't it?"

"Yeah." Nick scratched the stubble on his chin. "It doesn't take much to figure Eames for what he is. But I haven't been able to prove whether he's working independently or whether Stearns is paying him. And until you told me about the gold, I couldn't understand what either of them are after."

"And since Billie has the gold," Pat said, shaking his head, "she's smack in the middle of everythin'."

Nick hunched his shoulders. "Follow the Star M herd at a distance," he said. "When you get to Tucson, I want you to send for our old friend Tom Sandler."

Pat whistled. "You ready to spring a federal marshal on 'em? What about the sheriff at Xavier?"

"Stearns owns him."

"Damn!" Pat glanced at his friend, then look up at the horizon. "Nick, I've knowed you a long time. I ain't never seen you so het up over a woman before. You sure you ain't in love with that Meyrick gal?"

Nick was taken aback. Was it that obvious? Were his emotions written on his face for all to see—and laugh, that Nick Larabee had finally fallen in love? And to a woman who might be stirring the territory into open conflict just to add a few more square miles to her range? He shook his head, but when he opened his mouth to deny it, no words came out.

"Wal, I'd say I got my answer," Pat said. "If you ask me, you better get this damn thing straightened out before somethin' bad happens."

"No one asked you!" Nick shouted. Beelzebub pranced sideways, startled.

Pat steered his mount away from the nervous stallion. "Billie ain't the only one who can leave you sittin' in the dust," he said. "An' if that palomino dumps you, I might not be inclined to help you out."

"Sorry."

"I expect it's a trifle upsettin' for a man like you to fall in love and"—Pat moved his mount a few feet farther away—"not have the lucky lady drop pantin' at your feet like all the others. Mighty hard to get used to, eh?"

Nick stared at the other man's neck, wondering whether he'd be able to throttle him without spooking Beelzebub again. "You know, Pat, sometimes you can be damned annoying," he growled.

"Yeah, I know." Pat grinned. "Planning to go to Tucson any time soon?"

"You never know."

"She might shoot you. She was pretty mad the last time I saw her."

Nick grunted. Billie wasn't the only one who was mad. When he got her alone, he was going to get some answers from her—and a few other things as well.

Chapter 25

As the stage pulled away, Billie waved good-bye to Emma Lee and the children. "I hope they're going to be all right," she murmured.

"I'm sure they will," Rachel said, patting Billie's shoulder comfortingly. "She said her family will take care of them."

Billie, thinking of Rachel's long-absent brother, hoped Emma Lee's relatives would be more caring than Alan Laird had been for his sister.

Budge took his hat off and wiped his forehead with his sleeve. "Did you see the look on ol' DeWitt's face when he heard that you'd bought the Harndon place?"

"I sure did." Anger flushed Billie's cheeks and narrowed her eyes. "What do you want to bet that Stearns will know about it before the day is out?"

"I never bet on a sure thing," the Texan said. He took Rachel by the arm and turned her toward the wagon. "We'd best be gittin' out on the range."

"Not yet," Billie said. "I've got some business with the sheriff."

Budge wheeled to face her. "Don't you think you're

goin' off half-cocked on this? You ain't your pa, gal. You're goin' to regret—"

"You and Rachel go to the general store and get these supplies." Billie snapped, handing him a list. "I should only be a few minutes."

Budge shook his head sadly, but took the list without further comment. Rachel looked from him to Billie in confusion.

"Would someone care to tell me what's going on?" she asked.

"Jest Billie bein' her usual bullheaded self," Budge growled, taking her by the arm again. "C'mon, Rachel." He pulled her toward the general store, his long legs taking one stride to her every two. Rachel, her forehead furrowed with confusion and concern, glanced back at Billie over her shoulder.

"Bullheaded!" Billie gave a most unladylike snort and stalked across the street to the sheriff's office.

She opened the door and went inside, blinking for a moment in the sudden dimness. Then her vision adjusted, and she saw the sheriff's bulky figure sprawled back in his chair, his booted feet propped up on the desk in front of him.

"Afternoon, Jared," she said, loudly enough to cause him to jerk upright with a loud, honking snort.

"Whassa . . . Oh, Billie?" He rose slowly to his feet. "You gave me a start, girl."

She swallowed convulsively. Looking at the sheriff's coarse, unintelligent face, she realized that she couldn't put Nick's life in his hands. On her say-so, Jared Wallace would hang him, no questions asked. Territorial justice—quick and easy and final. She pushed away the vision of that leanly muscled body hanging at the end of a rope, that strong, vital personality sunk into the endless realm of death. Billie shuddered. No matter what Nick had done, no matter what he might be, she couldn't be the one to do that to him. Somehow she had to find a way to stop him herself.

Suddenly she realized that Jared Wallace had been talking for some time, and she hadn't heard a word he said. "What did you say?" she asked.

He sighed. "It weren't important. What kin I do fer you, Billie?"

She fumbled frantically for some reason to be standing here. Then her heart started to pound with excitement. She hadn't intended to tell him about the Apache, but it might just be a good way to discover where his loyalties lay. "Well, I . . . I came to tell you that the Harndons weren't burned out by the Apache."

"Not by 'Pach?" He stared at her in astonishment. "That ain't what I heard. There was Injun sign all over the place, and Eustace was missin' his hair."

"Then I suggest you go there and see for yourself, like Budge did," Billie said. "There were plenty of tracks, all right, but they were all shod horses."

"Shod!"

Billie nodded, watching the man's face narrowly. His expression shifted from astonishment to startled understanding, then went blank.

He rubbed his chin, his fingernails making scraping sounds on the bristles there. "Now, Billie, you know the 'Pach'll ride anythin' they kin raise, ketch or steal." With a grin, he added, "Why, some of them mounts might even be yourn."

"Yeah." Billie folded her arms over her chest. Well, she thought, she'd have to handle the rustlers without the law's help, that was certain.

"An' white men don't lift scalps," Jared pointed out.

"Not unless they want it to look like Apaches did the murdering."

"Now, I think you're jest a bit confused about this thing," the sheriff said. "But if it makes you happy, I'll send someone out to look at the place."

Billie nodded and turned to go. No doubt the man would find what the sheriff wanted him to find. All in all, she decided, it had been a most informative visit.

"Hold on, Billie," the sheriff called. She paused, her hand on the knob, and he said. "That's one wild story you're tellin'. You go spreadin' that around, and folks are goin' to think you've gone soft in the head."

"I suppose I have, at that," she murmured, opening the door to let a shaft of blinding-hot sunshine into the room. "Afternoon, sheriff."

She strolled slowly toward the general store, her attention focused on the office behind her. A moment later she heard a door open and close. Stealthily, she stole a glance over her shoulder to see Jared Wallace hurrying in the opposite direction.

"Going to tell your boss all about it, eh?" she muttered.

As she neared the general store, she saw Nick leaning against the side of the building. He was looking down at his boots. Maybe he hadn't spotted her yet. She paused, hesitating as she tried to decide whether she should flee or whether she should try to ignore him.

He looked up suddenly, his gold-flecked eyes narrowed with anger. "It won't do you any good to run," he said.

"I wasn't going to run," she lied. Holding her head high, she started to walk past him into the store.

He caught her by the arm. "I want to talk to you."

"I don't have anything to say to you."

"No? Well, I have some questions to ask, and you're going to give me some answers whether you want to or not," he growled, pulling her closer.

"Somethin' wrong, Billie?" Budge asked from the

doorway. Rachel stood behind him, peering over his shoulder.

"Nothing's wrong," Nick snapped.

The Texan's jaw tightened. "I ast Billie." He stepped forward to take hold of Billie's other arm.

Billie stood between the two tall men, feeling like an utter fool. "If you two will stop—" she began.

"Let her go," Nick said softly, staring into the other man's eyes. "This isn't your business, Budge."

"I think it is," Budge growled. "I don't want to call you, Nick, but Billie don't want to talk to you."

Rachel darted forward and pulled Billie from between the two men. "Oh, stop being stupid!" she cried. "Neither of you is going to do anything to anybody!"

They turned to her, identical expressions of annoyance on their faces.

She put her hands on her hips and faced them down. She wasn't going to tolerate this! Her brother and the man she loved were not going to get into a fight! "I thought you two were friends."

"Things are getting a mite confused all of a sudden," Budge said. "Namely, there's a lot of questions that need to be answered before anyone here kin be friends."

Nick crossed his arms over his chest. By God, Budge had a lot of gall! If anyone had sinister secrets here, it was Billie! And Budge was probably in it up to his neck.

Scowling, Nick turned to Rachel. "Rachel, get a room here in town. You're not going on the range with them."

She shook her head. "I'm going."

"I forbid it!" Nick growled.

"Oh?" Rachel lifted her chin defiantly. "You have no right to give me orders, Nick Larabee!"

"You know I do!" he shouted.

Rachel tilted her head back so she could look down her nose at him. "Really?" she asked. "Then why don't you tell these people why?"

Nick's hands tightened into fists. "You know I can't do that."

"Then you'd best go," Budge said. "An' don't let me find you hangin' around the herd, either. My men are right jumpy jest now. I'd shore hate to see you git shot fer a rustler when you was only comin' to visit friendly-like."

Nick's gaze moved from Budge to the others, lingering for a moment on Billie's face. "I'll be seeing you, Billie. Soon." His deep voice was like a sword sheathed in velvet, caressing, threatening.

"Don't bother," she said, ignoring the little shiver of dread that coursed down her spine. "I won't have any more to say to you than I do now."

"We'll see." He turned and stalked away.

Rachel took two steps after him, then stopped and covered her face with her hands. This wasn't the way things were supposed to work! she wailed inwardly. Why did Nick have to force her to keep that stupid promise? Couldn't he see that a little honesty could fix everything?

Billie glanced up at Budge. The Texan's face was set, his jaw as hard as granite. It had been obvious that Rachel was trying to force Nick into making a declaration. Had she pursued Budge only to make the other man jealous? It didn't seem the sort of thing Rachel would do, but Billie knew from experience that love could make a person do some strange things. Even hurtful things. She put her hand on Budge's arm briefly, almost sick with sympathy for the pain he must be feeling.

"Wal, we'd best be goin'," he said. His voice was harsh, but his hands were gentle as he steered the two

296

girls toward the wagon. "We kin make near ten miles before dark."

Later that night, when Rachel was sleeping, Billie went to join Budge atop the rock he'd chosen for a vantage point. He grunted to acknowledge her, but kept his gaze fixed on the horizon.

"I'm sorry about what happened today," she ventured.

He nodded. "I wondered about them two. They was never jest friends."

"No. But I think Rachel cares for you very much. You shouldn't turn away from her because of Nick."

He swiveled to look at her, surprise on his face. "What makes you think I'd change my mind? Honey, Rachel is the best thing that ever happened to me. I ain't about to let her go."

"But what about Nick?"

He shrugged. "Whatever she feels for him, she don't want to marry him. She wants to marry *me*. I never thought I'd be lucky enough that a gal like her would ever take a second look at a feller like me. I'll take her no matter what, and hope that someday she might come to love me half as much as I love her."

"That would be enough for you?" she asked.

"Yep."

There was absolute certainty in his voice. Billie picked up a stick and began making circles in the dust at the base of the rock. She envied the Texan. If only she could be the same! Then she could accept Nick's lovemaking with no guilt, no desire for anything more than what he was willing to give. And let him go when he was ready to move on. But she knew she wasn't built that way. She wanted his love. And that was the one thing he couldn't give her.

Suddenly realizing that she had written Nick's name in the dust, she scratched the stick through it irritably, erasing the telltale picture. She glanced at Budge and was relieved to see that he was once again staring at the horizon.

She frowned down at the hastily scratched lines, wishing she could obliterate her feelings so easily.

Chapter 26

"Wal, we got 'em to Tucson, gals," Budge said, watching the last of the cattle walk up the ramp into the railroad car. Rachel stood behind him, holding the wagon team's reins in one hand, her other hand resting lightly on the Texan's shoulder.

"Yes, we did," Billie said. "Although there were times when I had my doubts." She turned to the railroad agent, who was writing busily in a ledger. "Let's settle up, Mr. Simms. I've got men waiting to be paid so they can hurry up and spend their money."

Simms laughed. "They'll be broke by morning. They always are." He handed her the tally. "Sixteen hundred and seventy-two, all three-year animals. The market is good in California, I hear."

"I hope you heard right," Billie murmured, signing the tally and handing it back with the money she owed the railroad. There should have been over two thousand head of cattle on that train. Between the rustlers and the Apaches, she'd lost a fourth of her income for the year.

"Pleasure doing business with you, Miss Meyrick," Simms said, tipping his hat before walking away.

"Gonna be a tight year," Budge said.

"It sure is." Billie counted out a hundred dollars and held it out. "Here's your expense money for the trip," she said. "Get me a good price for my cattle, and maybe we won't be eating lizard this winter." Although her comment was meant to be a joke, both she and Budge knew how close to the truth it was; after she paid the men off, she'd be lucky if there was enough left to buy supplies for the rest of the month.

The train whistle sounded shrilly. With a tremendous gout of black smoke, the engine came to life, its great wheels squealing and slipping as they moved those first few inches along the track. Then they caught, and the train began to move forward faster. The whistle shrieked again.

Budge kissed Rachel soundly, then settled his hat more firmly on his head. "Take care of her for me, Billie," he said, then swung up into the nearest passenger car.

Rachel burst into tears. Billie put her arm around the other girl and gave her a squeeze.

"Come on, Rachel," she said. "He's only going to be gone two weeks, three at the most."

"That's not why I'm crying," Rachel sniffed. "It's . . . well, I'd gotten used to the smell of cows—sort of. But now they're gone, and I just realized that the smell hasn't gone away. Billie, it's me. *I* smell like a cow!"

Billie stared at her. "Well, so do I. What do you expect after a cattle drive?"

"I want a bath." Rachel pushed a strand of limp blond hair away from her forehead. "Now."

"All right, all right. A bath does sound awful good, I must admit," Billie said, linking arms with Rachel and pulling her toward the wagon. With identical groans of fatigue, they climbed into the seat.

The men were waiting on the other side of the cattle pens. Billie handed them their wages, admonishing,

"Now, try not to spend it all in one place."

With a whoop, they turned their mounts and galloped away. Billie knew they'd hit the public bathhouse first, then, arrayed in their finest clothes, head for the sporting district. She shook her head; it happened the same way every year. By morning they'd be broke, nursing throbbing heads and churning stomachs, and ready to get back to the ranch.

She slapped the reins against the horses' rumps, urging them into the traffic. Rachel grabbed at her hat as Billie expertly maneuvered the vehicle down the crowded street, where huge freight wagons rolled ponderously along amid throngs of smaller, faster buggys and carts. A stagecoach careened wildly by, nearly slicing off the back of the wagon. Dust rose with the driver's curses. Not to be intimidated, Billie shook her fist at the man and shouted something that made Rachel clap her hands over her ears in shocked embarrassment.

When her cheeks had cooled a bit, Rachel dared to ask, "Where are we staying?"

"Mrs. Petrie's Boardinghouse," Billie said. "Safest place in town; no one messes with Mrs. Petrie." She stiffened suddenly, spotting an elegant carriage that was stopped in front of one of the shops. Two women climbed down from the vehicle, one dark-haired, the other crowned with striking red-gold tresses.

"Watch out for that wagon!" Rachel shrieked.

Billie steered around the offending vehicle, again avoiding a collison by inches. "Damn," she muttered under her breath. What were Helena and Julia doing here? And more important, was Nick with them? Her throat tightened at the thought. She dreaded meeting him again. And yet she wanted to see him, to touch him with an intensity that made her body ache. Would she never be free of the man? Would his touch haunt her for the rest of her life, or would she become cold and hard like her father, sheathing her heart with iron so that no one could ever hurt her again?

"Billie, are you all right?" Rachel asked.

"Yes!" she snarled, pulling the wagon to a stop in front of the boardinghouse.

The house, a square, two-story structure with no grace or ornamentation to soften its blocky shape, was located in one of Tucson's newer sections. Like its neighbors, it was built of wood, not adobe. The landlady, after one horrified look—or perhaps sniff—at her boarders, sent them upstairs for a hot bath.

Afterward, Rachel climbed into bed, sighing with weariness. "I don't think I've ever been so tired," she mumbled, and was instantly asleep.

Billie was tired, too, but she had something to do—namely, find out why Helena was in Tucson right now, and if Nick was with her. She took fresh clothes out of the carpetbag and shook them out, but after two weeks in the well-packed case, the creases were there to stay. With a shrug, she put them on anyway.

After a moment's hesitation, she donned her jacket as well, slipping her pistol into one pocket and her derringer into the other.

She went down the back stairs so the landlady wouldn't see her, then slipped out to the stable and put her sidesaddle on one of the horses that had been hitched to the wagon. As the sun sank below the horizon, plunging the city into lavender twilight, she turned her mount north toward Main Street. It was on this broad, dusty avenue that Tucson's gentry built their mansions. Surely, she would find Rosswell Stearns's home among them.

She stopped to ask directions of a Mexican servant who was hurrying along the street, a basket of vegetables on his arm.

302

"The house of Señor Stearns?" the man repeated. "*Si*, just over there, Señorita." He pointed to a large Victorian house on the other side of the street.

"*Gracias*," she said, turning her mount toward the elaborate dwelling.

Surprisingly, the house was constructed of adobe bricks, only its tower and the intricate scrollwork made of wood. Surely, Billie thought, Stearns hadn't built this house. It had been designed by someone who knew adobe, and loved it enough to employ the most skilled of artisans.

Billie tied her horse up outside and rang the bell. A servant answered the door, looking her up and down with obvious disdain.

"What business do you have here, young woman?" he asked.

"None with you." Billie brushed past him and stalked into the foyer, shouting, "Helena! I want to talk to you."

"Now, just a moment, girl!" the man growled, catching her by the shoulder.

Billie shook him off, "Helena!"

The man reached for her again, but Helena came into the foyer then, panting a little from exertion. "It's all right, Ben. This is my daughter, Miss Meyrick."

He bowed. "My apologies, miss."

"No offense taken." Billie grabbed Helena by the arm and pulled her into the nearest room. It was the drawing room, even more expensively furnished than the one at the Dolorosa. "What are you doing here?" she demanded.

"Why, Rosswell wanted to come," Helena said, her brow wrinkling in confusion.

"Did Nick come with you?"

Helena shook her head. "He isn't even working for us any longer. Rosswell was terribly upset about it."

303

Billie frowned. So, Nick had gone out on his own. Maybe he'd made enough money from Star M cattle that he didn't need Stearns any longer. With an exclamation of disgust, she turned to go.

"Wait!" Helena cried. "Is that all you have to say?"

"Yes." Then, unable to stop herself from responding to the stricken look on Helena's face, Billie reached out and put her hand on the other woman's shoulder. "I suppose I should have said hello."

"Hello! Hello!" Helena raised her hands in exasperation. "Where are you staying?"

"Mrs. Petrie's Boardinghouse."

"I'll send a man for your things." Helena started for the door, but Billie held her back.

"We're fine where we are," she said, her brows contracting in a scowl. So Helena thought she could give orders, did she? Billie jerked her hand away from the other woman's shoulder as though it had been burned from that contact.

"But—"

"I wouldn't take a drink of water from that husband of yours, let alone stay in his house!" Billie put her hands on her hips. "I suppose it was your idea," she snapped.

Helena's mouth dropped open in bewilderment. "What?"

"Sending him over to buy me out!"

"Billie, I just want you to be safe, and happy. That ranch is too much for you to run alone—"

"Damn it to hell!" Billie shouted, several weeks' worth of frustration suddenly boiling over. A tiny part of her knew she was being unfair, but she couldn't help herself. "Just because you hate the place doesn't mean you have to try to take it away from me!"

"That isn't—"

304

"Or maybe you just want to erase the memory of my father to fix your own guilt!"

"I wasn't the only one at fault!" Helena cried furiously. "Do you think for one minute that I would have willingly left my own daughter?"

"What are you saying?" Billie felt as though someone had hit her in the pit of her stomach. "You didn't want to go?"

"Yes, I wanted to go. But I wanted to take you with me!" Tears streamed unheeded down Helena's face. "I hated Arizona. I hated what it was doing to you, and I hated Anton for allowing it to happen. Oh, Billie . . ." her voice broke. With an effort, she regained a measure of control. "He threw me out. He told me he'd kill me if I tried to take you away from him."

Billie stared at her, unable to speak. Could her father have been capable of such a thing? Even as the thought occurred to her, she knew it was possible. Pa had been a hard man, who tenaciously held onto anything that belonged to him. He loved his daughter, of that Billie was equally certain. How could he have done something so cruel? But her own experience gave her the answer: love was frequently cruel, frequently unfair and confusing.

Helena gathered the younger woman into her arms. "I'm sorry, Billie. Sorry for having to tell you about your father. I didn't intend to."

"I . . ." Billie took a deep breath, then another, and she was released from her immobility. Tears stung her eyes, spilling over in a hot flood. "I blamed you for everything! And it was him! Oh, God!"

"It's all right," Helena murmured. "Billie, please. Don't hate him. He didn't mean to—"

Billie felt as though the walls were closing in on her. "I've got to get out of here! I'll be back later, and we'll talk." Tearing out of Helena's grap, she whirled and rushed out of the room.

"Billie!" Helena cried.

Billie flung herself into her saddle and spurred her mount into a gallop, hoping the wind would scour the pain and rage from her. She hardly noticed where she was going, didn't see that the surrounding traffic had changed from elegant carriages and shining, expensive buggies to massive freighter's wagons. Suddenly a man ran into the road ahead of her, blocking her way. Her horse reared, nearly sending her to the ground. Before she could react, someone pulled her out of the saddle. Hard hands held her arms behind her, hurting her.

"Well, look who we have here," a familiar voice said in her ear.

She twisted to look over her shoulder. "Eames!" she hissed. "What rock did you crawl out from under?"

He jerked at her arms, forcing a gasp from her. "You should learn to curb that nasty little tongue of yours."

Billie kicked backward, aiming for his shin. Cursing, he lifted her, robbing her of her leverage, and began dragging her toward the edge of the street.

She looked around desperately, but this was the roughest section of town, where the women belonged to the highest bidder and the men kept their noses out of other people's business. No one was likely to help her here, least of all any of the hard-looking men who stood in the doorway of a nearby saloon, cheering Eames on.

He called to one of the watching men. "Get her horse, Ira. Tie him up with ours." Suddenly he stiffened and reached into her pocket, pulling out her pistol and derringer to a chorus of hoots from the other men.

"Better strip 'er down, see if she got any more!" one of them shouted.

"Ahhh, pretty girl like that, she got better weapons than a pistol 'neath them clothes," another man called. "Hey, Eames! Gonna share?"

Eames chuckled. "Not just now, boys. This one's special. At least right now."

Rosswell Stearns pushed his way through the knot of men in the doorway of the saloon. "What is going on here?" he demanded.

"Look what I found wandering around all alone," Eames said, anchoring Billie against his body with one arm.

Stearns stepped closer. For a moment Billie was almost glad to see him. Then, looking up into the glacial coldness of his pale eyes, she realized he didn't give a damn what happened to her. She opened her mouth to curse him, then closed it again. He wouldn't care about that, either.

"Indeed, this is a most fortunate coincidence," the Englishman said. "Bring her, Mr. Eames." He turned toward his carriage.

Eames didn't move. "No."

Stearns wheeled to face him. "No?"

"No. She and I have some unfinished business to tend to."

"Are you refusing to obey an order?" Stearns asked softly.

"You owe me," Eames snarled. "I'm taking her as payment."

"Pick another woman. I have a use for her myself, although"—Stearns's gaze slid over the gunman's face contemptuously—"mine is far different from yours."

Eames laughed. "You Englishmen don't know how to have a good time. For what I've got in mind, this little filly is perfect."

"Sorry, Mr. Eames." Stearns gestured, and three

307

men stepped out from behind the Englishman's carriage. They flanked Stearns protectively, their hands hovering near their holsters.

Eames laughed as two men slid out of the shadows of a nearby alley and faced Stearns and his bodyguards.

Stearns flicked a speck of dust from his sleeve. "Since neither of us intend to back down from our claim on Miss Meyrick, I suppose we shall . . . now, what do you Americans call it? Oh, yes—shoot it out. How shall we begin, Mr. Eames?"

Billie stared at the Englishman, chilled by his calm acceptance of the situation. She could feel Eames's body pressing against her back, stiff with anticipation.

"Tell you what," Eames said at last. "We'll compromise. I'll, er, have the use of the girl tonight. When I'm finished with her, I'll bring her to you." He smiled, a feral baring of his teeth. "As a favor, I'll see that she comes to you in a more cooperative frame of mind."

Stearns glanced at Billie's defiant expression. "How do you propose to do that, Mr. Eames?"

"Just leave it to me," the gunman said. "I know how to handle a woman like this. What do you say, Stearns? Do we have a deal?"

"An exceedingly equitable compromise," Stearns said. "I have rented a warehouse just south of the rail yard. Bring her there tomorrow." He turned away, and his bodyguards closed in behind him to protect his back.

Eames's men slid back into the darkness of the alley. The gunman set Billie back on her feet, but twisted her arm behind her to make sure she didn't slip away.

He tightened his grip enough to make her wince. "Come on, honey," he said. "It's time we got to know each other better."

Billie's arm felt like it was on fire, and every step she took caused a jolt of agony to run up her shoulder. She

308

could do nothing but walk beside him as he guided her down the street toward his hotel.

"Is this how you treat all your women?" she spat.

"Only the ones like you."

He dragged her around to the back door of the hotel. Once they were inside, he shifted his grip from her arm to her hair, pulling her head back brutally. He kissed her then, his teeth cutting into the soft insides of her lips. Her fists pounded his back, the sides of his head, but he only bent her farther backward.

He lifted his head so he could look down into her eyes. "I plan to enjoy you, honey. If you're nice enough to me, I might see that you enjoy it, too. Otherwise, it's going to be a long, long night for you."

"You mean make it easy for you?" she asked, frantically grasping for any opportunity to keep him from getting her into his room.

"Yes." Slowly, he loosened his grip on her hair. When she didn't try to get away or strike him, he moved his hands to her shoulders.

She gazed up at him with wide eyes, hoping she looked as frightened as she felt. "Will you promise not to hurt me?" she whispered.

"I promise that you'll learn to like what I do to you," he said, his voice thickening with rising passion. Slowly, he ran his hands down her back to her buttocks, pressing her against him so she could feel the hardness of him. "Feel what you do to me? I've wanted you since the moment I laid eyes on you."

Billie wound her hands into his fine hair, knocking his hat backward off his head. "You have?" she breathed, bringing her mouth to within a fraction of an inch of his. "It's kind of . . . exciting to be wanted like that."

"Damned if I'm going to wait another minute." He laughed, a throaty, exultant sound, as he peeled her jacket down her arms and tossed it away. "Come on, honey. My room is just over here. I'm going to . . . Ungh!"

His voice went up in a wail of agony as Billie jerked her knee up sharply, catching him squarely in the groin. Gasping for breath in great, gulping sobs, he clutched himself and sank to his knees.

Billie flung herself toward the door. A moment later she was outside, running down the street as fast as her legs would take her. She darted around one corner, then another, and bolted across the next street, nearly getting herself run down by a wagon in the process.

Like a rabbit pursued by a hungry coyote, she headed north, toward the safety of Mrs. Petrie's house. A cowboy, thinking she was one of the many ladies of the evening who plied these streets, tried to catch her by the arm. Billie tore away from him and ran on, leaving the startled man holding part of her sleeve.

Panting with exertion, she turned yet another corner. As she plunged wildly through the darkness of an alley, she bumped into something with such force that she nearly went down in a heap. A man's hard arms went around her, and she cried out. She struck out with her nails, feeling them connect, then her wrists were caught and held. Once again she lifted her knee, aiming for her captor's groin, but the man twisted so that the blow fell on his thigh.

"What the hell?" he growled, swinging her around and thrusting her against the hard adobe wall of the nearest building.

Billie gasped in shock, recognizing the velvet timbre of that deep voice. "Nick!" Her voice was hardly more than a squeak.

His body came against hers, pinning her to the wall behind her. "Well, well, well," he murmured. "Now isn't this my lucky night?"

Chapter 27

Billie's shock turned quickly to anger. "Let me go!" she cried.

"I can't do that, honey. After all, I came all the way to Tucson to find you." His mouth was poised over hers, his warm breath fanning her cheek. "I thought I'd have to search half the city for you, but you fell right into my arms. Like I said, it's my lucky night."

She pushed ineffectually at his chest. "Get your hands off me."

"Who were you running from?" he asked softly, ignoring her struggles.

"Eames. Now, get your hands off me. I've been pawed as much as I'm going to tolerate."

"Eames!" He moved away from her, but only to take her by the arm and pull her farther down the alley. "Did he hurt you?"

Although it was too dark for her to see his expression, the raw violence in his voice made Billie shiver. "No. And he won't be bothering any other women for a few days, either."

He chuckled, a harsh sound with more anger than humor in it. "Ah, yes, your little trick with the knee."

Summoning up a brief flash of bravado, she said, "If

you've got any ideas yourself, I'll do the same for you."

He slipped his arm around her waist, but it wasn't an embrace; his touch was hard, almost hurting on her already bruised flesh. "You already tried that, remember? And I'll never be stupid enough to let my guard down with you. See, I have an advantage over Eames, because I know what a deceitful and violent little demon you are."

Keeping his arm around her waist, he steered her out of the alley onto the better lit expanse of Meyer Street. Billie knew they were in the heart of the sporting district now. Other cowboys sauntered along, their arms around the girls they had chosen for the evening. Billie and Nick blended in with the others, seeming to be just another pair bent on romance.

He glanced down at her, his heart turning over at the sight of her lovely, heart-shaped face. Then his gaze moved to her torn sleeve, and fury rose up in him again. That bastard! he raged inwardly. He was going to settle with Eames, and soon.

Billie was frightened by his silence and by the barely leashed violence she sensed in him. "Where are you taking me?" she asked, struggling to keep the quaver out of her voice.

"To a nice, private place where we can have a long talk."

She tried to pull away, but his arm was like an iron bar, implacable, immovable. "I've got to get back," she cried, desperate to find some way out of her predicament. "Rachel's going to miss me!"

"That's a real shame." He pulled her into a narrow side street. A gate was set in the high adobe wall that bordered the alley, entrance to one of the old, Mexican-style houses that abounded in this section. He unlocked the gate and stepped into the courtyard beyond, dragging Billie after him.

312

"Why didn't you just take a room at the hotel?" she asked through clenched teeth.

"I wanted a place where you'd be comfortable."

"You mean where no one could hear me scream for help."

"Exactly." He pushed the door open and stepped inside, pulling her in after him. Once he had secured the door, he let go of her so he could light the lamp.

It was a tiny house, just one room and a storage alcove. A battered metal bed occupied most of the room, its pillows and counterpane a virulent shade of purple, trimmed in stained and wilted lace. Several dresses, as garish as the bedclothes, hung in the alcove. Billie turned to Nick, her face flushed with indignation.

"You're right," he said, sliding the smoke-blackened chimney into place. "This place belongs to one of Tucson's ladies of the evening. You should have seen the look on her face when she heard that I wanted to rent her house, not her body."

A number of emotions surged through Billie, the chief of which was outrage. But there was an undercurrent of fear, as well as a tiny upwelling of desire at the sight of the bed. Was he planning to talk to her, beat her, or make love to her? His expressionless face gave her no clue. For a moment she quailed, then pride made her lift her chin in defiance. She wasn't about to beg for mercy from him or anyone!

Putting her hands on her hips, she demanded. "Well, what the hell do you want from me?"

"You never give an inch, do you?" he asked, that hint of steel coming into his voice again. "I admire that." Suddenly he picked her up and tossed her onto the bed.

With a startled yelp, she scrambled for the far side of the bed. But he hit the mattress an instant behind her, grabbing the back of her shirt to haul her toward him.

He wrestled her down onto her back, using his greater weight and strength to curb her struggles. She tried to bite him, unsuccessfully, then felt her hands being pinned above her head.

"Now," he growled, "tell me about the gold."

Billie tried to arch her back, but he leaned into her, pressing her deeply into the mattress. After a moment she subsided, her breath coming in rasping gasps. So that's what he's after, she thought in despair. Gold. Not her, but gold. "I hate you!" she cried.

"I know, honey. Now tell me about the gold."

"I don't know what you're talking about!"

Nick's body was already reacting to the feel of her against him, and her struggles were only making it worse. If he didn't create some distance between them, he'd take her here and now, no matter what she wanted. Keeping his hands on her wrists, he moved to straddle her hips so he could look down into her face. Damn her! he thought savagely. She was staring right back up at him, nothing but aggrieved innocence in her beautiful green eyes. And still he loved her, wanted her.

"You're lying," he rasped.

"Talk about liars!" She arched again, not realizing that doing so only incited his passion even more. "You were taking my money—taking *me,* damn you to hell—while you were stealing my cattle!"

Nick was beyond outrage. His legs were trembling with the force of his frustrated desire, his chest heaving with every breath. "Why didn't you tell the sheriff, then?"

"How do you know I didn't?"

"Because nobody tried to hang me," he said. "Why didn't you tell him, Billie?"

"Because I wanted to shoot you myself!" she shouted.

He smiled. "You'd never shoot me, honey." His voice

was a caress, and he moved against her so that she'd have no question as to what he intended to do to her.

Billie gasped. Although she would have cut her arm off rather than admit it, that knowledge of what had happened to his body was having an effect on her. A slippery warmth invaded her lower body, nearly bringing a moan to her lips. Although she didn't dare look down, she knew her nipples had tightened into hard little nubs. She squeezed her eyes closed against sudden tears. And he hadn't even kissed her! Whore! She writhed frantically, but only succeeded in pulling her skirt up around her hips. When she felt the cool air on her exposed thighs she stilled, afraid he would turn and see what she had done.

"Tell me about the gold," he demanded. His gaze was no longer on her face, however; he, too, had noticed those upstanding nipples. His face tightened as he struggled to control himself.

"You tell me your secret, and I'll tell you mine," she whispered. Please, she begged silently, give me a reason to love you!

Nick shook his head slowly. Some small part of him stood clear of his blazing anger and his desire, telling him that he was being irrational, demanding things he had no right to ask of her when he'd been less than open about his own role in this thing. But he couldn't help himself. Right or wrong, he was determined to dominate her tonight. Somehow, he had to find a way to force her to acknowledge his claim on her, body and soul.

"I asked you a question, and I want an answer!" he shouted.

"You can go straight to hell!" she screamed back.

She was goading him, he thought in rueful admiration, actually goading him to see how far he'd go. Well, she was about to find out. He stared down at her, fasci-

315

nated by her defiant courage. He knew she was frightened. But he also knew she was aroused; he could see it in her eyes, in the hardened peaks that were plainly visible through her blouse.

With a groan, he slid down so that he was lying full upon her. Restraining both her hands with one of his, he sank his other hand into her hair to hold her head still. He didn't dare kiss her mouth—yet. Instead, he nibbled her ear, then kissed his way along her jaw to her soft white throat, stopping there for a moment to suck warmth to the surface of her skin. He felt a moan rise in her chest to be quickly suppressed, and smiled.

Raising his head so he could look down at her, he said, "If you won't give me the truth, I'll take something else from you." Deliberately, he slid his legs between hers, using his feet to hold her ankles wide apart.

Billie gasped as his groin came against hers. Even through his jeans she could feel the throbbing hardness of him. His primitive aggression sent shock waves of response through her, and it was only with a determined effort that she kept herself from arching into him, encouraging him. Then he reached down between their bodies to rub her mound, and she was incapable of controlling the surging wetness that followed his touch. Humiliated by her own weakness, she closed her eyes. Hot tears leaked out from under her eyelids.

Nick saw those tears. His hand went up to her face to touch one of those crystal droplets wonderingly. It was then that he kissed her. Billie wanted to turn away, but his mouth was so gentle, so beguiling, that she was unable to move, unable to do anything but part her lips and let him in. His tongue swept inside, claiming her, bringing her to a state of moaning desire, and it wasn't until some time later that she realized he had released her wrists. But instead of hitting him, her hands drifted

316

down to twine in the thick, tawny hair at the nape of his neck.

"Ahh, Billie!" he groaned. His tongue slid over her lower lip first, teasingly, then the upper, then darted back inside to plunder the sweet depths of her mouth.

She pulled him closer still. He sat up suddenly, drawing her with him, and began to unbutton her shirt. Too impatient even to pull it all the way off, he slid his hands inside and plucked at the ribbons of her camisole. In moments her breasts were bare. His palms moved over her aching nipples, the slight rasp of his skin urging them into even tighter buds. With a hiss of indrawn breath, he stripped off her blouse and camisole and tossed them to the floor.

He kissed her, his mouth slanting across hers with barely restrained passion, then laid her back down and removed her skirt and drawers. He leaned over her, gazing at her soft-fleshed nakedness, and the flaring heat in his tawny eyes made Billie tremble. Reaching up, she unbuttoned his shirt and pulled it open so she could run her hands across the corded muscles of his shoulders and chest, the ridged leanness of his belly. With a hiss of indrawn breath, she caressed the hard shaft that pressed so urgently against the fabric of his jeans.

He grabbed her wrists and pinned them above her head again, not in anger this time, but to keep her from touching him. "I can't take it right now," he rasped. "I want you too badly."

"But—"

"Shhh. Let me love you, Billie." He moved so that his chest was poised a fraction of an inch above hers. The fine golden hairs on his chest tickled her oversensitive nipples unbearably, and she gasped.

"Oh, God!" she cried, nearly mindless with desire.

"Easy, honey," he murmured. "We have all night,

317

and I don't want to waste a moment of it."

He slid down her body so he could take one of her nipples into his mouth, suckling it, flicking it with the tip of his tongue, then moved to the other to work his magic there. Billie arched her back, moaning with pleasure as he let go of her hands, freeing her to caress his shoulders and the long, flexing muscles of his back.

His tongue glided down over her ribs. Billie grasped his head, holding him against her for a moment, seeking respite. He paused, giving it to her. Then his mouth moved lower, and lower still, to taste at last the warm silk of her woman's flesh.

His flicking tongue was torment, delicious, incredibly exciting torment. It was too much to bear. She had to have him now, to possess and be possessed. She called his name over and over, her nails raking lightly over his shoulders as she tried to urge him to her. But he continued caressing her, his hands holding her hips to keep her still.

"Please. Oh, please!" she moaned.

Nick groaned, his control broken by her plea. He rose to his knees between her legs and unfastened his jeans with impatient fingers. In too much of a hurry now to bother removing anything else, he came down on her again.

"Do you want me, honey?" he muttered, rubbing himself against her moist cleft but not entering her. His eyes were slitted, almost closed with the strain of controlling his raging emotions.

"Yes," she whispered.

Still he didn't take her. "I've got to know if you belong to me. Tell me, Billie! Tell me, before I go crazy."

Billie could feel the velvet-sheathed hardness of him sliding along her flesh with agonizing slowness, teasing, tantalizing, promising. She arched upward,

318

gasping, "Yes, I belong to you! Yes, I want you! Please, Nick. Help me!"

He slid into her then, unable to resist a moment longer. She met him eagerly, wildly, straining against him as he thrust into her. Her hands slid down over his buttocks, pulling him even closer, and Nick thought he'd go crazy with the pleasure of it. His face taut with passion, he dug the toes of his boots into the bed for purchase and drove into her wildly. She screamed as the shuddering climax caught her, and he covered her mouth with his to catch that cry triumphantly. Then he buried his face in her hair and gave himself up to the sensations her throbbing depths were bringing to him.

"I love you!" he cried, his voice muffled against her neck. "Oh, God, Billie!" A moment later his own release caught him and he lunged into her again and again, then collapsed upon her, completely drained.

Billie held him close for a long time, reveling in what they had shared. He'd said he loved her! "Nick?" she whispered. He muttered something, and she realized he had fallen asleep. No matter, she thought. They'd talk everything out in the morning. As long as he loved her, everything would be all right.

She kissed his brow and rolled him onto his side. "I love you, too." With a sigh, she nestled her head against his chest and closed her eyes.

Nick woke with a start. The oil in the lamp had burned out, leaving the room dark but for the narrow shaft of moonlight that came in through the high window. Billie was sleeping, her breasts rising and falling with her breathing. Her hair had come out of the braid and was spread out across the pillow in a glossy raven flood. Beautiful, he thought. Beautiful and prideful and as unpredictable as a whirlwind. He

319

reached out to stroke lightly over one of her lush breasts, noting with satisfaction how the peak hardened in response, even when she was asleep.

Although his body was clamoring that he stay and wake her with love, he knew he had to leave. If she woke, he'd be tempted to ask her for the truth again. With cynical self-deprecation, he realized that he was afraid of what that truth might be.

Eames and Stearns, no matter how dangerous, were easier to face just now. Danger he could handle. Billie, or at least a criminal Billie, he could not.

He reached for his shirt, discarded at some point during that wild lovemaking, although he didn't remember doing it. Damn, he thought wonderingly, I didn't even take my boots off! He turned to look at Billie again, savoring the beauty of her face, serene now in sleep. Tenderly, he pulled the counterpane over her.

Please, God, don't let me find out anything bad about this woman, he prayed, knowing that even if he did, and even if he had to be the one to bring her to justice, he would always love her.

A moment later he slipped outside, closing the door softly behind him. He saddled his buckskin gelding, glad that he hadn't ridden the more conspicuous Beelzebub, and rode from saloon to saloon looking for Eames. He must have asked a hundred people if they'd seen the gunman before he found a man who nodded agreement and directed him to the Golden Garter.

The saloon was on Congress Street, in the very heart of the sporting district, and there was nothing golden about it. Housed in a hastily constructed adobe building, it was a gathering place for the toughest and most violent of Tucson's men. There were four horses hitched to the rail outside, two of which Nick recognized as Dolorosa mounts.

"Interesting," he murmured, tying his mount to the

rail with the others. Casually, as though he was supposed to be there, he moved among the horses, lifting each animal's left front hoof. With an indrawn breath of satisfaction, he found one with a notched shoe.

There was a shout of drunken laughter from inside the saloon, getting rapidly louder as someone approached the door. Nick melted into the darkness of a nearby alley. Four men stumbled out of the saloon and lurched toward the horses.

"I don' see why we got to go jes' when things're gettin' fun," one of them complained. "That li'l redheaded gal was jes' warmin' me up."

One of his companions made a rude noise. "You miss meetin' the boss like we's s'posed to, an' you gonna lose what that redhead was interested in."

"You mean his money?" a third man jeered. "He ain't got nothin' else of any account to offer a gal like that."

A scuffle ensued between him and the first man, a stumbling, cursing tussle in which the blows were more enthusiastic than accurate. Nick watched impatiently, cursing all drunks under his breath.

Finally the other two men succeeded in pulling the struggling pair apart and getting them into their saddles. The four men rode down the street, whooping and laughing.

Nick claimed his own mount and followed them. To his surprise, they headed toward the outskirts of Tucson. For a moment he hesitated, thinking of Billie lying warm and willing in that bed.

"You're a damned fool," he muttered to himself. But even so, he urged his horse in pursuit of the men.

Chapter 28

"What the hell are you doing here?" a woman cried, waking Billie from a deep sleep.

Startled, Billie jerked to a sitting position, clutching the counterpane to her chest. "Who are you? What are you doing here?" she demanded.

The woman grinned and put her hands on her hips. Her hair was an improbable shade of yellow, her dress cut so low in the front that the top arcs of her nipples were visible when she took a breath. "This here's my house," she said. "You the fancy lady that feller rented it fer?"

Billie stared at her blankly.

The woman made an impatient gesture. "C'mon, honey, saddle it and git it out of here. I've had a busy night, and I want my sleep."

Billie glanced around the room, but Nick was nowhere to be seen. Even his gear was gone. "I'm not . . . I didn't . . ." she closed her mouth hastily, unable to think of any reply that might possibly be appropriate to this situation. She slid to the edge of the bed, still keeping the counterpane between her nakedness and the woman. "Would you turn around, please?" she asked.

The woman cackled, but turned her back obediently. "New at this, honey? You'll lose that bashfulness soon enough."

Billie dressed hurriedly, then sidled toward the door. The woman looked her up and down, her penciled brows going up in surprise when she saw Billie's clothing.

"You *are* new at this, ain't you?" she exclaimed. "Let me give you a bit of advice, eh? Git yoreself some nicer clothes." She swept her hand to indicate the tawdry crimson splendor of her own dress. "Men likes things like this. They's goin' to think you're a schoolmarm in that getup." Sympathy came into her jaded brown eyes. "Or worse yet, pore."

"I see. I'll, er, try to correct that. Well, thank you very much, Miss, er, Mrs. . . . I really must be going now," Billie babbled. She fled, leaving the door open behind her.

She headed toward Mrs. Petrie's, fury quickening her steps. Nick had done it to her again! He'd used her, then walked away. Love! A convenient word, spoken carelessly in a moment of passion. Tossed off and forgotten without a care for the person to whom it had meant the world. And then he had sneaked away like the thief he was, leaving her to be humiliated in front of a . . . she didn't finish the thought. What difference was there between her and that woman, after all? A wave of revulsion went over Billie, nearly making her stumble. Whore, that was the name for her—and a stupid one, at that!

She was in a full-fledged rage by the time she reached Mrs. Petrie's, and nearly walked right over the cowboys who sat slumped upon the boardinghouse steps. The four men looked like they'd been through a stampede.

Billie put her hands on her hips. "I swear I've never

seen a sorrier-looking bunch. Spend all your money?"

"I don't recollect spendin' it all," Lester said, holding his head between his hands as though afraid it might fall apart. "But it's gone, that's fer sure. Did any of you fellers see if I had a good time?"

The other men shook their heads numbly.

"Where's Eliseo?" Billie asked.

Lester winced. "He headed down Agua Prieta way to git Isabel and the kids."

Billie, taking pity on them at last, spoke slowly and gently. "Go get the wagon, Squint. We're going home."

She went inside, moving quietly so as not to wake the other boarders, and found Rachel already dressed. The girl was pacing the confines of the bedroom, practically wringing her hands in agitation. She whirled when Billie came into the room.

"Where have you been?" she demanded. "You were gone all night!"

"I . . . had things to do," Billie said. A hot blush rose into her cheeks. Before Rachel could question her further, she grabbed clothes out of the bureau drawer and began stuffing them into the carpetbag.

Rachel took the clothes from her and folded them neatly before repacking them. "Does your nasty mood have anything to do with Nick, by any chance?"

"No!" Billie quickly changed into a split skirt and a clean blouse, then grabbed the carpetbag and headed downstairs. The men, moving with surprising efficiency considering their condition, had brought the wagon out front and were waiting beside it. Admittedly, some of them were leaning a bit to one side in their saddles, but she supposed they'd make it. She flung her burden into the back of the wagon and climbed into the seat. The moment Rachel joined her, she slapped the reins against the team's rumps and moved out into the street.

A short time later, they left the city behind and

headed out into the arid countryside. Brown, dessicated brush crackled as it was crushed beneath the wagon wheels, and even the mighty saguaro cacti showed the effects of the drought, their tough outer hides deeply pleated from lack of moisture.

A lone rider appeared on the crest of a nearby slope. Spotting the Star M's wagon, he turned and galloped toward them.

Billie shaded her eyes with her hand. "Isn't that Corporal Tillston?" she asked. A sharp stab of disappointment went through her, and she squelched it firmly. Fool! she told herself savagely. Even now you're waiting for Nick to come back!

"Is that the man who came to the ranch after his troop had been attacked by Indians?" Rachel peered at the rapidly approaching rider. "Yes, I believe it is. But he isn't wearing a uniform."

Tillston pulled up beside the wagon and tipped his hat. "Mornin', ladies. Thought I recognized yer rig."

Billie nodded. "Morning, Corporal. What can we do for you?"

"I jes' wanted to pay my respects, ma'am." The old man gave a hoot of laughter, adding, "An' it's jest Tillston. I mustered out a coupla days ago. Been in fer near twenty years, but the goddamn—'scuse me, ladies—army ain't worth a hill o' beans no more. Gone soft. Next thing they'll be kissin' the 'Pach 'stead of shootin' 'em."

"Well—" Billie began, but Tillston talked right over her.

"I'm headed up to the Santa Catalinas," the old man said. "Goin' to join up with a bunch of fellers aimin' to fix them 'Pach once an' fer all. Damn army ain't gonna do nothin'."

"About what?" Billie asked.

326

"Some old buffalo hunter found a pack of 'Pach up by way of Venera Peak."

Billie managed to keep her face and voice composed, but her heart contracted with dread. There was a valley in that section of the Santa Catalinas, a tiny, secluded place where Laughing Woman's band often sought haven.

"Venera Peak?" Squint asked. "I thought the 'Pach had all run to Mexico."

"So did ever'body else. But this old feller—"

"Were they braves?" Billie demanded. "Did he say they were warriors or women?"

"Who cares?" Tillston spat into the dust. "Nits grow into lice. It's time we wiped them murderin' savages out. Any of you fellers want to come?"

"I'll come," Creek Beuther said.

Billie turned to look at the cowboy. When she saw the icy glitter of hate in his eyes, she shook her head. "Creek, you don't want to do this."

"Yes, ma'am, I shorely do." Creek urged his mount beside Tillston's. "Come on, old man, let's kill us some Injuns."

"How 'bout the rest of you?" Tillston asked. When the others shook their heads, he wheeled his mount and headed for Tucson at a gallop, followed by Creek Beuther.

"Stupid, jest plain stupid," Squint growled. "Somethin' like that'll set the whole territory afire. What the hell do they think Geronimo's goin' to do when he hears about it?"

"I've got to try and stop it." Billie picked up her rifle, then slipped an extra box of shells into her pocket. "Cully, let me use your horse."

Rachel grabbed the smaller girl's sleeve. "Billie, what are you going to do? You aren't—"

327

"I'm going to Fort Lowell," Billie said, disengaging herself gently and climbing into Cully's vacant saddle. "Maybe the army can do something."

"They ain't hardly time," Squint protested.

"I've got to try," Billie said. "Stay close to the house. Don't let anyone in, and I mean *anyone*. And post a guard on the roof at night; we've got rough times coming." She settled her hat more firmly on her head, then spurred the horse into a gallop.

She headed for Fort Lowell, but the moment she was out of sight, she turned her mount northeast, toward Venera Peak.

Dawn came, a delicate feathering of apricot on the eastern horizon. Nick was forced to drop back lest the men notice they were being trailed. An hour passed, then another, and the gentle light of the dawn sun had intensified into blinding-hot radiance. Heat waves rose in the distance, distorting the landscape so that the ranks of towering saguaros seemed to be marching out of the depths of a vast, shimmering sea.

"Who the hell are you meeting all the way out here?" Nick muttered to himself.

His horse snorted and tossed its head. Nick saw the animal's flaring nostrils and asked. "Smell water, boy?" He loosened his hold on the reins, and the horse moved eagerly toward the base of a low ridge just west of them. There was a tiny spring at the base of the slope, the barest trickle, but it nourished a small wedge of greenery amid the desolation. Someone else had found it, too, for many of the bushes had been stripped of leaves and the ground bore the tracks of several horses.

Leaving his mount by the water, Nick pulled a pair of field glasses out of his saddlebag and climbed to the crest of the ridge. He lay on his stomach and peered into the mirage. Four mounted men toiled through the depths of the illusory sea, their figures eerily distorted by the heat waves. As Nick watched, two more mounted men rode out from behind a thick stand of cactus and joined them. One of the newcomers was Carson Eames.

"Not enough cover to hide a snake out there," Nick growled, lowering the field glasses to the ground in front of him. "Damn it to hell!"

Suddenly he heard gunshots. Snatching the glasses up, he put them to his eyes just in time to see the last of the four men he'd been following fall limply to the ground. The two remaining riders wheeled their mounts and rode directly toward Nick's hiding place.

"Well, well, well," Nick murmured. "Come on, boys." He slithered down the slope and led his horse to a spot behind the ridge, then returned to his vantage point.

The two men passed right below him, so close that he could have tossed a rock down on their heads. To his delight, they stopped to water their horses at the spring below. He lay on his stomach and peered cautiously over the edge.

"What about Stearns?" Eames's companion asked. He was a burly blond-haired man with one cheek scarred with the black peppering of a powder burn.

Eames shrugged his narrow shoulders. "I don't need him any more, just the girl. She's the one who knows where the gold is."

"Jest think of it!" the other man said. "A million dollars in bullion! Why do you think she hasn't used it yet?"

"What do you care, as long as you get to take it away from her?" Eames asked.

The blond man laughed. Eames stared at him coldly for a moment, then bared his teeth in a brief, feral smile that had no humor in it. Nick knew the gunman had no plans to share the gold with anyone; the other man was as good as dead.

Nick pressed his forehead against his hands for a moment. Billie was innocent! he thought, his heart swelling with exhultation. No one who had access to a million dollars in gold and hadn't used it—except to help someone in need, he realized with a swift flash of understanding—could have an avaricious bone in her body. His lovely, stubborn, courageous Billie! He was going to shake her until her teeth rattled, then make love to her all over again. And again and again—as many times as it took to make her acknowledge that they belonged together.

"What you goin' to do with the girl?" the blond man asked.

"Everything," Eames said.

They guffawed lewdly. Nick's hand twitched toward his gun, but he restrained himself. He could never take both men in a fair fight, and he couldn't shoot a man in the back no matter how badly he needed killing. So, cursing himself for his damned stupid scruples, he watched Eames and the other gunman ride away. Toward Tucson, and Billie.

When they were out of sight, Nick retrieved his mount and headed back toward Tucson, swinging slightly to the north to stay out of their sight. Every instinct screamed at him to push his horse into a gallop, but wisdom told him that he'd only end up losing his mount in this arid heat. Patience, he counseled himself. You'll get to her first. You have to!

Suddenly he stiffened, spotting a broad lane of churned dust marring the surface of the ground just ahead. He urged his horse into a trot and reached it a few minutes later. He leaned far out of the saddle and peered at the ground, frowning. At least twelve men had passed this way, heading northwest mighty fast.

"What the hell are they doing out . . . Hey!" The exclamation was torn from him at the sight of a lone rider, just visible on the horizon. He seemed to be following that wide trail that led upward into the Santa Catalinas. There was something familiar about the way that person rode . . . Muttering under his breath, Nick pulled out his field glasses and trained them on the distant figure.

"Billie!" he hissed between clenched teeth, seeing the full curve of her chest, the long-dark braid flopping behind her as she leaned over her mount's neck.

Dropping the glasses back into his saddlebag, he kicked his horse into a gallop.

Chapter 29

Billie heard shooting up ahead. She hadn't made it in time! Pushing her horse as much as she dared across the broken, rocky ground, she made her way toward the far end of the little valley from which the gunfire came. Finally she was forced to leave her mount behind and continue on foot. She was close enough to hear the shouts of the men and the frightened shrieks of women and children. Billie began to run.

Her breath coming in quick pants from exertion, she scrambled up the lower slope of the hill that bordered the valley. When she reached the crest at last, she flung herself down on the ground and peered over the edge. She looked down on a scene that would haunt her for the rest of her life.

As she had feared, the only Apache in the valley were old men, women and children. The vigilantes rode through the camp, killing everything in their path. The old men caught up weapons and fought bravely, desperately, but were brutally cut down. Billie watched with horror as a mounted man, his rifle held like a club, galloped toward an Indian woman and her young child. The woman turned and ran, clutching the screaming child to her chest. It was Laughing Woman.

The man caught up with her and swung the rifle back for the killing blow.

"No!" Billie cried. She threw her rifle to her shoulder and fired in one automatic motion. The man somersaulted off the back of the horse, his body going in one direction, his rifle in another.

Billie reloaded and fired again. And again, and again. A pile of spent shells began to grow beside her. Still the killing of the women continued. Suddenly there was the report of a gun from the ridge to her left, a steady, rapid fire that could only come from a repeating rifle.

Billie flinched, expecting one of those bullets to hit her. But the newcomer was aiming, not at her, but down into the valley. Billie didn't question her good fortune; she threw another shell into the breech and fired, emptying another saddle. The men below reacted to the unexpected attack, diving off their mounts to take shelter. They began returning the fire, their bullets spattering the rocks beside Billie.

She peered at the ridge to her left and saw her rescuer slip from behind a clump of rocks and run toward a boulder that was halfway between him and her. The men below saw him, too; he ran the last few yards in a hail of bullets.

"Nick!" Billie cried, catching sight of the newcomer's face at last. Her voice was a silly little squeak that even she could barely hear.

He leaned his back against the rock and reloaded his rifle. Then he looked at her. The expression on his face was so worried, so full of love that she nearly left her shelter and ran to him.

"Are you all right?" he called.

Her heart swelled with joy. He had come for her! He had chosen to stand with her. "I'm fine." Her voice shook a little from reaction. "How about you?"

"I'm just fine, honey." He flipped onto his stomach and slid his rifle around the edge of the rock to fire down into the valley. "I don't suppose you'd consider leaving?" he asked between shots.

"Not until the women and children are safe." Billie risked a peek over the edge. "They've taken shelter in that gully over there, but they're pinned down."

"What would your pa say about this?"

She shrugged. "Like I said, Pa didn't hold with shooting women and children. He'd expect me to do what I felt was right."

Nick's rifle was empty. Billie began firing her own gun now, keeping the men pinned while he reloaded. If only she and Nick could hold on until nightfall, just an hour or so! Then the Apache women could escape, and she and Nick could slip away into the darkness, mysterious attackers whose identities would never be known.

Nick finished reloading. She dropped back to let him take over. This time he saved his bullets, only firing when one of the men showed an inclination to leave his bolt hole. So, Billie thought, he, too, was just trying to hold them off until night came. And he was careful not to hit anyone he didn't have to, aiming to scare, not to kill. Cushioning her cheek on her hand, she lay on her side and watched him. He worked coolly and efficiently, the long, smooth muscles in his back rippling beneath his shirt with his every movement.

As though feeling her regard like a physical touch, he glanced at her for a moment before returning his attention to the valley below. "I love you," he called. "Want to get married?"

She gasped. It was the last, absolutely the last thing she'd expected him to say. After everything he'd put her through, after stealing her cattle and running her half crazy with his demands and rejections and . . . and . . .

335

"How dare you ask me that?" she cried furiously. "I ought to shoot you!"

"I'll buy you a rifle just like mine," he wheedled.

To her surprise, she felt tears running down her cheeks. She scrubbed them away with her sleeve. "Go on, get out of here! I never want to see you again!"

He only smiled maddeningly and fired again, drawing in his breath with satisfaction as he sent a man diving to the ground on his belly.

He dropped down to reload, and Billie rolled on to her stomach and squirmed back to the edge. A man bolted from behind a rock and sprinted toward one of the few horses that hadn't fled the valley. Billie fired carefully, and her bullet kicked up a little gout of dust ahead of him. He dodged, but she reloaded and fired again, this time right between his feet, and he dove behind a stand of cholla cactus. Billie could hear his howls all the way up here.

"That was downright unkind, honey," Nick called.

Scowling, she refused to answer. The minutes rolled by. With infuriating slowness, the sun sank toward the west. The mountains' jagged shadows crept across the valley like great, grasping fingers. Billie and Nick took several more turns at keeping the men pinned. During one of her rests, Billie turned to Nick again.

"I thought I told you to leave," she called.

He fired twice, then dropped down as an answering spate of bullets whined over his head. "You're stuck with me, boss lady."

"Oh, really? Are there a few of my cattle you think you've missed?"

"The only thing I've missed is you." He popped up and snapped off another shot, then dropped down again. "When we get out of here, I'm going to take you to my bed again, and I'm not letting you up until you agree to marry me."

336

Despite her outrage, Billie felt that treacherous molten heat rise into her limbs at the picture his words evoked. Oh, if only she could trust him! Why did he want to marry her now, when before he'd always run away when it came time to make a commitment?

"It's going to be dark in a few minutes," he warned. "Get ready, honey."

Billie reached into her pocket and pulled out her remaining shells. Fifteen shots. She lined them up on the rock beside her.

Dusk came quickly, rolling across the valley in a dark violet wave. The Indian women and children, silent as ghosts, rushed out of their hiding place and ran toward the ridge where Billie lay. Cursing, the vigilantes began firing at them. Billie and Nick shot back, desperately trying to keep them from following the Indians. Billie could hear the women and children clambering up the slope below her, vulnerable now. She fired and reloaded faster than she ever had before, her hands working like machines.

Then the first of the Apache women reached the crest. She glanced at Billie, but ran past without speaking, several children following at her heels. More women, more children came. Laughing Woman was last. She knelt beside Billie for a moment, her work-roughened hand coming out to stroke the other girl's cheek.

"Good-bye, Cactus Flower, friend of my heart," she murmured. Then she was gone.

Billie knew she would never see Laughing Woman again. Tears seared the inside of her eyelids. She scrubbed the back of her hand across her face, forbidding those tears, then inched up farther to fire again. Bullets spanged the rocks all around her, and something hit her in the temple, hard. With a gasp, she squirmed backward. Something hot and wet trickled

337

down her face and dripped onto her shoulder. She touched her face. Her hand came away wet, stained with dark blood.

"Billie! Let's go before they get here!" Nick's voice came out of the shadows nearby, but she was dizzy, disoriented, and couldn't focus on anything.

Then Nick grabbed her, pulling her upright with a force that made her head spin sickeningly. He hauled her after him. When she stumbled, he tucked her beneath his arm and kept running.

His horse was tied beside hers. He tossed her onto her mount's back and climbed into his own saddle. Then he got his first good look at her. Blood covered one side of her face, and the front of her shirt was soaked with it.

"Oh, my God!" Gently, he lifted her in front of him, cradling her against his chest. Taking the reins of her horse, he led it behind him as he spurred his own mount into motion. Fear for her made his pulse hammer in his ears. He had no idea how badly she was hurt, didn't know if moving her like this would kill her. But he had to take the chance; if those men caught up with them, her death would be a certainty.

He pushed the pace as much as he dared, trying to stay to the rocky places so as not to leave a trail. The moon rose, and its light made her blood-covered face look like a ghastly death mask. Her eyes were closed, and for a moment, for a moment . . . He thrust his hand beneath her shirt. But her heart still beat, sure and slow, and the skin of her breasts was warm against his palm.

She murmured, "Lecher."

His breath went out in a hiss of relief. There didn't seem to be any immediate pursuit just now, so he stopped the horses and climbed down, still holding her. Tenderly, he washed her wound with water from his canteen and examined it. A bullet had creased her head just above the temple, but despite all the blood, the wound was superficial. She had obviously taken quite a knock, but would recover after a few days' rest and a god-awful headache.

"You'll be fine, honey. It's just a crease." Suddenly he clasped her to him, burying his face in her thick, fragrant hair. "I thought . . ."—there was a constriction in his chest, making his voice hoarse—"I thought I'd lost you!"

She shook her head slightly and was surprised by how painful the small movement was. "Stupid," she mumbled.

He grunted, peevish with reaction. "Let's get out of here, if you're feeling good enough to insult me."

When she was once again settled in the saddle before him, Billie pressed her face against the warmth of his chest. The dizziness intensified with the motion of the horse, and she whimpered.

"Billie, what is it?" he demanded.

"My head . . . so dizzy," she moaned.

"I'm taking you to a doctor."

"No!" She stiffened, then instantly regretted it. She pressed her hands to either side of her head in an attempt to calm the whirlwind that was going on inside. "Home. Got to get home."

Nick's hands trembled on the reins. God, to see her in such pain! If only he could take it from her! "Don't be an idiot," he said, his voice harsh. "You need a doctor."

"No! Home . . . fast as we can. Rachel . . . danger." Billie squeezed her eyes shut, trying to hold on long enough.

Nick stiffened. "Rachel is in danger?"

"The gold . . . he'll come for the gold." God, her head felt like it was going to come off. "Nick! I'll be all . . . right." She clutched at his collar, desperate to make him understand. "Promise . . . take me home. Please!"

"All right, honey. I'll take you home," he soothed. "As fast as I can. Rest now."

Billie let herself drop into the dark whirlpool that beckoned. She was not quite unconscious, at least, not all the time. She was aware of the rhythmic movement of the horse beneath her, the warmth of Nick's strong body against her cheek, even the passage of time from darkness to light as night turned to morning again. But it was too much effort to rouse herself, even to open her eyes.

Secure in the protection of Nick's arms, she let herself drift at last into the dreamlessness of a deep, healing sleep.

Chapter 30

"Billie, can you hear me?" Rachel asked.

Billie opened her eyes, then cautiously moved her head from side to side. The pain was still there, but it was muted, and the dizziness was gone. Then Nick moved into her line of vision. He rushed to her, gathering her into his arms.

"Ahhh, honey! We were so worried," he murmured.

She leaned into him, reveling in the hard strength of his arms. Then she pushed him away and smoothed her mussed nightgown. "What day is it?"

"Thursday," Rachel said.

"I slept two days!" Billie cried. She glanced at the light slanting in through the gunport. "More than two; it's afternoon! What's been going on? Has anyone tried—"

"Easy, honey," Nick soothed. "Everything's fine."

"Don't you tell me everything's fine, Nick Larabee!" she said.

"Larabee?" Rachel whirled to look at Nick. "You haven't told her?" she demanded, putting her hands on her hips.

"Well, I haven't exactly had a chance—" he began.

Billie looked from one to the other in confusion.

"Tell me what?"

Rachel glared at Nick. "His name," she said. "His real name. Alan Nicholas Laird."

"Laird? He's"—Billie drew in a deep, shuddering breath, then shrieked—"he's your brother?"

"Yes."

He held out his hand. "Now, Billie, don't get upset—"

"Where's my gun?" Billie flung the covers aside. "I'm really going to shoot him this time!"

Grinning, Nick caught her in his arms and held her against his chest, ignoring her struggles. After a few wild moments she stopped and leaned her head on his shoulder, panting with exertion.

"Are you going to listen now?" he asked.

She nodded. He laid her back on the pillows and sat down on the edge of the bed.

Rachel put her hand on his shoulder. "Let me tell it," she said. When he nodded, she sat down beside him and clasped her hands in her lap. "You see, Billie, the men who killed our family weren't Apaches. Oh, they were dressed as Apaches, war paint and all, but two of my . . . attackers had blue eyes."

Billie sat up straighter. "The man in town—the one with the raspy voice . . . he was one of them!" Her startled gaze went to Nick. "That's why you killed him!"

"Yes," Nick said, a fierce look coming into his tawny eyes. "And because of what he tried to do to you."

Rachel shuddered in remembrance. "When I sent Nick a telegram telling him what had happened here, I warned him that things were not as they seemed. We decided that I should try to find a place at one of the ranches. One of the ranchers was behind the attack, we were sure. If I could only identify the men who had done it, perhaps we'd know who had paid them."

342

"You let me think . . ." Billie took a deep breath. "Why couldn't you trust me, Rachel? I thought we were friends."

"Ask my brother," Rachel said.

"I made her promise not to tell you." Nick spread his hands wide. "I didn't know who to trust."

"Lack of trust sure didn't stop you from . . ." Billie glanced at Rachel and blushed. Nothing was going to make her finish that sentence.

Rachel laughed. "You ought to see the look on your face!"

Scowling, Billie settled back onto the pillows. But the frown was there only to mask the happiness that filled her. What happened before today didn't matter. She knew that Nick loved her. His admiration and desire hadn't been false, nor had his feelings. At this moment, she would forgive him anything. But she wasn't about to let *him* know that.

"I thought you were an outlaw," she said. At Nick's stare of outrage, she added defensively, "Well, what else was I supposed to think with you poking around, asking too many questions and turning up in places an honest man wouldn't be?"

Nick leaned over her, his voice lowering to a growl. "You had your own secrets, honey. Between your friendship with the Apaches and the gold, I didn't know what to think."

"Those men tortured my uncle," Rachel said, her voice trembling with remembered pain and horror. "They tried to force him to tell them something, but they failed."

"The gold was the reason for everything that happened, wasn't it, Billie?" Nick asked.

"Yes. That damned gold!" These two peopole had lost so much because of it. "Eight years ago a smugglers' pack train came up here from Mexico. But

343

someone learned about it, and a bunch of outlaws set a trap for them. Most of the Mexicans were killed, but not before they hid the gold. Pa and Rowan Laird found one of them. He'd been gut-shot, dying. They brought him back here and we gave him what little comfort we could. He became delirious. All he could talk about was the gold."

"He told you where it was?"

She shook her head. "Oh, I know the general area where it's hidden, but it's scattered over a dozen square miles of canyons and arroyos. The outlaws searched for it for years without finding so much as a single coin."

Nick rubbed his chin thoughtfully. "I'm surprised they didn't go after your father and Uncle Rowan years ago."

"Who said they didn't?" Billie touched the spot where the bullet had scored her and winced. "Pa and your uncle Rowan were old hands. Real scrappers, as Budge would say, who didn't take kindly to anyone trying to force them to do anything."

"They killed those men? All of them?" Rachel's voice was a squeak.

Billie sighed. "Rachel, in those days there was no law here, no safety but what a man made for himself."

"Didn't they try to find the gold for themselves?" Nick asked.

"Well, sure. But they had no better luck than the outlaws. After a while, they realized that they were chasing a dream and gave it up."

Nick leaned forward intently. "You paid Mrs. Harndon in gold."

"How did you know about that?" she demanded.

"Answer me!" His voice was sharp, urgent. This was the last, lingering doubt he still held about her, and he wanted it settled.

344

Her chest swelled with indignation. "That five hundred dollars was what the Mexican was carrying on him. We didn't dare spend it or even keep it in the house lest it bring every gold-hungry renegade down on our necks. I only gave it to Emma Lee because she needed it so badly." She glared at Nick. "And despite what you might think of me, I didn't take her ranch from her when she was down. I'm only holding it for her until Shep is old enough to take over."

"I'm sorry," he said.

Not caring whether Rachel saw or not, Billie leaned forward and kissed him lingeringly. "Me, too," she murmured.

"I'll go see to dinner," Rachel said, her eyes brimming with moisture. "Don't let her get up, Nick."

"I won't." Nick's warm, gold-flecked gaze never left Billie's face as his sister left the room and quietly closed the door behind her. He leaned toward Billie. As he came closer, she sank back against the pillows.

"I want that rifle," she said.

"As soon as I can manage." He smiled. "Does this mean you'll marry me?"

"Maybe. Nick, what are we going to do about Stearns? We can't go to the sheriff; Stearns owns him."

"I know. I sent for a federal marshal." The fierce look came back into his face. "Did you think Stearns owned me, too?"

"Never." She grinned up at him, thinking that no one would ever believe a man like this could be bought by anyone. "I thought you were stealing on your own account."

His breath went out in a gasp of outrage. "You are the most infuriating woman—"

"I know." She looked up at him from under her lashes. "Will you talk French to me?"

"French?" he asked, bewildered.

"Did you think you were only going to get to use it on Julia?"

"So that's it." He leaned closer, holding himself over her with braced arms. "I'll talk all the French you want. I'll whisper it over every inch of your body until you beg me to stop. Will that do?"

"It's a start."

"How do you feel, *cherie?*" he murmured.

"Stronger." Billie reached up to trace the strong contours of his jaw and the warm, sensual curve of his mouth. "But I'm not sure I forgive you yet for not telling me who you really are. What you put me through!"

He laughed. "You thought I was in love with Rachel. My own sister!" Bending his head, he ran the tip of his tongue upward along the satin curve of her throat.

"Wait!" she gasped, holding him away with braced arms.

"What is it now?" he demanded in exasperation. Couldn't she see how badly he needed her just now?

"I . . . I'll never be the kind of woman you're used to. I'll never sit in the house and make doilies and things—"

"I don't want doilies, Billie." He increased the pressure on her arms, desperate to get close to her again. "I want you. Whatever you are, whatever you do or don't do, I want you. Forever."

Billie wound her arms around his neck, and he came against her in a rush.

"Je t'adore, Billie. *Je t'aime, Je t'aime."* He dropped tiny little kisses on her chin, her lower lip, then fastened his mouth on hers hungrily.

Billie pulled his shirt down along his tensed arms, ripping a button from it in her haste. He stripped the garment off and discarded it, murmuring things in her ear she no longer tried to understand. She wanted him,

346

wanted him with a desire that was nearly savage in its intensity. Although she tried to pull him down on top of her, wanting to feel the delicious weight of his body, he resisted.

Billie whimpered in frustration. His weight shifted, and his hands were on her breasts, his warm, strong hands. He slowly untied the ribbons on the bodice of her nightgown. With a single, sweeping movement, he slid the interfering fabric down and away, leaving her naked to his hungry gaze.

And then he did what he had promised, murmured things against every inch of her heated, silken skin until neither he nor she cared what language he spoke. He explored her with his lips and tongue until there was no place unknown to him, no nerve untouched, no reaction unplumbed.

Billie cried out, writhing under his ministrations, then pushed him onto his back and began her own trembling exploration of his hard male body. He groaned, half crazy from the sweet touch of her hands, the silken heat of her so close, so willing. Finally the delicious torment became too much to bear. He grasped her wrists, imprisoning her hands against his chest, and stared up into her passion-glazed eyes for a long, breathless moment.

"Oh, God, come here!" he growled then, pulling her astride him and slipping into her with a smooth, strong thrust that made her moan with pleasure.

She buried her face in the curve of his neck and gave herself up to the sensation that was rapidly building in her lower body as he loved her with gentle power. The first ripples of her climax caught her. Nick felt them, too, and the knowledge of what was happening to her tore aside the last remnants of his control. They cleaved together, shuddering, crying out with the force of their passion.

"I love you, I love you," he moaned into her hair.

Billie was too drained to lift her head. "I love you, too," she whispered against the moist skin of his chest. Her eyes closed. "So sleepy." With an effort, she opened her eyes again. "Nick? Stearns is going to try something, I know it. He won't let the gold go without a fight."

"Don't worry about him. We've got guards posted. He can't come at us without us knowing, and an army couldn't pry us out of here." He stroked her hair tenderly. "Go to sleep, honey. I'll take care of you."

She was vaguely aware of Nick pulling the covers up over them both before sleep claimed her once again.

Billie woke to darkness. It must be long after midnight, she realized, for the house was completely quiet. Nick lay beside her, his long body sprawled out over most of the bed. Careful not to wake him, she slid out from under the blankets and dressed, then padded barefoot out to the main room. She was starved. She'd fix herself something to eat, then climb back into bed and wake him up.

After lighting the lantern that hung over the table, she saw Rachel had thoughtfully left out some biscuits and a slice of ham. Billie jiggled the coffeepot. Hearing the slosh of good, thick, leftover brew, she lit the stove and put the pot on to heat. The aroma of coffee soon filled the room.

The trapdoor over her head opened. Lester Manon peered down into the room, whispering, "Do I smell coffee?"

"Want a cup?"

"I shorely do. This watch is getting mighty tiresome."

Billie took two cups down from the cabinet and

348

moved toward the stove. "I'll come up. I could use a breath of night air."

He slid the ladder down through the trapdoor. Billie handed him his steaming mug, then, balancing the other cup in her left hand, climbed to the roof.

The moment the trapdoor closed behind her, Lester put his hand over her mouth and pulled her against him. Her cup went flying, dark coffee spilling out to stain the pale adobe. Before she had a chance to struggle, he gagged her with his bandanna, then tied her hands behind her with a piece of rawhide.

"Sorry, Billie," he whispered. "But Stearns'll pay me five hundred dollars for takin' you to him. I got debts, bad debts to bad folks." He slid the ladder over the edge of the parapet until the lower end touched the ground.

She wriggled furiously, but was helpless to stop him as he lifted her to his shoulder and climbed down from the roof.

Chapter 31

Lester Manon led Billie into Rosswell Stearns's elegant study and pushed her into one of the plush velvet chairs in front of the desk. Billie shifted her weight, unable to repress a moan at the hideous discomfort of her bound arms. It was full morning, brilliant sunshine spearing in through the big window.

"Remove her bindings," the Englishman said.

Lester slit the rawhide thong securing her wrists and ungagged her, then handed the kerchief to Stearns. "You might want this," the cowboy drawled. "She's madder'n a wet cat."

"Did Larabee come back with her?" Stearns held the cloth disdainfully between his thumb and forefinger. With his other hand, he held out a packet of money.

Lester counted it, then slid the packet into his shirt pocket. "You offered me five hundred to bring her here, and that's what I did. Anythin' else you want to know, you git yoreself another boy." Turning on his heel, he stalked out of the room.

"You could have saved yourself five hundred dollars by killing him before you paid him," Billie said.

Stearns raised his gray-flecked eyebrows. "Miss Meyrick, you know very well that I would never do such a thing. No matter what happens, that money belongs to him." He turned to a nearby cabinet and took out a bottle of brandy. "What will you have? Sherry, perhaps?"

Billie shook her head. "Let's not waste time, Mr. Stearns. Get to the point."

"Very well. I want you to lead me to the gold."

"What if I say I don't know where it is?" she countered.

"That would be most unwise. Although I think you are a woman of remarkable determination, you have weaknesses, Miss Meyrick." After pouring himself a snifter of brandy, he sat down in the chair behind the desk and regarded her coolly. "You have become quite attached to Miss Laird and Mr. Larabee, have you not? No matter how careless you may be about your own life, I don't think you would be quite so reckless with theirs. And let us not forget dear Helena. A lovely woman, and quite charming, but she is replaceable, you know."

His words sent a hot stab of terror through Billie. She knew, knew as surely as she knew her own name, that he wouldn't hesitate to carry out his threat. And Helena would be first. "How could you? She's your wife!"

"But, Miss Meyrick, her fate is in your hands, not mine. If she is . . . discarded, that will be your doing."

"You're a cold bastard," she hissed.

He took a sip of brandy. "I assure you that my birth was perfectly legitimate. As for being cold, well"—he stretched his lips in a humorless, sinister smile—"it does allow one complete freedom of action, does it not?"

Billie looked down at her bare feet, not wanting him to see how badly he frightened her. Then she thought of her father and how he would have faced this man, and brought her head up with a jerk. "Why the rustlers?" she asked. "Why did you try to buy my ranch?"

"I think you know."

She stared into his pale, emotionless eyes. For all her abhorrence of his morals and his methods, she understood this man. "You wanted to squeeze me dry," she said. "You wanted to force me to go after the gold to keep my ranch."

"Thank you, Miss Meyrick. I'm glad you credit me with as much intelligence as I do you." He held the snifter up to the light, admiring the warm amber glow of the liquor within.

"And the Harndons? Why did you burn them out?"

He shrugged. "When one hires violent men, it is sometimes difficult to control their every act. I offered to buy the widow's land as recompense for what I was unable to prevent. I certainly was not interested in her paltry few acres of dust."

She nodded. It made a twisted kind of sense, she supposed. Honor, as Stearns saw it.

"Now, Miss Meyrick, let us get back to business. I have a map here. Just show me where the gold is located, and I'll set you free."

Billie knew he'd kill her the moment he got his hands on the gold. No matter that she didn't know where the gold was—he'd never believe it. She had to get him away from his army of gunmen, out into her territory. She'd show him that there were things more precious than any treasure, things like water and shade and knowing the way home. "I won't tell you where it is," she said. "But I'll take you to it."

He sighed. "Why must you make this difficult?"

"Why?" A grin of pure unholy joy lit her face. "Because I don't like you, and I'm damn well going to make you sweat for what you want."

The door was flung open suddenly. Helena rushed

into the room, followed by Julia. The English girl sat down in the settee near the door and smirked at Billie.

Helena ran to her daughter. "Are you all right?" she demanded. "He hasn't—"

"Helena." Stearns didn't shout, but there was a note of anger bubbling just beneath the surface of his deceptively quiet voice. "This has nothing to do with you. Go to your room."

"I won't!" Helena cried, placing herself between him and Billie. Tears ran down her face, and her knees trembled with fear of her husband, but still she faced him. "You're not going to hurt her! I'll kill you first!"

Julia clapped her hands. "Oh, how droll!"

Billie jumped to her feet and tried to pull Helena out of the way. "Mother, don't. It won't do any good."

The Englishman half-rose from his chair. "Mr. Jenks!"

"Boss?" One of the house guards appeared in the doorway.

"Take my wife to her room. See that she stays there."

"Yes, sir." The man grabbed Helena by the arms and dragged her toward the door.

Helena struggled wildly. Her elbow caught the man in the pit of his stomach, and his breath went out with a gasp.

Billie threw herself at the man's legs, catching him just behind the knees. He went down in a heap, his head striking the edge of a nearby cabinet.

"Mother, run!" she shrieked. "Nick's at the ranch!"

As Stearns rushed around the desk, Helena raised her skirts high with one hand and bolted for the door. Julia tried to grab her as she went past, but the older woman lashed out with her fist, catching the English girl on the nose. Shrieking, Julia fell against her father with a great flailing of arms and lace petticoats.

Billie scrambled to her feet and raced for the

354

window. With a roar, Stearns flung Julia to one side and hurled himself after his captive. His hand closed on Billie's arm, jerking her to a halt. Dragging her after him, he headed for the front door to alert his men. But he was too late; outside, there was a confused babble of men's voices, then the sound of a galloping horse's hoofbeats headed away from the house.

Stearns flung the door open just in time for Billie to see her mother astride the running horse, her white legs exposed nearly to her hips, her glorious red-gold hair streaming behind her like a banner. In a moment, horse and rider had cleared the gate and headed out into the countryside.

"Stop her!" Stearns shouted.

Two men jumped on their horses and galloped after the rapidly retreating pair.

Billie screamed, "Go, Mother! Show them how a Meyrick can ride!" Then she began to laugh. "You bastard, you thought you'd married a porcelain doll, didn't you?"

"Larabee won't do you any good," Stearns snapped, twisting Billie's arm behind her back cruelly. "He'll just get himself killed."

Despite the pain, Billie managed to laugh again. "How many men are you planning to bring, Stearns? Who can you trust," she gasped as he tightened his hold on her arm, "besides me?"

He stared at her, surprise coming into his pale eyes. "Have you lost your wits?"

"My pa always said an honest enemy was better than an unfaithful friend any day." She shook her hair back from her face. "How many men are you going to bring with you? Think about it, Stearns—a million dollars in gold. Do you know what the sight of it can do to a man? How many can you handle if they decide to take it for themselves?"

"Ahhh." He loosened his grip, but retained his hold on her wrist. "Mr. Gowan, Mr. Bullock, get your mounts and come with us."

Billie smiled with satisfaction. Only two. She'd done it! Greenhorns, both of them, and Stearns the worst of the lot. Three inexperienced men against one girl who had cut her teeth on this range. Fair enough, she thought.

Chapter 32

"How much farther, Miss Meyrick?" Stearns asked.

"As the crow flies, seventeen or eighteen miles. On horseback . . ." Billie shrugged.

She had led them into the range east of the Dolorosa, a desolate maze of canyons, arroyos and the dry, stark humps of hills that had lost even the scanty covering of brush they normally wore. It was late afternoon now, the shadows reaching long fingers across the dessicated ground. Billie welcomed the fall of night just as she had welcomed the passage of every hour, for time was her ally. Nick was coming for her. She knew it as surely as she knew her name. And then Stearns would be finished.

"I've never seen clouds like that," Stearns said, indicating the sky to the east. "Will we be getting rain soon?"

She braced her bound hands on her saddle horn and looked toward the hazy purple outline of the Rincon Mountains, where towering masses of white, slow-boiling clouds had collected around the peaks. A lone cloud had broken away from the pack and moved out over the land. A gray curtain of mist hung below it, but the moisture evaporated before it reached the ground.

"Maybe," she said. "But not today."

"Mr. Stearns!" One of the gunmen pointed toward the west, where a faint plume of dust rose over the ground. "Someone's followin' us."

"Larabee." The Englishman unbuttoned his jacket, exposing his holster and pistol. "Kill him."

"No!" Billie cried. "If you do, I won't go another foot."

Stearns lips thinned. "Then I won't need you, will I?"

One of the gunmen grabbed her by the hair and put his pistol to her temple. "Should I do it, Boss?"

Billie looked at Stearns, hoping her face didn't show the black terror that twisted her stomach. But she had to save Nick! Without him her life would be as dry and sere as the brush underfoot, her heart a wasteland. "Go ahead," she said through clenched teeth. "At least I'll have the satisfaction of knowing you'll never see that gold."

"Let her go," Stearns snapped. "Get Larabee, you two. Bring him here unharmed." His cold gaze went back to Billie's face. "Will that do, Miss Meyrick?"

She nodded, unable for the moment to find the strength to speak. Stearns took her reins from the man who was holding them. As the two rode away to do his bidding, he led her to the narrow line of shade near the wall of the canyon.

"You are only delaying the inevitable, you know," he said.

Billie shrugged. "A day, an hour, even a minute is better than nothing. You never know what'll happen." Showing the edges of her small white teeth in a grin, she added. "Maybe even God will take a hand."

"Pshaw, Miss Meyrick. God wouldn't bother."

Billie shrugged again and lapsed into silence. If only she could grab the Englishman's gun and get off a warning shot to Nick! But the man must know exactly

358

what she was thinking, for he made sure there was plenty of distance between them.

An hour later the gunmen returned. Nick's hands were bound before him, his horse led by one of his captors. A swelling bruise marked his right cheek.

"Boss, he was comin' so fast he ran right into our little trap," one of the gunmen said, urging Nick's horse beside Billie's so that one gun could cover them both.

Nick leaned toward her, his tawny eyes warm with love and concern. "Are you all right?" he asked.

She nodded.

He looked at her closely, seeing her fear-shadowed eyes and the reddening touch of sunburn on her cheeks and nose. Awkwardly because of his bonds, he took his hat off and placed it on her head. His fingers lingered for a moment on the silken glory of the unbound hair that cascaded in dark ripples down her back.

"Mother made it to the ranch all right, I suppose?" she asked.

"She sure did." Reluctantly, he dropped his hands back to his saddle horn. "She came riding over that ridge screaming like an Apache, her skirt rucked up to her waist to show one of the nicest pair of legs I've ever seen."

Stearns pressed his lips into a thin line. "We can cover a few more miles before dark. Which way, Miss Meyrick?"

Billie glanced toward the cloud-shrouded peaks of the Rincon Mountains again, then pointed to the mouth of a nearby canyon. "That way."

They made less than a mile, however, before the failing light made it too dangerous to go farther on this broken, stony ground. They made camp in a fold between two hills, building the fire in a shallow depression scooped in the earth. Billie and Nick, their hands still bound, sat together on one side of the fire, Stearns

359

and the two gunmen on the other.

"No tea?" Billie asked when Stearns reached for the coffeepot.

The Englishman shrugged. "Coffee is preferable to tea that is improperly prepared."

"Are you planning to go back to England?" Billie nearly added, "after this is over," but just couldn't get the words out.

"No. I've come to like it here. With judicial purchases of land and water rights, I can come to control a tract of land nearly as large as England. A heady thought, is it not?" He cupped his large hands around the coffee mug. "And I shall do everything in my power to improve the primitive conditions here."

"Is that why you offered a bounty on Indian scalps?" Nick asked. Billie jerked in surprise, but he shook his head to warn her to silence.

"Of course," Stearns said. "I'll not allow those savages to run freely in my territory."

"So you'll exterminate them." Nick brought the heel of his boot down on a scorpion that was scrabbling toward Billie's bare feet. "Crush them like insects."

"Yes." Stearns smiled.

Billie took a deep, calming breath. And he called the Apache savage! "Do you really think you can kill us and remain in the territory?" she demanded. "Arizona isn't as uncivilized as it was a few years ago. We'll be missed, and people will be asking questions."

"The right answers will stop all the questions, Miss Meyrick," he said. "If one enjoys a certain social position, people want to believe what one tells them."

"Some people, maybe," Nick growled. "But I sent for a federal marshal. He won't care if you're king of England."

For the first time, Stearns looked disconcerted. His pale eyes flamed with rage for a moment, then he regained his usual cool demeanor.

"I expect a federal marshal is as amenable to persuasion as other men," he said. "If not, I'll just have to be satisfied with England, shan't I? With a million dollars' worth of gold, that shouldn't be difficult."

"How did you hear about the gold, anyway?" Nick asked. "Your hired rogues were working long before you got here."

Stearns sipped his coffee and grimaced with distaste. Putting the cup to one side, he clasped his hands over his knees. "An Englishman by the name of Jack Longwood was the leader of the outlaws who attacked the smugglers' train. For years he searched for the gold without success. Then, nearly destitute, dying from some painful malady, he returned to England to beg help from his distant cousin."

"You?" Nick guessed.

Stearns nodded. "Of course, he died soon after telling me about the treasure—"

"I bet," Billie muttered.

"Imagine my surprise," the Englishman continued, "when I discovered I was married to the former wife of one of the men who knew where the gold was hidden." He picked up a stick and fed it absently to the flames. "I made inquiries, hoping to find a suitable property to purchase—to give me a reason for going to Arizona, of course. When I heard that the Dolorosa was available, I bought it immediately and sent Mr. Eames, a contact from an earlier, ah, venture in your country, ahead to prepare the way."

"Was it Eames's idea to torture Rowan Laird, or yours?" Nick asked, his jaw clenching in cold anger. God, if he could only get his hands on Stearns's throat! "What about killing the whole family? Did you tell him to do that?"

"Certainly not. Believe me, Mr. Larabee, I prefer a

subtler way. I only sent him to hire men and begin the rustling operation to get things stirred up. Chaos, you know, gives one considerable room to work." Stearns sighed. "But it seems the lure of the gold was too much for Mr. Eames. He had designs of his own."

"Don't you think he still does?" Nick's teeth showed in a humorless grin. "I'd watch my back, if I were you."

The two gunmen peered nervously into the surrounding darkness. It was obvious that even these hard men feared Carson Eames. Billie shivered; so did she. The man was vicious, without compunction or conscience. Even Stearns had *some* sense of morals, twisted though it might be.

"Mr. Gowen, you take first watch on that rock over there," Stearns said. "I suggest that the rest of us get some sleep."

Nick picked up the blanket he and Billie had been given and spread it upon the ground. He sat down on it and held out his bound arms to her. She went to him, kneeling in front of him so he could slip his hands over her head and gather her against his warmth.

He lay down, bringing her with him. Rage did a slow, fiery dance in his veins when he saw the raw skin of her bound wrists and the bruises that marked her forearms. Stearns was going to pay for doing this to her, he vowed, Every bruise, every insult would have its reckoning. Fiercely, he pressed her close againt his chest.

"I love you," he murmured in her ear. "No matter what happens, I will always love you."

"Shut yore mouths!" the remaining gunman barked. "Don't say nothin' the rest of us cain't hear, or I'll have to sleep betwixt you."

Billie rubbed her face against the fabric of Nick's shirt. With his heart beating against her cheek, slow and steady, she felt as though nothing in the world could hurt her. Courage seeped back into her. It couldn't end like this, with her and Nick dead—not Nick, his lean, powerful body, his infuriating, wonderfully sly humor stilled forever—and Stearns getting away to lord it over his neighbors with that damned haughty face that dared anyone not to believe him. Somehow they'd get away. Somehow they'd find a way to beat Stearns and his henchmen.

She stared fiercely at the leaping orange flames of the fire, hoping to convince herself it would really happen.

"Wake up," Stearns said, nudging Nick's shoulder with the toe of his polished boot. "It is past daybreak."

"Get your damned foot away from me or I'll tear it off," Nick growled. His voice was so savage that Stearns took a step backward in surprise.

Billie roused slowly, groggy with exhaustion and the heavy, frightening dreams that had haunted her sleep. Nick lifted his bound hands over her head and rose to a sitting position, then climbed stiffly to his feet.

"Come on, honey," he said, pulling her to her feet.

For a moment she leaned against him, unable to stand. But the sight of Stearns put steel in her spine, and she straightened, reaching up with bound hands to rake her hair into some semblance of order. She wouldn't let this man think he had defeated her. Oh, he had the power of life or death over her, but he'd never have the satisfaction of breaking her. But it was hard not to give in to the fear and fatigue, hard not to let the tears flow. Her bottom lip quivered. Then Nick brushed against her, and the warm strength of him firmed her resolve.

After a breakfast of sweet, mouth-searingly hot coffee and dry biscuits, the gunmen shoved the captives toward their mounts. Nick boosted Billie into her saddle, then climbed slowly, painfully into his own.

363

Turning his head so that the others couldn't see, he winked at her.

The sneaky devil! she thought admiringly. Acting like he was half crippled when she knew he was as strong and agile as ever. Her sagging spirits lifted. They *would* spend a lifetime together. Stearns, Eames, all the outlaws in the world were not enough to stop that dream from becoming reality. A plan began to form in her mind. Oh, it was risky, all right. But as her pa used to say, the things not worth taking a little risk for aren't worth having.

"Which way, Miss Meyrick?" Stearns asked.

She turned to look at the Englishman with narrowed eyes. "Well, I'm not exactly sure," she hedged. "Some of these canyons look an awful lot alike."

He drew his pistol and aimed it at Nick's head. "Which way, Miss Meyrick?" he asked again, his voice as cool as ever.

Billie pointed east, toward the massive blue outline of the Rincon Mountains. "That way," she said.

Stearns nodded. "Very good." He grasped her horse's reins and headed in the direction she had indicated.

They traveled without speaking, the only sound the noise of their horses' hooves against the stones. Billie wrapped her bound hands around her saddle horn and dozed in the stifling heat, rousing only when Stearns demanded directions. Again she pointed east, toward the mountains. Big, black-bottomed clouds were building up over the peaks ahead, their anvil-shaped tops rising far up into the sky. Lightning played through their depths, brilliant yellow splotches against the dark vapor.

"Looks like rain, Boss," one of the gunmen said.

If Billie hadn't been so tired, she would have smiled.

364

And Stearns said that God wouldn't take a hand in this!

"How much longer before we reach the gold?" Stearns demanded.

She glanced at the storm clouds, trying to gauge how long it would be before they arrived. "Two hours," she said, pursing her lips thoughtfully. "Maybe three."

Stearns nodded and moved forward again. Billie glanced back at Nick and saw that he was staring at her, a worried frown on his face. After making certain that none of the others could see her, she smiled at him.

Their gazes caught, held for a moment, then his eyes widened. She was going to try something. Dread made his heart hammer wildly. He didn't care about the danger to himself; he'd taken crazy risks before, faced odds worse than these, but not with Billie's life at stake.

He shook his head slightly, desperate to warn her off, but she only smiled wider before facing forward again. Muttering a curse under his breath, he glared at the back of her head. Whatever idea she had in that sneaky, reckless mind of hers, he'd better be ready to back her up. But if they got out of this alive, he was going to give her the walloping she deserved.

Ducking his head, he surreptitiously began rubbing his bindings on his metal belt buckle.

Chapter 33

"This is the place," Billie said.

"Here?" Stearns demanded eagerly. "Where? Where is it hidden?"

She pointed at an arroyo just ahead, a deep, jagged gully that wound upward into the hills. "In there."

"We'll never get the horses down there," Stearns said, dismounting. He tucked his shotgun into the crook of one arm and lifted Billie down from her horse with the other. "Bring the shovels, gentlemen." Pulling her with him, he entered the arroyo.

The gunmen dragged Nick out of his saddle. Holding him securely between them, they hurried after their boss. A drumroll of thunder sounded as they slithered down the steeply sloping walls of the arroyo closed around them. Although the sky over their heads was still clear and blue, the air was charged with static.

"Where is it?" Stearns asked.

Billie felt the tension in the hand with which he was holding her elbow, and knew she'd have to be careful. Despite his seemingly emotionless face and voice, the man was teetering on a hair-trigger of violence. One mistake on her part, and they all might end up dead.

"I need to find a certain rock." She walked slowly

367

along one steep wall, ostensibly scanning the face of the hill above, but really searching for a sharp bend in the arroyo itself. Please, God, she prayed, let there be one!

Another peal of thunder fairly shook the ground. The air had become heavy and humid, pregnant with the threat of the coming storm. Billie saw a twist a few hundred yards ahead, a sharp dog-leg of a turn that was perfect for her needs. She stopped, crying, "There! See it? The rock shaped like a coyote's head?"

The gunmen squinted up at the arroyo wall. Finally one of them shook his head in confusion. "I don't see no coyote's head," he growled.

"Damn the rock!" Stearns said, impatience creeping into his voice. "Where is the gold?"

"Right there." Billie pointed to a sandy spot in the middle of the arroyo floor. This was the most dangerous moment, the time when Stearns might kill them before finding out if the gold was actually there.

She glanced up to find him staring back at her, a slight smile on his face. "Not yet, Miss Meyrick," he said softly, as though reading her mind. "I'll wait until I see the gold. Just in case you've been tempted to lead me astray."

"Why would I do that, Mr. Stearns?"

"For revenge." He smiled again. "Perhaps just for fun."

Thunder boomed again, and she smiled back at the Englishman.

Stearns pointed to the patch of sand. "Untie Mr. Larabee," he said. "Then start digging, all of you."

"Why us?" one of the gunmen complained, slitting Nick's bonds with his knife. "We ain't . . . hey!" he stopped, gaping at the twin bores of the shotgun Stearns was aiming at him.

"You didn't think he was going to share, did you?" Billie taunted.

"Miss Meyrick, do shut your mouth," Stearns said. "You two, throw your weapons over here. Slowly, now. Use your left hands, please."

Their gazes on the wide barrels of the shotgun, the men unbuckled their holsters and tossed them toward Stearns's feet.

Billie glanced up at the Englishman from under her lashes. "Want me to pick them up for you?" she asked.

He chuckled. "Dear girl, even with your hands tied, I wouldn't allow you within ten feet of a gun. Gentlemen, if you please," he said, motioning toward the sandy spot with the shotgun.

They began to dig. Billie watched the hole grow larger and deeper, and wondered how long it would be before Stearns figured out that there was nothing there. She fidgeted nervously, gaining an admonishing order from her captor to be still. Would that damned storm never get here? Dear God, if there was any justice at all, do something before those men hit rock! As though her prayer had been answered, the sky grew dark, and a tremendous peal of thunder fairly shook the ground.

Big, fat drops of water began to fall, making dark splotches in the dust. Suddenly, as though someone had turned an enormous bucket over on their heads, a torrent of water fell from the sky. Billie raised her arms, lifting her face to the stinging cascade, welcoming it. Coincidence, luck, or divine intervention, she'd take it!

Nick and the others were digging in water now. One of the gunmen straightened and called, "Ain't no use, Stearns! We cain't do nothin' in this!"

"Dig, damn you, or I'll shoot you where you stand!" Stearns shouted.

They began working again, slinging water-heavy sand over their shoulders only to have the walls of the hole collapse as fast as they cleared it. Billie saw Nick glance at her over his shoulder. His tawny hair was

369

dark with water, lying sleekly against his skull, and his shirt was plastered wetly to his body, revealing the flexing muscles of his arms, the waiting tenseness in his back. Reading the question in his eyes, she shook her head slightly. Wait, she prayed silently. Please, wait. It's almost time.

Suddenly she detected a rumble beneath the mutter of the thunder, more a vibration than a noise. Then the storm attacked with renewed fury. A towering black cloud moved slowly across the peak of a nearby hill toward them. Straight, wide ribbons of lightning crawled downward from it to lick the ground, white-hot flares of murderous incandescence. Nick and his companions stopped digging to stare in wonder at the power of it, and even Stearns had a look of awe on his face.

Billie laughed, a wild, defiant sound that made all four men turn toward her. "Not like the rain in merrie old England, is it, Stearns?" she shouted, pointing toward the bend of the arroyo. A vast roaring came from that direction, eclipsing even the thunder.

Startled, Stearns whirled.

Nick, realizing with startled horror what Billie was doing, hurtled into motion, knocking the two gunmen aside. As he ran toward her, he saw a wall of dark, foaming water crash around the bend, carrying brush, uprooted trees, even rocks with it. He slammed into Stearns, sending the man sprawling and the shotgun into a pool of water, then caught Billie around the waist and carried her toward the arroyo wall. He clambered as high as he could with one hand as the floodwaters thundered toward him.

"Put your arms around my neck," he gasped, pulling her between his body and the arroyo wall.

Billie obeyed, slipping her bound hands over his head. He dug his fingers into cracks in the rock and

370

hung on as the crest of the torrent reached them. It tore at his legs with horrible force, threatening to rip him from his precarious perch. He gritted his teeth and hung on, groaning with effort, his arms feeling like they'd be pulled from the sockets at any moment. Only the thought that Billie, too, would be lost gave him the strength to retain his hold.

Something crashed into his side, nearly knocking him loose. He saw Stearns's terrified face and reached out, grasping the man by the hair and bringing him against the rocks.

"Hold on!" he roared. "Let go, and you're dead."

Stearns clutched at the rocks desperately. Nick let go of the man's hair and found his handhold again.

Billie pressed her mouth against his ear. "The rawhide around my wrists is wet. I think I can work it loose . . . there!" she said triumphantly, tossing her bindings away.

She twisted around so that she faced the rocks. Taking a deep, calming breath, she began to climb, wedging her fingers into precarious holds and pulling herself upward. Nick moved with her, using his body to shield her from the churning water. Thank God they were on rock and not dirt! he thought, watching a whole segment of the arroyo wall to his left slide into the flood.

Billie's feet slipped, and he pressed her against the rocks with his body until she regained her footholds. They steadily moved up after that, inch by precious inch. When they neared the top, Nick reached up to grasp the edge with one hand while he heaved her upward with the other. Billie scrambled to the top and reached down to help pull him up beside her.

He wasn't looking at her, however, but at Stearns. The man was losing his hold. In a moment or two, he'd drop back into the rushing water. The bastard deserved to die, Nick told himself savagely. Let him drown. But, watching Stearns's piteous, desperate struggle for life, he couldn't do it. Killing the man in a fair fight was one thing, but watching him die like a rat in a trap was something else entirely. Sighing, Nick climbed back down. Anchoring himself with one hand, he reached out with the other.

"Give me your hand!" he shouted over the roar of the flood.

The Englishman looked up, startled, then heaved himself high enough to grasp the proffered hand. Nick gasped as the man's full weight hit him. God, he was heavy! Groaning, the muscles of his powerful shoulders straining, he pulled upward. Stearns's free hand groped among the rocks, found purchase, and held. Nick pulled at his arm, urging him higher.

"Come on!" he shouted when Stearns hesitated. "There's no telling when this wall might come down!"

That got the Englishman moving. Nick climbed ahead of him, reaching the top in time to reach down and grasp Stearns's collar and drag him over the edge.

"Nick!" Billie grabbed him around the waist, pulling him several feet away from the edge.

Nick dropped Stearns, who lay motionless upon the streaming ground, and gathered Billie into his arms. He kissed her cheek, her lips, tasting salt from the tears that were mixed with the rain on her face. She strained against him, sobbing, reveling in the feel of his searing mouth against her chilled skin.

The torrent of rain slackened. With a final roar of thunder, as though disappointed that its prey had escaped, the storm moved away. Nick and Billie clung to one another, watching the great cloud head west to pound the lower rangeland with its fury.

Stearns groaned and sat up. Nick let Billie go hastily and went to kneel beside him.

"Are you all right?" he asked.

Stearns nodded. "I think so."

"Good," Nick said, taking his belt off and securing the Englishman's hands together.

"Mr. Larabee, you saved my life," Stearns said. "You have nothing to fear from me."

Nick checked the bindings carefully. "Now I don't."

"What do you plan to do?"

"I'm going to turn you over to the federal marshal," Nick said, reaching out to pull Billie against his side. "And then I'm going to spend the rest of my life with this woman, secure in the knowledge that you're spending the rest of yours in the prison in Yuma."

"Now, surely that won't be necessary," Stearns protested. "You have my word that I will never harm you or yours. I shall return to England and forget all about my unfortunate sojourn in this benighted corner of the world."

"Yesterday you liked it here," Billie snapped. "You were going to control an area the size of England, remember?"

He ignored her. "Truly, Mr. Larabee, you will gain nothing by turning me over to the authorities. I'm a rich man. If you let me go, I shall see that you never want for anything. Just name your price."

Nick shook his head. "There's nothing I want from you."

"Oh, come now, young man! You are what is called a drifter, a man with few possessions and little future except for what Miss Meyrick offers you." Stearns cocked his head to one side and regarded Nick curiously. "How will you feel when people say—as they surely will—that you seduced your way into the Star M?"

Billie stiffened with outrage, but Nick put his finger across her lips to prevent her from answering.

373

He turned back to Stearns. "They can say anything they damn well please," he growled. "My name is Laird, not Larabee, and I'm not quite as poor as you think."

"Laird!" The Englishman exclaimed.

There was a low, chilling laugh from the rocks behind them. A moment later Carson Eames stepped into view, his pistol held ready. Nick pushed Billie to one side and crouched, ready to leap.

"Don't try it," Eames said. "Nick Laird, eh? Now isn't that interesting?"

Chapter 34

"Untie me, Mr. Eames," Stearns said.

The gunman laughed. "You've got to be joking."

"I know where the gold is." Stearns held his bound hands out.

"You fool!" Eames sneered. "Do you think she'd take you to it just because you asked her nicely? Christ, man, she walked you right into a trap and you were too blind to see it coming. And you think you're so damned smart!" With his free hand, he unfastened his rain slicker and pushed the edges apart, revealing the twin holsters that crisscrossed his narrow hips.

Stearns looked up at Billie. "Is this true? There is no gold down there?"

She nodded. "I was buying time. I even told you that. You just didn't listen, Mr. Stearns."

The Englishman bent his head, almost seeming to shrivel in upon himself. For a brief moment, he looked old and tired. Then he shook himself and looked up at her again, his old icy calm back in place. "Do you know where it is?"

"No. Neither did my pa, and neither did Rowan Laird."

"But the Mexican—"

Billie chopped the air with her hand impatiently. "He was delirious by the time they found him. He talked about the gold, sure—about how it looked, how it smelled, how badly he wanted it. Everything but where it was."

Eames laughed again. "If he believes that, he's an even bigger fool than I thought he was."

"It's true!" She glared at Eames, her green eyes flaring with hatred. "You killed the Lairds for nothing."

Eames's cold gaze moved to Nick. "Ahh, yes. That brings us back to your friend here. Laird, eh?"

"Yes." Nick crossed his arms over his chest. "You've been a busy fellow, haven't you? Rustling cattle, burning ranches and killing innocent people—have I missed anything?"

"Well, there was raping your sister, but that was only a diversion."

Nick went very still. Fearing that he was going to launch himself at Eames, gun or no gun, Billie pressed herself against his side. Every muscle in his body was tense, hard as rock under her hands. But he only said, "I suppose it was you who killed Lew Purcell."

Eames shrugged. "The old fool didn't have sense enough to stay out of other people's business. He was getting too close."

"Is that how you work?" Nick asked softly. "Shooting men in the back?"

"Only when necessary." Eames met the cold hatred of Nick's gaze and smiled. "Even if I had faced him, he wouldn't have had a chance."

Nick's entire being yearned to kill this man. "But I would."

"You're not fast enough, Laird."

"We'll never know unless we try."

"Nick, don't!" Billie whispered urgently, tugging on his arm.

He ignored her. "Yours isn't the first reputation that hasn't been earned. You have to face a man head on to deserve a name as a fast gun, not murder women and children and old men. But maybe that's the part you can't handle, eh?"

"I can handle it, all right," Eames snapped, baring his teeth in an animal snarl.

Nick didn't reply. He just stood and smiled down at the gunman, a derisive smile on his lips. But inside, where Eames couldn't see it, there was the sick taste of dread. Again he had to risk Billie's life. Damn, if only she wasn't here! His revenge against his family's killer meant nothing if she got hurt in the process. But he had no choice; if he didn't find a way to make Eames face him fairly, she didn't have a chance, anyway.

A red spot of anger appeared high on Eames's cheekbones. "I could shoot you right now, Laird."

"Well, do it, then," Nick growled. "Either that or throw me a gun. I'm tired of talking to you."

With his free hand, Eames reached down and began unbuckling his spare holster. "Winner takes all, then? The girl and the gold?"

"If you win, I won't be in a position to say no, will I?" Nick asked.

"No." Eames grinned, staring at the front of Billie's blouse where the wet fabric clung to the lush curves of her breasts. "She's one hell of a woman, isn't she? Got some hard edges, maybe, but a couple of weeks with me ought to smooth them out some."

Nick merely held out his hand for the gun. Eames tossed the holster to him, keeping his own pistol ready.

"Nick, please!" Billie pulled on Nick's arm frantically. "This is crazy! You can't do this!"

377

He jerked away from her and began putting the gun belt on. When she tried to take hold of his arm again, he turned to face her, and the raw fury on his face drove her back a step.

"Go sit over there with Stearns," he said. "And stay there."

His voice was quiet, even gentle, but Billie didn't dare disobey. Whirling, she ran to the Englishman and sat down beside him.

"Can he do it?" Stearns whispered.

"I don't know!" Her fist pounded the ground beside her. "I just don't know!"

Nick was ready now, the gun belt hung low on his lean hips to bring the fancy pearl-inlaid handle of the pistol within easy reach of his hand. He indicated the other man's drawn gun. "Is that what you call a fair fight?" he asked.

Eames smiled. "Just making sure you don't try anything." Slowly, keeping his attention on Nick's hands, he slid the pistol back into his holster.

Although Billie wanted to cover her eyes, she forced herself to watch as the two men faced each other. Their bodies were relaxed, their hands held motionless at their sides. Only their eyes showed any indication of what was going to happen.

"Call it, Billie," Eames said.

"No!"

"Call it." Nick's voice was harsh, commanding.

Billie closed her eyes for a moment. This was the final torment! If Nick died, it would be at her word. Then she opened her eyes to gauge the two opponents, searching for a way to help her love. As she hesitated, she thought she saw a tremor in Eames's left hand. Was it fear or impatience? Either way, it was a crack in the man's armor.

"Do it!" Stearns hissed, unable to stand the tension.

But she waited a moment longer. Eames's hand moved again, a tiny but perceptible twitch.

"Now!" she shrieked.

The guns roared, their reports so close together that she couldn't tell which had fired first. Then a red blossom of blood appeared in the center of Eames's shirtfront. The gunman stared down at himself in disbelief. He staggered, then braced his legs and used both hands to raise his pistol for another shot.

Nick planted another bullet an inch below the first, and Eames fell backward, his gun flying from his nerveless fingers. Nick walked over the sodden ground and stood over the dying man.

"You not only have to be fast," he said as awareness and life drained from Eames's face. "You have to shoot straight, too." Stooping, he closed the dead, staring eyes before going back to the others.

Billie felt very strange. Her face felt stiff, as though she, not Eames, had died, and she was having trouble drawing breath. A great roaring blackness swooped down at her like the desert wind, and she fought desperately to hold it at bay.

Seeing how white her face had become, Nick ran the last few feet and snatched her into his arms. "It's all right, honey," he said. "Don't faint on me now."

"I've never fainted in my life!" she said, and promptly did just that.

Chapter 35

Billie and Nick sat at the Star M's well-scrubbed table, blinking with weariness. Rachel and Helena kept putting food and steaming cups of coffee before the tired pair, determined to hear the whole story before allowing them to go to sleep.

"You should have seen her," Nick said. "Leading those three men into an arroyo when she knew a flash flood was coming." He took a bite of biscuit before adding, "Took me along, too, the bloodthirsty little savage."

Helena glanced toward the room where Stearns had been secured. "What's going to happen to him?" she asked. For a moment, her normally laughing green eyes flashed fire just like her daughter's.

"He'll spend a damn long time in prison," Nick said. "Pat should be back here with the marshal in a day or two, and we can shake our hands of him."

"And Eames?" Rachel asked.

"Dead." Nick held out his arms and she ran to him, hiding her face against his shoulder. Silent sobs shook her body. "It's over, honey," he murmured. "Now we can live our lives. What do you want to do?"

Rachel wiped her face with her apron. "I'm going to

marry Budge. We're going to rebuild the house at Redesware and then fill it with babies."

Billie put her arm around Helena's waist. It would take her awhile to come to terms with what her father had done, and with her mother's weakness for letting him get away with it. But it was time to put the past aside and look to the future, and she decided she wanted Helena to be part of that future. "What are you going to do now, Mother?" she asked.

Helena sighed. "Well, with Rosswell bound for prison and Julia run away . . . she knew all about what her father was doing, you know. It was she who paid those men to ruin your dresses while they were looking for the gold here." She touched her daughter's hand lightly before moving away to take another pan of biscuits out of the oven. "She was jealous of you, and thought that would keep you away from the party—and Nick."

"Billie's never been able to keep away from me," he said complacently. "Although she tried."

Billie glared at him with mock outrage, then returned her attention to her mother. "Why don't you stay?" she asked. "You can shed Stearns quickly enough."

"Oh, Billie, don't you understand? I don't belong in Arizona. I still don't like the heat, the Indians or the lack of culture. As soon as possible, I'll be going back to Europe." Helena smiled tremulously. "But I'll come back to visit, if I may, and not years from now, either."

Nick slipped his arm around Billie's waist and pulled her into his lap. "Won't you at least stay for our wedding?" he asked.

"I gather this is not going to be a protracted engagement?" Helena asked.

"I'm going to claim her as fast as I possibly can." Nick's deep, slow voice was fiercely possessive, so full of sensual promise that Billie blushed and tried to bolt from his lap.

He pulled her back down, pinioning her against him with strong arms, and continued, "Budge is due back next week. We can make it a double wedding. Then we can start filling this house with babies, too."

Billie relaxed against him. "Does that mean you want to stay in Arizona?"

"I like it here. And Stearns has agreed to sell us his ranch."

"You have enough money to buy the Dolorosa?" she demanded.

He grinned. "That, and a Henry repeating rifle for my bride, little barbarian that you are."

"I don't know, Nick. All those windows—"

"I'll keep you safe." His hands moved restlessly on her waist. "And busy."

Smiling, Helena and Rachel tiptoed out of the room.

"All night?" Billie breathed. She put her palms on his shoulders, enjoying the way the heavy muscles moved under her hands.

"All night," he said, the velvet promise in his voice sending a shiver down her spine. His hands moved over her back in long, slow strokes. *"Ma belle,"* he whispered in her ear. *"Je t'aime, je t'aime."*

Billie looked up at him from under her lashes. Her hands moved up to twine in the thick, tawny hair at the nape of his neck. "Do you think anyone would notice if we started on those babies a week early?" she murmured.

"Who cares?" He rose to his feet, bringing her up with him, and turned toward her bedroom. He stopped in the doorway and looked into her eyes.

"Do you love me?" he asked fiercely.

She sighed. "Yes. More than anything in this world."

"Cherie!"

HEARTFIRE ROMANCES

SWEET TEXAS NIGHTS (2610, $3.75)
by Vivian Vaughan

Meg Britton grew up on the railroads, working proudly at her father's side. Nothing was going to stop them from setting the rails clear to Silver Creek, Texas—certainly not some crazy prospector. As Meg set out to confront the old coot, she planned her strategy with cool precision. But soon she was speechless with shock. For instead of a harmless geezer, she found a boldly handsome stranger whose determination matched her own.

CAPTIVE DESIRE (2612, $3.75)
by Jane Archer

Victoria Malone fancied herself a great adventuress, but being kidnapped was too much excitement for even Victoria! Especially when her arrogant kidnapper thought she was part of Red Duke's outlaw gang. Trying to convince the overbearing, handsome stranger that she had been an innocent bystander when the stagecoach was robbed, proved futile. But when he thought he could maker her confess by crushing her to his warm, broad chest, by caressing her with his strong, capable hands, Victoria was willing to admit to anything. . . .

LAWLESS ECSTASY (2613, $3.75)
by Susan Sackett

Abra Beaumont could spot a thief a mile away. After all, her father was once one of the best. But he'd been on the right side of the law for years now, and she wasn't about to let a man like Dash Thorne lead him astray with some wild plan for stealing the Tear of Allah, the world's most fabulous ruby. Dash was just the sort of man she most distrusted—sophisticated, handsome, and altogether too sure of his considerable charm. Abra shivered at the devilish gleam in his blue eyes and swore he would need more than smooth kisses and skilled caresses to rob her of her virtue . . . and much more than sweet promises to steal her heart!